Praise for Liz Trenow

'Extraordinary, fascinating . . . deeply rooted in history'
Midweek, Radio 4

'An assured debut with a page-turning conclusion'
Daily Express

'Liz Trenow sews together the strands of past and
present as delicately as the exquisite stitching on the
quilt which forms the centrepiece of the story'
LUCINDA RILEY

'Totally fascinating . . . a book to savour'
KATE FURNIVALL

'A novel about the human spirit – Liz Trenow paints
with able prose a picture of the prejudices that bind us
and the love that sets us free . . . Splendid'
PAM JENOFF

'An intriguing patchwork of past and present, upstairs
and downstairs, hope and despair'
DAISY GOODWIN

THE SILK WEAVER

Liz Trenow's family have been silk weavers for nearly three hundred years, and she grew up next to the mill in Sudbury, Suffolk, which is the oldest family-owned silk company in Britain and one of just three still operating today. Liz worked as a journalist for regional and national newspapers, and on BBC radio and television news, before turning her hand to fiction. She lives in East Anglia with her artist husband, and they have two grown-up daughters.

Find out more at **www.liztrenow.com**, like her Facebook page at **www.facebook.com/liztrenow** or join her on Twitter **@LizTrenow**.

LIZ TRENOW

The Silk Weaver

PAN BOOKS

First published 2017 by Pan Books
an imprint of Pan Macmillan
20 New Wharf Road, London N1 9RR
Associated companies throughout the world
www.panmacmillan.com

ISBN 978-1-5098-2325-3

1 3 5 7 9 8 6 4 2

A CIP catalogue record for this book is available from the British Library.

Typeset by Palimpsest Book Production Limited, Falkirk, Stirlingshire
Printed and bound by CPI Group (UK) Ltd, Croydon, CR0 4YY

Visit **www.panmacmillan.com** to read more about all our books
and to buy them. You will also find features, author interviews and
news of any author events, and you can sign up for e-newsletters
so that you're always first to hear about our new releases.

For my two wonderful daughters, Becky and Polly

ACKNOWLEDGEMENTS

First of all I must thank my agent, Caroline Hardman of Hardman & Swainson, who made certain that this novel – which is very close to my heart – found the best possible home with Pan Macmillan. I am really enjoying working with Catherine Richards, my new editor there.

This book was my first foray into the eighteenth century and involved extensive research. I read masses, of course, and visited many exhibitions and libraries – there's a list at the end of the book – but I also had assistance from numerous individuals, only some of whom I have space to mention here.

I am eternally grateful to the welcome shown to me by the residents of Wilkes Street: Sue Rowlands, who lives in the house where my forebears began their business – and on which I have based Monsieur Lavalle's residence – and her neighbours, John and Sandy Critchley.

The textile expert and author Mary Schoeser piqued my interest in Anna Maria Garthwaite and gave me an intro-duction to staff at the Victoria and Albert Museum's National Art Library, where I was thrilled to discover the final, unpublished manuscript by the previous curator of textiles, the late Natalie Rothstein.

Richard Humphries lent me several valuable books on eighteenth-century weaving and The Weavers' Company, and my brother David Walters (former MD of the family silk company) checked technical aspects of the weaving passages. Martin Arnaud corrected my French phrases and added some colourful eighteenth-century French curses. Mark Bills, Curator at Gainsborough's House Museum in Sudbury, was very helpful and my artist husband David Trenow made sure that the drawing and painting scenes made sense. All inaccuracies are entirely mine (see my note on the history that inspired *The Silk Weaver*, at the end of the book).

As always, I am hugely grateful to my family and friends (especially 'The Grumpies') for their unswerving love and support.

PROLOGUE

Anna rests her head on the cushion and traces her finger along the stems of daisies and the nodding heads of blue-bells embroidered onto its calico cover. The silken threads, though worn and coming loose in places, still hold their colours and gleam in the sunshine.

'Bluebells and daisies,' she sings to a familiar nursery rhyme tune. 'Bluebells and daisies. They all grow here, they all grow here.'

They are seated together on the old chaise longue in the window of the vicarage sitting room. This is where her mother likes to work at her embroidery, although she has to hold the frame further away than normal because her belly is so huge and round these days. She says that it is because she is growing a new brother or sister but Anna cannot believe it possible that there could really be a child inside her mother's body.

She is bored. Because of this baby bump they cannot go for their usual walks together across the heath or down to the marshes to collect wild flowers for pressing, as her mother says it gives her backache. Neither can they do much gardening, which Anna also adores. She loves getting her hands dirty making soft beds in the black earth into which they scatter tiny seeds. She cannot believe that these little specks will grow into beautiful flowers next year, but her mother promises they will, just like she's promised about the baby.

'Wait and see, my little one,' she says. 'Have patience and you will find my words are true.'

Although she is only five, Anna has already learned to name many wild flowers and some garden varieties, too. The ones she finds easiest to remember are those which perfectly describe the flowers themselves and seem to roll off the tongue: love-in-a-mist, snapdragon, foxglove, hare-bell, forget-me-not, wallflower, ox-eye daisy. Others she finds more difficult to pronounce and has to say over and over again before they come out right: delphinium, convol-vulus, asphodel, hellebore.

She returns her attention to the cushion. How different these two flowers are: the perky little daisy with its open face of tiny white petals around a yellow nose; the closed heads of the bluebells – more purple than blue, she thinks – hanging from a stem that seems barely able to carry their weight.

'What flower would you like to be?' she asks her mother. 'A daisy or a bluebell?'

'A bluebell, because it smells so sweet.'

'I'd rather be a happy daisy than a droopy bluebell,' Anna says. 'Besides, daisies flower all summer, and bluebells are only here for a few weeks.' She hums the little rhyme to herself a few times and kicks her feet.

'When will you teach me how to sew flowers like you do?'

'Sit up, and I will show you right now,' her mother says.

She puts the needle between the thumb and finger of Anna's right hand, guiding it with her own fingers. Then she helps Anna's other hand hold the frame flat, just like she does.

'We are doing a simple chain stitch for the stem,' she says, guiding the hand with the needle so that it pierces the calico just so. The needle disappears, pulling the green silk behind it, and then is pushed through from the back, emerging, as if by magic, just beside where they made the previous stitch. They do it again, and a third time, and Anna can see how the stem is growing before her very eyes.

But when she insists on trying without her mother's guiding hand, everything goes wrong. The stitches go everywhere and the needle loses its thread. She throws it down in a temper.

'I hate sewing,' she grumbles. 'Can we do drawing instead?'

Just then, her mother's body seems to go rigid, and she gives a sharp gasp. 'Run to the church and fetch your father,' she says through clenched teeth. 'Quick as you can. I think the baby is coming.'

Even years later, Anna cherishes the memory of that day and that inconsequential conversation with her mother. Perhaps it was important because this was the last time that she had her mother to herself, before Jane arrived. But what she remembers most, as clear as if it were yesterday, is the cushion with its embroidered flowers, and the silks glimmering in the sunshine.

LONDON 1760

I

There are many little civilities which a true gentleman will offer to a lady travelling alone, which she may accept with perfect propriety; but, while careful to thank him courteously, avoid any advance toward acquaintanceship.
— The Lady's Book of Manners, 1760

The carriage pulled to a sudden halt, and for a moment Anna dared to imagine that they had arrived.

But something was wrong. In the distance could be heard a great deal of commotion: deep-voiced male shouts and the screech of women's voices. They could see nothing from the windows and no one came to open the door. The four travelling companions sat without speaking, trying not to catch each other's eyes. Only the silent sighs of irritation and tiny tics – the tapping of toes, the drumming of fingers – suggested that this delay was out of the ordinary.

After a few minutes the gentleman of the middling sort cleared his throat impatiently, took his cane and knocked briskly on the ceiling of the carriage – *rat-a-tat-tat, rat-a-tat-tat*. There was no response. He leaned out and hollered upwards.

'Coachman, why are we stopped?'

'We'll be on our way shortly, sir.' He did not sound convinced.

They waited a few moments longer, until the gentleman huffed and sighed again, stood up and let himself out of the coach, telling his son to stay with the ladies. Anna heard him exchange words with the coachman, and five further minutes passed. When he climbed back inside, his cheeks were so flushed she feared he might be about to suffer a choleric turn.

'Nothing to worry about, ladies.' His tone was falsely calm. 'May I suggest, however, that you pull down the blinds.'

The carriage began to jerk backwards, forwards and sideways with such violent movements that the four of them were thrown about like butter in a churn. It seemed that the coachman was attempting the almost impossible task of turning around a coach and four on this narrow highway.

The shouting outside became louder. It was hard to make out any words, but at times it took on the rhythm of a chant, angry and menacing. What sounded like stones seemed to clatter on the cobbles around them and, even more alarmingly, against the carriage itself. One of the horses whinnied sharply as if in pain. The hollering came closer now, and Anna could make out a single syllable repeated again and again. It was shocking how such a plain, everyday word could sound so very threatening in the voice of an enraged crowd.

The coachman was hollering too, urging the horses to push on, pull back, hold hard. Everyone inside the coach remained tensely silent as they tried to brace themselves

8

against the jolts. Both gentlemen stared fixedly forwards; the lady turned her face downwards towards her lap, her eyes sealed tightly as if in prayer.

Although she too was trying to remain outwardly composed, Anna could hear her own heart hammering in her chest and her knuckles, clutching onto the strap above the window, shone white in the gloom of the interior. She began to wonder whether this sort of thing was a regular occurrence in the city; she had heard there were demonstrations and mobs that could become violent, but never thought for a moment that she might directly encounter one.

Finally the carriage set off again at a great lick, but with the blinds still drawn it was impossible to see in which direction they were now travelling. 'My dear sir, please tell us what was happening,' the lady said, looking up at last, her breathing ragged. 'Do I understand that our coach was the object of the commotion?'

'Have no fear, my dear lady,' the gentleman said smoothly. 'We were in no danger. There was an obstruction in the road. The coachman has decided to try another route into the city.' The colour of his face had returned to normal, but Anna didn't believe a word.

'But why would they be shouting about bread?' she ventured. 'And why would they choose strangers as the focus of such an attack?'

'It is not for us to presume.' He pursed his lips and would not be drawn further, so the four lapsed into another heavy silence.

Now, she began to worry about their delayed arrival. Cousin William was due to meet her at the Red Lyon public house, but how could she get word to him that they were well over an hour late? She had eaten nothing but a slice of bread and a small lump of cheese since breakfast and her stomach was rumbling so loudly that she feared that her companions would hear it, even over the clatter of wheels on the cobbled street.

At last the coach pulled to a halt and she heard the shout, 'Spitalfields Red Lyon, Miss Butterfield.'

She climbed stiffly from the carriage and waited while her luggage was unloaded from the rear and placed beside her. In just seconds, the coachman shouted a cheery farewell and they were gone. The carriage and its passengers had become a haven of safety and protection and as she watched it turn the corner and disappear from view she felt abandoned and a little afraid. She was on her own in this great city.

Around Anna and her cases flowed a seemingly unending stream of people. Some walked at a leisurely pace in twos and threes, absorbed in conversation, while others, apparently engaged on urgent errands, scurried quickly, dodging between the groups.

She found herself entranced by the cries of the street pedlars. A woman waved a bunch of sweet-smelling herbs in front of people's noses, shouting, 'Buy my rosemary! Buy my sweetbriar! A farthing a bunch to sweeten your home.' Some cries even sounded like poetry: 'Pears for pies! Come feast your eyes! Ripe pears, of every size, who'll buy?'

In her village, people would stop to gossip with travelling

salesmen – it was one of the best ways of discovering what was going on in neighbouring villages, who had died, who had married, who had borne children and how the hay, corn and fruit harvests were faring. But here in the city it appeared that everyone was too busy to chat.

Every kind of produce seemed to be for sale: boxes and baskets, brushes and brooms, Morocco slippers, matches, saucepans, wooden spoons and nutmeg graters, doormats, chickweed and groundsel for bird seed, oysters, herring, ropes of onions, strawberries, rhubarb and all manner of other fruit and vegetables and, most enticing of all, delicious-smelling hot loaves, baked potatoes and meat pies that made her stomach rumble all the more.

Apart from the traders and a few beggars, no one was taking the slightest notice of her. A lone woman waiting on the roadside in the country would have received several offers of help within a few moments. Here, it was as if she were invisible, or something inanimate like a statue or an island around which the human river was forced to navigate. Among this mass of people her presence was of no conse-quence at all. *I could disappear*, she thought, *and no one would ever be the wiser*. It was a curious feeling, both fright-ening and freeing all at once.

And the noise! The clatter of drays and carriages across the cobbles, the shouts of hawkers and women hollering at their children. In the hubbub it took a little while to make sense of any words, and now Anna began to realise why: much of it was not in English.

She looked around. Across the road, although it was not yet dusk, a crowd of drinkers had gathered at the Red Lyon

Inn, spilling into the street, tankards in hand, engaged in conversations animated with much raucous laughter.

Behind her, high brick arches fronted the pavement and, through them, she could see a cavernous interior dense with tables and other wooden structures. It looked like a market, but Anna had never seen such an expanse of stalls. Just two dozen filled the square at Halesworth, even at Michaelmas, yet there looked to be well over one hundred here. Although trading had ended for the day and the stalls were now empty, pungent smells of herbs and vegetables, stale fish and rotting meat wafted across the road.

Minutes ticked by on the cracked-faced clock above the market. Her stays were tight, her stomach empty, she had a raging thirst and she was beginning to feel light-headed. She shifted her weight from toe to heel and from foot to foot as she had learned during long hours at church, and prayed that William would come soon.

Time passed and she fell into a kind of reverie. The next thing she knew, she seemed to be on the ground, vaguely aware of someone kneeling by her side and cradling her head, with another person standing close on the other side, fanning her with his cap. It took her a few moments to understand where she was.

'Oh dear, I am so sorry to be a nuisance,' she mumbled, starting to push herself up.

'Do not be troubled,' the young man said. 'We are keeping you safe.' He spoke something unintelligible to his companion who disappeared, returning shortly with a cup of water which she sipped gratefully.

'Are you having a home?' the young man asked. 'A family? Or a friend, perhaps?'

'I am come to stay with my uncle, Joseph Sadler of Spital Square,' she said, her wits now slowly returning, 'and my cousin William was to meet me here.' The young man spoke some further incomprehensible words to his friend, who left them again.

A glorious thought slipped into her confused mind: perhaps they were speaking in tongues, just as the Apostles described? She'd always considered it an unlikely story – just an allegory, like so many tales in the Bible – but something rather like it did indeed seem to be happening to her. She smiled to herself. *The Lord does indeed move in mysterious ways.*

A crowd had gathered now, but with this young man's arms around her she felt curiously unafraid. She could see that he was clean-shaven and gentle of demeanour. His eyes were the deepest brown, like horse chestnuts freshly released from their cases. Although wigless and not, as far as she could see, dressed as a gentleman, his dark hair was neatly tied back, and he spoke to her tenderly and smiled often, to reassure her. There was a sweet, musty smell about him; not unpleasant but strange, nothing she could recognise.

The second boy returned, panting, 'He come.' Not wanting her cousin to find her on the ground, and since she was now feeling considerably recovered, Anna tried to stand. The two young men gently put their arms around her waist to help her up.

At that moment a loud shout came from the edge of the crowd. 'Make way, make way. Let me by.' As William appeared – for indeed it was he, a tall, thin-faced young man in a powdered wig – his face darkened.

'How dare you? Take your hands off the young lady at once,' he bellowed, and a fist whipped past Anna's nose into the boy's face. He grunted and fell away, nearly taking her with him but for the strong left hand of William holding her arm painfully tight. He aimed another punch at the second boy, who fell in an untidy heap at their feet. The crowd gasped and drew back.

'Now get out of my sight, cabbage heads,' William bawled, lashing out with his boots as the crowd tried to drag the boys to safety, 'and if I ever catch you touching an English lady again, I'll string you up by your webbed feet.'

'Do not be so harsh, Cousin,' Anna whispered, shocked by his violent response. 'They were helping me. I had fainted from the heat.'

'Dirty frogs,' he growled, barking instructions about the baggage to a man with a pushcart. 'You should never have allowed it. You have much to learn about how a young lady should comport herself in the city.'

'Yes, I expect I do,' Anna said, in what she hoped was a conciliatory tone. He grabbed her arm again and began to drag her along the road with such haste that she had to trot to keep up.

'Hurry along, Anna Butterfield. We have been waiting for hours. I cannot imagine why you did not send word of your arrival earlier. Had you done so you would not have caused this trouble. You are most terribly late and supper has gone cold.'

Fortunately it was but a few minutes – at William's pace – from the Red Lyon to Spital Square. They stopped outside a house with a wide shop frontage: bow windows either side of a grand front door set with bottle-glass, and double pillars that supported a porch to shelter callers from the rain. On a board hanging below the porch was written in elegant gold script: *Joseph Sadler & Son, Mercers to the Gentry*. They were here at last.

She turned to go up the steps, but William grabbed her arm once more and pulled her onwards, opening a smaller side door that led into the darkness of a long entrance hall. They passed two doors on the ground floor – probably leading into the shop area, she assumed – up some stairs to a wide landing, and through yet another door into the dining room.

Uncle Joseph stepped forward first, welcoming her with a formal handshake and a smile that disappeared as soon as it had arrived, as though it were an infrequent and unexpected visitor. He was a daunting figure: tall and portly, whiskered and bewigged even at home, high-collared and tail-coated, with a well-rounded stomach held tight under his embroidered silk waistcoat. He must once have been a handsome man but good living had taken its toll. His jowls drooped and wobbled like a turkey's wattle.

'Welcome, dear Niece,' he said. 'We hope you will be happy here.' He waved his hand proprietorially around the sumptuously furnished room, in the centre of which a deeply polished oak table laden with silver glistened in the light of many candles.

Anna dipped her knee. 'I am indebted to you, sir, for your generous hospitality,' she said.

Aunt Sarah seemed a kindly sort with a smile that, unlike her husband's, appeared quite accustomed to her face. She kissed Anna on both cheeks. 'You poor thing, you look weary,' she said, standing back to regard her up and down. 'And your clothes . . .' She gave a little sigh and her eyes turned away as if the sight of Anna's dress was too terrible to contemplate, even though it was her Sunday best. 'Never mind. You shall have supper now and a good rest after your long journey. Tomorrow we can see about your wardrobe.'

She has the same voice as my father, Anna thought, with the slight lisp that seemed to run in the family. She was his younger sister, after all, but it was difficult, without staring, to divine precisely which features they shared. The lips, perhaps, or the eyebrows? Certainly not the stature. Sarah was very much shorter and more rounded while her father was angular and long of limb, proportions which Anna had inherited and which, she knew, were no advantage for a woman. But the familiarity of her aunt's features helped Anna feel at home.

Cousin Elizabeth made an elegant curtsey.

'Please do call me Lizzie, Cousin Anna. I am so looking forward to having an elder sister.' On her lips the lisp sounded sweet, even endearing. 'A brother is no use at all,' she added, with a poisonous glance across the table. William returned a scowl which, in truth, did not seem to have left his face since their first encounter.

Lizzie would be around fourteen years of age, Anna calculated. A pretty little thing, she observed, round-faced like her mother but much slighter, all auburn ringlets and cream lace, six years younger than her brother and four years younger than herself. Sarah had borne several other children, she remembered, but these were the only two who had survived. She recalled her father sighing over his sister's letters: 'Another child gone into the arms of our Lord. Alas, poor Sarah. If only they could live somewhere with healthier air.' In church, he would name Sarah's lost babies out loud, beseeching God to care for them in heaven.

Anna understood from this litany of sadness that child-birth was something to be dreaded, perhaps more than anything else in the world. Yet how could it be avoided, she wondered, when one grew into a woman and became settled in the proper manner?

They sat down and Joseph poured goblets of a liquid the colour of ripe plums. 'Claret', he called it. As her uncle raised his glass with a toast 'to the arrival of our dear cousin, Anna', she took a tentative sip; it was sharper than communion wine but tasted delicious. She ventured another and yet another until she found herself becoming quite warm and relaxed.

'You poor things, I cannot imagine the trials you have been through these past few months,' Aunt Sarah said, handing around a plateful of cold meats. 'I do hope that dear Fanny's last few weeks were not too difficult?'

The warm glow disappeared as a vision of her mother appeared in Anna's mind: ghostly pale and skeletal, propped against the pillows and struggling to contain paroxysms of coughing, gasping for every breath and unable to speak or eat for the congestion in her chest.

It had been a long and lingering illness: a slow decline followed by apparent recovery, bringing new hope, only to be dashed by further decline. Throughout it all, Anna and her sister Jane had nursed their mother, trying as best they could to shield their father who, as the village vicar, had plenty of problems of his own: difficult parishioners, the demands of his diocesan masters and the need to shore up the ruinous fabric of the church.

The exhaustion of caring for her mother and running the household had kept Anna from dwelling too much on the tragedy ahead. When it finally came, Jane took to her bed and wept, so it seemed, for several weeks. Nothing could console her except for the sweetmeats she consumed by day and the warmth of her sister's embrace in their shared bed by night.

Their father, Theodore, though hollowed-out and grey in countenance, continued about his daily work, the only difference being that he retired earlier to bed than usual. Once or twice, in the dead of night, Anna would hear heartrending sobs through the wall and longed to comfort him. But she resisted the impulse, sensing that he must be allowed to embrace this misery without needing to keep face for anyone else.

As for herself, the anticipated collapse into despair never really happened. She rose each day, washed and dressed and did her chores, made meals for the family, organised the funeral tea and tried to smile when people commented on how well she was coping. But inside she felt empty, almost indifferent to her own misery. Grief was like sleep-walking through deep snow, its landscape endless and unchanging, every step painful and exhausting. The world seemed to become monochrome, colours lost their hue, sounds were muffled and distorted. It felt as though her own life had been taken, along with her mother's.

Dragging herself away from these painful recollections,

she turned back to the dining table, and her waiting aunt. 'Thank you, madam, she was peaceful at the end.' As she said it, she crossed her fingers in her lap. It was an old habit from childhood, when she believed it might save her from God's wrath when lying. But then she uncrossed them as she realised that her words had a certain truth: the lifeless form laid out on the bed had indeed looked peaceful, now that all pain had gone.

'And my dear brother, Theo? How is he coping with his loss?'

'His faith is a great comfort, as you can imagine,' Anna ventured, although she knew well that the opposite was true: his faith had been sorely tested these past few months.

'It is a cruel God, indeed, who takes with one hand while purporting to offer solace with the other,' her uncle said.

'Each to their own, my dear,' Sarah muttered.

'It is an interesting conjecture, all the same.' William's eyes glittered, alert for the challenge, his thin lips in a sardonic twist. 'Just what *is* the point of God, when all's said and done?'

'Shush, William,' Sarah said, sliding a glance towards Lizzie and back again to her son. 'Save such debates for your club fellows.'

A silence fell over the table. Anna took a couple of rather larger sips of claret. 'I do hope you will forgive me for my tardy arrival. The coach was held up by a commotion, and we had to find another route into the city,' she said.

William looked up sharply. 'What kind of commotion? Where was this?'

'I do not know exactly where, I am afraid. It was as we

entered the city, and we could not see anything from the coach on account of having to draw down the blinds. There was much shouting – something about bread, I thought I could hear.'

'Sounds like another food riot,' William said. 'Probably those Frenchie weavers again, like last month. They're always revolting. Have you heard anything, Pa?'

Joseph shook his head, jaws working on the generous spoonful of meat and potato he had just stuffed into his mouth. 'If they didn't waste so much money on Geneva, they would have plenty for bread,' he muttered. 'And it would help if those Strangers would stop stirring things up.'

William took out his watch, put down his knife and spoon with a hurried clatter and pushed back his chair. 'Forgive me, I am late for the club,' he said, grabbing his jacket and bowing slightly in Anna's direction. 'We will meet again tomorrow, dear Coz. In the meantime do try to stay away from cabbages. They can cause the most odorous indigestion.'

Anna puzzled over this until, later, she recalled his 'cabbage heads' jibe. Why he should be so vitriolic towards two innocent and indeed most helpful young men was a mystery, but so much of this new world was unfathomable that it made her feel quite dizzy to contemplate.

After the meal Lizzie was deputed to show her the rest of the house – the upper floors at least, for the ground floor was entirely devoted to Uncle's business and the basement, she presumed, was the domain of the servants. The building stood four storeys tall and, although deep from front to back, it felt less spacious than her own dear vicarage and nothing like so homely. She admired the opulent silk hangings, the elegant furniture, the painted wainscoting in each of the main rooms and the shutters on every window, but the overall effect was to make the place darker and more formal.

Next to the dining room, at the front of the house above what she presumed to be the shopfront, was a wide, elegant drawing room with a cast-iron fireplace and marble surround. Out of the window, Anna could see the street and the small square of grass with a few young trees which, she thought to herself, no doubt afforded the house its grand address. And yet the building was attached on either side to others so that it was difficult to see where one started and the other ended. *Land must be very scarce in this cramped city*, she thought to herself, *that even in such prosperous areas they cannot afford to be separated from their neighbours by even a few feet.*

'Do you have a garden?' she asked.

'It's just a patch of mouldy grass and a tree,' Lizzie replied quickly. 'I can show you tomorrow.'

'I love to sketch natural things.'

'There is little to inspire an artist,' Lizzie said. 'Although I know where we could see flowers and fruits in great abundance.'

'Where is that?' Anna asked.

'At the market. All sorts, from farms and Strangers' gardens and from foreign countries too, piled high in their thousands. It is a wonderful sight.' Lizzie laughed suddenly.

'I do not suppose that is what you had in mind for a painting?'

'Not really,' Anna said, pleased to be talking of lighter matters after so many serious hours. 'Although I should love to see it.'

'Mama will not let us enter the market; she says it is common. "'Twould not be decorous for a young lady."' Lizzie mimicked her mother's tone, crinkling her pretty features into a grimace. 'I think that's silly, don't you? But I shall ask if we can visit our new church tomorrow, so we can pass by.'

Anna demurred. It would be unwise to appear disloyal to her aunt at such an early stage. 'I could turn my pen to architectural scenes instead, but I do find the perspective of buildings such a puzzle, don't you?'

Lizzie's face fell, her smiles gone as quickly as they arrived. 'I would love to be able to draw, but my tutor is so scornful of my attempts that I scarcely dare to try.'

'Then I shall teach you,' Anna said.

'Oh yes,' Lizzie said, instantly recovered. 'I should like that very much.'

After her tour of the house Anna begged leave to retire.

'Of course, you must be exhausted,' her aunt said. 'But I must warn you that your chamber is up many stairs, and it is rather plain. We are short of rooms because the ground floor is given over to the business. We hope to move shortly, to an address more suited to Sadler and Son's status, do we not, my dearest?' She smiled at her husband but his face remained impassive. 'Lizzie, why don't you show Anna to her room? Her luggage is already there and I shall send the maid at once with water.'

They climbed a narrow wooden stairway to the very top floor, which Lizzie called the 'old weaving loft'. It had been converted, she said, now that Uncle Joseph had finished with the weaving and turned to selling finished silks for his living. The room, next door to one shared by the cook and Betty the maid, was indeed small and plain, with a wooden chest of drawers, a side table with a bowl and ewer, an upright chair and a bed that, although simple, looked marvellously inviting to her weary limbs.

After Lizzie had clattered back down the stairs, Anna opened the casement, took a long breath of warm night air and sighed deeply, releasing the muscles of her face that had grown painful from holding a polite smile.

She climbed under the covers, but sleep was slow to come.

The bed was short, the horsehair mattress lumpy and the blanket smelled unaired. But if not as comfortable as her feather bed at home, she was at least warm and safe. What more could she want for?

It was certainly warm in this attic on a hot July evening. Little breeze stirred the air, even up here on the top floor. The noise from the street was astonishing – did people in the city never rest? It seemed hardly to have abated since she first stepped from the coach this afternoon: brays of laughter from boisterous gangs of young men, the shrill calls of women and wails of children, the howling of dogs and keening of cats, the clanging of coaches and the hammering of handcart wheels on the cobbles. In her village all would be quiet at this time of night except for the rhythmical boom of the breakers when the wind was in the east.

What an adventure it had been. Despite the sorrow of leaving and the heaviness in her heart which had not lifted since her mother's death, she could not help being a little excited.

'Life has much to offer a talented young woman such as you,' her father had said as they sat together that last evening. 'There is so much to see and so much to learn, much in the world to savour and enjoy. But you will not find it here in this little community. You must go and seek your fortune in the city.'

'Like Dick Whittington, I suppose?'

'Indeed,' he laughed. 'And if you become Mayor of London, then you must invite us to your grand residence. But remember you can come home whenever your black cat leads you here.'

Even though the first day on the road had been perfectly straightforward and without incident, every small event came as a surprise for a novice traveller. She had been instructed to refrain from conversing with the other passengers for fear of encouraging intimacy, but it was so rare to spend time in the company of strangers that she could not prevent herself from scrutinising them, as covertly as possible to avoid appearing rude.

All ages of human life seemed to be represented in the cramped space of the stagecoach. Next to her on the bench was a stout gentleman who studied his newspaper in a self-important kind of way, harrumphing with disapproval at what he read and digging her in the ribs whenever he turned the page. After a while he fell asleep, tipping alarmingly sideways onto her shoulder before stirring and sharply pulling himself upright, only to repeat the process every few minutes.

She could not see the faces of the two women on his other side but knew they must be herring girls from Yarmouth, unmistakeable from their odour and redness of hand. On the opposite bench, two stout housewives from Bungay occupied sufficient space for three and chattered unceasingly all the way to Ipswich. Each jiggled a small child on one knee and a baby on the other.

The children whined incessantly before falling asleep with dribbles of snot streaming unchecked from their noses, while the chubby cupids took it in turns to cry: piercing, disturbing sounds in such close proximity. In between wails these babes would bestow cherubic smiles upon any who caught their eye, and all would be forgiven until the next bout of yowling. When it went on for too long, their mothers would yank down their tops and stuff the wailing infants' faces into the exposed folds of disconcertingly white flesh.

A withered elderly gentleman had levered himself into the narrow space next to the two ladies and, when he too fell asleep, Anna feared that he might be silently squeezed to death, with no one the wiser until all had disembarked.

To reserve her stares and pass the time, she took out the pocket Bible her father had pressed into her hand at their parting. Her faith had evaporated during the long nights of her mother's agony, and had never returned, but the familiar phrases of the epistles were comforting. As she opened the scuffed leather cover she saw for the first time that he had inscribed inside the frontispiece, in his vicar's spidery hand: *To my dearest Anna, God keep you and hold you.* Tears prickled behind her eyelids. *When will I see the dear man again?* she thought. *How will he cope, with just Jane to care for him?*

Although she was only five at the time and had witnessed little of her mother's labour, she understood that her sister's birth had been long and arduous. When she finally arrived, the baby was blue and limp. Defying all expectations, her sister survived and slowly gained strength and weight. It was not until much later they discovered that the difficult birth had left long-lasting effects: Jane's right side was weak and she walked with a limp, dragging her foot painfully behind her. And although sweet-natured, she was slow in her mind, struggling to understand those things that others found simple, and never managing to learn reading and writing.

How will she manage the household without me, strange little creature that she is? Anna thought to herself. *Will she understand Father's needs? Will she stay well? And will she find company and friendship with other girls in the village, now that I have gone?* How she missed them both, already.

When they finally reached the staging inn at Chelmsford, the portly gentleman took her hand to help her disembark.

'May I help with your overnight case?'

'Thank you very much,' she replied, grateful that someone had taken even a slight notice of her. 'This is this one. I suppose the portmanteau and hatbox will stay on the coach for the onward journey in the morning?'

'That is the usual custom, if you have informed them.'

He picked up her shabby canvas bag and his smart leather case and walked with her across the yard towards the front door of the inn. 'Pardon me, madam,' he said, 'please do not think I am too forward if I offer a nugget of advice?'

'Dear sir, any advice is most welcome, for I am unfamiliar with the customs of the road,' she said.

'Then may I recommend that you might ask for your meal to be served in your room? The tap can become somewhat rowdy and may not suit your gentle temperament.' As if to prove his words, a roar of voices accosted them as he pushed open the door. She hesitated on the threshold but he took her arm and gently led her between the crowded tables through a fog of tobacco smoke towards a serving hatch. He shouted over the hubbub to a surly-looking woman Anna assumed to be the innkeeper's wife and, shortly afterwards, a scruffy boy appeared and showed them upstairs. As they parted on the landing, Anna said, 'You have been most kind, sir.'

'May you rest well, madam,' he said, with a slight bow.

The little exchange had so cheered her that she barely noticed how small and sparsely furnished was the room, how grey the bedsheets from too many launderings. When it arrived, the cold mutton was greasy and the potatoes pocked with black eyes, but she was so hungry she cleaned the plate without a thought. The candle stump they supplied quickly burned out and she found herself facing a long, disturbed night, trying to ignore the bedbugs as they celebrated the arrival of new flesh, and listening to the tap room below becoming ever more lively.

When she slept, finally, she dreamed of returning home to find all unchanged, the vicarage full of activity and laughter as it once had been, the fires lit, the family foursome intact. She fell into her mother's embrace, smelling the mingled aromas of laundry soap and garden herbs that, to Anna, spelled love and security.

When she woke in the early hours and realised where she was the tears came at last, wetting her pillow with long, racking sobs that seemed to shake her whole body. How could she think of leaving that beloved place? But how could she return to it, when she would never again feel her mother's warmth?

Yet next morning her mood seemed to rise with the sun. She was sorry to discover that the kindly gentleman was not joining them again, but stepped aboard the coach full of optimism at the prospect of another day of travel, even venturing a smile at the only other passenger, a smartly dressed lady. After twenty-four hours of barely speaking to another person she would have welcomed a conversation, and was disappointed when the lady immediately took out her spectacles and opened her book.

She turned to her own thoughts, excited at the prospect of seeing at first hand all that she had heard about the great metropolis, and of making the acquaintance of her uncle and aunt, and her two cousins. After being confined to the house caring for her mother for such long, dutiful months she yearned to spread her wings and see the big city, and they had generously offered her this opportunity.

In the early afternoon, they stopped at a village to pick up two gentlemen who appeared to be father and son, and the coachman invited the ladies to disembark for what he called 'a fine view of the city'.

At first, Anna could make out only the River Thames, reflecting the sun like a silver snake along the valley beneath a reddish-brown pall of smoke. As her eyes adjusted to the distance, she could discern ribbons reaching out towards them and in every other direction. After a few moments she came to realise, with astonishment, that these were streets of houses, in their hundreds, even thousands. The numbers of people all these buildings might contain was barely imaginable. In the densest part of the city before them, along the river's edge, barely a speck of green could be seen; not a tree, not a field in sight.

How will I ever survive in such close proximity to so many others, all breathing that smoke-filled air? she wondered. Her village had but three hundred souls, with fields and woods occupying all the land to one side, sand dunes and the great empty sea to the other. *What will I find to paint, in a place with no flowers or trees, no butterflies or birds?*

Turning restlessly in the attic bed, she felt empty and emotionless, as though travelling at such an unaccustomed pace had caused a part of her soul to be left behind. She had waited so long for her 'big adventure' to start. But now that she was actually here, everything seemed so strange and unfamiliar, even frightening, that she longed to be back in the comfortable familiarity of the countryside.

2

A lady ought to adopt a modest and measured gait; too great a hurry injures the grace which ought to characterise her. She should not turn her head on one side and on the other, especially in cities, where this bad habit seems an invitation to the impertinent.

– The Lady's Book of Manners

Anna woke early with the sun pouring through the windows of the attic room, wondering at first where she was. And then she remembered. All was silent downstairs and even the restlessness of the city seemed to have been stilled. It must be very early, she decided, and climbed back into bed to wait until she could hear the family stirring.

The events of the previous few days ran through her head: her father's sorrowful face and her sister's tears as they parted; the yowling babies in the coach; the kind gentleman at Chelmsford; the frightening chants of the crowd and the swift evasive action by the coachman. She wished she understood why the townsfolk were so angry about bread. Surely this was something everyone, even the poor, could make for themselves?

And those French boys, at the Red Lyon. Her cousin

had treated them harshly but in the new light of the morning she felt more generously disposed towards him: surely he had only been concerned for her safety in the heat of the moment and had meant no harm?

Recalling that strange turn of events, she found it surprising all over again that she had not felt more alarmed on finding herself in the arms of a stranger – and he not even a gentleman. She smiled to herself, remembering how tenderly the young man had spoken to her, the warmth in his eyes and the sweet, nutty smell of him, like dried beech leaves in the late autumn sun.

She must have drifted off again, for the next thing she heard was the maid knocking at the door, with a fresh jug of water. She quickly washed and dressed, and went down-stairs to find the family already seated at the most sumptuous of fast-breaking meals she had ever encountered: no fewer than three sorts of breads, butter, honey, marmalade and cherry jam, oatmeal with sweet cream, smoked herrings, cold veal pies, grilled kidneys and coffee. This last was a most fashionable drink, she had heard, but she found it to be dark and bitter-tasting. She would have preferred tea and just a slice of bread and honey, but felt it impolite not to taste at least a small piece of everything they pressed upon her. By the end of the meal she was afraid her stays – already well worn – might give out completely.

Aunt Sarah outlined her plans for the day: 'First thing after breakfast, we must see about your wardrobe.'

'You are very kind, but I do not wish to put you to any expense,' Anna said hurriedly, since she had but the few pounds Father had pressed into her hands before she left.

'I have two other dresses, a blue and a brown, and several shawls and bonnets.'

'You are in the city now,' Aunt Sarah said firmly, 'and you must be attired accordingly. We cannot have people mistaking you for a maid, can we? You must wear the best of silks – what else would the niece of an eminent mercer be wearing? Besides, you are of an age now to be settled –' Lizzie giggled into her hand '– and I am sure I need not explain why your appearance is of the greatest possible importance.'

Sarah helped herself to a further generous slice of pie. 'This morning, my dressmaker will measure you and show us her patterns, and then we shall go downstairs to the shop to choose the silk. I think five dresses might suffice for the moment – two day dresses, two evening gowns, and a further gown and jacket for Sunday – do you think so, Husband? And of course a cape for cool evenings.'

Joseph grunted into his newspaper but Lizzie was listening intently. 'Which dressmaker are you using?'

'Miss Charlotte, as usual. She is my favourite,' Aunt Sarah said.

'Do make sure she offers the latest fashion, Mama, and the right kind of design: a small floral pattern, perhaps, or fine stripes. And with lots of lace; it is so pretty close to the face.' Anna wondered how the girl had become such an expert at her young age.

'Have no fear, dearest. By the time we have finished, your cousin will be the talk of the town.'

'Oh, it's so exciting!' Lizzie cried. 'I wish it was me, getting new dresses.'

Anna felt more alarmed than excited. Fashion had not

entered her world before; anyone dressed too modishly in the village was considered to be puffed up, and it was not in her character to enjoy being thus noticed. Besides, the wet and windy weather at the coast was never kind to fine fabrics, and any form of headwear needed to be firmly tied around the chin.

She felt as though she were a doll being discussed and dressed for the pleasure and enjoyment of others, regardless of her own feelings or views. But she had to accept, at least for the moment, that this was the fact of the matter: she would have little or no say in what happened from now on because she was both physically and financially dependent on her uncle's hospitality. Obedience had never come naturally – her lack of it had often led her into trouble in the past – but everyone had her best interests at heart, she told herself, so she must follow their advice as best she could, so that she could learn the ways of this new world.

Although it had never been articulated openly, she knew full well *why* she had to submit to her aunt's attentions; why she must do her duty. Jane would never marry and would need to be looked after for the rest of her life. Their father had spent most of his savings on doctors' fees trying to restore his wife to health, and little was left in the coffers to rent a home when he became too old to preach and they had to leave the vicarage.

The family was dependent on Anna making an advantageous marriage, but she wondered whether that notion would ever coincide with her own longing to spend the rest of her life with someone she truly loved. She'd recently attended the wedding of a former schoolmate, a lavish affair paid for by the groom, an older man with large estates in

North Suffolk, receding hair and an already expanding waistline. The girl had smiled bravely throughout the day and appeared to be entranced by her new husband, but the thought of sharing affectionate moments with such a man had made Anna shudder inside.

Lizzie was banished to her lessons with a tutor while upstairs in Aunt Sarah's bedroom Anna was stripped to her stays and every part of her body, even the circumference of her head and the length and breadth of her feet, was measured and recorded by the seamstress, Miss Charlotte.

I will never make an elegant society lady no matter how beautiful the new dresses, she thought, regarding herself with dismay in the full-length glass. Her limbs were too long, her feet and hands too large, her fingernails short and roughened by housework, her wide-set eyes too bold and an inconstant shade of blue. 'The colour of the changing seas,' her father would tease her. 'I can always tell when stormy weather is approaching.'

Despite daily applications of lemon juice, the freckles that splattered her nose and cheeks were as bold and abundant as ever and her hair, although an acceptable shade of blonde, curled in unruly corkscrews that were almost impossible to restrain beneath a bonnet.

I really do look like a servant girl. Or at the very best the hard-working daughter of a country vicar, which of course I am.

'She'll need two sets of stays as well, don't you think?' said Aunt Sarah, frowning at the well-worn undergarments.

Anna could not remember how many years they had served – probably since the first time she'd been persuaded that a young lady should wear stays. She'd objected at the time but eventually obeyed because she knew it would please her mother, in whose life there seemed to be so little pleasure and so much pain. How long ago that girlhood seemed, and yet she was still only eighteen years old.

Miss Charlotte continued her measurements without comment. A petite woman of indeterminate age, with small, intelligent eyes, she herself was modestly attired without even a bonnet, her dark hair tied into a neat bun that allowed just a few curls to escape, softening her plain face. After Anna dressed again, she was invited to sit at the dressing table where Miss Charlotte had set out pages of coloured drawings of skirts, bodices, gowns, coats, bonnets, hats and shoes in a confusing range of styles. 'These are the latest designs for young women. Is there anything here that takes your eye, Miss Butterfield?'

They all looked the same to Anna: the bodices over-puffed and over-ruffled, the skirts so wide and so gathered around the waist that she'd never be able to move without tripping over. And how would she get dressed each day without the help of a lady's maid?

The hats were so large that the wearer would have to take care passing through doorways, and they could certainly never be worn outdoors except on an entirely windless day. The shoes were so high of heel she felt sure she would trip with every step, and they would bring her head in line with that of the tallest man.

Miss Charlotte and Aunt Sarah were engaged in a complicated discussion involving words like *cornet*, *à l'anglaise, pelerine, stomacher, rabat* and *stole*, that Anna had never even heard before. *I must take lessons in fashion*, she thought, *if I am ever to take control of my own appearance.* Perhaps Miss Charlotte would agree to be her guide; she seemed a sensible sort.

Following much debate they chose four designs and Anna nodded assent, although in truth she could never imagine herself wearing any of them. Aunt Sarah pronounced herself to be well satisfied. 'And now we will go downstairs to choose the silks,' she announced.

The first room they entered, at the rear of the house on the ground floor, was a very untidy office panelled with shelves sagging under the weight of leather-bound ledgers. At the window, overlooking the courtyard garden, was a table with a disarray of fabric samples, books and papers heaped upon it. In the centre of the room were three high wooden desks at which sat William and two other young men, at their accounts. As the ladies entered they put down their quills and leapt to their feet.

'Gentlemen,' said her aunt. 'This is my niece Anna Butterfield, who has come to live with us. And you already know Miss Charlotte, my dressmaker.'

'Pa, it's Ma and the girls to see you,' William shouted in a vulgar manner, and after a short pause Joseph appeared from a panelled cubicle, with that passing smile that disappeared like a mirage.

'Welcome to the beating heart of Sadler and Son, Mercers to the Gentry, of Number Four Spital Square,' he boomed. 'This is where we make the money to keep our ladies in the manner to which they are accustomed, isn't it, lads? Now, back to work with the lot of you while we go next door to look at dress silks for my pretty young niece.'

It was the almost overwhelming aroma that first accosted Anna's senses: a concentrated essence of that same dry, sweet, nutty smell, she realised with a jolt, of the young man who had helped her yesterday. Now she understood: this was the smell of silk, the heady bouquet of confidence and prosperity. But the young man had not appeared to be wealthy and was not clothed in silk, as far as she could remember.

She forced her mind to concentrate on what her uncle was saying: 'This is where we keep samples from all the best master weavers in the area, so that we can show them to designers and dressmakers who supply the most superior people in the land. We had a commission from the Duke of Cumberland's agent last month, did we not, my dear?' he said to his wife. 'And each week brings further rumours of a royal engagement. A royal wedding would certainly perk up trade.'

Everything in the room was designed to impress. At the wide bow window was set an elegant oak table and damask-covered chairs clearly intended for the top people's backsides, or at least the backsides of the top people's agents. Wide oak floorboards gleamed with polish where they were not covered with a brilliantly patterned deep-red Persian carpet. On shelves around the room was arrayed a visual feast: a dazzling display of samples and rolls of silk in a rainbow of vivid, luminous colours, glittering golds and silvers, in all manner of designs and patterns.

'Well, what do you think, young Anna?' her uncle prompted. 'We pride ourselves on dealing with the very best.'

'It's beautiful,' she said. 'But where does the silk originally come from? I mean, before it is woven?'

'Well now, there's a question!' He pointed to a large square frame hung above the main doorway. A brass plaque announced it to be: *The Life Cycle of the Silkworm*.

Inside the case, set out in a circle, were preserved specimens of the insect in its twelve stages, starting at the top with the moth. *The moth lives but one day and never flies*, read the label. *In its short life, its sole purpose is to mate and lay eggs. From these hatch tiny, thread-like caterpillars that do nothing but eat mulberry leaves and multiply many times in size, before spinning hundreds of yards of the finest thread into a cocoon. Most cocoons end up as raw silk* – a small hank of which, twisted and tied with a pink ribbon, was displayed inside the case – *while others are allowed to hatch into new moths so that the cycle can start all over again*.

She read all of this with growing astonishment. 'How extraordinary,' she said. 'Where do all these moths and caterpillars live?'

His great booming laugh continued for several embarrassing seconds. 'Dearest Anna, you have much to learn. Do you hear, Wife –' he turned to Aunt Sarah '– our niece thinks we have silkworms munching away in the garden!' This was not at all what she had suggested – the notion was clearly ludicrous – but she bit her lip.

'We do not keep the worms, nor do we spin the thread or weave it, my dear. The raw silk comes by ship from the East, places like Constantinople and China; it is spun and woven here in London.' Anna knew all about wool, which, of course, was shorn from English sheep, and linen, which was produced from the flax that grew in the fields. But she'd never stopped to imagine where silk came from, and was astonished to learn that it originated in such exotic lands.

'My father and his father before him were master weavers, as was I, before I became a mercer,' he went on. 'We have silk in the blood.'

'But where are your looms now?'

'Long gone, my dear. Haven't been near a loom or held a shuttle for years. I tired of dealing with journeymen and apprentices – the trade is now so dominated by the French and they can be such a treacherous lot. No, there is more to be made from buying and selling, so when William joined me in the business, we sold the looms and turned to mercery, as you see before you.'

Behind the door were shelves on which were stacked dozens of leather-bound ledgers. He pulled one of them down, laid it on the table and opened it. 'See here, Niece. These are just some of the designs we have supplied to the top people in society.'

As he turned the pages, she could see that each contained coloured drawings on squared paper with, on the opposite side, a list of complex instructions and abbreviations. On some of the pages were pinned clippings of fabric: the silk, she assumed, that had been woven to the painted design.

Meanwhile, Aunt Sarah and Miss Charlotte had been choosing samples of fabric, laying them out on the other end of the table. 'Look, Anna, tell us what you think,' said her aunt. In the light from the window the silks shimmered before her eyes like a thousand butterfly wings. Anna was so dazzled that she found herself almost unable to distinguish between the various patterns.

'Come now, you must have a preference,' her aunt prompted. 'Or we will have to choose for you.' Anna pointed vaguely in the direction of the colours that she liked to use when painting landscapes: leaf green, sea blue, burnt umber, red ochre. By sheer luck it appeared that she had made the right choice. 'Most suitable for a young lady,' Miss Charlotte said approvingly, 'and perfectly *à la mode*.'

Next morning at breakfast Lizzie announced that she wanted to show Anna their church.

'Do you not think it would be sensible to wait until your cousin can wear one of her new gowns?' said her mother gently. 'They should be ready in a day or two.'

'But it is so hot,' Lizzie whined. 'I was indoors at my studies all day yesterday, and I would so love a little distraction.'

'Then go into the garden,' Aunt Sarah said. 'It is shady there.'

'There's nothing to see or do in the garden, you know that.' The girl turned to her father with a pretty, pleading smile, her head on one side, ringlets bobbing. 'Please, Papa. We wouldn't go far. Just to the church and back again. We won't say hello to anyone, I promise.'

Joseph muttered, 'Can't see that any harm could come from it.'

'Just for a couple of hours, then,' her mother conceded. 'And don't be late for luncheon.'

Anna was grateful to Lizzie for pleading the case. For two days now she hadn't taken a single breath of fresh air. At home, she would be out and about every day, collecting eggs and vegetables, walking down the street to the village store for milk and tea, and back along the beach. Besides, the little exchange had been most instructive. Joseph was clearly prey to his daughter's charms and out of loyalty Sarah would not contradict him, in front of the family at least. Anna could see now that her cousin could become an important ally.

She was certainly pleased to have Lizzie at her side as they stepped out. The streets were just as noisy, bustling and chaotic as the day she'd arrived.

'Watch the ground to make sure you don't step in anything. And don't catch anyone's eye – especially the beggars – they'll only target you,' Lizzie said, leading her briskly between the crowds, crossing the carriageways fearlessly and deftly avoiding the carriages and wagons that appeared with great speed from each direction. At last they came to a junction, and Lizzie pointed down the street ahead. 'There it is. Christ Church. It was completed but ten years ago, or twenty, I am not entirely sure. Is it not beautiful?'

The building was truly awe-inspiring. The spire reached so high that Anna's neck soon ached from peering upwards to the pinnacle; the white stone gleamed almost dazzling white in the sunshine against the blue of the sky above and the dreary grey streets below. As they climbed the wide steps up to its massive pillared portico she felt very small and humble, as though she were about to enter a palace, or somewhere she did not deserve to be.

They eased open the heavy wooden doors and stepped inside. It was blessedly cool and quiet, with that dusty smell of ages that seems to pervade all churches, even new ones.

Their village church, a wooden-roofed flint-work building with a single nave, much reduced amid the ruins of its medieval origins, could seat just one hundred souls. This one must surely seat a thousand, perhaps more. Rows of box pews were ranged down the centre and side aisles, above which were wooden galleries almost certainly containing yet more benches.

They appeared to be entirely alone and their footsteps echoed in the soaring, sunlit space. *What a splendid reverberation there must be when all these people recite the Lord's Prayer or intone the psalms,* she thought, recalling the timid quaverings of her father's congregation.

Lizzie sat at a bench and invited Anna to join her. 'What do you think?'

'I think it is magnificent,' Anna whispered. 'More like a cathedral than a church. Do you come every Sunday?'

The reply was shocking in its honesty: 'Oh no, only occasionally,' she said. 'Mother comes when she wants to pray for something good to happen, Father comes because it beholds him to be seen here from time to time, he says, and I like to meet my friends here.'

'And William?'

'Refuses to come, ever. Says science is his God, whatever that means.'

'Is that what he meant when he said that God was an interesting conjecture?'

'He talks all kinds of nonsense. I don't listen to him. He has so many theories; each time he comes back from his club he has a new one. All learned from his cronies, no doubt.'

'What kind of a club is it?'

'From the smell of him I think they do little more than drink port and smoke cigars. He claims it is a mathematical society, but my guess is that their calculations are mostly about gambling odds.' Lizzie stood up suddenly. 'Let's go to the market before it's too late. Some of the stalls pack up at lunchtime.'

'But I thought . . . ?'

'I don't care what Mother says, and you want to see the flowers, don't you?'

As they approached the market building Anna became apprehensive.

'Won't we become the object of people's attention?' she whispered. 'What if someone sees us and tells your mother?'

'Dearest Anna, have you not noticed how I am dressed today?' In truth she had not, but now she could see that Lizzie was wearing a plainer gown than usual, and her hair was tied under a simple cotton bonnet, much like her own. 'We look like a pair of country lasses, don't we?' Lizzie chuckled. 'No one will take any notice of us. But hold your breath,' she shouted over the hubbub of traders' cries. 'Thank goodness it's not Friday, for the fish smells even worse then.' Anna kept her eyes lowered, unwilling to look too carefully at the bloody carcasses and dead fowl, the displays of liver and intestines and the decapitated hogs' heads with their blank eyes and mouths stuffed with apples.

The smell became sweeter, even fragrant. Here, fruit was piled into pyramids of every hue: apples in a rainbow of varieties from palest yellow to brightest scarlet, thin green pears as well as rosy round ones, blushing peaches, deep ruby plums, aromatic quinces, golden apricots, greengages, mulberries, blackberries and figs, oranges and lemons. Stands of sweet pink rhubarb stood guard at either side. Each stall was an individual work of art, each trader competing for the finest display.

They passed along a row of vegetable stalls every bit as artistic and colourful as the fruit: salads in all shades of green, cucumbers, leeks, celery, carrots and cauliflower, deep green curly kale, bright red tomatoes – never seen in Halesworth market – and towering constructions of cabbages in every shape, size and colour.

'Why would someone call another person a cabbage head?' she asked, recalling William's jibe.

'Don't say it too loudly, it's rude,' Lizzie whispered. 'Where did you hear it?'

'Just someone in the street.' This was not a lie, at least.

'Some people call the French people cabbage heads because they eat a lot of it – it makes them smell, too.'

'But why are they so unpleasant about the French?'

'Dearest Coz, you have so much to learn,' Lizzie said, taking her arm. 'Half of France is in London these days, although I don't really understand why they should choose to leave their own country. Many are weavers, good weavers too, which doesn't please the English. I suppose people resent them, think they have funny ways.'

Further along, they found an aisle of flower stalls. Anna loved to study the wild flowers that grew in the fields and marshes around her village, but knew little of garden varieties save those that somehow thrived in their neglected vicarage garden: snowdrops and primroses in spring, delphiniums and roses in summer. At first, the blooms on these stalls appeared exotic and unfamiliar but, as she looked closer, there were among them some that she recognised: lavender, catmint, pinks, lily of the valley, heartsease, auriculas and sweet peas. She found herself smiling at them, like old friends, their vibrant colours and aromas transporting her back to summer days in the village.

On their way out she noticed a wooden staircase in one corner and looked upwards to see where it led. Above them, beneath the roof of the market, was a gallery with further stalls. The railings were hung with what looked like pieces of old cloth.

'Why are they selling rags?' she asked.

'They're not rags, silly. They're clothes.'

'They're all torn and dirty.'

'Oh, Anna. Don't you know anything? That's because they are second-hand clothes. But there's still value in them, so people sell them on.'

'That's horrible. To wear clothes others have worn. And not even family.'

'Some people don't have the choice. They are not as lucky as we are, to have new clothes. Come, we must hurry back now. Mama will be listening for us with her eye on the clock, counting every second.'

As they turned the corner into Spital Square Anna's stomach did a small somersault. At the side of the square were two young men sitting on a wall in the shade of a large tree, kicking their heels and laughing at a private joke.

As they approached, the eyes of one of them widened in recognition, and she saw that his cheek carried a purple bruise. He stood and took off his cap, making a small bow. Long dark hair fell around his face.

She could feel Lizzie tugging at her arm, whispering, 'Come *on*, Anna. You must not talk to French boys.'

'Mam'selle,' he said, in that curious accent. 'I hope you are now fully recovered?'

'I am well, sir, thanks to your help. I wanted to apologise . . .' She gestured in the direction of his cheek, their eyes met and they smiled at each other. For a fleeting, astonishing second, Anna felt as though she had known this stranger for ever.

'*De rien*, it was nothing,' the young man said quietly, his gaze falling to the ground.

Lizzie pulled again at her arm, as Anna racked her brain for something more to say so that she could prolong the moment.

'May I know your name?' she asked.

'My name is Henri,' he said. 'Henri Vendôme. Silk weaver. *À votre service.*' He made another small bow.

'And I am Anna,' she said. 'Miss Anna Butterfield. And once more, thank you for your kindness.'

'It was my pleasure,' he said. '*Au revoir*, Miss Butterfield.'

She allowed herself to be dragged away. So he was a French silk weaver. His eyes might have sparkled with mischief, but he did not look at all likely to demonstrate or be violent. The very opposite, in fact.

'Whatever were you thinking, talking to a stranger like that?' her cousin chided.

'He helped me when I fainted the other day. It would have been discourteous not to stop and thank him.'

'It would have been wiser not to have done so.' Lizzie looked around furtively. 'Let us pray we were not observed. It would cause such a scandal.'

3

Make industry a part of your character as early as possible: Be officiously serviceable to your Master on all occasions: if possible prevent his commands, understand a nod, a look, and do rather more than is required of you, than less than is your duty.
— Advice for apprentices and journeymen OR A sure guide to gain both esteem and an estate, 1760

As the girls disappeared around the corner Guy began to dance around his friend making squelchy kissing noises and jerking his hips suggestively.

'*Tais-toi, crapaud.*' Henri chased him and punched him sharply on the arm.

'*Pourquoi?*' Guy said, punching him back. '*Elle est belle, non, la jeune Anglaise?* Another addition to your crowd of adoring admirers?'

'*Ça n'a pas d'importance, idiot.* I helped her, nothing more.' Henri walked away, struggling to persuade himself that this was true. In fact, he had not stopped thinking about her since that first encounter.

Her name was Anna, niece of the mercer Joseph Sadler; that much he knew from his bruising encounter with her cousin William, just a few days ago. One piece of the riddle was in place. But the rest of her was a puzzle. She dressed as a maid but spoke like a lady. Unlike most English women of her class she had been polite enough to acknowledge and thank him and would have talked for longer, he reckoned, had the younger girl not been nagging her. She was tall – almost as tall as himself – skinny and not, at first glance, especially pretty, with all those freckles and eyes that seemed undecided as to whether to be blue or green. In fact, there was little remarkable about her, and yet he could not put her from his mind. She appeared demure and modest, even though she came from a family he'd heard were ruthlessly ambitious and the most snobbish social climbers of the area.

'Jumped-up weaver, nothing more than the rest of us, that Mr Sadler,' Monsieur Lavalle had grumbled one day, on returning from delivering some silks to the Spital Square establishment. 'Just because he's got a few dukes and duchesses wearing his stuffs.'

Henri never discovered quite why M. Lavalle, normally a peaceable man, should have been moved to speak so strongly against the mercer. He imagined there had been some snub about the quality of the silk he'd been offering to Mr Sadler, or perhaps he suspected that the mercer was importing foreign fabrics. But it wasn't one's place, as a journeyman, to question your master.

'*Pas si vite, Henri.* Why such a rush?' Guy called, running to catch up. 'We still have fifteen minutes.'

'I must hurry back,' Henri said. 'I was only sent to deliver the lustrings to Shelleys. I still have two feet of the damask to weave by dusk.'

'Surely you don't need light to weave your miracles.'

Henri's cheeks coloured. At the time he'd been so delighted by M. Lavalle's compliment that he had unwisely repeated it to Guy. Now it seemed he would never live it down.

'It's such a dark purple it's impossible to see dropped threads by candlelight, and it's got to be ready first thing in the morning. See you tomorrow?'

'*À demain*. Shall we return to meet your new English sweetheart again? Or will it be the one you were lusting after last week?'

'*Vas au diable*,' Henri cursed cheerfully as they parted and he headed towards Princes Street. It always gave him a happy feeling, safe inside, walking these streets, the silk weavers' streets – *his* streets – rows of houses with warp winders hanging over the doors, the songs of birds in their cages and the clatter of looms from the long-light lofts high above the street.

Henri regarded M. Lavalle as a father figure and was only too aware that he owed everything to the master weaver. He barely remembered his own father, who had died when vainly trying to save his sister from drowning in the Bay of Biscay during their flight from France.

Through much subterfuge they had managed to escape from the foul-mouthed *dragonnades* for whom they, along with all other Protestant families, had been required to provide lodgings. It was supposedly to ensure they had renounced their faith but it also resulted in penury as they were forced to sell their looms to make room for the soldiers, and meet their endless demands for food and wine. To refuse would mean a beating or worse. His elder sister disappeared one day and never returned. He'd heard people whispering, although he did not at the time understand what they meant: that she'd refused a soldier's advances and paid for her virtue with her life.

'We have nothing left to stay for,' his father had whispered late one evening as the soldiers snored in their beds. 'It is time for us to leave, while we still have a few livres remaining.'

They trudged sixty miles to the coast under the cloak of three long, cold nights, resting during daylight to avoid capture, and arrived at the port only to learn that the ship for which they had bought tickets had been wrecked. They spent the last of their savings bribing the captain of a small fishing smack – five hundred livres before embarkation, and the promise of a further five hundred on arrival in Plymouth.

These things Henri knew from what his mother, Clothilde, had since told him. All he remembered of that terrible journey was being carried through the surf in the dead of night by a gruff captain with enormous hands and then hauled through a narrow trapdoor in the deck down into the pitch-black bilges of the ship, the stink of rotten fish and the fearful sting of the kippering salt on which they crouched. She had recounted how, before leaving the port, they'd been advised to stand stock-still, in perfect silence, immediately beneath the main beam of the deck above so that their skulls should not be pierced by the swords that customs inspectors would thrust between the planks to detect stowaways.

Sometimes, Henri's dreams were haunted by other

memories: the whites of his parents' eyes in the darkness as the smack bucked and rolled, his mother's retching, his sister's terrified whimpers. And how, as the ship pitched even more violently, they were thrown against the side of the hold, the trapdoor was blown open and they were plunged into a torrent of freezing ocean water. He would always waken at this point, crying out and struggling for breath, knowing that this had been the end of his life as he had once known it.

It was only many years later that his mother managed to steel herself to describe what happened next. They hauled themselves on deck through the trapdoor, battling the cascades of water crashing over the ship, only to discover that the fisherman and his boy had disappeared, presumably washed overboard by that first devastating wave. Their only hope was to lash themselves to the mast and pray that they would ride out the storm, but before they could do this another mountainous surge hit them, dashing twelve-year-old Marie over the side of the ship and into the darkness. His father had immediately jumped in to rescue her, but both had been carried away in the swell, never to be seen again. The last of the family's savings went with them.

Clothilde's memories of how they survived the storm were vague, but eventually they were shipwrecked on the coast of what he now knew to be the county of Kent and hauled to safety by salvage hunters. They must have been sorely disappointed to discover that their sole bounty was a woman and a small boy, half dead from exposure, but one of the families took them in and nursed them back to life.

Henri could remember little of what happened over the

next few months. They found shelter in an abandoned shed on the edges of a small town and his mother seemed to give up all hope, weeping day and night and never venturing out, while he went scavenging for food, clothes and blankets.

Then, one day, he was caught by a market trader who accused him of thieving and dragged him by his ears to the home of the Town Clerk. Although Henri had by now learned a few words of English they were nothing like sufficient to explain that he had only been waiting for discarded food, and that he and his mother were starving because they had lost everything at sea.

The Town Clerk, a barrel of a man with bloodshot eyes, a heavily powdered wig that sat lopsided on his head and a white beard that cascaded over his chest, bellowed at him, 'So, what do they call you, boy?'

Terrified, Henri managed to mutter his name.

'Onry? Ain't that a Frenchy name?'

Henri nodded.

'How'd you get here, then?'

He understood the question and tried to find the words to reply but failed, and instead tried to mime the motion of a boat tossing in a storm. As the man continued to shake his head in bafflement Henri was overcome with fear and frustration, and began to cry.

Then the miracle happened. A young woman came through the door with a tea tray. As well as the teapot, tea plates, cups and saucers, sugar bowl and milk jug, the tray contained a plate of sandwiches and another of small biscuits. Captivated by the sight of such deliciousness passing so close to his face, Henri's tears dried in an instant.

He found his mouth watering and heard his stomach rumbling. It was all he could do to prevent his hands from reaching out to grab a small piece.

'Oh,' she exclaimed. 'I didn't know you had a visitor, Father. Shall I bring another plate? He looks famished.'

There was an agonising silence as the two of them regarded the urchin in his bare feet and rags, his limbs so thin they might snap at any moment.

The man grunted. 'I suppose you'd better, m'dear. Come and join us. I need you to translate.'

Henri stood obediently as they seated themselves by the fireside, eating everything that was passed to him, and drinking a whole mug of milk while trying to answer the questions the man fired at him. The girl's French was rudimentary and some of the sentences she translated made little sense, but he responded as best he could. As the interrogation continued, haltingly, it became clear that many of Henri's replies were also becoming lost in translation.

Eventually he managed to convey to them that he and his mother were fugitive Huguenots, his poor drowned father having been a silk weaver in their home town, and that his mother had worked as a throwster in the same trade, twisting the finest single silk threads together on her wheel to make yarn of the correct *denier* as required by the weaver. Even though his hunger was clearly apparent they found it hard to believe that he and his mother had no home and, literally, not a *sou* to their names, and survived from his begging and scavenging.

'We must do something for him, Pa,' the girl said.

'It's the workhouse for them, I reckon.'

'But didn't you hear what he said about his mother? She has a craft and would earn a living if she could find work.'

'There's no throwstering around these parts, my dear.'

'There is in London. What about Uncle? He works in the silk trade, doesn't he?'

'*Pssht.* He don't want vagrants turning up at his door, Louisa. Enough of this, lad. I'll let you off the charge of pilfering if you do as I say. Bring your mother here and we'll take you to St Dunstan's. At least you'll get food and a bed there.'

As the girl showed him to the front door she whispered, 'Don't go to the workhouse, it's a terrible place. You'll get separated from your ma there. Go down the side steps and come to the kitchen door. *Cinq minutes.*'

She met him at the threshold, thrusting a brown-paper package into his hand.

'Good luck,' she said. 'Now get out of here before Father catches you.'

On his way back to the shack he hid in a copse and carefully unwrapped the package. Inside was pure treasure, better than any gold. It contained a loaf of stale bread, a large chunk of cheese and a girl's drawstring pocket holding a single silver shilling and a piece of paper on which were written the words: *My uncle, Nathaniel Broadstone, silk weaver, 5 Marks Lane, Bethnal Green, London. Do not mention my name.*

The journey took four days of walking and hitching lifts from cartiers because the stagecoach tickets cost more than the shilling would cover, and it was evening by the time they found their way to Bethnal Green. It had been raining all day and they were soaked to the skin. The man who answered the door regarded the ragged and sodden pair suspiciously.

Fear tightened Henri's voice into a squeak. 'Please, sir, we come to see Mr Broadstone.'

'And who are you, may I ask?'

'Henri Vendôme, sir, and my mother, Madame Clothilde Vendôme.'

'And so, madame, why have you brought your son to my doorstep?'

She shook her head.

'Speak, woman.'

'We cannot say, sir.' How could he betray the girl's kindness?

The man shook his head. 'If you cannot say, then why should I help you? Be off and stop pestering me.'

They endured an uncomfortable and terrifying night huddled in a doorway, trying to avoid the attention of the many unsavoury characters that seemed to populate the streets after dark. A bitter rain lashed down unceasingly and the noises of the city were strange and fearsome to their ears. More than once, Henri wished himself back in the Kentish shack, and that he had never met the Town Clerk or his daughter, who had given them such hope of a new beginning only for it to be so rudely dashed in this noisy, foul-smelling place.

And yet, in the morning, the sun came out and warmed them dry, and they stopped at a market stall to buy a couple of hot pies with their last few pennies. As Henri struggled to order in English the woman smiled and, miraculously, replied in fluent French. A fellow countrywoman! It was the first time they'd heard their own language, from a native speaker, since being washed up on these shores.

'*C'est gratuit*,' she said, handing over the pies. 'Keep your pennies. You look a little down on your luck.'

Clothilde burst into tears. '*Oh, merci madame, merci mille fois! Dieu vous bénisse.*'

Through her sobs, the story poured out in an incontrollable stream of words, as though a barrage had been unstopped. Finally she was able to express herself, to tell her tale to a sympathetic ear.

'*Ah, les pauvres*,' the woman said, at last. 'But take heart, madame. You still have your lovely boy at your side. And you are in the best place for a new start.'

Mon Dieu! They could barely believe what she told them. This was a place where many thousands of French and Flemish refugees had settled over the decades, fleeing persecution just as they had done. The English followed the same religion as theirs, more or less, and, at least officially, were welcoming, even if the locals were not always so sympathetic.

This area, just outside the city walls, she said, was where most of the French congregated. There were churches and charitable organisations and, best of all, literally hundreds – '*des centaines, à chaque coin de rue*' – of silk weavers, warpers, throwsters, merchants, mercers.

She held her hands wide to express the scale of what she was trying to convey. 'There is work for everyone here,' she said. 'London is crazy for silk.'

When, finally, Henri and his mother took their leave, she advised them to head for the French church in Fournier Street, a short walk away in a place called Spitalfields. The church elders would be able to help, she said. They followed her instructions and headed for the tallest building in the distance.

As they drew near, Henri's eyes were pulled heavenwards by the extraordinary tower, tiered like a wedding cake, with its tapering spire above almost touching the clouds. It made him feel quite dizzy. Apart from its spire the building looked more like a palace: broad granite steps led up to a door made for giants, surrounded by massive pillars that would take several Henris to join their hands around. The whole building was brilliant white, whiter than a new fall of snow, and glowed like a beacon in the sunlight among the dark, noisy streets of the city.

As they stood, in awe, Clothilde began to weep all over again. 'It's too grand,' she said. 'However can a pair of vagrants like us enter such a place?' But Henri dragged her up the steps. 'How can we know if we don't try, Maman? What else can we do?'

Just as they reached the doors, a tall, black-frocked priest emerged.

'Can I help?' he said, peering down at them.

'We look for French church.'

'Then you're in the wrong place, laddie. This here is Christ Church,' the man said, pointing behind them. 'L'Église de l'Hôpital is just along there.'

It's hard to believe that was ten years ago, Henri thought to himself as he sauntered down Lamb Street and Browns Lane, turning right into Wood Street, avoiding the route that would lead him past the kiosk selling sugared almonds. The girl at the stall was undoubtedly pretty but she had at first resisted his flatteries. Then, after weeks of dedicated flirting, he'd managed to steal a sweet, almond-scented kiss. More recently, she'd allowed him, with much giggling and a little high-pitched squeal, to feel her breast. But, as so often, and in a way he did not quite understand, once the game was won he'd begun to find the girl's attentions a little burdensome. His thoughts were already turning elsewhere.

At the far end of Wood Street the English church glimmered in the sunlight just as it had on that day. As he passed Fournier Street, he could see L'Église de l'Hôpital itself, a fine building on the junction with Brick Lane, still standing tall and proud above the terraced rows of weavers' houses.

As an apprentice Henri had not been allowed to leave the house on a working day but, now that he had graduated to become a journeyman, he was often asked to run errands: taking and returning messages to and from weavers or mercers, collecting and delivering additional supplies of raw silk to be twisted by throwsters and of warp beams and thrown silk to weavers, bringing back woven silk ready for packaging and sale. He revelled in these new freedoms. M. Lavalle trusted him implicitly and depended on him to help teach the other apprentices from time to time.

'*Bonsoir, Henri*,' M. Lavalle called from the office at the front of the house. It was barely half past four, but Henri knew when it was wisest not to argue.

'Apologies for my tardiness, sir,' he said, poking his head around the door. 'Shelleys kept me waiting twenty minutes but the sun still sails in the sky. I have three hours yet to complete that damask. *Pas de problème*.'

M. Lavalle looked up from his ledger, peering over his glasses. As usual, when not seeing customers, he was casually dressed in baggy trousers and a waistcoat that had seen better years, his favourite deep-crimson velvet cap concealing his balding pate. He was not a handsome man, but his pudgy, deeply lined face and irregular complexion spoke of a life of hard work and pleasures enjoyed: good food, plentiful drink, and the contentment of loving and being loved.

He smiled benignly at his protégé. He'd watched the emaciated, lice-infected urchin boy whom he'd first encountered emerging, like a silk moth from a cocoon, into an intelligent, lively young man with a remarkable aptitude for hard work, who had completed his seven-year apprenticeship with ease and was now well on his way to achieving his own mastership.

As an established member of the Huguenot community in Spitalfields, M. Lavalle was an elder of the French church which had, over time, developed clear protocols for helping the hundreds of destitute compatriots who arrived every year. Each family would be issued with second-hand clothes and boots, and would be fed and cared for at a parishioner's home for a number of weeks until they were able to find work and fend for themselves.

M. Lavalle remembered that first meeting with perfect clarity. The dreadful state of the mother and child had touched his heart: their skinny frames, ragged clothes and desperate eyes. He had gladly offered to act as their temporary host, especially on learning that they had come from the same region of central France as his own forebears. Not that he'd ever lived there himself; his parents had escaped before he was born, shortly after the persecution of Protestants first began.

In those days, before so many thousands had followed them, the English were very welcoming. But with successive waves of immigration, and French people now outnumbering native speakers on some streets, the welcome had worn thin. Even though the guild had lifted their ban on 'Strangers' and M. Lavalle, like many other French masters, was now accepted as a Freeman of the Company of Weavers, resentment had grown, and divisions had formed.

The streets of Spitalfields could become treacherous late of an evening, when the young gallants had been supping in the taverns for a few hours. At the very least, insults could be thrown: he'd not infrequently been called a 'cabbage head', 'froggy' or 'French piss pot'. Only the other day he had picked up a pamphlet entitled 'Considerations upon the Mischiefs that may arise from granting too much indulgence to Foreigners', which he had skim-read, briefly, before consigning it to the fire in disgust.

Through M. Lavalle's introductions Clothilde soon secured work as a silk throwster. She was already experienced and her skills were much in demand, especially as she was prepared to put in the hours and could turn out yarn quickly, with a consistent twist. Within weeks her reputation had grown sufficiently to guarantee regular work and she was earning enough to rent an independent lodging. M. Lavalle helped them find a small room in a house off Brick Lane.

For the first time in many months she discovered something to live for, something to relieve the grief that had almost destroyed her mind. The knot of fear that seemed to have taken up permanent lodging in her belly began to ease, and Henri even caught his mother smiling from time to time.

He was sent to the church school, where he quickly learned to speak and write English, also showing a special aptitude for arithmetic and a great curiosity for the natural world. Even at that young age, all who met him were charmed by the boy. He, in turn, came to learn that by being willing and good-natured, by offering his sweet smile, he could make the world go his way. When he turned twelve, M. Lavalle offered him employment as a drawboy in his own weaving loft.

From dawn until dusk Henri would sit under a loom and, on the command of the weaver, pull the correct lashes that were laced to the simple. These, in turn, produced the figured design of the cloth and, even in those early years, he was full of questions, wanting to know how the design was translated from the painted original, how the figure harness worked or why this or that denier of silk was always used. It was this evident interest, his application to work and a maturity beyond his years that encouraged M. Lavalle to take on Henri as an apprentice without demanding the usual premium.

This act of generosity had been well rewarded: in the main the lad had obeyed the rules of the indenture, the requirement to be 'modest, civil, clean and above all obedient to his master', and, over time, M. Lavalle had entrusted him with increasingly complex work, which he could now weave with great accuracy.

At nineteen, when Henri completed his indentures, he'd gratefully accepted M. Lavalle's offer of full-time work as a daily-rate journeyman, and accommodation. When he was ready, Henri would present his 'master piece' to demonstrate that he had gained all the skills necessary to be admitted to the Worshipful Company of Weavers as a master weaver, and he would then be able to set up on his own in business, and employ other apprentices and journeymen. But as a widower with no sons of his own, the fancy had been growing in M. Lavalle's mind of late that Henri might, one day, inherit his business.

M. Lavalle's only surviving child, Mariette, had always viewed Henri as the older brother she'd never had. But lately, at nearly fifteen, her responses had subtly changed. She had, more than once, commented on Henri's good looks, his striking Breton colouring, the thick black hair that had grown so long that he was obliged to tie it back as he worked, and the intense, questioning chestnut-brown eyes that seemed never to miss a thing.

When once she always had a snippy retort to Henri's banter, it now seemed to reduce her to a fit of girlish giggles. If he paid a simple compliment, such as appreciation of the food she placed on the table in front of him, her cheeks would flood with pink.

M. Lavalle watched these changes, feeling out of his depth in this new phase of his child's life, and wishing for the thousandth time that his wife were still alive to deal with it. In a few years' time the pair would make an ideal match. Once Henri had achieved his mastership he would be in a position to start the process of handing over the business and slipping into gentle retirement, reading his books and warming his feet by the fire. He could not think of a better outcome.

Henri climbed the two flights of stairs to the top landing, and then up the ladder, pushing open the trapdoor into the weaving loft. Every inch of this room was familiar to him, every smell and sound, the way the light fell through the windows onto the looms in different seasons and weathers. Eleven years of his life had been spent in this large, airy space that stretched the width of the house, with its rough-hewn wooden floors, dormer windows across the front and two skylights angled into the roof at the rear. Three sturdy wooden looms, two spinning wheels and a rack holding wound warp beams occupied the floor area almost entirely, leaving only narrow walkways between.

The walls to each side were covered from floor to ceiling with boxes of bobbins, shuttles and pirns, all carefully labelled by colour, twist and denier. Empty warps were suspended from the ceiling, ready to be sent out to the winders. These beams, too awkward to manoeuvre down narrow stairways, would be eased through the wide case-ment window and lowered to the street below on ropes from a gantry. The reverse operation was used for returning the wound warps ready for mounting on a loom.

The windows were thrown wide open this sultry July afternoon – being at the top of the house, hard beneath the tiles, the loft was always too hot in summer or too cold in winter. Under the looms were straw pads on which the drawboy and apprentice slept. At the end of his indentures, Henri had graduated to the privilege of a truckle bed in a small box room in the basement of the house, next to the kitchen, where it was never too cold nor too warm and was close to supplies of bread and cheese which, if taken in moderation, could evade the cook's suspicions.

'*Merde*, it's hot up here today,' Henri said, closing the trapdoor with a gentle thud.

The drawboy, who normally worked the lashes and simples, had taken Henri's absence as an opportunity and was asleep on his pallet. Benjamin, the apprentice for whom he had responsibility for tuition, sat dully slumped at his loom, upon which he was supposed to be weaving a basic grey taffeta lining for gentlemen's waistcoats.

'How's that tabby going?' Henri said, peering over to see for himself. 'Whatever have you been up to? I've been gone an hour and you've barely woven an inch.'

'Broken warp thread,' the boy muttered. 'Took an age to find. They're the devil to see in this colour.'

Henri examined the woven fabric more closely. 'Make sure you pull that heddle firmly after each pass of the shuttle, to press the weft taut against itself. No skimping or the fabric will turn out uneven and it shows badly on a plain silk like this. Take care Monsieur Lavalle has no excuse to dock your dinner again.'

The boy was lazy and already half starved for being rude to his master; he was the spoiled only son of an English mariner and spoke longingly of going to sea, but his father had decided that the silk business would be more profitable and less dangerous. Henri doubted he would see out the full seven-year indenture, but it was a feather in his own cap that M. Lavalle had entrusted him with the boy's training and he was determined to persevere while he remained.

He nudged the drawboy awake with his toe. 'Lashes time, *gamin*.' The boy groaned and rubbed his eyes, then stirred himself into his position beside the loom.

For the next few hours the three boys worked hard, each concentrating on their tasks, the only sound the clack of the shuttles, the rattle of the treadles manipulated by Henri's feet, as if he were an organist, and his terse instructions to the drawboy about which of the dozen numbered simples of the figure harness to pull: '*cinq, cinq, un, sept, dix, dix*.'

They all knew that, as the sun lowered behind the roofs of the houses on the other side of the street, the light would quickly fade and weaving would have to stop. On rare occasions when a deadline was immutable they could weave by candlelight, but the going would be slow and the quality jeopardised. Fine silk threads, only visible because of their lustre, would become almost impossible to see by the flickering light of a candle. More than once, Henri had been forced to reweave a piece because of the faults he had discovered the following day, and M. Lavalle would fly into a rage at the waste of precious silk.

Later that evening, after a supper of boiled eggs, apple pie and ale followed by a short game of backgammon with M. Lavalle and Benjamin, Henri retired to his basement room. The cook was still clattering about the kitchen next door, clearing up, laying the fire and preparing vegetables for the following day, but the noise of domesticity never troubled him. He found it comforting; a reminder of how, as a boy in France, he would listen to his parents talking and moving about in the house below his bedroom, long before their troubles began.

Henri closed his eyes and wondered how his mother was faring this sultry night. A year ago the widow had been courted by one of her customers, a weaver from Bethnal Green, whose wife had died, leaving him with five small children to raise. But he was pockmarked and ill-tempered and she'd been wary of his attentions. Even though grief still cast a long shadow over her heart she had found her place in society, taking on voluntary work at the French church and making a good living as a throwster, while no longer being responsible for Henri's upkeep. Now in her late forties, she had grown to relish her independence and had no intention of taking on responsibility for a new family. So, when the widower proposed, she had refused him.

Unfortunately he took her refusal as a personal slight and she had received no work from him ever since. And he seemed to have told his friends, too, because commissions from other regular customers also dried up from that moment. She was a proud woman and rarely complained, but Henri could hardly fail to notice that she had been forced to give up the second room of her lodgings, which meant that she had to work, eat and sleep in a single cramped and airless space. There was little food in her cupboard, and he would slip her a loaf of bread or a couple of eggs whenever he could.

He'd mentioned it to M. Lavalle, who had tried to send as much work as he could in her direction. What Henri now wanted most in the world was to gain his mastership and then raise enough money to rent his own house and his own looms, to provide his mother with the comfort and security she so desperately deserved.

Of late he had spent the moments before sleep imagining himself in the aromatic embrace of the sugared-almond seller but this time, when sleep finally came, it was of the English girl that he dreamed, the girl with the bold gaze and blue-green eyes, the girl who spoke like a lady but dressed as a maid. She took his hand and led him into a room hung on all sides with the most beautiful silks he had ever seen, sumptuous satin grounds figured with intricate, elegant and delicate floral designs in intense, lustrous colours, the kind that took months to weave just a few yards of, that cost hundreds of pounds and was commissioned only for dukes and duchesses, bishops and royalty.

He woke, in the dark, knowing that the dream was his future: to achieve his Freedom and be accepted into the Weavers' Company, he would have to create, design and then weave without fault such a fabric as one of these, as his master piece.

4

Do not be too submissive to the dictates of fashion; at the same time avoid oddity or eccentricity in your dress. There are some persons who will follow, in defiance of taste and judgement, the fashion to its most extreme point; this is a sure mark of vulgarity.
— The Lady's Book of Manners

Anna had been dreading the day when her gowns would be ready, when she would have to forgo her comfortable linen skirts and jackets, the cambric petticoat worn soft with washing and the boned stays grown flexible with age.

Worse than that, the thought of having to ask the family's maid to help her dress twice a day, once in the morning for her daytime outfit and then, before supper, into an evening gown, troubled her deeply. Betty was sweet and willing – in some ways Anna felt more of an affinity with her than she did with the rest of the family – but it was the prospect of being so entirely dependent on someone else that she could not bear.

At the vicarage they'd had just a day-cook and a maid, with no live-in help – her father cherished evenings when they could enjoy the peace and privacy of a family home. Her aunt's relationship with the servants seemed inconsistent, veering between being domineering and over-familiar, and it was difficult to know how she should treat them. Either way, she did not relish the thought of having to share her most intimate times, of dressing and undressing, with another.

Homesickness weighed like a boulder in her chest; a constant, almost physical pain that could only be relieved, temporarily, by reading or conversation. Other distractions seemed precious few. The life of a London lady in polite society was, as far as she could tell, devoid of purpose, endeavour, excitement or intellectual stimulus. She had no friends to talk to apart from Lizzie, who seemed solely interested in gossip, clothes and other frivolous matters. If she tried to engage the girl in discussion about novels, or the latest news in *The Times*, Lizzie would chide her: 'Why so serious, Anna? Cheer up! You've always got your nose in a book, and who cares about silly wars or politics, or what the Scots are up to now?'

Occasionally there were guests at supper, when subjects might be discussed such as the shocking excesses of the gin-drinking poor, or the shameful greed and violent tendencies of journeymen weavers. Once or twice she had tentatively ventured to contribute to the conversation or ask a simple question: 'What are the weavers demonstrating for?' or, 'How can poor people afford gin, and not bread?'

Each time, Uncle Joseph had been dismissive: 'Why would a girl want to trouble her head with the nastier aspects of our world?' he'd say. 'You must engage your mind with more pleasant matters, Niece. Fashion, music, art. These are more suitable topics.'

After leaving the table with the other ladies to play whist

or gossip about the latest French hat styles, she could hear the men's discussions raging next door, and longed to be there with them instead, eager to learn how city life, trade and politics worked. But, for now, she stopped asking questions and contented herself with close reading of the newspapers her uncle brought into the house each day.

She read reports of a slump in the silk business partly caused by the illegal smuggling of cheaper French imports and how thousands of weavers were out of work and even starving. Bread riots, such as the one they had encountered, were apparently becoming commonplace. Some silk masters, it was claimed, hired untrained people, sometimes women and children, to avoid paying the rates demanded by journeymen.

There were stories of stonings, sabotage and even what the paper called a 'skimmington': when a weaver accused of working below the agreed rates was tied to a donkey backwards and driven through the streets accompanied by the 'rough music' of jeering journeymen hammering pots and pans. It sounded violent and horrible and, much as she felt sorry for those who had not enough money to live on, she fervently hoped that such problems would not affect her uncle's business.

The ache of homesickness was worst at night, when the house was locked and barred and the rest of the household asleep, but the alien sounds of the city filtered through the ill-fitting windows of her little garret bedroom. Dogs howling, drunken louts brawling and the catcalls of what

William referred to as 'women of the night' kept her wide awake, intruding even into her sleep.

She hoped against hope that she would, in time, become used to this strange new world, but for now she lay sleepless for hours at a time, and her thoughts inevitably turned to Suffolk. She missed her mother, of course, like a hole in her soul. She could still summon that dear face, the wispy hair, the vague, slightly distracted look, the gentle, calming voice. From her mother she had learned how to draw and paint, how to appreciate all living things, how to recognise wild flowers and cultivate a kitchen garden, how to sew and bake. All these skills she was determined to cherish, holding them close to her heart as the precious legacy of her mother's love.

She missed the countryside: the sea with its violent turns of mood and ever-changing shoreline; the constant, comforting *shurrush* of reeds rustling in the marshes and the shallow brackish lakes loud with the calls of wading birds; the heathland with its changing colours – the fizzing yellow of spring broom, the delicate dog rose in pale pink and white, the fiercer pink of summer willow-herb and finally the brilliant purple heather, spread across the sandy land like a blanket.

She missed the companionship of the village, too, the comings and goings at the vicarage, her friends from church, her sister, their dog Bumbles, her art lessons with Miss Daniels and, most of all, her father.

As she had grown towards adulthood, Theodore had come to confide in his elder daughter, grumbling about the demands of the more eccentric and wayward members of his congregation and bemoaning the impossible requests sent down from on high from his diocesan masters. He invited her to sit at his side during meetings with the accountant about the family's finances, with his lawyer discussing legal issues relating to the church and sometimes at parish council meetings if there was a particularly thorny issue to be debated.

'You are the only one I can trust, dearest, and I need you to be my eyes and ears, so that you can guide me as to whether I am making the right decisions,' he said, more than once.

So she had watched and listened, learning how a negotiation could be successfully achieved without an opponent even realising that they had acceded; how to bring a conversation back from the diversion of a personal hobby horse without the speaker feeling they had been ignored; how to understand the elements of simple accounting and the basic tenets of legal judgement.

In his darkest moments Theodore would admit that his faith had been tested by her mother's persistent illness, and would debate with her the morality of continuing to preach when assailed by such doubts. In better times, they talked late into the night of literature, of politics both local and national, of philosophical ideas, of the exciting new understandings of science and nature being discovered. Although not artistic himself – she had inherited that talent from her mother – he gladly supported her desire to learn, paying for her lessons with an old lady in the village who had become something of a local celebrity for her book of floral illustrations.

She missed her privacy. A vicarage is a public place with plenty of comings and goings but, despite this, there were always quiet corners where each member of the family could enjoy their own company. Here, in the more confined quarters of the Spital Square house, the only place she could be alone was in her bedroom. But if she spent too much time there, and was discovered by Lizzie or her aunt, she would face questioning. Why had she retired to bed? Was she feeling unwell?

Most of all she missed her freedom. She was desperate to find out more about her new surroundings, to explore the streets and, particularly, to find subjects to draw and paint. With the cook's help, she created a still-life tableau on the dining table with plates, mugs, a loaf of bread and some peaches, but she had to deconstruct it each mealtime and was never able to replace it again in precisely its original form.

She sketched the rooftop view from her bedroom window, struggling to find the perspective of all those angles; she painted Lizzie in her favourite yellow damask gown, head bent over her tapestry frame. Figures were always so difficult and the light in the house, with its heavy furnishings and small windows, was often poor – it made her appreciate all the more those masters of the internal space, the Rembrandts and Vermeers, whose paintings she had seen reproduced as engravings at Miss Daniels' house.

But what really fired her artistic imagination were growing things, trees and flowers: the way that light and shade played through the tracery of their stems, the leaves in shapes of endless variety and infinite shades of green, and the colours of their petals, sometimes subtle, sometimes bold.

The last watercolour she had made before leaving Suffolk was of the green coils of columbine that twined unchecked along the vicarage fence, and she had been pleased with the painting's strong sense of movement, accented by brilliant white flowers with their delicate pink stripes. Her father had lavished praise, and requested that he could hang it on his study wall, 'to remind me of you when I am lonely'. She had already decided that her first London drawing – when she was satisfied that she had created something good enough – would be sent to him for a birthday or Christmas present.

Here in the London house there was little opportunity to observe growing things. All was stifling stillness and propriety, and her aunt's instructions were uncompromising: she was not allowed to venture into the streets without being accompanied by Lizzie, or Betty, and without a clear purpose and timetable. But Lizzie was at her studies each morning, and Betty had her work to do, so, more often than not, Anna was left to her own devices.

The heatwave persisted and she found herself nodding off even during daytime. It felt as though her life was slipping away.

Aunt Sarah had promised that when she was 'properly attired' they would go visiting. Anna dreaded the thought of such formalities, of pretending to be someone she was not, of making polite conversation with strangers, but anything would be better than this isolation and confinement. So when her aunt received a note from Miss Charlotte announcing that the gowns were ready for collection, she was surprised to find that the dread had been overtaken by a sense of excitement.

It was just a short walk – no call for a chaise, her aunt

said – but the day was warm, and by the time they reached Draper's Lane she was starting to perspire uncomfortably.

The sign above the door read: *Miss Charlotte Amesbury, Costumière*. Through the glass of the single bow window she could see what appeared to be a group of fashionably attired ladies and gentlemen, but as they entered the front door she realised that the figures were dressmaker's dummies. The gowns were beautiful, but so adorned with gathers, ruffles and lace that she wondered how anyone could manage their daily lives wearing them. She prayed that the dresses that had been made for her would be simpler in design.

Alerted by the tinkle of the bell attached to the front door, Miss Charlotte appeared almost instantly from a back room, welcoming Anna and her aunt with a broad smile.

'Good day, Mrs Sadler, Miss Butterfield. All is ready for you, if you would like to come through.'

She seemed so confident and energetic that Anna struggled to put an age to her – certainly no older than thirty-five, she thought to herself. Yet she wore no wedding ring. How had this woman managed to set up such a successful business, apparently on her own account, and remain so independent? At their previous meeting she had warmed to Miss Charlotte's calm, composed manner. Now, she wondered whether she might become an ally, or even a friend, in this strange and confusing world.

They were led through to a large, airy room at the back of the shop, where the boards were covered with a worn carpet. One side of the room was furnished as a modest kind of parlour with four chairs, their seats upholstered in faded blue velvet, set either side of an empty fireplace. The other corner was curtained all around with long hangings of white calico.

'Do take a seat, please,' Miss Charlotte said. 'Can I get you something cool to drink?'

As they waited, Anna noticed a miniature dressmaker's dummy on which hung a tiny coat in dark plum damask silk with velvet collar and cuffs and pearl buttons.

'What a beautiful jacket,' she exclaimed. 'He is certainly going to be a very proud little fellow, wearing that.'

The seamstress, engaged with the pouring of elderflower cordial into three glasses, paused and looked up. 'Yes indeed,' she said quietly, her pale cheeks colouring. 'It is a present for his seventh birthday. I hope he likes it.'

After a further brief exchange of politenesses Aunt Sarah said, 'We had better proceed, Miss Charlotte. Show us how you plan to transform my country bumpkin niece into a fashionable young lady about town.' She added, almost as an aside, 'Quite a challenge, I grant you.'

Anna felt her cheeks flush. *Why was her aunt so determined to undermine her confidence?* Miss Charlotte, quick to notice, took her arm gently and steered her away towards the curtained area. 'It is my pleasure to dress such a charming young lady,' she said with a reassuring smile. 'Are you ready, Miss Butterfield?'

Behind the curtains, carefully hung from wooden hooks and covering every part of the walls, was an array of gowns and petticoats in brilliant colours, *like an artist's palette*, Anna thought. On a long side table were displayed a number of undergarments: white cambric chemises, stays, hoops, lace-edged cuffs and pinners, and two embroidered stomachers.

'If you put on this new chemise, then I will help with the stays and hoops,' Miss Charlotte whispered. 'Don't be concerned. It is not so complicated.'

She turned away discreetly while Anna undressed. As the garments came off, one by one, she felt vulnerable, as though she were stripping off her old self to become a blank canvas. She took one of the chemises from the table and slipped it on gratefully. The feel of the soft white cambric, so fine that it could be feathers stroking her bare skin, was comforting, and she found the courage to clear her throat gently, indicating her readiness.

She went to put on the new stays with the opening to the front, as was her habit, but Miss Charlotte shook her head and reversed them so that the laces were at the back. 'You can lace them to the front when you are dressing yourself,' she whispered, 'but just for now we must give you the perfect shape.'

She pulled the laces so tight that the whalebones cut sharply into Anna's sides, and she felt she would never be able to breathe properly. At the same time she noted with some alarm how her small breasts were pushed into a new and surprisingly voluptuous shape. After the stays came the hoops, hung from straps at the shoulders and tied in place at the waist, forming modest oblongs projecting from her hips on either side.

'It is my belief that hoops will become smaller yet,' Miss Charlotte said, busying herself with the ties at the side. 'They may go out of fashion entirely before long, but we have provided you with two sets for the moment. You will find them very convenient for pockets.' She handed Anna a pair of simple cambric pouches with tapes to be tied around the waist so that they lodged beneath the arch of the hoops on either side.

There followed a petticoat in plain cream silk, ruched along the hem and tied at the waist, and then Miss Charlotte announced that they were ready for the gown. From two of the hooks she took down a confection of flounces in pale yellow damask.

'I think you will be pleased with this one,' she said. 'This is the *robe à la française*, as we discussed. Sackbacks are so terribly elegant, and absolutely *à la mode*.' Anna had never worn yellow before – she thought it made her skin look unhealthy – but Miss Charlotte assured her that it was absolutely the latest thing because it gave her a 'fashionable pallor'.

She had to admit that the gown fitted beautifully, the pleats at the back falling in a gentle drape from her shoulders, the sleeves tight to just below the elbow, the bodice wide until it met at the front with panels of reversed fabric that Miss Charlotte called 'robings'. She used tiny hooks and eyes to link the front panels together right down to the waist and then tied flounced linen cuffs edged with lace to each elbow. Below the waist, the petticoat peeked through the edges of the skirt at just the right height to show Anna's toes.

'It is the done thing to show your feet these days,' Miss Charlotte said. 'You will have a pair of embroidered slippers to match the dress, but the heels should not be too tall, since you already have a certain height.'

Finally, after much tweaking and primping of the fabric around the shoulders, waist and sleeves, she pronounced the gown properly fitted.

'Will I have no stomacher, no modesty piece? Or a handkerchief or shawl, at the least?' Anna whispered, placing her hands over the expanse of flesh still remaining uncovered by the bodice. A new, deep cleavage had appeared between her breasts, which seemed to protrude in the most immodest manner.

'Covering up is for ladies of more mature years, and might appear prudish or frumpy on a youthful frame.' Miss Charlotte smiled. 'Please do not worry, Miss Anna. Let us see what Mrs Sadler thinks.'

As the curtains were pulled back Aunt Sarah's plump face, so grumpy in repose, lit up with a brilliant smile.

'Oh, my dearest niece,' she breathed, fanning her perspiring face. 'What a wonderful transformation. All the young men will be queuing up to make your acquaintance. We shall be fighting them off, shall we not, Miss Charlotte?'

How shall we fight them, Anna wondered, *whoever 'they' are? Perhaps with the axe used to cut firewood at home, or the hatchet Father employs with such savage vigour against invading bramble bushes?* The memory made her smile.

'What sort of hat should she have, do you think?'

Miss Charlotte disappeared behind the curtains and returned with a round box. 'My milliner has provided us with a few samples. She says, and I agree, that it should be nothing too elaborate for a lady of Miss Anna's youthful charms.' She took out a straw bonnet with a narrow brim. 'This milkmaid style is all the rage these days, perhaps you have noticed.' She placed the hat on Anna's head, tilting up the brim in a jaunty fashion at front and back, and tying the ribbon – a delicate cream the same as the petticoat – in a loose bow at her chin. Anna smiled self-consciously, wondering at the strangeness of a fashion combining yards of luxurious, costly silk with a simple countrywoman's hat.

She turned obediently as they discussed her figure: the shape of the bodice, the cut of the sleeves, the length of the hems, and found her mind distracted by a powerful childhood memory of cardboard dolls that could be dressed in a range of cut-out dresses, hats and shoes. She and Jane would delight in ensuring that the outfits were as bizarre and uncoordinated as possible, with clashing colours, matching nightgowns with fancy hats or galoshes with ballgowns. Right now she felt like one of those paper dolls, a one-dimensional toy, with a fixed grin and rigid outstretched arms.

She felt a sudden urge to grab her old clothes and run back to Suffolk and her father. It may have been, as he'd been so careful to explain, a life without prospects, but at least it was her own life, not a life in which she was merely the plaything of others.

Instead, she took a deep breath. 'It is a beautiful gown, Miss Charlotte. Thank you so much.' The seamstress acknowledged the compliment with a graceful nod and the hint of a smile. 'You have been so generous, Aunt Sarah,' Anna went on. 'I shall write to my father this evening and tell him how kind you have been.'

There was a second formal gown in cream with stripes and brocaded flowers in a more usual, more modest style, and two further gowns for daytime or at home; softer and more flowing in pale blue lustring and sea-green alamode, worn without hoops, and for which Miss Charlotte had provided a pretty white apron and matching neckerchief to cover the décolletage. There were three round caps, too, in lace-edged cotton, with lappets that could be pinned up or tied beneath the chin, and four sets of white silk stockings.

The following morning, at breakfast, Aunt Sarah announced that she and Anna had been invited to take tea with Mrs Hinchliffe, mother of William's best friend, Charlie.

'Can I come too?' Lizzie cried.

'Of course not,' her mother said. 'You will be at your studies, as usual.'

'That's so *unfair*. Their house is so pretty, and Susannah plays so well on the harpsichord.'

'Your time will come, when you are eighteen, Elizabeth. Now –' Aunt Sarah turned to Anna '– I think it is a day for the cream brocade and that pretty little milkmaid bonnet with the cream ribbon. Miss Charlotte is so clever, don't you think? It's perfectly fashionable and has the advantage of not adding to your height.'

'Charlie will be paying attendance, I don't doubt,' William said, with a knowing smile.

'If he is not at his studies, Mrs Hinchliffe said.'

'Oh, he'll be there. I've already primed him. Anyway, he's always boasting about how little time he's required to spend in chambers.' William took a large bite of pie and went on talking with his mouth full. 'He'll make a good catch for you, Coz. Definitely his own man, lives for the moment and all that. His mother's rich as Croesus. Proper old money.'

'Don't be so vulgar, Will,' his mother chided. 'Gentlemen do not discuss money in mixed company.'

'But isn't that what this is all about? Finding a rich husband for our country mouse? Just don't mention Purple Velvet.'

Anna dropped her face to her lap, trying to contain her fury. It was enough having to deal with her aunt's caustic comments, but whatever had she done to deserve William's constant sniping?

'Purple Velvet?' Lizzie asked.

'Nag that Charlie lost his shirt on at the weekend,' William explained. 'Dead cert, he said, and he persuaded a few others to back it, too. Not me, though, luckily. He nearly got beaten up yesterday evening.'

Uncle Joseph, who had been harrumphing quietly throughout the conversation, weighed in sharply. 'That's quite enough, William. Finish your breakfast and get down-stairs to work.'

✻✻✻

'Well, look at you now, Miss Anna,' Betty said, standing back after fixing the bonnet with hatpins. 'Quite the young lady about town, if you don't mind me saying so.'

'It's so hot with all these layers on,' Anna complained, fanning herself. 'I'll never survive.'

'You won't have to walk. Madam has asked me to call a carriage.'

'Is it far?'

'Just a couple of miles, as far as I know. But she likes to make an impression, does Mrs S.,' Betty added, with a discreet wink.

Anna was greeted with an approving smile from her

aunt, and as they stepped outside, ready to cross the pavement into the carriage, two gentlemen passers-by stopped in their tracks, doffing their caps. *How extraordinary suddenly to be so noticeable*, she thought to herself, *all because of a new dress.*

The windows in the carriage were open and the coach clattered along the cobbled streets attracting a refreshing breeze. As they passed the end of Paternoster Row she spied the spire of Christ Church, white and elegant, soaring into the sky, reminding her that since her arrival in London two Sundays had already passed. She had little faith in God these days but attending the weekly service was almost second nature. After church was the most sociable time in the village, when everyone gathered to exchange greetings or engage in longer conversations. Here in the city, it seemed, there were few such opportunities for informal mingling. She would ask if she could go next Sunday, she decided: it might offer a moment of freedom, or even the opportunity of meeting other people.

The coach paused for a moment, giving her time to observe the scene in the street alongside. A gaggle of about thirty men, working men she assumed from their apparel, were gathered on the pavement around a single figure standing on a box. Beside him, another man held up a handmade placard with rough lettering: *Bold Defiance*, it read. *Fair pay for all.*

Red-faced, his mouth wide open in a shout, the man on the box was attempting to make himself heard above the clamour of the street. From time to time his audience raised their arms above their heads, chanting and punching raised fists.

'Ruffians,' her aunt said. 'Best to pull down the blind, dearest. Don't want to draw attention, do we?'

Just as Anna reached up for the cord, one of the men turned and looked her directly in the eye. The face was familiar, and she imagined for a split second that he recognised her, too. Then she realised: it was Guy, the French boy who had been with Henri the day she arrived, and again at Spital Square.

She wanted to wave, to call out and ask after his friend, but it was impossible with her aunt beside her. The coach began to move and, as the chanting faded into the distance, Anna was left wondering whether perhaps Henri had been there, too, with that group of angry young men. But why? She longed to meet the French boys again, to find out what the gathering had been about, but such a meeting seemed so unlikely, now that she was being groomed into a proper society lady.

She gave a quiet sigh, straightened her back and looked forward, readying herself for the ordeal of 'taking tea'.

5

What I shall next recommend to you is frugality, the practice of which is expedient for all, but especially for such as you, who are, like the silk-worm, to spin your riches out of your own bosom. The neglect of trifles is suffering a moth to eat holes in your purse, and let out all the profits of your industry.
— Advice for apprentices and journeymen
OR A sure guide to gain both esteem and an estate

The sound of Guy's distinctive whistle from the street below pierced through the busy clack of looms, the hubbub of the street, the draymen's calls, the barking of dogs and the song of caged birds.

Henri put down his shuttle, and went to peer out of the loft window.

Guy gestured energetically. 'Come down. I need to tell you something.'

'I'm right in the middle of a figure. Can it not wait until this evening?' Henri shouted, exasperated.

'No, it's *about* this evening. *C'est très important.* Come down. *Juste une minute.*'

'*Bon Dieu*, what is it now?' Henri muttered. Telling the drawboy to take a break and get a drink of water, he took off his shoes and tiptoed as quietly as possible down the wooden ladder so as not to disturb M. Lavalle, who was sweating over his accounts in the downstairs office. His master might generally be lenient, but he didn't like to take liberties.

His friend was pacing the pavement, unshaven, long hair pulling free from its loose plait and flailing around his face. Guy was always behind with his rent and sometimes earning barely enough to feed himself, Henri knew.

'What's so urgent? Are you not well?'

'Never better, *mon vieux*.' Guy lowered his voice to a hoarse whisper. 'Listen, it's good news. We've written a *Book of Prices*, you know, set down rates for every kind of work, and we're going to get it printed and give a copy to every master in the area, to make them pay a fair wage, for a change. We're pretty sure the Company will back us this time. There's a meeting this evening. You must come.' He twisted his felt hat fiercely between his fists.

Henri sighed. 'I'm way behind, Guy.'

'It will take only half an hour. Every signature is really important if the Company is to agree it. You have to come.'

'Where is it, then, this meeting?'

'The Dolphin, Bethnal Green. There's a room on the second floor they're letting us use.'

'It's not that calico chasing lot, none of that? I can't afford to get caught up in any protests.' The growing taste for printed calico was bad news for the silk trade and, the previous year, Guy had had a near escape when out with a gang of older weavers who'd thrown *aqua fortis* onto the cotton dresses of society ladies. Two had been arrested and one was hanged.

'Nothing like that. It's only to sign a petition so that we can get official backing for the Book,' Guy said, squeezing Henri's arm urgently. '*C'est légal. Fais-moi confiance.* Go in by the side door and up the stairs. I'll be there. Promise me you will come.'

At seven o'clock Henri nervously climbed the rough wooden stairs and entered a dark room packed with men huddled around a central table, in the light of a single candle. Their gaunt, desperate faces and the stink of unwashed poverty reminded him why he was here. His signature was a small thing to offer, if it helped to alleviate their troubles.

M. Lavalle had been supportive when Henri had told him where he was going. 'I've heard of this Book,' he said. 'It is probably a reasonable way of trying to keep the peace, so long as the weavers do not set their expectations too high. They have to accept that this is a volatile market, and the fluctuations have to be borne by us all.'

'You do not mind if I add my signature to the petition?'

'So long as that is all you do, my boy.' M. Lavalle had given him a fierce look over his spectacles. 'Beware of becoming involved in any march, or other actions of protest. It is too risky at a time like this, when you are on the brink of gaining your Freedom.'

'*Ne vous inquiétez pas*, I will take care,' Henri had said.

He spied Guy in the shadows at the edge of the room and pushed his way through the crowd towards him.

'*Merveilleux*, you are here!' Guy embraced him forcefully, then shouted, 'Friends, this is *mon cher ami* Henri Vendôme, journeyman working for the esteemed Monsieur Lavalle, hoping soon to gain his own mastership. He is here to sign the petition.'

Several dozen faces turned to look. M. Lavalle was well known, and his reputation high among both customers and weavers.

Guy took his elbow and steered him through the throng to the table. 'Read this.' He pulled forward a thick wedge of manuscript paper, roughly bound with string. Beside it was a separate single sheet. 'Then make your signature here.'

To the Upper Bailiff and Assistants of the Worshipful Company of Weavers, Henri read. *Please be informed that, in seeking a Peaceable Manner in which to resolve the Current Difficulties, we, the undersigned, do beg your Agreement and Support in the Publication of the attached* Book of Prices, *being a list of the Prices agreed to be paid for Making the different kinds of Work in the various Branches of the Weaving Manufactory.*

The main document was around forty pages of close-lined script in columns laying out the prices for every conceivable type of silk under the many specialisms of weaving: the two main groups, the Black Branch and the Fancy Branch, followed by the Persians, the Sarsnets, Drugget-Modes, Fringed and Italian handkerchiefs, Cyprus and Draught Gauzes, and Plain Nets. It was a work of enormous detail and must have taken many days and many heads to agree and many hands to write down. Glancing through it to check the weaves with which he was familiar, Henri thought the prices seemed reasonable.

He took up the quill, dipped it into the inkpot, and signed.

Later that evening, after a meal of cheese with shredded buttered cabbage and some new season's potatoes, Henri asked M. Lavalle if he could spare a few minutes to look at the design for his master piece.

He had been working on it for several weeks, and his master's opinion was critical. Technically the design was good, he knew, although possibly a little too complicated. He'd been so keen to demonstrate his weaving prowess that he had incorporated as many complex techniques as he could. But it was the aesthetic aspect with which Henri was less confident: he sensed, without knowing quite how, that it fell short of his ambition.

On a table by the window he set out his sketches of flowers, leaves, swags and ribbons, and pieced together in order the several sections of point paper with its tiny squares that he had meticulously painted with watercolours and a fine brush, showing how the design would translate into woven fabric. Then he handed his master the handwritten pages describing how the warps, wefts and simples should be set up on the loom.

He tried not to fidget as M. Lavalle read in silence, occasionally lifting his head and checking the point-paper design. Finally, the old man finished reading, straightened his back, removed his velvet cap and brushed back his thinning hair.

'Well, boy,' he said, 'I am impressed. Technically it would be a fine piece of craftsmanship, well beyond anything normally expected from someone of your experience. I know how capable you are, but might it not be better to make something simpler, easier to set up, quicker to weave, less likely to go wrong?'

Henri shrugged, suddenly deflated. 'I wanted to create something unusual, something really eye-catching.'

'A few years ago the mercers would have been fighting each other for it.'

'A few years ago?'

'When rococo was all the rage; the bolder and more ornate the design, the better. These days the ladies are after a much lighter touch. The new *naïf*, you know, simplicity, realism, delicate elegance.'

Henri felt the ground shifting beneath him. From the start of his apprenticeship he'd always admired the large, colourful designs of the famous masters of the day, such as James Leman and his father Peter. He realised now what a fool he'd been: fashions had moved on and he hadn't even noticed.

'Why do you think I prefer to weave damasks, plain silks and satins? They might not pay so well, but they are a lot less trouble because the designs don't change with every season,' M. Lavalle went on. 'Take a look at what society ladies are wearing these days, and you'll see what I mean.'

Henri shrugged his shoulders again. It all seemed so unfathomable.

'Anyway,' M. Lavalle said, folding up the point papers and setting them with the sketches in a neat pile on the table. 'You will do what you think best. You are a very talented weaver and I would have no hesitation in recommending your Freedom, here and now. Almost any of the designs you have woven in the past year would prove you are technically capable. But if you really want your master piece to establish your reputation and set you on your way to a fortune, then you may have to give it some more thought.'

Mariette looked up from her sewing as they entered the parlour. 'What did you think, Papa? Will Henri's piece be a sensation?'

'I will allow him to speak for himself,' M. Lavalle said, jamming his hat onto his head and making for the front door with his pipe and tobacco pouch. 'I'm going for some air before we lock up.'

Henri looked into Mariette's sweet, expectant face. He knew how much she admired him, like an older brother, but these days he had a vague and growing sense of a new kind of intimacy in the way that she responded to him: the teasing smile she sometimes wore, the way she cocked her head, the sideways glance of her eyes.

These subtle changes disturbed him. Mariette was still a child, growing prettier by the day, this was true, but in his eyes nothing more than a cherished and sometimes annoying younger sister. He felt sure that, in time, M. Lavalle would be seeking a good match for his daughter, the son of a wealthy and well-established weaver or mercer, perhaps, who could expect to inherit the business.

'Well?' she said.

He sighed, trying to find a way of telling her without betraying the fact that he felt totally dejected.

'Surely it is not *that* bad?'

'No, not at all,' he said quickly. 'Your father says . . .' He hesitated and then tried again. 'He says it's technically good, but I think the design is old-fashioned.'

'That is a certainly a problem.'

'What I really need is someone who can predict next season's fashions.'

She laughed. 'You'll need a soothsayer, then. No one can predict the whims of fashion.'

'Then who decides what society ladies will wear?' he said, shaking his head. 'It is so confusing. How does anyone work it out? Surely they cannot just imagine it out of nowhere.'

'I suppose there are people of influence who come up with the ideas in the first place, and then everyone else follows them,' she said.

'And who are these people of influence?'

'Mercers, designers, people in the trade . . .' She tailed off. Then, after a moment, she gave a little yelp. 'That's it. I know just the person!'

'Who's that?'

'Miss Charlotte. She was a friend of Maman's and she made my Confirmation gown but I have not seen her much of late,' Mariette gabbled. 'She lives in Draper's Lane.'

'But I cannot afford to pay for her advice.'

'I will ask her,' Mariette said, putting her hand on his arm with a confidential smile. 'As a favour for a special friend.'

Next evening after supper, Henri walked to Draper's Lane and stopped outside the shop: *Miss Charlotte Amesbury,*

Costumière. After ensuring that no one was watching, he peered through the small windowpanes at the models inside.

As he studied the lustrous drapery and elegant finishing of the gowns, the delicate designs of the fabrics with their lifelike flowers and leaves and their swirls of fine ribbons against backgrounds of cream or pastel damask, he realised with a sense of growing despondency that he must have spent the past ten years in a kind of dream. Why had he not, until now, taken more notice of the designs that fashionable people were wearing? He had been so keen to master the technical complexities of his craft that he had entirely forgotten the real reason why people love silk: it makes the wearer both look and feel beautiful.

He became aware of a pair of bright eyes peering back through the window. A slight, dark-haired woman was beckoning to him, indicating that he should come into the shop. He shook his head, but it was too late: she was at the doorway.

'Is there anything I can help you with, sir?'

'I was just looking,' he muttered.

'Anything in particular? Perhaps something for yourself? For a special occasion? I have some beautiful silk brocade waistcoats which would look well on a fine young gentleman like you.'

He knew it was just sales talk but he hesitated, intrigued by the bold, straightforward approach of this young woman and flattered that she would even consider that he might have the means to buy himself a silk waistcoat. She seized on his hesitation.

'Why not come in for a moment? I can show you some designs you might like to consider, with no obligation whatsoever. You will never know, unless you see them for yourself.'

Once inside, she drew from the shelves several waistcoats in the most stunning colours and designs of brocade that he'd ever seen, laying them out across the counter and smoothing them with a fond hand, as though they were her children. She led him to a long mirror on a stand and held up one of the waistcoats against his chest.

'How the bright colours emphasise your dark looks, sir.' She spoke with such certainty, as if she truly believed he was the sort of person who might wear such a thing, and not a lowly French journeyman in scruffy linen breeches and serge waistcoat.

'Madam, I must be honest with you,' he said at last. 'I cannot afford a waistcoat as fine as these. Please let me introduce myself. I am Henri Vendôme, journeyman weaver. My master's daughter, Mariette Lavalle, mentioned your name and said you might be able to help.'

The professional mask broke into a genuinely warm smile. 'I wondered as much,' she said, producing from her pocket a note. 'Mariette wrote to me this morning. You are most welcome, Monsieur Vendôme. She clearly thinks highly of you. How is the family faring? I have not seen them since her mother was so untimely taken.'

'They are well, thank you. Mariette is growing up now – she is nearly sixteen.'

'How the time passes. Now, how can I help you?'

As he explained his desire to find a fashionable design for his master piece that would help to establish his reputation, her pale cheeks coloured. 'I am flattered that you consider me qualified to advise you. I am only a seamstress, but will do my best.' She led him to the dressmaker's dummies he'd spied through the window. 'What do you see?'

'I see a very fine silk damask in the most delicate pale yellows and greens,' he said, feeling the quality between his fingers. 'Are these the latest colours?'

'Indeed they are, but what about this one?' She indicated the third gown.

'I see a coloured floral brocade on a deep cream damask ground weave,' he said.

'And the design?'

'I see flowers . . .'

'What *kind* of flowers?' she pressed.

'Simple ones, such as one might see in a garden, or in the fields.'

'You're getting the idea, Monsieur Vendôme. The new designs are lifelike, not stylised as in the past. Rococo is gone, naturalism is the new style.' She ran her finger over the delicately woven daisies and harebells. 'You see how small the designs are, just life-sized or less? A few years ago the fashion was all about exaggeration. The bigger the better, with giant flowers: roses the size of peonies and peonies the size of cabbages. Ugh!'

She reached over the counter for a bonnet and placed it on her head at a jaunty angle, pulling the ribbons beneath her chin so that the brim curved either side to frame her face. 'What do you see now?'

'A straw bonnet?'

'Who wears this kind of bonnet?'

He shook his head.

'It's a countrywoman's bonnet, of the style frequently worn by milkmaids. Young society ladies cannot get enough of them. Imagine, rich folk pretending to be poor milk-maids? It's silly, of course, but all fashion is playful, and that is part of its charm.'

In just five minutes, Miss Charlotte had opened his eyes to an entirely new understanding. He thanked her warmly, promising to give her regards to M. Lavalle and Mariette, and walked back to Wood Street with his head spinning in an unsettling combination of uncertainty and excitement. One thing was now quite clear: the design for his master piece would be very different from the one on which he had been working.

But how and where he would find that new design, he had no idea.

Four days later Guy arrived just as Henri, Mariette and M. Lavalle were enjoying coffee and honeyed oat cake in the parlour after supper. They offered him a square of cake, which he ate hungrily in two bites. M. Lavalle invited him to have a seat and join them in taking coffee, but Guy remained standing, restlessly shifting from one leg to the other.

'What news of the Book, lad?' M. Lavalle asked.

'The petition worked, sir. The Weavers' Company Court of Assistants met last night and gave it their endorsement. Now it is going off to the printers. You'll be getting your copy very soon.'

'I shall cherish it,' M. Lavalle said. 'It shall take pride of place on the shelf next to the Bible, and we will read from it every night before dining.'

'Don't tease him, Papa,' Mariette said. 'It is a serious matter, this Book, is it not? Oh, do sit down, Guy, and have another piece of cake. You are making me nervous with your jiggling.'

'Apologies, Miss Mariette,' Guy said, perching on a chair, and reaching for the plate. 'It is indeed a matter of life or starvation for us journeymen,' he went on. 'Not all masters are as scrupulous as you, honoured sir.'

'I am well aware of it, my boy,' M. Lavalle said. 'And, sadly, neither are all mercers.'

There was an uncharacteristic bitterness in his words and, as no one was sure how to respond, silence descended on the little room. Eventually Guy ventured: 'Have you further news?'

'I've learned what was also on the agenda for the Court of Assistants this morning,' M. Lavalle said, reaching for his clay pipe and charging it carefully with a pinch of his favourite twist.

'And that was?'

'A report into the increase in smuggled French silks over the past six months,' he said. 'It seems that more and more mercers are prepared to evade import duties in order to turn a quick profit, and at this rate there will be little or no work for masters, let alone journeymen, in this country.'

'Which mercers are they? We should demonstrate.'

'Demonstrations lead to violence, as you know only too well, Guy,' M. Lavalle chided. 'And violence achieves nothing. What we need is for the law to be upheld.'

'Why is French silk so much in demand, when our silks are just as good?' Mariette asked.

'Your guess is as good as anyone's,' her father replied.

'People suspect that it is all the more desirable precisely *because* it is restricted.' He shook his head. 'It doesn't make sense, I admit, but such are the whims of the wealthy. Anything rare or hard to buy is especially prized, whatever the quality.'

'What are the Weavers' Company doing to stop it?' Henri asked.

'They refused to name names but I believe they suspect who are the worst culprits and may send inspectors. It's an unpleasant task, and will cost the Company good money but it is worth it if they can get a few convictions, to deter others.'

'The sooner the better,' Guy muttered. 'They are destroying us, *les salauds*.'

As Henri went to the door to say goodbye to his friend, Guy gave a crude wink. '*La petite Mariette*, she's growing prettier by the day.'

Henri put his finger to his lips, closing the door.

'She's all eyes for you, my friend, you have to admit it. You could be in there in a flash.' He pumped an index finger through a circle of fingers and thumb.

'*Silence, sac à vin.* She is the innocent daughter of a man whom I esteem as a father. I will not have you talking of her like that.'

'Touched a nerve, have I? Remind me not to mention *la belle Mariette*, the nun of Wood Street, ever again.' Guy started down the steps. 'Oh, I nearly forgot,' he added, turning back. 'Talking of pretty girls, guess who I saw the other day?'

'By your own account there are so many women desperate for your charming company, I cannot for the life of me think.'

'Not one of mine, one of *yours*.'

'And who is that, then?' It would be the sugared-almond seller, he felt sure. He'd managed to avoid her for nearly ten days now.

'The English girl you rescued in the street a few weeks ago. What was her name?'

'Anna,' Henri said a little too quickly.

'Aha! So you remember her well, my friend,' Guy chortled, delighted. 'Yes indeed, the fair Anna. She was in a carriage that stopped right beside me on the street. She seemed to recognise me and I tried to wave but it moved on.'

Henri forgot to pretend that he was not intrigued. 'A carriage? Did she look well? Was she alone?'

'She looked *délicieuse*, my friend, dressed up to the nines, in one of those milkmaid's bonnets that are all the rage. She was with her fat aunt, the wife of that two-faced mercer Sadler, *en route* to show her off at some society tea party, I don't doubt. They'll have her wed to some rich bastard before you can say "private income".'

'Two-faced?'

'I'll wager you half a livre that he's one of the mercers Monsieur Lavalle was talking about, my friend. He's got it coming to him.'

Watching him walk away, Henri noticed a new arrogant swagger to his friend's stride. Hopefully, once the *Book of*

Prices was distributed and the masters were obliged to pay fair rates, he would settle down and get on with making a living, instead of complaining all the time.

Guy's barbed comments about the English girl pained him. She had seemed so straightforward, with none of the airs and graces most girls seemed to have. Still, she was far beyond his reach, so he may as well stop thinking about her.

Which was more easily said than done.

6

*Never sit gazing curiously around the room when paying a call,
as if taking a mental inventory of the furniture. It is excessively
rude.*

　　　　　　　　　　　　　　　　　– The Lady's Book of Manners

Anna gazed up at the enormous space above their heads,
the soaring columns stretching vertiginously upwards to
support rows of barrel vaults on either side. The ceiling, of
ornate white plasterwork with gold-painted decoration at
every corner, was even taller; she found herself wondering
how they had ever managed to construct it at such a height.

The whole effect, light-filled and – she struggled to find
the right word – numinous, that was it, was perfectly
designed to make you feel as though you were in the presence of something greater than yourself. Her father had
once used the word to describe his own church at certain
times of year, when the rays of the setting sun would reach
through the west window, suffusing the altar with a warm
glow.

'You don't need prayers and hymns to summon up spirit-
uality when it's like this,' he used to say. 'That sunset is
doing me out of a job.'

She understood exactly what he meant. Although she struggled to believe in the existence of God, she could always find solace in nature: the rising and setting of the sun, the light of the moon, the shape of a leaf, or the sound of the dawn chorus.

The minister droned on, his words almost indecipherable as they reverberated through the huge space.

The format of the service was recognisable but curiously different; she suspected that Christ Church was 'higher' than her father's deliberately modest approach to worship. But the sound of the organ – so much more powerful than any she had previously heard, save for the time they had visited Norwich – was utterly thrilling, filling the church with muscular chords that seemed to vibrate through her body. The organist appeared to have perfect mastery of the lofty golden pipes hidden inside the carved wood casing high above the entrance porch at the west end of the church.

She'd been delighted to discover that she knew most of the hymns and, emboldened by the mighty sounds of the organ, sang out with the strong soprano voice she'd developed from leading the church choir at home. Halfway through the first hymn she noticed that Aunt Sarah and Lizzie, flanking her on either side, were barely audible. Were they such infrequent churchgoers that they were simply unfamiliar with the tunes? Perhaps it simply wasn't seemly to sing so loudly? She toned herself down to a whisper, listening to the choir and wishing that she could be among them.

Aunt Sarah had regarded her with barely concealed astonishment, the previous evening, when she'd expressed her desire to attend Sunday service.

'Is tomorrow a special day?'

'No, nothing special.' All she really wanted was an excuse to get out of the house.

'Of course, you would have been required to attend every Sunday at home, you poor dears,' Sarah said. 'I don't suppose it's very comfortable, that draughty old village church your father runs. He used to write of how your mother found it hard to tolerate the cold. Never mind, we shall take you to Christ Church tomorrow, won't we, Lizzie? It's all so very beautiful, and –' her face brightened at the prospect '– many well-connected people attend.'

Uncle Joseph and William, having awkwardly agreed 'to keep the ladies company', had subsequently discovered important reasons why they were unable to do so. So here they were, the three women of the family, all dressed up in their Sunday best. Anna had chosen her most modest gown – the blue damask – but even so had been obliged to borrow a shawl from Lizzie to cover up the wide expanse of décolletage. On her head she wore her new milkmaid's hat.

Aunt Sarah had insisted on powdering Anna's forehead, nose and chin, and then rouging her cheeks and lips. After so much primping, Anna felt more appropriately dressed for a trip to the theatre or the music hall than for church.

Now, strategically placed in a row halfway back from the altar – 'so we can get a good view of the important people in their boxes,' her aunt had whispered – Anna was able to peer discreetly at the other worshippers. When the minister quoted the passage from Matthew about it being easier for a camel to pass through the eye of a needle than for a rich man to enter into the kingdom of God, she reflected wryly that few around her were likely to end up in Heaven. *If he's looking down at us, he'll have an amused smile on his face*, she thought. Everyone seemed so over-dressed for Sunday worship, adorned in such fine silks, satins and lace, wigs and bonnets that she began to appreciate what kept so many weavers, mercers, dressmakers and drapers in business.

Her mind wandered back to the tea party at the Hinch-liffes' two days before. It had not been a comfortable experience. Even before they arrived she'd found herself unsettled by the glimpse of Henri's friend Guy in the mob shouting for 'fair pay' and after that, all the way to Ludgate Hill, her aunt had chattered endlessly about the Hinchliffe family, until Anna began to feel quite uneasy about meeting the people with whom her aunt was so obviously entranced.

In the space of the fifteen-minute journey she learned that Mr H. was a highly successful mercer who frequently supplied fabrics for lords and ladies, bishops and Members of Parliament and even, on one memorable occasion, the old king's mistress, the Countess of Yarmouth; that, as William had vulgarly explained, he had 'married well' to a woman of considerable means in her own right, and that his success was due, at least in part, to his wife's family associations; that their elder son, Alfred, had joined the family firm and had married equally well; that the younger son, Charlie – 'the same age as my William, and they are *such* good friends' – was 'an extremely eligible young man' currently studying for the law; and that their daughter Susannah, who must be seventeen years by now – 'my, how the time passes' – was already so highly accomplished on the harpsichord that people came from 'literally miles around' to hear her, and Mrs H. had high hopes she might be presented at court next year.

'She's such a sweet young thing. You are similar in years, dear Niece, so I am perfectly certain you and Susannah will become the very best of friends.'

But Anna had stopped listening, because their carriage had passed into the shadow of an enormous structure, the largest building she had ever seen. Even by tilting her head she could not see the top of its tall towers, and it seemed to take an age for the carriage to pass its immense length.

'My goodness, whatever is that?'

'St Paul's,' her aunt said impatiently. 'You really must listen to what I am telling you, dearest Niece, so that you are fully prepared for your introduction to the family.'

She had heard of St Paul's Cathedral, had learned from one of her father's books about how it had been rebuilt to a grand new design by the famous architect Sir Christopher Wren after the Great Fire, and read in the newspaper that the famous Italian artist Canaletto had lately come to London to paint it, but had never imagined that she might see it for herself. Nothing could have prepared her for its massive bulk of glistening stone towering over the city street. Christ Church had been impressive enough, but this was in another league altogether.

'Sorry, Aunt, please go on. I really am listening,' she said, tearing her eyes away from the extraordinary sight.

Shortly after this they drew to a halt at their destination: a fine four-square building with wrought-iron gates. It was a world away from any house she'd ever visited before. Instead of whitewashed walls or wooden panelling, the walls of the hallway were covered in pink and white striated marble, the floor a chequerboard of black and white tiles. The 'morning room' was deeply carpeted, its walls covered and furniture upholstered in opulent shades of green and blue silk damask.

Mrs Augusta Hinchliffe, a tall, horsey-faced woman with a prominent nose, artfully concealed her lack of natural beauty by the application of make-up and the distraction of an ornate confection of hair on top of her head. By some happy miracle the daughter, Susannah, had failed to inherit the maternal nose and was, as Aunt Sarah had described her, a 'sweet little thing' who seemed, both physically and in personality, completely overshadowed by the forceful presence of her mother.

After the formality of introductions and the taking of chairs as directed by their hostess, two maids in immaculately starched uniforms appeared with teapots and plates of tiny saffron biscuits, and began pouring the tea into porcelain cups with handles so delicate that Anna feared to grip hers too tightly in case it shattered between her fingers.

'How do you find our great city?' Mrs H. asked her. 'It must seem very exciting after your quiet life in the countryside?'

'I like it very well, thank you, ma'am.'

'And I am sure you have already been introduced to many interesting people since you arrived? Your dearest aunt and uncle are so well respected in their community.'

'Indeed she has,' Aunt Sarah jumped in before Anna could reply. In truth she had met barely anyone outside of the family, with the exception of Henri and Guy, who would surely fall outside Mrs H.'s category of 'interesting'.

'Charles will be joining us very soon,' Mrs H. went on. 'He is such a good friend of your cousin William, as you know.' Although the prospect made her nervous, Anna couldn't help being a little intrigued by this 'man about town' who bet on the horses and lived 'for the moment'. He sounded lively, if rather raffish, and likely to be quite entertaining.

Mrs H. began to recount how the family would be going to Bath for the whole of August to escape the heat of the city, and their plans for introducing Susannah into society. Aunt Sarah nodded along, apparently admiring every pronouncement and endorsing every opinion the other woman expressed. But it was when Augusta mentioned Thomas Gainsborough, the society portraitist who currently lived in Bath, from whom they were considering commissioning a portrait of Mr Hinchliffe as Upper Bailiff of the Worshipful Company of Mercers, that Sarah's smile seemed to tighten into a grimace of burning envy. A couple of days ago Anna had heard her aunt mention the notion of going to Bath and Joseph's response: 'Absolutely not, Sarah, do you think we are made of money?'

Fortunately the conversation now turned to the Mercers' annual dinner in September, who else was likely to be there and who would be organising the seating plan for the tables. The way they examined and dissected the subject, it seemed that one's entire future could be defined by the people with whom you shared company for a single evening.

Anna turned to the daughter, who had barely spoken a word. 'I am so pleased to meet you, Susannah. My aunt tells me you are a very fine musician.'

'I play a little,' the girl whispered, her eyes to the floor. 'The harpsichord, mostly.'

'You must play for me sometime.'

Susannah nodded, and an awkward silence fell between them.

'And are you musical, Anna?' Mrs H. interjected.

'I play the pianoforte and on occasion the small chamber organ in church, but very poorly,' she replied, praying that she would not be invited to perform. 'My real love is for painting.'

'She has made a very fair representation of our Lizzie,' Aunt Sarah said. Anna blushed. The portrait she'd painted for fun was truly dreadful but, to her great embarrassment, her cousin had insisted on showing it to her parents.

'I prefer to paint natural things, trees and flowers,' she replied.

'I must show you our garden, dear Anna,' Mrs H. said, waving her hand in the direction of the French windows. 'We do love our flower borders. We have lately made the acquaintance of a famous botanist, a German fellow called Georg Ehret, who lives in London these days. Mr Hinchliffe recently made the purchase of that print.' She pointed to the wall behind Anna. 'We hope it will be the first of many.'

It was a curious composition: a showy, pink-flowered Christmas rose with dark serrated leaves overshadowing a modest yellow winter aconite. Above hovered a peacock butterfly, surely the most unlikely sight, Anna considered, in early springtime when those two plants would be flowering.

But it was not the curious composition that thrilled her,

it was the draughtsmanship. Each part of the plants had been represented so realistically that she could almost feel them between her fingers: the rough edges of the hellebore leaves, the delicate yellow stamens, the veins of the petals. At last, she thought, someone who shared her joy of drawing plants.

Her musing was interrupted by the entry of a very tall, thin-faced young man in a royal blue silk damask topcoat and powdered wig.

'Good morning, ladies,' he said, making a formal half-bow. 'I hope you will permit me to join you?' His long nose was unmistakeably inherited from his mother.

'Charles! How delightful to see you again,' Aunt Sarah said, offering her hand. 'Do please meet my niece, Anna Butterfield, lately come to the city from Suffolk.'

'Enchanted, Miss Butterfield,' he said, with a smile that seemed to soften the severity of his features. 'William has told me of your arrival. I do hope you find our great city to your liking?'

'Please sit down, Charlie,' his mother urged. 'You make me feel uncomfortable, looming over us like that.'

His mother poured a cup of tea and offered him a biscuit – he took two – as he responded politely to Aunt Sarah's inquiries about his legal studies. He turned to Anna, saying he now regretted very much that the family would shortly be leaving the city for the summer but, since he and William were such good friends, he was sure they would soon have the opportunity to become better acquainted in the autumn.

She smiled, while taking care not to meet his gaze directly. Although not handsome, not in any respect, he was certainly striking; the phrase her aunt had used – 'a fine figure of a man' – seemed perfectly apt. But there was little kindness about his eyes; they were too piercing, too close-set either side of that prominent nose, and the cheeks were sunken so that in a certain light he looked almost cadaverous. The Adam's apple bobbed conspicuously in his long neck whenever he spoke.

Nevertheless, he seemed to be well mannered, genial and easy in conversation, and this confident demeanour, no doubt a consequence of his family's comfortable position in society, did much to make up for the deficit of physical advantages.

'I return to my earlier question,' he said, taking a seat beside her. 'I hope you find our great city to your liking? There is so much to enjoy, is there not?'

'I'm afraid I have seen little of your great city, as yet,' Anna replied. 'But I understand that there is much to be learned and enjoyed. I look forward to making its acquaintance.'

'Eloquently spoken, Miss Butterfield.' Charles laughed with a horsey snort. 'But let me give you a warning. There are parts of London with which you must certainly avoid making any acquaintance. Not everyone in this city is as genteel as those in this drawing room, nor is it everywhere the peaceful place that I imagine to be the country town or village such as your own. Sadly, not all of us are so fortunate. There is a dark underbelly of crime and misery in London which a young lady such as yourself should hope never to have the misfortune to encounter.'

Anna's curiosity was piqued. Perhaps Charles was more compassionate than she had at first thought. 'Pray, tell me more,' she said. 'Why is there such misery? Why is nothing done to alleviate the suffering?'

That startling snort again, more like a donkey this time. 'What a charming sentiment. But do you not think that people should hold their fate in their own hands?'

'To an extent—' Anna began, but he continued talking over her.

'If people are lazy and indolent, surely they deserve nothing better? If they commit crime, they should expect to endure the appropriate punishment. Are we not responsible for ourselves in this life? Ours is a civilised society; we are not savages who give themselves up to the fates, or depend entirely on some God-like figure to save us, I am sure you would agree, Miss Butterfield.'

'As a matter of fact, I believe that it is the mark of a civilised society to care for its underprivileged members,' she said. 'And, in the end, as Christians, we must surely have faith that it is only God that can save our souls.' Her words, spoken with some passion, dropped loudly into a room gone suddenly silent. Anna felt her cheeks reddening. It was not polite to disagree with someone on first acquaintance, she knew, but she found she did not care overly much. Charles crossed and re-crossed his lanky legs uncomfortably as the general conversation slowly resumed. To his credit, the face that had fallen so blank with astonishment at her pronouncement now lit up with an amused smile.

'I see you are a young woman of strong views, Miss Butterfield. I look forward to many further such lively debates. But –' he lowered his voice to a whisper and leaned in towards her '– perhaps not in front of Mama?'

Anna found herself agreeing with a slight nod of the head and a raised eyebrow. She liked him better already.

She'd been hoping to return the conversation to the subject of the German botanist, and perhaps be invited to take a turn around the garden but, just then, the ornate silver clock on the mantel struck twelve times.

'Midday already,' Aunt Sarah exclaimed. 'We must not outstay our welcome, dearest Augusta. Our carriage will be waiting outside.'

'Must you go so soon?' Mrs H. said. 'I was just going to suggest that Charlie and Susannah could show you the garden, before luncheon.'

Anna opened her mouth to plead for just ten more minutes, then closed it again, knowing that it would only irritate her aunt. Nothing in city society was spontaneous, she was learning; all must be carefully planned and executed, because anything unexpected might endanger the established order of things.

'I am sure we would both enjoy that very much, but it is so terribly hot today and I regret we have matters at home to attend to,' her aunt was saying, standing to make her intentions perfectly clear and patting her skirts to ease out any creases. 'When you return from Bath, perhaps.'

Charles stood, offering his hand to Anna. She took it, embarrassed by the formality but knowing that it was expected. What she had not anticipated was that he would hold firmly onto her fingers and raise them, albeit briefly, to his lips. This forwardness made her feel mildly queasy. Already he was acting as though she owed him some kind of intimacy. *The man is powerful, certain of his place in society, used to getting his own way*, she thought to herself, *not a person to get on the wrong side of.* She would need to tread carefully around him.

At last the sermon came to an end, they sang a further hymn and were given the final blessing. Before she knew it, they were filing out of the church. Just as they reached the great doors to the outside, Anna caught sight of a familiar figure with dark hair tied back in a plait appearing from the organ loft stairs, but as she moved forward with the crowd the figure disappeared from view. Then, as her aunt exchanged pleasantries with other members of the congregation, and she and Lizzie waited in the welcome shade of the portico, she saw him again, walking directly towards them.

'Miss Butterfield,' he said, taking off his cap and making a small bow. 'It is much pleasure to see you again.' He was still dressed in his plain brown work clothes with scuffed shoes and no wig.

Lizzie cleared her throat loudly. 'Anna, you should not talk to this boy,' she whispered.

'Monsieur Vendôme, is it not? Did I see you coming down from the organ loft? Are you the organist?'

'Hah! I do wish it so.' His laugh was infectious; she found herself smiling along with him, although she did not know why. 'I am asked to help here because the under-beadle, the usual organ blower, is, how do you say it? *Indisposé.* They pay me a few *sous.*'

'Organ blower?'

'Who works the bellows. With big levers –' he held his

arms out wide '– to make the pipes to sound. I do this at my church – the French church.'

'I thought you were a silk weaver?'

'So I also have strong arms,' he said, with that teasing grin again. His gaze had locked with hers in a way that seemed to shut out the world around them.

'But this is an Anglican church . . . surely . . . ?'

'I am Protestant too.' It was not said sharply but she felt a pang of guilt all the same. 'The Lord does not know any difference.'

'Of course. I am sorry . . .'

Lizzie tugged at her sleeve. 'Anna, we must go. Mother is coming.'

'Goodbye, Monsieur Vendôme,' she called.

'*Au revoir, ma belle demoiselle*,' she heard him say through the bustle of the crowd. '*À bientôt*.'

7

Drawing, like music, should be cultivated early. Its advantages are the habits of perseverance and occupation, which it induces; and the additional delight which it gives to the works, both of nature and of art.

— The Lady's Book of Manners

My dearest daughter,

My heart brims with happiness and I feel trebly blessed to receive not one, but two letters, as well as your charming drawing of the garden in Spital Square, which is already pinned above my desk. You have captured the perspective well, especially the windows at the back of the house, and the light and shade of the mulberry tree is excellently drawn.

Your descriptions of Christ Church were so evocative that I could picture it easily. I dearly hope that I may come with you to that 'numinous space' one day. Perhaps we could also visit St Paul's Cathedral, if it is not too far.

Your new gowns sound beautiful and I would love to see my girl all dressed up in her fine silks and milk-maid's bonnet. Jane was green with envy when I read

*her this passage of your letter and I have already
written to Sarah to thank her for her generosity.*

*All is well here but for your absence, which leaves
this house very quiet. It seems an age since you left even
though only four weeks have passed. Your sister is doing
her very best to look after the house and we are
muddling along with the help of Mrs M. and Joe, who
I can see trying to tame the garden outside as I write.*

*My only concern, dearest Anna, is that I detect a
certain loneliness in your words. Call it a father's
intuition. You write of spending time with your cousin
Lizzie, and of taking tea with the Hinchliffe family,
but there is no sparkle in what you write. As I have
always insisted, there is no compulsion for you to stay if
you are unhappy. But I would urge you to be patient:
allow yourself time for settling in, and give it a further
six months before making any decision. You have a
questing soul and I am sure that there will be much to
fascinate you in the city, once you get used to its ways.*

*You say that the garden is the only outdoor space in
which you can paint, which is unfortunate. I know how
much it means to you, to observe and paint the natural
world. Would you like me to ask my sister if she can
help you find a solution?*

*Write again soon. Your letters lift my spirits! God
bless.*

Your loving father

The letter only served to heighten Anna's loneliness. The
dear man! Although she had tried to conceal any hint of

her unhappiness in her letters, he knew her too well. What she would give to see him once more, with Jane by his side.

I know how much it means to you . . . the natural world. The words reverberated in her head. This lack of freedom, of space, of green plants and open sky made her feel like a plant deprived of sunlight. The only glimmer of hope was that she might be able to visit the Hinchliffes' garden – but now they had left for Bath and would not be back until the beginning of September: a whole month to wait.

One particularly hot morning, the walls seemed to bear in on her, crushing the breath from her body. She tried to read in the garden in the shade of the tree but, as the sun moved around, the heat became too much to bear. She went upstairs to read, but even with the casement at its widest the air at the top of the house was even hotter and muggier than in the garden. She lay on the bed and closed her eyes.

On hot days like these in Suffolk, once her chores were done, she might wander on the beach with Bumbles, throwing him sticks and perhaps even paddling in the sea. Behind her eyelids she could almost see the sun glittering like a million diamonds on the sea's gently rippled surface, the delicate filigree of foam on the flat, wet sand left by the waves as they reached and receded. Sometimes she might persuade her mother and Jane to accompany her and the three of them would set out with a picnic and a large rug to spend the afternoon on the sand or in the dunes, gossiping and laughing, or quietly reading, relieved from the heat by the sea's cooling breezes until the strength of the sun had abated.

The memory caught in her throat – *Mother is dead, and*

those days will never come again. She took a deep breath, trying to summon the salty, seaweed tang of the beach, but all she could detect was the heavy odour of sewage and horse dung which clung to the city on these hot, airless days.

I can bear it no longer, she said to herself, feeling close to tears. *If I don't get into the fresh air, just for a little while, I will suffocate.*

A sudden, reckless thought sprang into her head: what if she dressed as a maid, as she had that first day? If she could get out of the house without being noticed, she would be able to wander at will, for she knew no one and no one knew her. She tried to ignore the idea but it became insistent, her imagination taking flight as she saw herself wandering freely through the market, with its stalls of brilliantly coloured fruits and flowers.

Earlier, at breakfast, her aunt had announced that she would be out visiting for most of the morning. The men were in the office as usual and Lizzie was at her studies. If she didn't go now, the moment would be lost.

Quickly, before she could lose her nerve, she removed her gown and took out her shabbiest linen dress and apron, tied an old cotton bonnet closely around her face and placed her sketchbook and pencils under a handkerchief in a small basket so that, if challenged, she could simply claim that she had gone out to buy a few items of shopping. With her heart pounding in her chest, she slipped noiselessly down the three flights of stairs, and out of the front door into the blinding sunlight.

Despite the pounding heat, her heart lifted as she turned the corner out of Spital Square. She was free, walking unnoticed among the throng. The sense of anonymity she had found so daunting on first arrival now felt wonderfully liberating. She strode purposefully, keeping her head bowed so as not to meet anyone's eye, holding her line along the pavement save when necessary to avoid the street hawkers and beggars who stepped into her way.

The market was but a few streets away, so she was certain of not losing her way. Sure enough, the odours of rotting fish and putrid meat wafting on the air confirmed that she was growing closer. She rounded two corners of the market square until more fragrant scents indicated that she was nearing the area of fruit and flower stalls that she and Lizzie had discovered last time.

Once again, as she entered through the arches and her eyes grew accustomed to the shade of the great hall, she found herself dazzled by the rainbow of intense colours, her nostrils assailed with sweet, delicate perfumes. She moved slowly along the aisle in a blissful daze, oblivious to the bustle of the market and the cacophony of stallholders' cries. Her eyes were so busy that the rest of her body seemed to lose all awareness and all her earlier self-consciousness and fear of being discovered were forgotten.

Her gaze was caught by a type of fruit she did not recognise. The woody-looking apples with rosy cheeks and a small coronet seemed plain enough on the outside but one had been cut in half to reveal inside a mass of juicy crimson seeds threaded with strands of bright yellow flesh.

'Them's pomegranates, miss. From Persia. Have a taste,' the stallholder said, offering her a handful of red seeds. 'Just a shilling each to you, dearie. How many would you like?' Anna backed away, shaking her head, but he continued talking. 'Or what about a guava? Now there's a cunning fruit – looks like a lumpy green apple but tastes like heaven. Or a grape, perhaps? Delicious little morsel. And not just good for making wine.' He pulled a couple of pale green fruit from the bunch and popped one into his mouth, holding a small bunch out to Anna.

'Our cook says all fruit should be stewed or baked to prevent sickness.'

'Then your cook's behind the times, miss, if you'll forgive me for saying. These fruits would be ruined by cooking, as all fashionable folk know. Now, what everyone's talking about are these,' he said, brandishing a bristly-looking thing which appeared to Anna more like a cudgel than a fruit. 'Pineapple. Once tasted, never forgotten.'

'How much is it?' Anna asked, thinking she might buy a present for her uncle and aunt.

'Five shillings, miss, and cheap at the price, given that it makes a tasty snack for a right crowd of folks. This little beauty has travelled all the way from the shores of Africa.' *How ridiculous*, Anna thought as she hurried onwards, *a fruit that costs the same as half a pig, or the weekly wage of a maid.*

She came upon a small stall that she had not noticed the previous time. It was a display of wild flowers so artfully arranged that she was instantly transported back to the country fields she knew so well. There were the tall yellow bracts of fennel with their delicate hair-like leaf fronds, sprays of goldenrod in a sharper yellow, the pink of the open-faced mallow and the modest heads of harebell in deeper purple. The desiccated stems of teasel, with their prickly seed heads, were entwined with columbine, elegantly coiling upwards to their showy white flowers.

Even more than the stunning variety of colours, both vibrant and subtle, what excited her artist's imagination was the dizzying variety of forms: of stems, leaves, blooms and seed heads. She found her fingers twitching to commit this beauty to paper.

Tucked in a corner was a large bunch of one of her favourites, Solomon's seal, surprising at this late stage of summer. She loved it not only for its graceful, arching stems and tiny white bell flowers, but because of the biblical story attached to it. Indeed, her own mother would brew tea from the dried leaves as a healing drink whenever any of the family had suffered stomach problems, or as a poultice for bumps and bruises.

As her eyes wandered over the display she was able to imagine, for a moment, that she had actually walked from the fields onto the sandy margins of the North Sea. Here was the sturdy sea lavender that forms a purple carpet over the marshes every July, the bold upright stems of yellow tree lupin, the prickly sea holly with its delicately veined blue-grey leaves and thistly flowers, the white willow herb, its seed heads curling open into downy arcs, and large bunches of the tough wiry heather that carpets the heath-land around the village in such a dramatic display of purple and pink that visitors will walk from miles around to see it.

A harsh voice close by startled Anna from her reverie. 'You going to buy anything, missy? Two bunches of lavender for a penny.'

Anna looked up into the eyes of a burly, ruddy-faced woman behind the stall. 'Sorry. I was just looking.'

'Lookin' don't make me a livin', miss, if you get me drift? Just gets in the way of me other customers.'

Anna muttered a further apology and went to take a step but her feet stumbled and she almost fell, just managing to save herself by putting a hand out to grab the side of the stall. She yelped as her skin brushed painfully against the heads of prickly thistles.

'Whoops,' the stallholder cried, pulling her upright with a powerful hand. 'Nearly had us over then, you did. Are you feeling a bit faint, miss? You've gone a funny colour. Terrible hot today, ain't it?'

She led Anna to the side of the stall and pulled out a rough wooden stool.

'Sit down and gather your senses for a moment. I'll get you a cup of water.'

Anna sat, gratefully sipping the tepid water, still light-headed yet feeling strangely elated by her discovery. Here, laid before her on a table, was everything she desired for her palette. If only she could paint it, right here and now.

'You feeling better, miss?' The tone was kinder now, less impatient.

'I am, thank you very much,' she said. 'But I wondered . . .'

'Yes?'

'I wondered if I could stay a while and try to sketch your beautiful display.'

'Sketch?' She looked askance. 'You some kind of artist? You ain't going to put me in it, is you, like that naughty Hogarth fellow?'

'Oh no, I just love to draw and paint flowers,' Anna hurried to reassure her. 'It wouldn't take many minutes.'

'So long as you keep out of me way, you can take all the time you like, dearie. Might be a nice little lure for me customers,' she muttered as an aside.

As Anna began to draw her hands and fingers seemed to move almost automatically, linked to the perception of her eyes by unseen threads that bypassed conscious thought. The flowers quickly began to take shape on the page – the arcs of stems, the serration of leaves and shades of light filtering through translucent petals – and relief spread through her neck and shoulders like a balm. The world around her receded into a dim, barely perceptible background.

She had filled a whole page with sketches and was trying to capture the way that the convolvulus twined through the sturdier stems of the teasel when an extraordinary idea began to take shape. It was a pattern of intertwined stems and flowers such as she had once seen in a hedgerow not far from home, a network of forms that seemed to reflect the wonderful beauty and unity of the natural world.

Ten minutes later, a heavy hand on her shoulder made her nearly jump out of her skin.

'Sorry to disturb, miss, but I have to nip off for a mo. Call of nature, you understand. Would you mind me stall for a few moments?' The woman pushed past, and was gone.

The interruption broke Anna's concentration, bringing her back to the world around her. She looked up with alarm, realising that she had absolutely no idea how long she had been sitting here. She'd heard no peals of midday church bells, but then she had heard nothing of the sounds of the market either, so absorbed had she been in her sketching. Was it lunchtime already, perhaps? Was the family sitting at the table, looking accusingly at the empty chair?

The woman seemed to be gone for an age. How could it possibly take so long? She put away her sketchbook, moved the seat behind the stall and sat with her head bent low, praying that no customer would stop. She had no idea what to do or say. After what felt like half an hour, but was probably only a few minutes, she began to pace, anxiously peering through the crowds for a glimpse of the stallholder returning.

Finally, she could stand the anxiety no longer. Ripping the page out of her sketchbook, she scrawled on the back: *Sorry to leave. Please take this in gratitude for letting me sit by your stall.* Then she laid it on the display and hurried to the next stallholder along. 'The lady there asked me to keep an eye for her but now I have to go. Would you mind?'

She almost ran through the market, down the steps and back along the streets, only remembering just in time to slow to a more graceful pace and gather her breath before she reached Spital Square.

She entered the front door without being noticed and stepped into the profound darkness of the hallway, felt her way to the bottom of the stairs and tiptoed upwards, trying to avoid the slightest sound on the treads. Still half blinded from the bright sunlight, she tripped on the top step and nearly fell. She caught herself with the banister and paused, with heart in mouth, fearing that she had been heard. But there was no sound and she had already reached the foot of the third set of stairs, the ones leading up to her attic, when she heard her aunt calling from the main bedroom, 'Is that you, Anna dearest? Luncheon will be served in fifteen minutes.'

'Yes, it is me,' she said, holding her breath. 'I will join you very shortly, Aunt.'

Hurriedly, she removed her bonnet, changed out of her 'maid's disguise' and into her best dress, retied her hair into its bun and fixed a crisply starched lace pinner onto her head. She gave her face and hands a quick rinse from the fresh jug of water Betty had kindly replaced since the morning, and slipped downstairs to join the family in the dining room.

Lunch was a tedious affair. The room was so hot and airless that the company seemed to have little appetite and less conversation. Exhilarated by the adventures of the morning, Anna felt deflated – if only she had someone to share her excitement with. William appeared even more taciturn than usual, and only Lizzie chattered on, complaining about the weather and the Latin declensions her tutor had been forcing her to learn. 'It's a dead language, whatever use can it be?' she whined. 'It's not fair. And when I too am half dead from the heat anyway. I hate her.'

She turned to Anna. 'I suppose you have had a lovely morning, Cousin. I was so jealous of you. What did you buy?'

Anna's heart nearly stopped. 'Buy? I did not buy anything. I have been reading in my room.'

'But you had a basket on your arm, when you returned just now. I thought you had . . .' The girl faltered, seeing the flush rising on Anna's face, and her mother's look of confusion. 'Oh . . . I must have mistaken you for someone else,' she ended, unconvincingly.

Surprisingly, nothing further was said, either during the meal or immediately afterwards. Later, when they had gone into the garden for some air, Lizzie whispered, 'I am so sorry . . . I thought Mama knew you had gone out. Will you get into trouble?'

'Do not fret, Cousin,' Anna replied, trying to sound braver than she felt. 'I am sure everything will be perfectly understood.'

It wasn't until teatime that Aunt Sarah summoned her to the drawing room, and Anna was not invited to sit down.

'Do I understand that you left the house on your own this morning, without a chaperone?'

Anna had already decided that honesty was the only policy. 'It was so hot that I thought I might die if I had to stay inside any longer. So I took a short walk, just for a little air. It was hardly any time at all.'

'That is beside the point. Have I not stated, quite clearly, that it is unseemly for you to be out in the streets alone? You have no knowledge of the city and its ways, and could be lured into any kind of danger. And yet you choose to ignore my advice.'

Anna lowered her face; it was easier to bite her lip that way. She had already decided that trying to defend herself would only lead to more trouble. The silence became almost suffocating.

'Have you nothing more to say for yourself?' Sarah's voice rose with irritation. 'You seem to have no idea of the consequences of your actions. Just imagine should you have been seen by someone? Out on your own, with no chaperone? We would never have lived it down.'

The words came out of her mouth before she could stop them. 'But I know hardly anyone in the city, Aunt, so there is little chance of my being recognised.'

Aunt Sarah's face turned an ugly puce colour, the perspiration on her brow glittering in a beam of sunlight. 'Don't be impertinent, girl,' she said sharply. 'It does not become you.'

She blotted her forehead with a lace handkerchief and sighed. 'My poor brother has obviously neglected your proper education in the ways of polite society, so I will have to teach you. When everyone has returned to the city in September, we will arrange tea parties and dinners to make sure that you are introduced to all the right people. That is how things are done in the city. Until then, you will only leave the house in the company of another member of the family or Betty, and then only with my permission. Do I make myself clear?'

8

Whatever was the English girl doing, leaving a piece of her sketching paper among the wild flowers?

Henri had come to the market to acquire a cheap pair of breeches for the drawboy, who had snagged his only pair on a nail head in the floorboards of the weaving loft. Mariette had pronounced them unrepairable and the lad was too embarrassed to venture to the market himself. Eventually, after much discussion over the breakfast table, M. Lavalle lost patience.

'Oh, for heaven's sake,' he shouted. 'Why are you making such a to-do about this, boy? Is your bottom such a thing of beauty that young ladies may faint at the sight of it?'

The lad began to cry.

'Shall I go?' Henri asked. 'It will take me but a quarter hour and I will be back at my loom before you have noticed my absence.'

'Thank you for relieving me of this irritation,' M. Lavalle sighed, handing his coin pouch across the table.

Henri made for the gallery above the main floor of the market, and was halfway up the wooden stairs when he glanced across the stalls below and spied a figure sitting among the flower sellers. He could not see the face, which was bent over a book, but the incline of her neck, the pallor of her skin, and the long, elegant fingers were instantly recognisable.

He stared for a while, and then climbed to the top of the stairs and walked around the gallery, past the second-hand clothes sellers, until he was almost immediately above the English girl. She could not see him but, just fifteen feet overhead, he had a perfect view. All now became clear: she had a drawing pad on her lap and was sketching the flowers.

And what drawings they were! He could see at once, even though they were only outlines and had not yet been coloured in, that she had somehow managed to capture the shape of each stem, leaf and flower so as to render them instantly recognisable even for *un ignorant* like him, who had never studied the natural world except in the designs which he wove. And they were nothing like the realistic depictions this girl was producing.

He watched, transfixed, as the lines flowed onto the page in strong, powerful arcs, then pale, delicate curves and even lighter strokes for shading of stems, leaves and petals, bringing their shapes to life with extraordinary, three-dimensional veracity. She worked fast, almost feverishly, as if hungry to capture the forms, and the page was soon filled with vignettes of different plants.

If I could draw like that, I could make my fortune as a silk designer like Leman or Baudoin, Henri thought to himself. Another idea flashed into his mind: *Perhaps she could show me?* before he dismissed it. *Idiot!* he cursed himself. *Why would an English lady want to teach a poor French weaver like me?*

All the same, as he watched, he found it all too easy to daydream: how he might sit beside her, how she might gently place her hand over his to guide it across the paper . . .

She turned to a blank page and started on a new design, drawing two bold, meandering lines equidistant from each other diagonally from the top of the paper to the opposite corner at the bottom and then two more, crossing the first, from the other corners, to make an open, curved trellis pattern. She followed each of those lines with lighter strokes either side and shaded them; it was soon clear that she was drawing the sinuous stems of a climbing plant. He followed her eyes as she looked up at her subject, the columbine entwined with the teasel, and could see that she was now reproducing its heart-shaped leaves and delicate bell-like flowers with their translucent petals, shading them with tiny strokes until they too became instantly recognisable.

Soon, more plants began to appear on the page, interlaced through her trellis pattern: bold-faced ox-eye daisies and nodding bluebell heads (although there were none of these on the stall), the curled petals of a dog rose flower and some fronded leaves so fine, like the hair of a baby, from a plant that he did not recognise. It took him a little time to understand why her work was so true to life, so compelling: while the drawings in themselves were perfect, she also reflected the imperfections of nature, the torn leaf, the faded bloom, the crushed or folded petal.

Henri was spellbound. He forgot the heat and the smell of the market, the drawboy's breeches, M. Lavalle's irritation and the coin pouch hanging heavy in his pocket. The pressing deadline for the brocade he was working on today was suddenly unimportant.

The notion dawned on him slowly, but once he realised the potential of what he could see on her page, he could barely contain his excitement. Although the girl was surely unaware of its significance, this was the most beautiful, elegant and delicate fabric design he had ever seen in his life. It captured exactly what the dressmaker Miss Charlotte had been talking about: the wild flowers, the look of the countryside, the realistic rendering of the images and the beautiful curving lines of nature that surely – his face flushed at the thought – reflect the perfect shapes of a woman's body.

The naive simplicity of it made his heart thud in his chest. He could almost see the design already transposed with dots of paint onto the squared point paper, and how the loom and its lashes should be set up to weave it.

Then, all at once, an astonishing idea overcame him with an almost physical intensity, making him giddy. It was the perfect design for his master piece. Already he felt a strong sense of ownership. It was meant to be his.

But how? Should he just approach her and ask if he could buy it? Would she be offended? Or would she just laugh in his face?

At that moment he saw the fat woman striding away from the stall. The girl moved her stool behind the table out of his sight. What was she doing now? He dithered, rooted to the spot by indecision. Within a few minutes she reappeared, pacing the gangway in front of the stall. Then she disappeared behind the stall again and reappeared with her basket. He saw her tear out the page from the sketch-book with *his* design on it, scribbling a few words on the back so hastily that he could not read them, and placing it face up among the flowers. Before he knew it, she was gone.

He was about to follow but, from observing her fretful demeanour, instinct told him that any interruption or inter-vention would not be welcomed. Besides, the drawing was still there on the stall, like a white bird stretching its wings in a flower-strewn field. The stallholder had not returned.

Hurrying as quickly as he could without drawing atten-tion to himself, Henri rounded the gallery until he reached the wooden stairs, slipped down them and made his way towards the stall without knowing precisely what he was going to do when he reached it. And then, to his dismay, he saw the trader approaching with her wide-hipped stride from the other direction. He was so close to the stall by now that he could almost reach out and take the sketch without her noticing.

'Oi! Put that back, boy!' A man's harsh shout came from the other side of the aisle. 'That was left for Mags, that was.'

With a sudden turn of speed, the ruddy-faced Mags was upon him, snatching the paper from his hand. 'Give that here, you thieving little cur,' she said, smacking him across the head so hard that he stumbled and fell among the trampled mess of rotting fruit and discarded plants. He scrabbled away to avoid the kick that followed, and crawled

out of sight beneath a nearby stall, trying to catch
breath.

'So, what have we here, then?' Breathing heavily from
her efforts, she glanced at the sketch and turned the paper
over. 'That little missy done a runner, then?'

'Asked me to keep an eye out,' the man said.

The pair of them examined the drawing for a few
moments and began to argue about its value.

'What'll you give for it?'

'Don't you want it, then?'

'Looks like scribbles to me. A load of nothing.'

'Then I'll give you nothing for it.'

'Cheeky sod. I'll tear it up, shall I?'

'No!' Henri found himself shouting. He jumped up from
his hiding place, holding out M. Lavalle's purse. 'I'll buy it
from you.'

The woman's fearsome demeanour softened in an instant.
She knew her smile could charm men into spending far
more than they had ever intended when buying flowers for
their sweethearts. She could almost smell the pork chops
the boy's money would buy for this evening's supper.

'Two shillings,' she pronounced. The man beside her
whistled quietly between his teeth.

'Two pennies, more like,' Henri replied, remembering
the errand on which he'd been sent. He had not checked
how many coins were in the pouch but from its weight he
judged there were not many, and he must not return without
having purchased breeches for the drawboy.

'One shilling, then,' the woman said, standing foursquare,
her feet wide across the aisle.

'Thruppence,' Henri said, pulling back his shoulders to

make himself as broad as possible. 'I have other purchases to make and that is all I can afford.'

She fixed him in the eye and held up the piece of paper, twisting her hands on each side as if to tear it.

'Sixpence, then,' he blurted out, as if his life depended on it.

The woman hesitated, examined the piece of paper again as if to convince herself that it was not worth more, and then, to Henri's great relief, said, 'Done.'

The drawboy pranced around the loom loft, jiggling his hips and singing an old French song, apparently delighted with his green serge breeches, even though they were several sizes too large and had to be held up with an old lash cord. They were already well worn, shiny at the knees and buttocks, and might not even last long enough for him to grow into them, but none of this seemed to dim his happiness.

Henri could take no satisfaction from the boy's childish pleasure, sullied as it was by the guilt he felt at having spent M. Lavalle's money on the English girl's sketch without prior permission. The breeches had been the cheapest he could find – only nine pence – and now he faced the dilemma of how to own up about the other sixpence. He had no money of his own to repay the debt – having given all of the fee from his labours in the organ loft to pay his mother's rent – but fully intended to do so just as soon as he was able to earn it.

On his return M. Lavalle had been engaged with a

customer, so he'd simply handed back the purse without having to explain. It crossed his mind, fleetingly, that he could claim the breeches cost a shilling and thruppence, but his master would then think him a fool for paying so much. The problem gnawed at him for the rest of the morning, but the magic he'd felt while watching the English girl was still wrapped around his heart. He didn't want to share that with anyone, at least for the moment.

Before lunch, he went to his box room and carefully took out the piece of paper from under his shirt, where it had been tucked all morning. The enchantment was still there – the delicate fronds of leaves, the curled petals, the curving stems – and his heart began to race all over again as he imagined them translated into a fabric design. He would make a start on marking up and painting-in the point paper this very evening, after supper. Then he could show M. Lavalle the sketch and the design, and it would be an easier task to persuade him that the sixpence had been well spent.

In the end, the decision was taken from him. At lunchtime, M. Lavalle invited the drawboy to show him his new breeches, slapped him on the backside approvingly and said, 'They should last you until you are a man.' Then he turned to Henri, in a perfectly casual way, and asked how much they had cost.

'Nine pence, sir.' Henri's appetite suddenly disappeared. 'They were the cheapest I could find.'

'Then, if I am not mistaken, there is a further sixpence to account for.'

Henri took another bite of bread, giving himself time to think. 'May I speak with you in private, after lunch?'

M. Lavalle nodded assent, but Henri could sense the

question hanging over the table like a cloud for the rest of the meal. Even Mariette seemed to have little to say. At last, it was finished and the others dismissed.

'Well, boy? Where is my missing sixpence?'

'Please forgive me for spending your money without permission, master. I will repay it just as soon as I can – when I get another request to be organ blower.'

'I have never questioned your *honnêteté, tu sais*. But I need an explanation.'

Henri took a deep breath, and began. 'I have been thinking much since our discussion about my design. Mariette suggested I should ask the dressmaker Miss Charlotte Amesbury, whom I think you know?' M. Lavalle nodded. Henri hurried on. 'She showed me how the newest vogue is for realistic-looking representations of natural forms, flowers, leaves and so on.'

'Indeed. Fashions change with the wind these days, as I have said before, but that is certainly the way they are blowing right now.'

'So I decided to start again, change my design to something more fashionable. The problem is finding a designer to help me.'

'You won't buy much of a designer's time for sixpence. You know this, do you not?'

Henri reached inside his shirt and pulled out the sketch paper. 'But I have something which I believe may make a good start.'

M. Lavalle unfolded the paper and smoothed it out on the table. Two long minutes passed, as the *tick-tock* of the grandfather clock in the corner seemed to grow louder and louder.

At last, the old man looked up. 'Am I to take it that this is what you spent my sixpence on?'

Henri nodded.

'And may I ask who sold it to you?'

He struggled to find the right words to explain, with M. Lavalle having to ask him to start again several times: how he had seen a girl drawing beside the flower stall, how she had given it as a gift for the trader who didn't want it, and how he had offered sixpence to save it from being torn up. He omitted to identify the girl or mention that he already knew her, albeit only slightly, or that she was the niece of the despised merchant Sadler. There was no point in complicating matters for the moment.

'Did the girl give her name?'

'I would know her again,' Henri replied, trying to avoid a lie. 'But why does this matter, sir? Since I paid for the drawing it is surely mine?'

'Of course it matters,' M. Lavalle spluttered. 'You may have paid for her sketch but you have not paid for the right to reproduce it in cloth. If you hope to get the fabric commissioned and widely distributed, do you imagine that she will not recognise it, and wonder how you came by it?'

Henri shook his head, crestfallen. 'Of course, you are right. I will have to ask her permission.'

'And hope that she does not seek to charge you in addition for reproducing it,' M. Lavalle said. His words were not meant unkindly, Henri knew; his master was being realistic. 'Great riches are not the only route to happiness,' he'd once told him. 'A clear conscience is the path to a good name and a contented life.'

Guy was panting as though he'd run a mile. 'I need to speak to M. Lavalle. I have news of much interest. May I come in?'

'It is late,' Henri said. 'He may already have retired, and I am busy.' The last thing he wanted was to listen to another rant from his friend about the scandal of journeymen's pay.

'Please. It's important,' Guy pleaded.

M. Lavalle appeared at the top of the stairs. 'I was about to treat myself to a drink of *chocolat* before bed. Would you two both like to join me? Mariette, do we have enough milk?'

Guy smirked. '*Alors.* Now will you let me in?'

When they were settled in the parlour, Mariette brought a tray with cups of hot milk into which she had melted shavings from a precious lump of chocolate given to M. Lavalle the previous Christmas by a yarn merchant grateful for his continuing custom. The dark treasure was kept hidden in the coolest place in the basement, its use allowed only sparingly.

M. Lavalle took a sip and murmured his appreciation, '*C'est délicieux, ma petite,*' before turning to Guy. 'So, now you can tell us your very important news, my friend.' He took the scruffy piece of paper offered to him. Glancing over the old man's shoulder, Henri could read the heading: *Soie de Lyon*, followed by a list of a dozen names. Halfway down was written, *Jsph. Sadler & Son.*

M. Lavalle skimmed it, sucking the breath through his teeth. 'These are important men. Why are their names on this list?'

'They have imported French silk, sir, from Lyon, without paying the duty. That is what we believe.'

Henri forgot to breathe, for a second. The great Joseph Sadler, breaking the law? He cared little for the man and his pig of a son, but the scandal could spell disaster for his niece.

M. Lavalle sighed and scratched his head beneath the velvet cap. 'This is dangerous information. Where did you get it?'

'Last week I was at the chophouse with some friends talking about the *Book of Prices* when someone said it was a waste of time because French imports would have us all in the poorhouse before long,' Guy said. 'Some fellows at the next table heard our talk and said they could help us: they had information about who was buying French silk.'

'And from where did their information come, may we ask?'

'They are workers at the port of London, sir. They see everything coming in and going out. They noticed many packages, rolls of fabric addressed to London mercers, which were not marked for import duty, so they opened one or two and discovered that it was French silk. Some of the lads thought they might make a few bob in blackmail but they got cold feet and decided it was safer to approach the Weavers' Company about it.'

'And did they do this?'

Guy nodded.

'I was at a Freemen's meeting two days ago. Surely it would have been mentioned?'

'That's the point, sir. Nothing has happened. The lads

are assuming the Company has buried it because of the important names.'

M. Lavalle shook his head. 'Not that I have heard. But do I now take it they sold *you* the list instead, right there, in the chophouse?'

'The journeymen's group bought it, from their campaign funds,' Guy said. 'The group who put together the *Book of Prices*.'

'And what do this group propose to do with it now?' M. Lavalle asked.

'That is why I am here, sir, to seek your advice. You know these people. What is the best way to proceed?'

M. Lavalle took a long sip of chocolate and wiped his moustache with his kerchief.

'I need to give this some serious thought, Guy. It requires careful handling or it will go off like gunpowder and innocent people might get injured. I need to talk to some of my fellow Freemen, those whom I can trust. Come back at the end of the week, Sunday afternoon, would you? We shall talk more, and perhaps drink more *chocolat*. Can your group wait?'

'I will ask them tonight. But I fear that unless they see some action soon, they will take matters into their own hands. French imports are taking the food from their children's mouths, they say, and it is time the authorities showed a firm hand. All of their protests have been met with deaf ears, and their patience is running out.' He made a small bow. 'Thank you for your time, Monsieur Lavalle. The *chocolat* was delicious, Miss Mariette. Goodnight to you all.'

As they parted for bed, M. Lavalle whispered to Henri,

'Your friend is among hotheads. I fear he may get into trouble. You have read the newspaper reports about the cutters, and the group that calls itself the Bold Defiance? The Guards are becoming impatient with their protests and if they are caught, they will be shown no mercy. Please warn him to be careful.'

At the foot of the stairs he turned back to Henri. 'I know that he is a good friend of yours, but if Guy persists with these associates, you would be wise to distance yourself from him. I have high hopes for your future, my boy. It would break my heart to see you getting into trouble.'

Guy's list was not mentioned again nor, to Henri's relief, did he reappear. He noticed, however, that M. Lavalle was frequently out of the house. Henri hoped he would be able to settle the matter quietly, so that Guy could disengage himself and there would be no scandal that might affect Anna's family.

Over the following days he found excuses to visit the market as often as he could. Each time Anna did not reappear he was disappointed and yet, at the same time, slightly relieved.

He decided instead to send a letter. It took him a whole evening to write and rewrite, with much agonising over the unfamiliar English words and their spelling. Finally he was satisfied, but then delayed a further two days, trying to summon the courage to deliver it.

At last, when he reached the end of a weave half an hour earlier than expected, he could allow himself to procrastinate no longer. Several times, *en route* to Spital Square, his heart faltered. What would he say should he meet her in the street or, worse, at the doorstep? *I have a letter for you?* Or would he just blurt it out: *I bought your drawing from the stallholder at the market. Can I have your permission to use it as the design for my master piece?*

It was a simple enough request, after all. So what was it about this girl that made him feel so awkward, so nervous and unsure of himself?

9

Opinions vary regarding ladies' withdrawal to the drawing room after the meal while the men indulge in port, cigars and masculine conversation. The best advice is to follow the lead of the host and hostess.

— The Lady's Book of Manners

Anna read the last page of her book, slapped it shut, and sighed. There was still more than an hour to kill before suppertime.

She'd read the novel several times and each time had found it more disheartening. Poor, sad Clarissa, pressured by her family into marrying the vile Robert Lovelace. Was that all life was about for a young woman: being hawked around the marriage market? And was it the only alternative to poverty, ignominy and death?

She tried to remind herself that her own situation was very far from that of tragic Clarissa's. There was no coercion, for a start; she was here in London entirely of her own volition, and in the care of a loving and generous family who, although they might expect it, were not by any means pressuring her to get married. She could change her mind and return home at any time and, for the meanwhile at least, she had hardly met anyone, let alone a villain like Lovelace.

So why could she not shake off this feeling of being so entirely undermined? She did not recognise her former self any more, the chatty, cheerful girl always ready to challenge and question, sometimes getting into trouble for it but never doubting for a moment the love of her family and friends. When once she had felt so confident of her place in the world – albeit the small world of the village – here in the city she was floundering, directionless, uncertain how to behave, even of what to think. *Am I losing myself?* she wondered. *Perhaps this is what happens when you grow up?* Or was it just that she had not yet found her place in this society?

She went to the open window, looking out across the rooftops, which sometimes helped to ease her loneliness. *There is a world out there just waiting to be discovered.* Once she found her feet and had learned the ways of the city, she would be more able to determine how to enjoy it.

A small movement in the street below caught her eye and she leaned further out of the window to peer over the parapet. Someone was crossing the square, making straight for their front door. He looked familiar, even from this height, and when he turned his head as if to check whether anyone was watching she knew instantly that it was the French weaver. Observing his easy, confident stride, the bare legs below the breeches, the modest linen jacket with white shirt and loose kerchief at the neck, and the dark plait that fell onto his neck, she couldn't help recalling the moment she had come to her senses finding herself in his arms, the unfamiliar but somehow comforting smell of him, and the strange language he spoke to his friend.

He had a piece of paper in his hand, probably an invoice for silks woven, she assumed. Because of the porch overhang she could not see whether he actually knocked on the door, but moments later he was returning across the square. He had just disappeared from sight when she heard the light skip of Lizzie's feet on the stairs, and a knock at the door.

'Anna, are you there? I've something for you.'

'Come in,' Anna called, turning from the window, picking up the book again and opening it at a random page.

'It's been delivered by hand,' the girl said, handing her a letter.

'Thank you, Cousin,' she said, trying not to betray the unsettling feeling in her chest, a kind of fluttering, like the wings of a tiny bird.

'Won't you open it now? *Please?* I am burning up with curiosity.'

'I can only quench your fire when I have discovered myself from whom the letter comes, and what it says. Please close the door as you leave.' The girl pulled a face, emphasising her disappointment with each clomp of her feet descending the wooden stairway.

Anna held herself very still, taking slow breaths, for several minutes. Even then, she could not stop her hands from shaking when she finally allowed herself to pick up the letter. She broke the seal and opened it.

Dear Miss Anna,
 This is me, Henri Vendôme, the silk weaver. It is dificult to explain, but I am wanting to speak you

about matter of importance. It is possible we meet,
please? Can you reply at my adress your anser, yes or
no? I hope very much yes.
Henri

Her immediate instinct was to laugh at his terrible spelling, but she checked herself. The boy's first language was French, after all. She herself could barely speak a single word of his tongue, or any other language come to that, so what right did she have to be critical?

As for the content of the letter, she was consumed with curiosity. Whatever could this matter of importance be? She had already learned that people in the city only mixed socially with those of the same level: lords with lords, merchants like her uncle with other merchants, manual workers with other manual workers. This inflexibility seemed a pity: it would probably be more fun to spend time with Henri and his friend Guy, she thought wistfully, than at the tame little tea parties her aunt would organise.

She barely knew him and yet each time she'd found herself in his presence she had felt a strange familiarity, as though she had been acquainted with him in another life, long ago. Had she met someone else who looked like him, which might account for it? However much she racked her brain, she could find no conclusion. So perhaps that sense of intimacy was only a consequence of his rescuing her, in those confusing few hours of her first day in London, nothing more?

So rapt was she by these tempting, perplexing thoughts, and the dilemma presented by this unexpected turn of events, that she barely noticed time passing. The bell rang for supper, and she hurriedly concealed the letter under a pile of papers.

The table was laid with the usual mouth-watering generosity: cold meats, hams and salted beef, fresh loaves from the market, a steaming pile of boiled potatoes, green beans and slices of braised marrow. Uncle Joseph, usually the first to reach for the meat and pile his plate high, sat with his hands in his lap. His attention seemed to be elsewhere. When urged by Sarah, he muttered irritably that he had little appetite this evening, and would she please leave him be.

While everyone at the table – Sarah, Lizzie, William, Anna and the two clerks – helped themselves and began to eat, their spoons clattering in the uneasy silence, Joseph's empty plate seemed to glare in reproach.

Sarah tried once or twice more: 'Are you not well, Husband? Why not try some of Cook's new sweet pickle with a small piece of cheese, my dearest, just a little?' And, later, 'These peaches are perfectly ripe – they will rot if we do not have them tonight. Take just a small slice, won't you, to keep up your strength?' Each time Joseph snapped back, 'Stop nagging, Sarah.' Or, 'Am I not allowed an evening without appetite?'

William and the other boys talked about their work in language comprehensible only to themselves, her aunt was utterly distracted and Lizzie seemed close to tears. Anna could not wait for the meal to be over.

The ladies left the table and went to the drawing room

and, shortly afterwards, William and the other boys could be heard making their way downstairs – probably heading out to a coffee house, Anna thought enviously, as the front door slammed. Sarah took out her embroidery but sat with the frame in her lap, her gaze unfocused, making not a single stitch.

At her mother's urging, Lizzie went to the harpsichord and played a few notes, but kept making the same mistakes and soon gave up. Anna opened a book and tried to read but the text danced in front of her eyes. All she could see was his curly handwriting: *your anser, yes or no? I hope very much yes.*

Even with both of the sashes raised, the air in the room was thick with unease, hot and hard to breathe. Anna suggested a game of backgammon and Lizzie leapt eagerly to take the box from its shelf.

'I won't join you this evening, I am afraid,' Aunt Sarah said, replacing her embroidery frame in its basket. 'I must attend to your father. He seems so very out of sorts.'

Shortly afterwards, raised voices could be heard from the next room. Anna and Lizzie tried to continue their game, but soon gave up the pretence and sat in silence, sharing only an occasional raised eyebrow or troubled glance. The conversation was clearly audible through the cracks in the wainscot.

First, her uncle's deep rumble: 'Leave me be, Wife. It is nothing for you to be concerned with.'

'It *is* my concern if my beloved is unable to eat,' Aunt Sarah said more gently. 'Please, tell me what ails you.'

'It is nothing. I will be in better spirits come the morning.'

'I *must* know, dear Husband. I will not rest until you tell me.' There was an extended silence during which Lizzie took Anna's hand, seeking comfort. Then came a shocked shriek: 'Whatever is *this*, Husband? Who sent it?'

'The Mercers' Company.'

'I cannot believe my eyes. Are you sure it is meant for you?'

'My name is on the envelope.'

'It accuses you of illegal trading and failing to pay the proper import tax. Surely that cannot be correct?'

Another long pause.

'I shall die if you keep me in suspense like this, Joseph! Tell me they are mistaken.'

'It's a load of codswallop. Bloody outrageous.' The outburst caused both girls to flinch, his voice so loud and aggressive that even their own candles seemed to flicker in its blast. 'What right do they have to interfere like this? It was William's suggestion and I agreed with him. It is *my* business, *my* right to decide what I buy and to whom I sell!'

Sarah's voice in response was surprisingly calm and meas-ured. Anna could imagine how she was having to hold herself in, tighter even than her stays. 'Should you not have cautioned William that paying the correct duty is the law of the land? Do you not have a reputation to consider, Husband?'

'It is a ridiculous law, totally discredited. They say it's intended to protect English weavers, but how can we obey the law when all society is crying out for imported fabrics?'

'But what in heaven's name is wrong with English silk, pray?'

'Perhaps the French designs are more refined, but the

real reason is because they are rare and difficult to get hold of – because of the law.'

'That sounds like a stupid law, then.'

'Which is why every mercer in the land ignores it. You want us to prosper, do you not, to move to a better area, take a large house in Ludgate Hill like the Hinchliffes? How can we prosper if we do not supply what the market demands?'

'Then surely you should complain to the Company, dearest Husband? You are well respected among your peers, your voice should carry weight. Was your name not being whispered for Upper Bailiff in a year or so?'

'I *have* complained, many a time, in Council. But recently there have been petitions, and the pressure from the weavers is becoming difficult to ignore. They are afraid of riots.'

'Surely they will not bow to such threats?'

'Alas, there is little choice, when the law is the law.'

The conversation lapsed and then they heard a single sob, followed by low conciliatory murmurs from Joseph.

Lizzie whispered, 'Is he in terrible trouble, do you think?'

'I am sure it is just a mistake,' Anna whispered back, trying to sound more confident than she felt. 'Your father is well respected. Nothing will happen.'

'But if he has broken the law, will he go to prison? William too? Whatever will become of us?' A tear fell onto Lizzie's flushed cheek.

'Hush, little one,' Anna said, putting an arm around her. 'As with all things, this will pass.' She remembered her father using these same words, attempting to comfort her when her mother was critically ill. Her mother died shortly afterwards. Things did indeed pass, but that did not stop you mourning them.

She slept fitfully that night. In just a few moments of overheard conversation the world seemed to have altered irrevocably. She had been growing accustomed to the family and the city, and was feeling more secure – even if overly constrained – and looking forward to September when there would be more social diversions as people returned from their country retreats. But the future that had felt so solid had now become shifting, like standing on a riverbank when the ground which had felt unyielding underfoot might suddenly give way and leave you calf-deep in treacherous mud.

Next morning at breakfast her uncle announced that Sarah was suffering from a headache and would be staying in her chamber, at least until lunchtime. Betty had taken up a few morsels to tempt her appetite. Joseph and William ate quickly; they were going to a meeting, he said, and would be gone most of the day.

When the two girls were left alone, Anna asked, 'Did you manage to sleep, dearest Cousin?'

'A little,' Lizzie replied. 'I had a nightmare about Papa going to gaol.'

'I do not think that at all likely, dearest. Besides, do you not imagine that your father and William are even now on their way to sort out the matter?'

Anna could not decide how to respond to the French boy's letter. Her mind vacillated wildly. One minute she felt it better to ignore the request, to avoid becoming involved in something of which her aunt would certainly disapprove; the next she was determined to find out more, even at the risk of incurring her aunt's wrath.

What remained unchanging was the feeling of over-whelming curiosity about this ordinary French journeyman whose face and physical presence seemed so improbably familiar to her. It was impossible to resist. Returning to her room after breakfast, she tore a sheet of paper from her sketchbook and wrote:

> Dear M. Vendôme,
>   Thank you for your letter. I will be at Christ Church on Sunday and may be able to speak with you after-wards, but only if my aunt is not accompanying me.
> I hope you will understand.
>   Yours etc.
>   Anna Butterfield

She folded the piece of paper and tied it with a piece of ribbon. But how to deliver it? Somehow she had to find an excuse to leave the house. She returned downstairs to Lizzie's room.

'Is your tutor coming at ten o'clock as usual?'

'Worse luck. I am too tired and do not feel a bit like doing my studies.'

'It will make a good distraction for you, and perhaps this afternoon we could do some painting? I will go with Betty to the market to buy some flowers, shall I? I cannot trust her to get the right kind.'

'Should you not check with Mama?'

'Let's not trouble her as she's feeling unwell. If she asks, I am reading in my room. Is that clear?' She fixed her cousin with a strong look, and was rewarded with a nod of agreement.

She ran downstairs to tell Betty about her plan, then up to her room to get changed into what she'd now come to think of as her 'maid's disguise'.

When they reached the market, she left Betty with strict instructions to spend a long time making her purchases and then to wait at the pie stall when the clock of Christ Church struck twelve noon. She wasn't entirely sure where Wood Street was, but remembered the direction in which the boy had gestured that day when they met on the steps of Christ Church, and surely it could not be far.

She hastened to the farthest point of the market, on the corner of Lyon Street and Paternoster Row, and then headed up Church Street, past the huge white bulk of Christ Church towering over the other buildings. The heat seemed even to have silenced the songbirds that usually sang from their cages, but through the open loft windows high above the street she could hear the clack of countless looms – a sound that Lizzie had pointed out on their first day – as the weavers thrust their shuttles back and forth.

Soon she found herself on a wider highway called Brick Lane, a bustling thoroughfare of carts and carriages, street merchants, temporary market stalls, beggars, shopfronts, inns and chophouses. Hawkers were everywhere shouting their wares: 'Eels, smelts and whiting, fresh today,' or 'Hats and caps! I buy, sell or exchange,' but she was careful, as Lizzie had instructed her, never to meet their eyes.

Picking her way between the traffic and the crowds, she marvelled at how, in just a few short weeks, she had become accustomed to this extraordinary city, the throng of carts and carriages, the press of people, the smells of horses, rotting meat and fish mingling with wood smoke and tobacco. And yet she knew that just a mile away was open country: gardens, fields and woods. If she kept on walking, she might find somewhere like home, coloured in shades of green instead of the drab grey and brown of the city.

She became so wrapped up in her thoughts that she found herself striding along as she would at home but, when she was next able to see through a gap in the streets, the spire of Christ Church appeared further away than she had expected, and rather more to the left than she had remembered.

At last, after asking several people, she found her way to Wood Street. Since arriving in the city she had been intrigued by the numbers boldly displayed on the door of every house. In the village every building had a name that gave a sense of its occupants and its location: Five Bar Cottage, Butcher's House, High Elms Lodge, Little Barley Farm. Just living at a number seemed so anonymous, so dull.

Today, however, she discovered how necessary they were, when every house looked the same. And here it was, number 37, a tall, narrow house in a terrace of identical brick build-ings, each with a basement window peering up to the pavement, three further storeys and the long dormer windows of the weaving loft stretching the full width of its roof.

It looked respectable enough, she observed, although it seemed to lack a woman's touch: there were no singing birds in the windows, no pots of flowers in the porch; the sills were dusty and the woodwork definitely in need of a lick of new paint.

Glancing quickly around to check that she was not being observed, Anna ascended the few steps and was about to slip her note under the front door when it was opened from the inside by an elderly man, his greying hair tied into a plait under a red velvet cap.

'*Bonjour, mademoiselle. Je peux vous aider?*'

'I just wished to deliver this note, sir,' she stuttered, trying to gather her composure. 'To Monsieur Vendôme.'

A look of gentle amusement crinkled the corner of the old man's eyes; a look that made her suspect that he knew exactly who she was and what the letter was about.

'Do you wish to speak to him in person?'

'Oh no,' she said hastily, 'I do not wish to disturb him on a working day.'

'Then may I say from whom the letter is come?'

'I am Anna. Anna Butterfield.'

'What a pretty name,' he said. 'I shall make sure Henri receives it, Mam'selle Butterfield.'

Emboldened by the success of the morning, Anna planned her next move with meticulous care. After lunch she spent nearly four hours helping Lizzie create a reasonable likeness of the arrangement of wild flowers she had purchased in the market. Her pupil had little patience for careful observation and Anna had resorted to drawing much of it before allowing her to apply the watercolour.

When it was finished, they took it to Aunt Sarah – it would help distract her from her troubles, they agreed.

'What a marvellous talent you have, dearest daughter,' Sarah cried, holding the painting at arm's length to better view it. 'If you do some more, we shall stage a little showing of your work. And we had better get you a new dress for that, hadn't we?' Lizzie clapped her hands with glee.

Aunt Sarah swivelled her feet out of the bed and stood up. 'I declare that your little painting has so cheered me that I believe I shall be able to rise for supper.'

Later, as Lizzie hugged her with genuine gratitude, Anna knew this was the moment to take the girl into her confidence. She explained about the letter in which the French boy had asked to see her. She could not refuse for fear of appearing rude, she explained, so she had agreed to meet him after church. On condition that Lizzie would be her chaperone this coming Sunday, and agree to keep secret whatever took place there, Anna would continue the drawing and painting lessons until she deserved her new frock.

Lizzie grumbled that it seemed a most unwise course of action, although she had no option but to agree.

That night Anna found it hard to sleep again, her head full of the day's excitements and imaginings about the French boy's mysterious words: *a matter of importance.*

She had finally dropped off when she was woken by sudden, harsh shouts from the street outside, a sharp, shocking crash and the ominous clatter of breaking glass. She heard her aunt's terrified scream from the bedroom below, followed by a bellow of rage from her uncle, and then William's voice, a panicky commotion of shouts and the thunder of footsteps on the stairs.

Peering into the darkness, she caught a glimpse of shadowy figures disappearing around the corner of the square. With shaking hands, she lit her candle, pulled on a shawl and descended the wooden stairs. Aunt Sarah and Lizzie were huddled on the landing, Lizzie pale-faced and trembling, her mother restless with anxiety, occasionally leaning over the banister to shout instructions: 'Call the night watchman!', 'Have a care, Husband, they may be violent,' and, 'For Lord's sake, do not go out into the street.' Raking her cheeks with her fingers, she wailed, 'Dear God, whatever will become of us?'

They descended to the drawing room and lit as many candles as they could find to dispel the shadows which now hung full of menace, and waited in tense silence, listening for sounds of activity on the ground floor below.

Eventually they heard the chirpy voice of the night watchman at the front door, her uncle's deep tones and then a clear, 'Not to worry, sir. We'll soon apprehend the scoundrels. Now, please go inside and lock all your doors and windows. I will return just as soon as we have any news.'

As Joseph entered the drawing room he seemed to be tucking something into his pocket. 'Nothing to worry about, my dears. Thank heavens all our windows are shuttered, so it is only the fanlight above the front door that has been broken. William is putting up a board to make it secure.'

'Is this about the French silk, Papa?'

Anna's aunt and uncle exchanged glances.

'I don't know to what you are referring, Daughter, but if it is something you have overheard, it is all wicked lies,' Joseph blustered. 'This is just stupid vandalism, so do not let me hear you repeating anything about this ever again, do you understand?'

Anna had always been a little afraid of him, his over-bearing presence and intimidatingly loud voice, but now, for the first time, she could see that he was vulnerable. What would the consequences be for his business? And for those around him – his family, and herself?

Joseph took a deep breath and set his shoulders, regaining his composure. 'Now there is nothing more to be concerned about, my dear ones, so I think you should return to bed for your precious beauty sleep. William and I will wait for the night watch to return.'

Next morning, after a scanty sleep, Anna woke early and was first to breakfast. Betty had laid eggs and bread on the table, and returned to the kitchen to collect the cheese and cold meats. As Anna went to take her place, her eye was caught by something tucked behind one of the candlesticks on the mantel. It was a scrap of dirty paper, once crumpled but now smoothed flat and folded in two. Cautiously she moved closer, ready to turn away should anyone enter the room. She reached for the paper and unfolded it. The words, in large capital letters, were ominous and terrifying: *THIS IS FOR SELLING ILLEGAL FRENCH SILK, SADLER. CEASE NOW OR YOUR HOUSE WILL BE TORCHED.*

10

You cannot be too wary in the choice of him you would call your friend; nor suffer your affections to be so far engag'd, as to be wholly at his devotion. 'Tis dangerous trusting one's happiness in another person's keeping; or to be without a power to refuse, what may be your ruin to grant.

– Advice for apprentices and journeymen
OR A sure guide to gain both esteem and an estate

The heatwave broke, heavy grey-purple clouds rolling in from the west and blotting out the merciless rays of the sun for the first time in weeks. Soon enough, Henri could hear the rumbles of thunder, first in the distance and then drawing closer and closer until they seemed to be directly overhead. Then the rain started, drumming so loudly on the slates immediately above their heads that he and Benjamin had to shout over the noise.

The sky darkened like dusk, making it difficult to see the fine threads of silk. The drawboy shrieked in terror with each flare of lightning and was unable to concentrate on maintaining the proper sequence of lashes. It soon became clear that no weaving could continue until the storm had passed.

They took the boy down to the basement kitchen where the noise of the storm was more distant and, while the cook sat him at the table and warmed a cup of milk to calm his nerves, Henri took the opportunity of slipping next door into his room. There, he took out Anna's letter once more from its hiding place, carefully concealed with her sketch beneath his mattress.

When M. Lavalle had asked whether the letter contained the permission he sought, Henri had to admit that it was not yet agreed.

'I hope to meet her at Christ Church after the service on Sunday,' he said, cursing the red flush rising up his neck onto his cheeks.

'I see,' the old man said, with a knowing smile. 'She certainly appears to be a charming young lady, and her artistic skills are remarkable.' His face settled into a more serious expression. 'I trust you will approach this meeting in an entirely professional manner, Henri? She may dress like a maid, but from her accent and her bearing you must understand that she is not one of us.'

'It is a business proposition, nothing more, I can assure you,' Henri said, trying to believe himself. He was usually so self-assured with girls, so confident of his own good looks. He would often scheme for days to gain a girl's attention and bask in his success when it was finally given, but was usually disappointed to discover that once the game had been won the prize tended to lose its glister.

This time it was more complicated. He could not determine which made his heart race most: the prospect of seeing the girl again, of being close and hearing her voice, or the thought of getting her permission to use the drawing for his master piece.

The worst of the storm seemed to have passed when they heard Cook shouting, 'Henri, your master is calling for you.' He reached the top of the basement stairs to discover that M. Lavalle had opened the front door to a bedraggled figure. 'Come in, come in out of the rain, Guy. Whatever possessed you to venture out in this storm? You look like a drowned rat. Henri, where are you?' the old man shouted. 'Oh, there you are. Take the lad downstairs and get him dry, for heaven's sake.'

His friend's face, always pale, was now almost grey, the sockets around his eyes bruised purple, as though he had not slept for days.

'Whatever is the matter, are you unwell?' Henri said, leading him down to the kitchen. 'Here, take off your shirt and dry yourself. Cook, can he have some milk, please?' He handed over an old towel while the cook scowled disapprovingly at this further intrusion into her kitchen. With a martyred sigh, she poured the milk and handed the cup to Guy as he sat, shivering, at the table.

'Well?' Henri asked.

'I cannot talk here,' he whispered. 'May we go somewhere private?'

Henri slipped upstairs to ask M. Lavalle's permission to use the parlour.

'You may have a quarter hour, no longer,' his master said.

'Please tell your friend that in future he should call only out of working hours.'

'I understand, sir, and I am sorry, but I think this is urgent,' he said.

The old man nodded. 'Very well. Tell those other two lads that the storm has passed and they must return to work.'

'*Bon Dieu*, you look terrible. Whatever is it now?'

'I'm in trouble, my friend. I need your help.' The shirt hung too loosely on his friend's gaunt frame, but at least some colour was now returning to his cheeks.

'Last evening I was with my friends at The Dolphin, you know, having a few pints of ale.'

'Go on.' The story was becoming depressingly familiar.

'They got talking about the *Soie de Lyon* list; how impatient they were that nothing seems to have been done against these mercers who are doing us out of our living. I tried to remind them that Monsieur Lavalle was looking into it, like he said, raising it through the proper channels. But with each round they got more and more agitated, saying they were sick of waiting for the bloody Company to act while they starved for lack of work, and wanted to show the bastards that they meant business.

'I suggested we should write to each of the mercers on the list, not threatening, but just to tell them we know what they're up to. So someone found some paper and a quill and ink, and started writing letters there and then. They were that drunk by now, and hot for delivering them that very night. Honestly, it was like watching a kettle coming to the boil. You know the lid's going to fly off at any minute, but there's nothing you can do to stop it.'

'So, what happened?' Henri asked, dreading what was to follow.

'They ran out and began going from house to house, shouting and egging each other on, starting to pry open shutters and throw cobbles, you know, with the notes wrapped round them, and breaking people's windows. At one house they even set fire to a bunch of dried grass and stuffed it through a broken pane. They turned into maniacs,' Guy said, beginning to shiver again. 'I was terrified we might be caught.'

'Let alone that you might have killed someone, or burned a whole family to death. Did they attack Sadler's house?' Henri held his breath, dreading the answer.

'He got a stone through the fanlight with a note wrapped round it, nothing too serious.'

'For God's sake, why did you have to get yourself involved? Why did you go with them?'

'I thought I could stop them. I tried, honestly, but they wouldn't listen.' Guy chewed a fingernail. 'And then we saw the Watch coming round the corner.'

'Were you seen?'

'I don't know for sure, but the Guards called at my rooms this morning, when I was out making a delivery. My land-lady told them I'd be back in half an hour, so I just fled over here.'

'*Bon sang de bon Dieu.*' Henri shook his head. Guy was in deep trouble.

'I know, I know. I'm bloody terrified. If I get arrested, I'll never get work again.'

It could be a lot worse than that, Henri knew. 'Isn't it best to come clean, explain that you were trying to stop them, like you told me?'

'*Phuh*, you think they'd believe that?'

Henri could hear the rain gurgling down the gutters, splashing into the street outside. As his friend leaned closer he could smell his breath, rank with fear and self-neglect. 'I have come to make a request, as my oldest and closest friend.' Guy paused, struggling for the right words. 'The only thing that'll save me is an alibi, someone who'll say I was with them last night.'

Henri felt the blood leach from his face. 'You're asking me to *lie* for you? To the *law*?'

'It's my only way out.'

'Listen . . . even if I lie for you, any one of the others could swear you were with them, let alone all the other people who saw you out on the streets last night. It would be my voice against a dozen.' Henri's mind was in a turmoil of fear for himself, for his mother, for M. Lavalle, Mariette and all those others he might implicate.

'Please? Just do this one thing for me.'

The silence between them grew thick with mistrust. Henri went to the window, looking out at the rainy street and the houses opposite. With his back to the room, avoiding the look of desperation on his friend's face, he summoned the courage and the words to express what he knew he must say.

'You are my best friend. If the Guards call, I will vouch for your good character and good intentions, that's a promise, and I will tell them you tried to stop the violence. But I cannot lie for you.'

He heard the sudden scrape of the chair and Guy pushed past, almost knocking him to the floor. 'No thanks for your help, *friend*. Don't bother coming to me when you are in trouble.'

The slam of the front door brought M. Lavalle from his office.

'What's he been up to now?'

'He's been an idiot, that's all.'

'Is it about that list again?'

'I cannot say more, sir.'

'This may be difficult, but you must tell Guy not to call here again, Henri. I feel sorry for him, but he has not heeded our warnings and I fear for his safety. This is a dangerous business. You cannot afford to be connected with it.'

'Yes, sir,' he said. 'I understand.'

M. Lavalle knew not to press the point. From Henri's pallid cheeks and sweaty brow he could tell he'd been shaken by the encounter. Whatever had transpired, he would no doubt find out before long. 'You'd better get back to work, then,' was all he said.

❦

Henri felt sick with apprehension, dreading each knock at the door, but two days passed without event. Guy failed to appear at church on Sunday morning and, as the priest droned on, Henri tried to imagine where his friend might be: had he gone to ground like an injured fox, lying low at another friend's house, or perhaps out in the countryside, he wondered? It might be for the best that he stayed away, at least for a while. Much as he loved Guy, his politicking, his anger and resentment about the world of late had brought a sour note to their friendship.

The previous evening, taking supper with his mother in her rooms, as had become their habit of a weekend, he'd found the courage to talk about it. Clothilde was the only person, apart from M. Lavalle, whom he could trust, and she was quick to reassure her son that his decision was the right one. '*La vérité finit toujours par éclater*,' she said. '*Et vous éclate au visage*.' The truth will always come out and return to bite us.

As Henri crept out of the French church before final prayers his stomach churned with apprehension of a different kind. He ran to Christ Church, where the service was also drawing to an end, and slipped silently into the shadows behind the steps leading up to the organ loft. He wanted to be certain that Anna was alone, or accompanied only by her cousin, before allowing himself to be seen. Worrying about Guy had at least taken his mind off this meeting, but now the butterflies began to dance in his stomach once more.

He tried to imagine how she would respond, but found it impossible. Whoever knew how girls think, let alone English girls? Would she be cross when he admitted buying her sketch from the stallholder, or would she be flattered? He'd become so fixated on the design that he hadn't even considered what he would do if she failed to meet him or, worse, refused to give permission for him to use it.

The service ended and, as the ladies and gentlemen began to file past in their bright silk dresses and jackets, with their ornate hats and finely dressed wigs, he became painfully aware of his own shabbiness, in his well-worn linen jacket and plain serge trousers, with only a brown cloth cap to cover his head. They were his Sunday best, of course, but even so, how could she possibly allow herself to be seen with him?

As the church emptied he began to fear that she might not have come after all, but then he caught sight of her, hanging behind. She was with her cousin, the girl with the ringlets, but there was no sign of Mr or Mrs Sadler, or William, which meant that she would surely be looking out for him.

He inched back into the shadows, his feet itching to take flight, but before he knew it, she was standing in front of him.

'Monsieur Vendôme, how do you do?' she said, holding out a hand. He was so surprised that he hesitated to reciprocate and then responded just in time. Their fingers met briefly and awkwardly, and were quickly withdrawn.

'Miss Butterfield,' he said, feeling the blush deep into the roots of his hair. 'Please, my name is Henri.'

'Then you must call me Anna.' There was that bold gaze again, the one that seemed instantly to draw him into her confidence. 'And this is my cousin Lizzie Sadler. Lizzie, meet Henri Vendôme, the weaver I told you about.' Lizzie scowled and bent her head in acknowledgement but did not offer her hand.

Henri's mind went blank and an uneasy silence fell between them. All he knew was that he needed to own up about the drawing. He began trying to explain and then, words failing, pulled out the sketch that had been carefully folded inside his jacket, opened it and, with a shaking hand, held it out to Anna.

'But that is *my* drawing.' Her voice shrilled with recognition. 'The one I did in the market, the one I gave to the stallholder. How did *you* get hold of it?'

'I pay her,' he said, his eyes fixed on the drawing, fearful of raising them to hers. 'Good money. All – how you say? – above the boards. I was upstairs at the market and saw you sketching and, you know . . .' He ran out of words again, recalling the shimmering feeling of revelation he'd had that day as he gazed down on her bowed head, captivated by the designs emerging from the point of her pencil.

He steeled himself to look up and, with relief, saw that her expression was not one of anger, just genuine astonishment.

'Well, I am flattered, of course,' she said. 'But may I be so bold as to enquire *why* you wanted this paltry drawing of mine?'

'You know I am a silk weaver?'

She nodded.

'To become a silk master I must make a piece of weaving to show my skills. This is called my master piece. If they approve this, I am a Freeman and I set up in business for myself.'

'I understand. But what has my sketch got to do with this master piece?'

'It is difficult to explain,' he said, with a sideways glance at Lizzie. 'And there is but a few minutes.' Behind them, he could see the church officials snuffing the altar candles, folding the white linen cloths used for the Eucharist, gathering hymnals, preparing to close the church. He turned back to Anna and her smile, and found himself almost overwhelmed by the desire to take her hand.

Lizzie had wandered away, peering up the stairs leading to the organ loft. 'Can she go up?' Anna asked. For a second, her hand rested on his jacket sleeve. Even though it was withdrawn almost immediately the warm imprint persisted as a tingle on his skin.

'*Mais oui*. The organ will not sound unless someone is working the bellows.'

'Be very careful,' Anna warned.

'I will.' The girl disappeared, and they were alone.

Feeling suddenly bold, he led her to one of the benches that ran along each side of the church, where the sun pouring through the clear glass of the high-arched windows reflected off the high ceiling and white walls with an ethereal light. As they sat, side by side, it felt to him like the most natural thing in the world.

He reached into the pocket of his breeches and brought out the large piece of point paper onto which he'd attempted to translate a section of the design with dots of colour in each of the tiny squares. He unfolded it and smoothed it onto his knee.

'This is how we make a design for weaving,' he said, thrilling at the warmth of her as she moved closer to scrutinise it. 'It show us how to set up the loom, how to join the lashes which pull up the warp threads and allow the weft threads to go over them or under them and make the pattern.'

As he tried, in his halting English, to describe the very complex process in simple terms, he discovered that hand gestures were often easier and more eloquent. Glancing sideways to check whether she was understanding his descriptions, he found himself in danger of losing himself in her face: the serious blue-green eyes, the way she listened so carefully, the little cleft in her forehead that deepened in concentration.

He sensed that her interest was genuine, not forced. 'So the warp goes long-ways, the weft from side to side?' she would ask, or, 'The warp is the strength and the weft usually provides the change of colour?' or, 'So, if you want to make a solid block of the same colour, you just allow that weft thread to stay at the top?'

'Yes, but if this is too big, the fabric will . . .' He held his palms together, then pulled them an inch apart.

'It will separate, you mean?' she said. 'I'd be a hopeless silk designer!' Laughing with her, watching the way her face lit up, Henri felt happier in this very moment than he could remember ever being before. Time seemed to stand perfectly still. There was no feeling of urgency, just the thrill of sensing her curiosity, and his own desire to help her understand why this meant so much to him.

'Oh, if only you see the loom,' he said, exasperated by the inadequacy of words. 'This is how I learn, by watching other weavers.'

'No matter. I am learning so much already,' she said. 'The idea of weaving a design makes so much sense, because nature is never just a block of colour,' she said. 'Look at the flowers I've drawn here.' She pointed at the sketch still in her hand. 'This might be a pink flower, but to colour it in a natural way, I would have to use a dozen shades of pinks, oranges, reds and purples, even black, to give the shading which makes the shape look realistic.'

She had shaded the petals of the flowers so realistically that the blooms seemed to reach out of the paper towards him. Not a single leaf, stalk or petal were flat, all were three-dimensional, entwined around themselves, so true to life that you could imagine them swaying in the breeze. And not a single one was the same: she had reflected all the imperfections of nature, the torn frond, the curled petal, the bent stem.

She began to gather her skirts. 'They will be expecting us at home.'

He could not bear the moment to end. 'I have this question to ask,' he said. 'The question of importance.'

'Go on.'

They were standing now, facing each other, and he found himself suddenly tongue-tied. 'May I . . . that is, can you . . . is it possible to . . .' She was waiting, her face lifted to his, her expression gentle, encouraging. Eventually he blurted it out: 'I would like to use your design for my master piece, but first I must have your permission.'

She laughed, her face relieved. 'Of course you may. I should be delighted.'

Their faces were turned to each other, eyes meeting, just inches apart. He could almost feel the pressure of those soft lips on his. With any other girl he would have kissed her in a moment, even daring to reach a hand to her breast, but this time he felt curiously constrained.

Instead, he took her hand. She did not resist and she did not take it away; it rested there, dry and light, with a heat that seemed to sear upwards through his arm and into his whole body.

'Thank you,' he said.

'I am very flattered, sir,' she said, with a smile that left him breathless. They stood, unmoving, for a few further blissful moments, the sun shining down on them through the window, the only sounds the indistinct murmuring voices of the clergy far away in the vestry, the cooing of pigeons outside and the light clunk of Lizzie's fingers on the organ keys above. 'May I see the fabric, when you have woven it?'

'I like to invite you to Monsieur Lavalle's house, so you see it on the loom,' he said. 'But I think that may not be easy?'

A shadow passed over her face. 'I think perhaps you are right. I am sorry.'

He knew it was the truth, and there was little more to be said, but the thought that he might never meet her again left him bereft. After a moment, she took her hand gently from his. He watched, wordlessly, as she prepared to take her leave, smoothing her skirt, straightening her shoulders, checking that her hat was still at the right angle.

'I wish you all the best with your master piece.' Her smile was so sweet, and so regretful, that it seemed to suck the breath from his lungs. She called to her cousin: 'Come, Lizzie, it is nearly lunchtime.'

There was a clatter of feet on the wooden stairway and the spell was broken.

II

In conversing with professional gentlemen, never question them upon matters connected with their employment. An author may communicate, voluntarily, information interesting to you, upon the subject of his works, but any questions from you would be extremely rude.

– The Lady's Book of Manners

The encounter with Henri Vendôme had lasted no longer than a quarter of an hour, but whenever she was alone Anna found herself reliving every second of it, in minutest detail.

There was no doubting that it had left her unsettled. Here she was, trying to find her feet in an unfamiliar city, adapting to the expectations of society. He was a stranger from another social world, another country even, and she was well aware that by talking with him in that intimate way she had crossed the boundaries of acceptable behaviour, risked the wrath of her aunt and uncle and potentially put her reputation in jeopardy.

Lizzie had made no secret of her disapproval. 'Whatever were you thinking of, conversing all that time with the

French boy, for all the world to see, as though he were one of us?' she had asked, on their way home.

'He's a human being, Lizzie, just like you and me. He wanted permission to use my design for his weaving. I cannot see what is wrong with that,' she'd retorted, a little too sharply. 'Anyway, what would you like us to paint this afternoon?'

'So long as that is *all* he wants,' Lizzie had replied.

Anna barely cared. Those few moments in the church appeared gilded, glowing, a shimmering mirage. How easy she had found herself in his company, how plainly he had replied to her questions, struggling a little with the language, of course, but with such honesty.

Talking to him was like a breath of fresh air after the stiff conversations of her aunt and uncle, who somehow never seemed able to say exactly how they felt, or what they wanted, without embroidering their sentences with extra phrases and convolutions. Nothing was ever said directly. But with Henri, the conversation had flowed in a perfectly simple and uncomplicated way, as though she had known him for years.

She struggled to understand it: the tremor in her chest when she looked into his dark eyes, the way it had felt perfectly natural when he took her hand, like they were two halves meeting to make a whole. It had been thrilling and utterly irresistible.

That night she lay in bed, marvelling at this extra-ordinary turn of events. Could it be true that Henri thought her hastily drawn sketch good enough to recreate in silk? She felt flattered, and proud, that he showed such confidence in her design but at the same time it was alarming that she might hold some kind of responsibility for his future career. It would be the most important piece of weaving of his life, on which his acceptance as a silk master depended.

If only she knew more about weaving techniques, could understand what would translate into an elegant design, or even what would be considered fashionable. She'd been given a glimpse, as if through a chink in a door, into a wonderful new world of art and ideas, but the extent of her ignorance was like a lock preventing her from ever entering that doorway.

She tossed and turned as the thoughts tumbled around in her head. And then she remembered, with a realisation so powerful that she found herself sitting upright in bed, her eyes wide open. On her first day in this house Uncle Joseph had shown her the dozens of leather-bound sample books stacked on shelves in the company's showroom. Each ledger contained dozens of drawings and designs on squared paper and clips of the finished silk, which were pasted or pinned onto the pages. There must be hundreds of silk designs right here in this house, just three floors below her. What a tantalising thought. If only she could study them, to find out more about what makes a good design for weaving into silk.

She entertained the idea of asking Uncle Joseph or William to help her, but dismissed it almost at once. Uncle Joseph would tell her not to 'worry your little head about such matters' or, worse, might question why she was so curious about silk designs. William was so grumpy and miserable he would probably tell her to mind her own business.

But what was stopping her from going to look at the

sample books herself? Now? Everyone was asleep. The house was deathly quiet and pitch-black. She told herself not to be so impetuous, to wait until the morning and perhaps discuss it with Aunt Sarah. But the notion, once it took hold, would not let go.

She lit a candle, wrapped a shawl closely around her shoulders, and descended the stairs, carefully choosing the treads that she could trust not to creak. The most dangerous part was the upper landing, from which the other bedrooms led, but she managed to negotiate it without a sound. In her mind's eye she could see the ledgers on the shelf. They were almost within her grasp.

When she finally reached the ground floor, the door to the office was closed and she feared it might be locked. She took a deep breath to steady her nerves, turned the handle and eased it open.

At first, she did not register that the glow in the room emanated from another candle besides her own. A second later she sensed the presence of someone concealed behind its glow on the other side of the table. Before her legs had understood the need to take flight, the person looked up: it was cousin William, his face the colour of tallow, pinched into a grimace of alarm and immobilised in her gaze. She struggled to take in what her eyes were telling her: on the table in front of him was a money box, and in his open hand several gold coins.

In that same moment, he seemed to recover the power of movement. He picked up the money box and shoved it into a drawer underneath the table and then, slick as lightning, slipped the coins into the pocket of his robe where they fell against each other with a sharp clink. But also, in that fraction of a second, Anna comprehended what she had seen: William was stealing money. Even the flickering candlelight could not conceal the expression on his face: it was a look of naked guilt.

'Anna? What in God's name are you doing down here at this time of night?'

Her heart was pounding in her chest, but she managed to answer calmly. 'I might ask the same of you, William.'

'It is none of your business. You're not allowed in here anyway.' He turned away, as if to busy himself with some papers on the nearby desk. 'I suggest you take yourself back to bed and I'll say nothing more of it.'

She might have done so but for the anger. How dare he be so insolent, so unpleasant, when it was *he* who had been caught red-handed?

'Is it not my business to report that I have seen you taking coins from the money box?' she asked, astonished by her own audacity.

William turned back and stepped around the table towards her with clenched fists raised, his face puce with fury.

'Is that your answer?' she heard herself saying. Every muscle was straining to run, but she stood her ground. 'To beat me?'

For a moment he seemed to freeze on the spot, with fists still held high, but then his arms fell to his sides, his face contorted in confusion and – she now saw – a look of utter wretchedness. He slumped into a chair, rested his head in his hands and gave a loud groan. 'Oh Christ,' he muttered. 'Why don't you tell the whole world? I'm finished, anyway, so what difference does it make?' To her further alarm, she saw that his hunched shoulders were shaking.

This was a dizzying turn of events – William, the sophisticate, the tough man, breaking down in front of her? It would have been so easy to run away, but what gain would there be from that? Her original intention had slipped to the back of her mind. Now, she was really curious to know what was causing William such intense distress and why it had led him to help himself from the money box at the dead of night. She drew up a chair and waited until the sobs subsided.

William looked up, his eyes red and raw-looking. 'For Christ's sake, why are you still here? I told you to go back to bed,' he said, wiping his face with the sleeve of his night robe.

'I am concerned for you, Cousin,' she said.

'It is nothing to trouble your little head with.'

She ignored the slight. 'But it *is*, you see. I have seen it in your face these past few weeks. And it's brought you to theft, too, if I'm not mistaken. So, as a member of the family, I think it is of quite some concern to me.'

He sat, stony-faced, trying to stare her out.

'Unless,' she added quietly, 'you want me to ask Uncle Joseph?'

His fingers wrestled in his lap. 'How do I know you won't sneak on me anyway?'

'I give you my word, William. And I will do what I can to help you,' she said. 'Even if you don't seem to like me very much.'

He sighed deeply, causing the candle to gutter. 'I owe money,' he began. 'And if I don't pay it back, they're going to issue a writ to take me to court. I could end up in debtors' prison.'

'How much money?'

'Nearly two hundred pounds.'

Anna's head was spinning. Two hundred pounds! A small fortune. 'How . . . ?' she began.

'Gambling,' he said. 'I'm such an idiot. It was Charlie got me started, and one thing led to another. Just thought if I could only get a lucky break, I could clear the debts and never do it again. But it doesn't work like that and now some very powerful people are determined to bring me down, unless I pay up by the end of the week. Honestly, I don't know what else to do.'

She thought for a few moments, weighing up the possibilities. 'Wouldn't it be better to own up to your father, and ask him to lend you the money? You can pay him back a certain amount each week.'

'Haven't you learned *anything* about my father?' William scoffed. 'If he knew I'd been gambling, he'd throw me out on my ear.'

'He's not without his own shortcomings,' she said. 'What about that illegally imported French silk?'

His eyes widened. 'How do you know about that?'

'Never mind. I just know.'

There was another long silence before he started again, in a low voice. 'The thing is, it was me who ordered that silk. It was another wheeze to try to pay off my debts and Father was never supposed to know, but it got discovered and went horribly wrong. He's been covering for me ever since, trying to get me off the hook.'

It was Anna's turn to be speechless. William had risked

the reputation of his father, the business and the whole family just to feed his gambling habit? Now she understood perfectly why he had looked so queasy for the past few days. It was a truly dreadful state of affairs.

'Haven't you any friends who can lend you money?' She still disliked the man and would never condone his actions, but could not help feeling sorry for the miserable plight he'd got himself into. 'Can you not pay the debt back slowly, a few pounds each week?'

He gave a harsh, scornful guffaw.

'What is the worst that could happen, if you don't pay up?'

'They will beat me, perhaps to death. At least that's what they've threatened.'

'Surely Uncle would notice if the cash has disappeared?'

'I can cover it with accounting adjustments, until I can pay it back.'

'Not by gambling? Tell me you won't take that risk again?'

'I may be an idiot but I've learned my lesson now, of that you can have my assurance,' he said, looking her straight in the eye for the first time. 'No, I will pay back a little each week, and no one need ever know.'

She did not want to know what 'accounting adjustments' meant and neither did she want to appear to be excusing his dishonesty, but she was coming to understand that, apart from telling Uncle Joseph, this might be the only way for William to avoid a fatal beating. She gave an involuntary shiver.

'You will not mention this to anyone, Anna? Can I trust you?'

'I will say no more of this meeting, on two conditions.

First, that you do not mention my own appearance here tonight and, second, that you agree to help me with the mission on which I came in the first place.'

'And what might that be?'

In the most confident voice she could muster, she replied, 'I want to learn about how a silk design is translated into woven fabric, and what makes a good design.'

'May I ask why you wish to know these things?'

'I cannot tell you why,' she said. 'Except that I am an amateur artist and now that I am living in a world full of silk the subject has piqued my interest.'

The colour had returned to his face now and she saw that his expression was, for once, neither a smirk nor a sneer. It was a smile, an honest smile, a smile of respect. 'You want to look at these designs *tonight*?'

'Why not? I am wide awake, and we have the place to ourselves.'

'I will do my best,' he said.

He moved quickly now, lighting three more candles and retrieving several ledgers from the showroom. For the next hour he was as good as his word, explaining all that he knew about silk design. He showed her how each double-page spread held a copy of the original design, the coloured point paper and a sample of the finished fabric, along with written instructions about the colour, yarn and weave.

'First of all, the original design is translated onto these tiny squares and each one is coloured to represent the pattern that would be created by every movement of the warp threads, the ones that go lengthways,' he said. He described how the type of cloth would determine the number and proportion of warp and weft threads – 'for example, a satin has more warp threads than a tabby' – and how each colour requires a different shuttle. 'So, the more colours you have, the more complicated the weave and thus the more expensive the finished fabric,' he explained.

Patterns could never be wider than a single comber – the width of the loom – of between nineteen and twenty-one inches. 'And it must repeat well in width and length,' he added, 'to make it easier to weave without pucker, or distorting the design.'

'There's so much to remember,' she sighed. 'It would take a lifetime to learn it all.'

'Many of the best designers are also weavers,' he said. 'But there are books about the topic. I will see if I can find one for you.'

He went on to talk about the design itself: how it is important never to have too many picks – 'that's a single pass of the shuttle' – of one colour or this will result in a section of 'floating' weave which will be vulnerable to pulls and render the fabric 'unstable'. He also showed her how it is difficult to weave curves, especially shallow curves, 'when essentially you only have threads that go up and down or across', and how shading can require especial skills, particularly in the horizontal plane. 'It is simpler to shade with weft threads than with the warp,' he explained, although she struggled to understand exactly what he meant.

The more he talked, the more Anna became convinced that her own sketch would be impossible to weave. *All those curves, all that shading, all those colours*, she thought to herself. *Does Henri know what he is taking on, or will he have to simplify it to fit the difficulties of translating it into weave?*

William closed the ledger, stretching his back. 'Will that do for tonight?'

'Thank you, William,' she said.

'You will not tell, Anna, about . . . you know?'

'Your secret is safe with me, Cousin. But please take care. Stay out of trouble.'

'You have my word,' he said.

The following morning Anna was in the drawing room with Aunt Sarah, trying to read but struggling to keep her eyes open, when Betty arrived with the post.

The pretensions of the family never failed to amuse her – apart from the daily cook, Betty was their only servant, and thus expected to comport herself as butler, footman, lady's maid and under-servant, all in one day. Nonetheless, she appeared to manage it all with admirably good humour.

'A letter addressed to Mr and Mrs Sadler, and one for yourself,' she said, presenting the silver tray to Aunt Sarah with a curtsey. 'Would you take more tea, madam?'

'No, you may remove the tray now, thank you.' Aunt Sarah brushed her away with a flick of her wrist, and reached for the ivory letter knife.

The first, released from its crested envelope with great ceremony, was the formal invitation to the Worshipful Company of Mercers' annual autumn dinner the following week, the event that had been the subject of much discussion at the Hinchliffes' on their visit. Sarah examined for some minutes the thick, gilt-edged card with its heavy gold script, before asking Anna to place it on the mantelpiece.

'No, not there, dear. In the middle, where everyone can see it,' she said, sighing at her niece's failure to appreciate the simplest of social niceties.

Anna had heard no mention of French silk since the night of the stone-throwing incident. Perhaps, she thought, this invitation was an indication that all had been smoothed over. She very much hoped so.

'Your uncle and I are certain to have a most advantageous place at the high table because Mr Sadler is tipped to be Upper Bailiff next year. He is so very well respected, you know, and it is the highest position in the Company.' Sarah fanned her face with the envelope. 'Oh, my dear, it fills me with such pride to think of it. And I will have to look my very best at his side. I must commission a new gown from Miss Charlotte at the very earliest moment.'

She took up the second letter. 'And this one is from dearest Augusta,' she exclaimed, unsealing the folded note, and reading out loud: '*Now that we are lately returned from Bath, Charles, Susannah and I would be delighted to welcome yourself, Miss Sadler and Miss Butterfield for tea tomorrow afternoon.*'

'How very generous,' Aunt Sarah purred. 'Do you hear that, Anna? Charles will be joining us again. This is excellent news. He seemed most taken with you last time.'

'He is certainly a very pleasant young man,' Anna said, recalling the cadaverous face and the Adam's apple that bobbed so distractingly in his throat.

'I do so long to hear about their time in Bath,' Sarah went on. 'And whether Susannah was introduced to any suitable young men. Oh, and I wonder if they met with Mr Gainsborough to discuss Mr Hinchliffe's portrait. I should be most interested to hear of this. Indeed, I have considered whether we should commission him ourselves, to paint your uncle in his Upper Bailiff robes and regalia.'

Anna knew full well of Mr Gainsborough's reputation – he had painted many members of the minor aristocracy – and she doubted that her aunt had any idea how much such a portrait might cost. But the possibility was certainly intriguing: the chance of meeting the famous artist, or even watching him at work, would be a remarkable opportunity. She had seen reproductions of his work in magazines and although his portraiture was of no interest to her whatsoever, the depictions of nature in his backgrounds – especially those wonderful trees and skies – were second to none.

Sarah was reading the rest of the letter: '*Recalling Miss Butterfield's interest in matters botanical, I have also arranged for the artist Mr Ehret to visit at the same time. We pray for clement weather which will enable us all to view Mr Hinchliffe's garden together.*'

'How thoughtful. I am sure we will all enjoy that very much.' Sarah sounded unconvinced. But Anna's heart had begun to race with excitement: Georg Ehret, one of the most celebrated masters of botanical illustration! And she was to meet him tomorrow. She could scarcely wait.

The next day dawned grey and drizzly, and Anna spent the morning gazing anxiously at the sky, keen to detect any sign of the clouds lifting. Her stomach was full of butterflies.

Happily, by the time the carriage arrived the weather

was clearing, the sun dimly visible through a thin veil of mist. Anna brought with her two sketchbooks of different sizes and a set of newly sharpened graphites. Even Lizzie's persistent chatter for the entire journey could not dampen her sense of pleasurable anticipation.

Mr Ehret was already in attendance when they arrived: a tall, slim, middle-aged man with a prominent nose and rather bulbous lips, wearing a well-powdered wig and dressed soberly in a black jacket and waistcoat. On his feet were the shiniest black shoes she had seen in a long time.

At their entry he leapt to his feet, clipped his heels and, in response to Mrs Hinchliffe's introductions, made a short, formal bow to each of the ladies in turn, repeating in strongly accented English, 'Delighted, most delighted, I am sure.'

'Our gracious hostess informs me that you too are an artist, Miss Butterfield?' he said. 'And that you are interested in botanical drawing?'

'I am but a very amateur artist, sir. However, I have seen your work and am most honoured to meet you.'

'Would you care to sit with me,' he said, patting the place beside him on the chaise longue, 'so that we may talk about painting?' He glanced towards the window. 'And then, if the sun decides to oblige us, we may take a walk to admire Mr Hinchliffe's most admirable planting.'

Serious conversation was curtailed by the serving of tea and cakes, followed by further offerings and polite refusals. When she and Mr Ehret fell silent, her attention was drawn to the other side of the tea table where Susannah and Lizzie seemed already to have become the best of friends.

Lizzie was quizzing the older girl about the entertainments in Bath.

'For *how* many dances did you say he chose you?'

'Five, including the last.'

'Oh, he must be so very taken with you. Is he wonderfully handsome?'

'Tall and slim, with the deepest brown eyes imaginable.' Susannah lowered her voice, checking across the table to make sure her mother was not listening. 'He's in the Guards.'

'The ones who wear those wonderful red jackets?'

Susannah nodded, her cheeks blushing a similar hue.

'Oooh, you are so lucky,' Lizzie sighed. 'I cannot wait to be eighteen.'

'You must come with us to Bath next summer.'

Lizzie looked across to Anna. 'And can my cousin come too?'

Susannah laughed gaily. 'Of course! The more the merrier. It is *so* much fun.'

Anna forced herself to smile. From what she'd heard, the summer season at Bath was a market where mothers paraded their daughters in front of potential suitors like so many farmers showing off their sheep or cattle to meat buyers. The very idea filled her with horror.

The lively, informal conversation between Lizzie and Susannah only seemed to highlight her own difference: their shared enthusiasm for fashion, dancing and prospective husbands was a world away from her own, more serious interests in art, literature and the ways of the world. It made her feel even more like an outsider than ever.

At last the formalities were ended and as they set foot outside the sun came out to greet them. Losing her nerve at the last moment, she left the basket with sketchpad and pencils behind.

The garden was so much wider and longer than she had expected, hidden on all sides behind high brick walls. The parade of ladies, followed by Mr Ehret, strolled the gravelled paths between wide rectangular raised borders, exclaiming and sighing over the planting that, even in early September, provided a truly colourful display of Michaelmas daisies, dahlias and late roses as well as many foliage plants that Anna could not identify.

'My dear Augusta, this truly is a sight to salve the soul,' Aunt Sarah gushed. 'How fortunate you are to have a wide expanse for your palette. In Spital Square we have such a cramped little outdoor space it seems barely worth the effort of planting it.'

Towards the end of the garden the path led between a row of espalier trees laden with red and golden apples to a handsome, vine-covered pergola shading three stone benches. Anna manoeuvred a seat next to Mr Ehret once more, who immediately began to examine the leaves of the vine, already starting to take on autumn colours.

'You see,' he said, plucking a leaf. 'How the stalk has begun to go red from where it joins the stem, then gold towards the base of the leaf?' Anna nodded, eager to absorb his observations. 'And the leaf itself, it is such a beautiful thing, a fascinating study. The outermost points are the first to colour, and the area around the veins is the last,' he said, pointing out the reddening edges and the golden skeleton of veins leading out from where the stalk was attached.

'But there are still patches of green, between the red and yellow,' Anna said. 'How does that happen?'

'Well observed, Miss Butterfield,' Ehret said. 'The truth is we do not yet know why this happens in some leaves and not in others. There is much careful study among botanists to try to divine how and why leaves colour and die in the winter. It is one of many mysteries we have not yet uncovered. In the meantime the best we can do is record it as faithfully as possible. That is my modest role in the great scientific adventure.'

He held the leaf up against the sun. 'See how the light filters through in different ways, depending on the depth of colour?' he said. 'How the red is almost black, the yellow quite golden? And how the network of tiny capillaries now becomes clear?'

He leaned forward to point out another leaf, on which raindrops were still hanging. 'This is fascinating,' he said. 'Each drop of water acts as a magnifying glass, so that we see the capillaries even more clearly as we look through it.'

Anna was enthralled. 'For all my many hours of drawing, I feel I have been almost blind,' she sighed.

'Do not be concerned, my dear,' he said with a kindly smile. 'You have your whole life before you, and all you need to do is observe until you feel you know every detail of every leaf, every petal, every stalk. And then you must record, and look, and look again, and look yet again. From what I have been told you already have the talent, and I can see from the way you listen that you also have the passion to be a great artist one day.'

He reached into his inside pocket and pulled out a small sketchbook and a short, well-sharpened graphite with which he began, with the surest of hand, to draw in miniature the leaf with the drop of rain resting upon it.

'The serrations of the leaf go thus . . . this curl of the leaf needs to be shaded like this to give us depth . . . but where we see the back of the leaf, observe this, it is much paler . . . the veins all meet at the apex of the stem, not partway up, as with some leaves. And here are our raindrops, two – no, three – in descending diameter . . . I leave the white paper to shine through to show how they glitter and refract the sunlight . . . thus.'

This was the ultimate lesson from a master of his art, and Anna knew that she must try to understand and remember every word. At last, the sketch was complete. He signed it with a flourish, tore it from his sketchbook and presented it to her.

'For me?' she said, blushing.

He nodded.

'I cannot accept. It is too generous.'

'Of course you must, my dear,' he said, with the kindest smile. 'I made it for you.'

Before she could object any further, they were interrupted by a raucous shout. '*There* you all are! I've been looking everywhere.'

'Charles, my dearest,' his mother called, as the gangly frame came striding down the path towards them. 'We have been enjoying the late sunshine with Mr Ehret. Come and join us.'

Mr Ehret leapt to his feet in greeting, and Charles proceeded along the row of ladies, welcoming each in turn.

When he came to Anna he held on to her hand a fraction longer, taking it to his lips. She felt his gaze piercing her, immobilising her like a butterfly pinioned inside a frame.

'Miss Butterfield, what a pleasure. The city has been treating you well, I can see, for you are looking even more charming than I remember.' He sat down beside her in the space that Mr Ehret had vacated. 'Tell me what you have been up to since we last met.'

'Not very much, I'm afraid,' she replied. Although much had happened, none of it must ever be allowed to reach the Hinchliffes' ears. 'The city appears to be very quiet in August.'

'Indeed. All sensible people leave the city in summertime,' he said, apparently unaware of the affront his words might cause. 'And how is my good friend William?'

'He seems well, I think.' In fact, she had noticed, over the past few days, that her cousin appeared even more subdued than ever. At first she'd put it down to worry over the money he owed and the issue of the French silk, but at supper the previous evening he had looked sweaty and a little bilious, and he left much of his plate untouched. He had left the table early, as was his custom, but had not rushed out as usual. She longed to find the opportunity to ask him whether he'd been able to repay the money she'd caught him stealing, but the right moment never seemed to arrive. Before she could leave the table herself, she'd heard him climbing the stairs to his room, and he was not seen for the rest of the evening.

'Please tell him I will see him at the club tonight. He is expected. And may I call on you at the Sadler house, perhaps tomorrow or the next day?' Charles was saying.

'That would be delightful,' she said. The air had cooled as the sun slipped downwards in the sky, and she suppressed a shiver.

Before long everyone agreed that it was too chilly to remain in the garden and Aunt Sarah declared that it was time to leave. As they said goodbye, Mr Ehret gave another of his formal little bows. 'It was such a pleasure to talk to a fellow artist, Miss Butterfield. I do hope we have the opportunity to talk further in the not-too-distant future.'

'Indeed I would like that very much,' Anna said, her cheeks glowing pink from the compliment. 'I shall try to practise what you have taught me, Mr Ehret. And I shall treasure your sketch for ever.'

'My dear, I am unworthy of your flattery, but I thank you for it all the same,' he said, bowing more deeply this time.

Charles was invited for tea at Spital Square the following day.

Betty was dispatched to buy fresh tea, milk, cakes and sweetmeats. 'Girls, you will make the drawing room ready for our visitor,' Sarah instructed. 'Make sure the cushions are well plumped, and put out some appealing books and journals on the tables, my dears, so we may impress him with our wide-ranging interests. It often helps to stimulate a conversation of consequence. Lizzie, please practise your most charming pieces for the harpsichord in case we would like music to entertain us.'

When he arrived, Aunt Sarah insisted that Charles

should take a seat beside Anna on the settle and, after they had finished tea and endured a further uncomfortable ten minutes of polite conversation, Lizzie was cajoled into playing the harpsichord and Sarah picked up her embroidery frame, moving to a seat by the window.

'Don't mind if I leave you young things to chat among yourselves, do you? I need the light for such close work. This handkerchief has been promised to a friend and I cannot delay.' Anna observed these manoeuvres with amusement and a little unease. This was the carefully engineered opportunity Charles had been waiting for, even expecting.

'Miss Butterfield . . .' he began.

'Anna, please.'

The first time they met she had thought his eyes, so close-set either side of that prominent nose, rather piercing and unkindly, but his face seemed to have softened, the narrow cheeks filled out and less sallow.

'Anna. I have so enjoyed the opportunity of getting to know you a little better but there is an additional purpose to my visit. On Saturday week we – that is, my family and I – are attending the annual autumn ball at the Inns of Court and it would be so very delightful if you were able to accompany us.'

Anna felt the blush spreading across her chest, so vulnerably exposed by the low neckline of her dress, up her neck and flooding her cheeks. Despite her misgivings, she was flattered that Charles thought enough of her to invite her to such an important event, at the Inns of Court, no less. But a ball? As the implication began to sink in, her head filled with terror. She'd heard of the elegant French-style dances that city folk enjoyed, but the closest she'd come to anything like it was at the assembly rooms in Halesworth and there they only did the polka and other country dances. How could she attend a proper ball with so little time to prepare? She had only ever tried to dance the minuet once in her life; that had been enough for her to appreciate how complex it was, how it needed to be accomplished with confidence and elegance. She would make a complete fool of herself.

'Oh, sir,' she began. 'I do not think . . .'

'Charlie, please.'

'Mr . . . Charlie. I do not think . . . without a chaperone . . . my uncle . . .'

'Mr Sadler will be perfectly satisfied, do you not think, Mrs Sadler, when he hears that my mother, father and sister will be also there?'

'Oh, indeed,' Sarah responded instantly. She had been hanging on every word, of course, her embroidery neglected, the needle hanging loosely on its thread. 'I am sure this would be perfectly acceptable.'

By the time Charles took his leave, all was settled. Afterwards Aunt Sarah, flushed with excitement, called her into the drawing room. 'This is such a wonderful opportunity, my dear,' she fluttered. 'Just think, the Inns of Court – such a prestigious event. There will be so many important and influential people there. I am so pleased for you. We must make sure you are dressed in your very best. The sackback in the yellow damask, don't you think? You do look most alluring in it. But you will need something warm to wear for the journeys – the evenings are drawing in so these days. A cloak? No? You have no cloak? Oh my goodness, we must get Miss Charlotte onto the task immediately.'

She fanned herself so violently with her embroidery frame that the needle flicked from its thread into a far corner of the room.

'Charles is such a charming young man, do you not think? And with such prospects. A lawyer – just imagine? There is always work for a lawyer. We will have you settled by the end of the year, my dear, I can promise that. Oh, I cannot wait to tell your father.'

Anna's heart recoiled, but she held her tongue. She must write to him straight away, before her aunt could do so. She did not want to be 'settled', like a business deal. She wanted to be in love.

12

Be warily silent in all concerns as are in matter of dispute between others. For he that blows the coals in quarrels he has nothing to do with, has no right to complain if the sparks fly in his face.

– Advice for apprentices and journeymen
OR A sure guide to gain both esteem and an estate

It was at noon, when they ceased their looms for the lunch break, that they first heard the hubbub of voices, like distant thunder, billowing over the rooftops and reverberating through the streets.

'Whatever is that?' The apprentice Benjamin leapt from his loom bench and went to the window. As he opened it, the sound magnified into a roar over which individual, though not identifiable, shouts could be heard. Henri, Benjamin and the drawboy looked at each other, their eyes wide in a mixture of curiosity and alarm.

They peered down into the street below. Many of the neighbours were out on their doorsteps, some already walking towards the end of the road in the direction of the noise. The three of them tumbled down the loft ladder and the two sets of stairs to the ground floor, elbowing each other as each tried to be first. M. Lavalle was already on the doorstep.

'What do you think it is, master?' Benjamin asked.

'Word has it that the journeymen will march to Parliament today, to protest against a bill which will allow the import of foreign silks,' he said. 'The Company has already sent representatives, but it seems their pleas have fallen on deaf ears, so the journeymen are taking the matter into their own hands. I fear it may result in violence,' he sighed. 'Which will do no good for their cause.'

'May I go to see?' Henri said. 'So that I can report back to you?'

M. Lavalle frowned. 'I cannot stop you, my boy, for you are no longer indentured and are entitled to your midday break. But I must warn you that you do *not* have my blessing to join the march, no matter how persuasive the exhortations of your fellows. And beware, if previous demonstrations are anything to go by, there will be violence. Proceed with the utmost caution. Ensure that you are nowhere near any such eruptions or associated with any who take part in them, especially the Bold Defiance men. The Guards will crack down without mercy.'

'*Absolument, monsieur,*' Henri said, leaping down the steps. 'I will be most careful – and I'll be back within the half hour, I promise.'

At the end of the road he could already see the throng spilling across Red Lyon Street, creating an unholy crush in every direction. It was a gathering of humanity larger than Henri had ever seen, reaching out so far that he could not tell where it ended. *There must be well over two thousand men*, he thought to himself, their faces hungry-looking, their sunken eyes fiery with desperation. Many were clothed in little more than rags and some were even barefoot. What bitter irony, he thought, for men who wove the most sumptuous fabrics in the land.

They reminded him of the time when he and his mother had been close to starvation, how they had worn out their shoes walking to London and had gone barefoot until the French church took them in and clothed them. But he had never witnessed hardship on this scale. It was dizzying to comprehend. *How shielded I have been*, he thought, *how fortunate to have been taken in by Monsieur Lavalle.*

Angry coachmen, cart drivers and pedlars hurled volleys of abuse as they tried to push their way through the mob to reach the market. It made no difference: the crowd's attention was elsewhere, held by a tall, bearded man shouting through a conical loudhailer from a position high on the steps of Christ Church.

'We can brook no further delay,' he was calling. 'Letters and petitions through the official channels have made not a jot of difference to their lordships. They appear to care more for covering their own lazy arses –' the crowd booed and made farting noises '– and the tits of their mistresses in fine French silks –' more jeers, accompanied by vulgar gestures '– than they do for the poverty of their own countrymen.'

Henri scanned the throng until his eyes burned, trying to spot Guy. He had not seen his friend since that desperate night two weeks before, but felt sure he must be here, somewhere. If he could not see him, he feared he might have to assume the worst.

'Today is the opening of Parliament, so all the Members

will be there. But it must be a peaceful demonstration, you understand. There are to be no punches thrown, nor stones. A riot would only serve to undermine our cause. Do I have your word?' The speaker was rewarded with a murmur of agreement, even though some among the crowd were carrying sticks and stakes, which surely meant they were set for a fight. Their fearsome expressions and angrily muttered utterances underlined their obvious intent.

'We're going to get the bastards.'

'Yeh, make 'em suffer.'

'Show 'em they can't treat us like animals any more.'

'Fair pay for a fair day's work, that's all we want.'

'They've got to stop that illegal trade in effing French silk. It's ruining us.'

'It's starving us.'

'We've had enough.'

'We're going to tell 'em. Loud and clear.'

The clock on Christ Church sounded the half hour. As Henri went to leave, he heard a familiar voice: '*Henri, ça va?*' It was Guy, even thinner and more unkempt than before, but at least he was not in prison. Henri ran to his friend, embracing him. 'Where have you been? Did the Guards ever . . . ?

'Lying low. But enough time's gone by now, so I figured . . .' Guy gestured behind him. 'Why aren't you coming with us?'

Henri could feel the pull of the crowd, the excitement

and camaraderie. 'I am forbidden. I cannot afford to disobey
Monsieur Lavalle, not right now. You must take care, Guy.'

Guy scowled his disapproval. 'Will you obey your master
over your fellow workers, *par le sang de Dieu?*'

'It's not like that. You know why. I have to support my
mother – I cannot afford to lose my job.'

The drums had started again, dozens of colourful banners
were raised, and the crowd was moving, pressing forward
so that Guy began to be carried away with them. '*Maudit
cadavre pestiféré*,' he mouthed over the din, pumping his
fist in front of his crotch. 'When will you grow up to be a
man?'

The Red Lyon was packed with journeymen returned
from the demonstration, their faces ablaze with triumph
and ale: 'There was at least three thousand there, I swear
it.' And: 'Them lace makers came good to their promise
– a few hundred of them, I'd vouch, swelling our numbers.'

As far as anyone knew, there had been only one or two
outbreaks of violence and damage was restricted to a few
broken windows in the House of Commons. Five men had
been arrested, three of those later released without charge.
Despite this, all agreed the demonstration had been a great
success. 'We got them toffs running scared, didn't we?' they
bragged. 'So worried they sent for the Gunners.'

'Let's hope the sight of all those hungry men will scare
Parliament into action,' M. Lavalle murmured gloomily.
He'd insisted on accompanying Henri to gather information
about the demonstration, and, Henri assumed, to make sure

he did not get into trouble. 'Some cannot even afford to buy bread. If this goes on much longer, thousands will starve.'

'Surely they won't allow that to happen?'

'We do what we can at the church, but charity alone cannot address such suffering.'

On the way home they met Guy, clearly the worse for beer. 'Had a nice easy day, did you?' he slurred, veering across the street towards them. 'Looking after your own fat arse while we risked our necks to support our friends?'

'It was on my account he could not join you,' M. Lavalle said, stepping between them. 'I would not allow it because we have a deadline on an important commission and no one can afford to turn down work these days. But I was glad to hear that the demonstration was peaceful. I'm sure it will have the desired effect.'

'The desired effect, *mon oeil*,' Guy mumbled, swaying on his feet, his eyes trying to focus. He snorted and spat a fat oyster of phlegm at their feet, before gathering himself and meandering away.

What M. Lavalle had said was no lie. Henri and Benjamin had been working on a large order of silk for the newly rich colonials across the Atlantic Ocean. The work was so prestigious and the design so secret that M. Lavalle could not risk outsourcing it to other journeymen, and this meant that both of the looms at Wood Street were fully engaged and Henri had been unable to make any progress on the new design for his master piece.

Five days had passed since his meeting with the English girl Anna, and it now seemed to him like a dream, unreal and unlikely. But he found himself thinking of her much of the time, longing to be in her presence once again, to hear her talk in that forthright way; to tell her of the funny moments in his life and the sad, to share his hopes and fears, to talk about the guilt and sorrow he felt towards his old friend Guy.

The longing was worst at night, in the dark, in his truckle bed. It was then that she appeared to him again, placing her hand on his sleeve, the heat of it travelling up his arm and coursing through his body. When this translated into physical hunger he felt ashamed, as if sullying her memory, but could not resist pleasuring himself with the vision of her face before him.

With the morning would come reality and the sobering knowledge that, in all probability, he would never speak to her again. She had given permission for him to use the design, and that was it. She would marry some well-respected society figure, and he would go back to flirting with other girls – and so often finding himself disappointed – until he could make enough money to take a wife, probably a homely soul who would cook and sew, and care for him in his fading years.

He admired the drawing just as much as he had the first time he set eyes on it, but as the days passed he began to doubt his ability to weave it. He asked his master once again, was it good enough for a master piece? But the old man would not be drawn. 'It is a very fine piece of work,' he allowed. 'The girl has great talent. But it is your challenge to translate that into a fine piece of silk.'

Mariette positively bubbled with enthusiasm. 'Oooh, it's heavenly,' she shrilled. 'Completely wonderful. I want it for my new gown.' She looked up at him with those coy, dewy eyes. 'Is it your drawing, no, surely not? Wherever did you get it?'

When he would not reply, she pressed her point. '*Tell* me, Henri. Who exactly *is* this clever artist? Why are you so secretive?'

'I cannot tell you until the piece is finished,' he improvised. 'But then, I promise, the secret will be revealed.'

'You are such a tease. I hate you,' she cried, flouncing out of the dining room. As he crept past the parlour shortly afterwards he could hear the harpsichord being hammered inexpertly, with many discordant notes.

And then the realisation came to him. Of course! Why had he not thought of it before? The one person whose judgement he could really trust was Miss Charlotte. She met discerning customers every day of the week – it was her business to know what was in and what was out this season. Had she not been kind to him when he had called on her the first time? He remembered her words distinctly now: she'd told him not to hesitate should he need any further help, as she would be pleased to give it. He would show Miss Charlotte the design, and if she liked it, that would settle the matter.

Two days later, when the silk for the Americas was completed, taken off the looms, carefully packed and lowered to the street from the gantry for delivery to the mercer, Henri requested the afternoon off. They had been working long hours to meet the deadline, often by candlelight after the evenings had drawn in, and M. Lavalle was in a genial mood.

'You've certainly earned a few hours of liberty,' he said, pulling out his purse. 'On your way home, buy us some hot meat pies for our supper and a few bottles of porter besides. And why don't you invite Clothilde to join us? It's time to celebrate.'

As he left the house Henri felt his spirits rising. The prospect of a jolly evening with good food and strong drink was cheering, and his mother would be delighted with the invitation. Since her split with the widower Clothilde had rarely enjoyed much social company, and was very fond of M. Lavalle and Mariette. In fact, Henri had sometimes wondered whether his master had ever considered taking another wife – his mother would make the perfect candidate. She understood the silk business, could cook well and maintain a clean house and, despite the hardships and sorrows of her life, had kept her figure and her looks. But the old man was still grieving, it seemed. He never showed the slightest interest in other women.

He strode up Draper's Lane with greater confidence this time. Alerted by the tinkling of the bell, Miss Charlotte appeared immediately from a door at the back of the room.

'Monsieur Vendôme,' she said with a sweet smile. 'How delightful to see you again. What can I do for you today?'

Henri pulled Anna's sketch from his inside pocket, unfolding it onto the table in front of the window, smoothing out the creases as best he could.

'And what is this?' she asked, taking a seat.

'It is a drawing of wild flowers, although not by me, *bien sûr*,' he said. 'I think it may make a good design for silk but I like to have your idea, please? Will it work, do you think?'

She bent her head over the design, studying it with great care. 'It is a very charming sketch: so much delicate detail, and such naturalism.' And then, fixing him with her dark eyes, she asked, 'May I inquire who is the artist?'

His cheeks burned. 'I am sorry . . . I cannot tell.'

'What a delightful mystery.' A ripple of amusement flickered across her face. 'It is a woman's hand, I'd wager. But what I find so fascinating –' she peered more closely at the paper '– are these.' She traced her finger along the curving stems of bindweed that criss-crossed the sketch in a loose, informal trellis pattern around which the flowers and foliage were wound. 'It has reminded me of something.'

'Wait here a moment, would you?' She reappeared a few seconds later with an illustrated magazine in her hands and sat down, flicking through the pages until she found the one she was seeking.

'There, look,' she said, handing it to him.

It was a black and white etching: an extraordinary and apparently random collection of classical sculptures in a strange landscape of buildings, walls and roofscapes, with some anatomical drawings of the muscles of the leg on one side, and open books on the other. The scene had a deep border, which contained numbered boxes with draw-ings of flowers, candlesticks, faces – some quite comical – a pierced torso, a woman's skirt swirling about her legs, and what looked like a set of stays in various curvy shapes.

'What is this?' he asked. 'I have not before seen anything like it.'

'You have heard of the artist William Hogarth?'

'Indeed I have,' Henri said. 'Monsieur Lavalle has a print that he shows new apprentices: *The Fellow 'Prentices at their Looms*. He hopes it warn us about the dangers of idleness and drink.'

'That's the one. He has always had an interest in Spitalfields – he was born not far from here. His wife, Jane, has long been a customer of mine – such a charming woman and herself once an artist – and she recently had the goodness to bring me this magazine article about his new book, *The Analysis of Beauty*.'

'It looks complicated.'

'It is, rather, but Mrs Hogarth tried to explain it to me. Mr Hogarth has endured much criticism for being so arrogant as to try to define what constitutes beauty and good taste, but I think he has a point – that is what he's trying to illustrate in this print.'

'I will try my best to understand.'

'In a nutshell, that the infinite variety of curved lines in nature are far more pleasing to the eye than the straight lines and angles that humans create,' she said. 'These classical sculptures are full of curves, because they follow anatomy. Nature is full of curves, like these flowers. The furniture maker Chippendale knows it – here are his turned-wood chair legs.'

With rising excitement, Henri began to comprehend what Miss Charlotte was trying to tell him – that the curving plant stems criss-crossing Anna's design were the very essence of that beauty. 'And the curved lines in my sketch are just like that?'

'Exactly so,' she said, turning to the shelves along the back wall of the showroom. She returned with a bolt of cloth, and unfolded a short piece of beautiful, shimmering silk brocade, with a diamond pattern of lines infilled with floral designs.

'This is not unlike your design, but it has one thing missing,' she said. 'The lines are straight, the angles are sharp, and they contrast uncomfortably with the naturalness of the flowers. Your design is so much more pleasing to the eye, because it is set on a framework of naturally curved stems – what Mr Hogarth called the serpentine curve.'

He looked into her face and then down once more at the print, lost for words. When he picked up the sketch again, his fingers were trembling. 'So do you think . . . that this will make a good design for dress silk?'

'I think it will do very well indeed. It is unlike anything I've ever seen before,' she said, the smile lighting up her pale cheeks.

'Thank you very much. You have filled my heart with happiness.'

'It is my pleasure, Monsieur Vendôme.'

'Please. My name is Henri.'

'If you wish. In which case you must call me Charlotte,' she said. 'And, now that we are on first-name terms and I am not expecting my next customer for half an hour, will you take a cup of tea?'

She invited him into the large, airy room at the back of the shop, one side of which was furnished as a parlour and the other curtained with white calico, behind which, he assumed, her customers might hide their modesty during fittings.

She disappeared to put on the kettle and he was making himself comfortable, flicking through the fashion books on the table, when he heard the tinkle of the front doorbell. He cursed lightly under his breath – it must be a customer, whose arrival would surely put an end to this delightful sojourn with Miss Charlotte. Perhaps, had she not heard it, and he said nothing, the customer would leave of their own accord? But he began to worry whether the stranger might take advantage of being left alone for so long, perhaps being tempted to pick up a small bolt of cloth, a pair of gloves or a muff, and make off without payment.

'Miss Charlotte,' he called quietly. 'I believe you have a customer.'

She ran up the stairs, apologising breathlessly, and went through into the showroom, part closing the door behind her.

'Oh, Miss Charlotte, I am so sorry to arrive early; the walk was so much quicker than I remembered.'

That voice! Henri's heart seemed to stop in his chest. 'Are you engaged with another customer? I do beg your pardon. I can return later if it is not convenient.'

'Please do not concern yourself, Miss Butterfield. I was making tea for a friend, but that can wait. You have come to collect your cloak, have you not? It is all ready for you. Just let me fetch it.'

Charlotte re-entered the back room, went behind the curtains and returned with a dark blue velvet cloak with a ruby satin lining and a collar of black fur. 'I won't be a moment,' she mouthed to Henri, closing the door behind her.

The voices were now muffled but still audible. He found himself holding his breath as he listened, eager to catch every syllable. Anna expressed her delight at the cloak, and how well it fitted her, congratulating the seamstress. Charlotte suggested that a muff of the same black fur as the collar might be a useful accessory and it seemed that several samples were produced because both women began to giggle as Anna tried to choose. Their girlish laughs sounded to his ears like handbells pealing for joy. How he wished he could be there to share their fun and not skulking behind the door like a thief, stealing crumbs of her presence through the sound of her voice.

'This one is perfect. I'll take it.'

'Would you like to wear the cloak and take it today, or shall I arrange for it to be delivered?' Charlotte asked.

'I shall wear the cloak, but I do not think it is cold enough for a muff today, do you? I might look a little silly wearing it. Perhaps you could wrap it for me?'

'Of course, I'll do it right away.'

A long, agonising silence followed. And then a sharp, surprised, 'Oh!' and Anna's voice, quieter now: 'Excuse me, Miss Charlotte? Forgive me for prying. But could I ask you where this came from?'

A further pause, and then Miss Charlotte said, quite casually, 'Oh, that. It's just a draft design someone was interested in. They wanted my opinion on it.'

Henri felt his knees begin to buckle and he leaned back against the wall, taking deep breaths to try to dispel the giddiness threatening to overcome him. His sketch! He must have left it on the table beside the Hogarth print. How could he have been so careless?

'It is very familiar to me,' he could hear Anna saying. 'May I be so bold as to inquire who that person is?'

'Do you mean that you have seen it before, this design?'

'Indeed I have, Miss Charlotte.' After a moment, Anna began to laugh. 'May I take you into my confidence?'

'Of course.'

'It is *my* drawing.'

'*Your* drawing? But how, I mean where . . . ?'

'It now belongs to a French weaver, Monsieur Vendôme. He requested my permission to use it.' The sound of his name brought Henri to his senses. He felt compelled to explain himself to Miss Charlotte – and also to Anna. For a few seconds he hesitated, his fingers on the handle and then, taking a deep breath, he pushed open the door and entered the room.

There she was, just a few feet from him, taller than he remembered, resplendent in her fine new cloak. The look of surprise on her sweet face nearly took his breath away.

'Henri!' she cried. 'I mean Monsieur Vendôme. It's you.'

'*Mam'selle Butterfield.*' He bowed deeply, the way he'd seen gentlemen bow when introduced to society ladies. His neck and cheeks were burning. She was blushing too, almost the same deep red as the lining of her cape. '*Tout le plaisir est pour moi,*' he began, and then remembered to speak in English. 'The pleasure is all mine.'

'I did not know that you were acquainted with Miss Charlotte,' Anna said, looking from one to the other in confusion.

He rushed to explain. 'She is an old friend of my master's

family and has been of much help to me,' he said, glancing towards the seamstress, who was frozen in the act of wrapping her parcel, a piece of string still looped from her uplifted hand. 'I was taking advice from Miss Charlotte: if your design is good for a dress silk.'

Anna nodded, her face clearing. 'Ah, it is becoming clearer now.'

'She tells me the artist Mr Hogarth is very much favouring curves. He says they are the "essence of beauty".'

She laughed again, making his heart sing. 'But mine are simply the stems of ordinary columbine,' she said. 'I just sketch from nature.'

'But with such realism,' Miss Charlotte replied. 'That is a very special skill.'

'My own poor skills will be much tested,' Henri said. 'To make the same in my weaving.'

'I am sure that one of your experience will have no difficulty,' Anna replied and, for a moment, their eyes met in the way they had at Christ Church: a look of mutual understanding so powerful that it felt as if he could see right into her bared soul. In that second, the rest of the world seemed to recede into unimportance.

Miss Charlotte was rummaging through a drawer behind the counter. 'I have something here that might inspire you even further, Monsieur Vendôme,' she said, pulling out a small piece of silk and unfolding it onto the counter. 'It is the remnants from a gown I made a long time ago from French silk – legally imported, I might add.'

It was a bold pattern of large, blowsy and brightly coloured roses and peonies, surrounded by luxuriant foliage on an eggshell-blue background. The designs were power-fully realistic.

'I can see what you are thinking,' she said. 'This would not be considered fashionable today, but it demonstrates a technique the Lyonnaise weavers were using in those days – I think it was first used by a designer called Jean Revel – which allowed them to introduce shading. It was called *points rentrées*. Perhaps your Monsieur Lavalle will know of this, Henri?'

He lifted the silk close to his eye, regretting that he did not have with him the magnifying lens they used to scru-tinise the weave of fabrics. He recognised the technique: warp and weft threads of different shades were interlocked to create gentle, subtle edges to flowers and leaves, rather than the more usual method which created a defined line. He had seen it in the designers of an earlier age – Leman and the like – that he had studied during his apprenticeship, but evidently it had been abandoned as the fashion wheel turned to smaller, less brightly coloured floral designs.

It was as though a key had turned, unlocking the mystery. All he needed to do was to figure out how to rig the lashes and simples on his loom to recreate Revel's innovation on a much smaller scale, which would reproduce the shading effects of Anna's graphite pen.

'Miss Charlotte, *vous êtes merveilleuse*,' he said. 'You have answered my problem.'

'What is it you have seen?' Anna said. 'Do explain.'

'I will try my best,' Henri said.

'Then let us all listen in comfort,' Miss Charlotte said. 'Miss Butterfield, we were about to take tea in the parlour. Do you have a few minutes to join us?'

13

No young lady should go to a ball, without the protection of a married lady, or an elderly gentleman.
— The Lady's Book of Manners

My dearest father,

Today has been the happiest of my life so far in London, for I have made a friend. Her name is Charlotte, and she is a dressmaker — or more correctly I should call her a 'costumière', for that is what it says over the door to her shop. She has made all my gowns most beautifully and today I collected the most delicious velvet cloak with a fur collar and muff to match. I shall be the warmest girl in town!

She is really the most admirable person, independent and unmarried as far as I can tell and conducting what seems to be a very successful business all on her own account. Today, when I went to collect the cloak, she invited me into her parlour for tea and we had the most delightful conversation about art and fashion.

What I most admire is that she appears unconcerned regarding social status. Despite being in 'trade', as Aunt Sarah would say, Charlotte speaks to everyone: society

*folk and working folk, men and women, in the same
straightforward way without being patronising or
obsequious. It is as if, in her mind, all classes and both
sexes are perfectly equal. How wonderful it would be if
we were all to be treated so.*

*Please do not mention this to Uncle or Aunt for I am
sure they would not approve. But I am so delighted
with my afternoon that I simply had to share it with
someone.*

*Oh, and Aunt Sarah will doubtless write to you
regarding an invitation I have received to a ball at the
Inns of Court, by a young man called Charles Hinchliffe, a lawyer. She thinks he is the perfect match for me.
He is interesting, but I feel little for him, so although
she is very excited about this, please do not hold your
breath for news of any developments in that quarter!*

*Give Jane a big hug for me, and tell her that I will
write to her again very soon.*

Your loving daughter,
Anna

'You look like the cat that drank the cream, Anna,' Lizzie
remarked at supper, and Aunt Sarah added, 'You certainly
have a bloom to your cheek this evening, Niece. Have you
received some good news from home, perhaps?'

Anna managed to deflect their questions without lying:
'It is just that I am so delighted with my new cloak, dearest
Aunt, and the muff, that I cannot help smiling with the
pleasure of it. Thank you so much for your great generosity.'

Her letter told only one part of the story, of course: her
joy was two-fold. She had genuinely enjoyed getting to

know Charlotte better, and felt an increasing respect for her independent way of living, her confident manner and strength of character. She certainly would like to count her as a friend, although she had no idea whether the affection would be reciprocated.

But by far the larger part of Anna's elation, the part that made her smile for no apparent reason and caused a catch in her breath when she thought about it, was the serendipity of meeting with Henri. It felt like an unexpected and joyful gift, to have had the opportunity of being able to converse naturally with him, as an equal, without guilt or fear of being found out.

The content of that conversation had been fascinating and challenging: they started with a discussion about Hogarth's *The Analysis of Beauty*, with Charlotte giving her opinion on how it might apply to the world of fashion. This was followed by Henri's explanation of *points rentrées* and how he hoped to set up his loom to achieve the realism of her sketch. When Anna ventured to mention Mr Ehret, they both seemed to have heard of him and were impressed that she had actually had the chance to discuss botanical drawing with such a respected master.

Throughout all of the discussion, Anna struggled to tear her eyes away from Henri's face. She was simply captivated by him: the intense chestnut brown of his eyes, his olive skin and his broken English, his modesty and his easy sense of humour. She was enthralled by the breadth of his knowledge and obvious confidence when talking about his work.

When he spoke of his master and of his widowed mother it was with such love and respect that she immediately wanted to meet them, to tell them how fortunate they were to have such a young man in their lives. Now, she felt his absence as an almost physical ache and yearned to see him again, to get to know more of him and to share more of herself with him.

And yet, she remembered with a sudden unpleasant jolt, there really was no future in such a friendship. She was here in London to find a wealthy husband and it was madness to entertain fancies about a poor journeyman silk weaver, a Frenchman at that. Besides, in the eyes of her aunt, she was practically engaged to Charlie Hinchliffe. Sarah was convinced that the invitation to the ball, which was to take place in just three days' time, was a declaration of intent, and a proposal would shortly follow. Anna could not decide what she felt about such a prospect.

A part of her was flattered because Charles was undoubtedly what her aunt called 'a good match'. Before long he would surely be a man of some means – so long as he could curb his gambling habits – and would keep his wife and her dependents in some comfort. But, try as she might to reassure herself, she could imagine no joy in such a life. She would become mistress of the house and an elegant lady, an ornament in Charles's life to charm his wealthy clients and aid his rise in society. *How does any woman manage to endure such a pointless existence?* she sighed to herself. *I would surely die of boredom within a year.*

But what else could a woman do, when men seemed to hold all the power and all the purse strings? If only she had a skill with which she could earn a living, like Miss Charlotte. But apart from keeping house, doing laundry and cooking meals she had none, and who wanted to be a housekeeper for the rest of their lives? She could paint, of course, and improve her technique on the harpsichord, but there was no living in those aptitudes save perhaps becoming a governess, and that always seemed such a sad and lonely existence. She felt like a rat caught in a cage, tearing desperately and fruitlessly at the wire mesh walls, refusing to accept the inevitable.

Finding no solution, she decided to put the problem to the back of her mind and concentrate on more appealing matters.

For a start, she needed to address her concerns about the sketch for Henri. At Charlotte's showroom she had seen it with new eyes, and had become uncomfortably aware of its shortcomings. How poor it was, how amateur, how sloppily observed and hastily executed. She could instantly note its artistic flaws, the lack of symmetry, the unrealistic shapes of the leaves, the way that the stems were the same width as they curved from the bottom to the top of the page, not narrowing as they would in nature. How much better it could have been had she applied the lessons Mr Ehret had since taught her.

Before leaving Miss Charlotte's shop, she had asked Henri whether he would allow her to do further work on it, to make the floral figures even more naturalistic, perhaps to add some colour wash. He had protested that it was perfectly lovely as it was but had then concurred, so long as she did not change it too much. She promised to supply a new version to him within the week.

The following day, after breakfast, she retired to her room and sat at the table by the window, attempting to recreate the sketch. With each try, her confidence in its artistry diminished. *What on earth is wrong with me?* she berated herself, scrunching another wasted sheet of paper into a ball and hurling it at the wall. *I have no talent, no inspiration, no ability at all. What a mess. It's hopeless.*

She flung herself onto the unyielding mattress and closed her eyes. A sequence of images flickered on the inside of her eyelids: of the lines and curves flowing from Mr Ehret's pencil, of the raindrops gleaming, and of shades of red and orange spilling over the autumn leaves. She was in the Hinchliffes' garden again with Mr Ehret's voice in her ear exhorting her to 'look, look and look again'.

The bells of Christ Church, pealing midday, woke her from the reverie. She realised what she had been doing wrong, and what she now needed to do.

After lunch, she asked Betty to accompany her to the market. There, she returned to the wild flower stall – relieved to discover that the ruddy-faced woman had been replaced by a man – and spent nearly two shillings on bunches of sea lavender, yellow tree lupin, sea holly and heathers of different hues. Returning home, she carried up to her room a large pitcher of water, and arranged the flowers into a display that lifted her heart, calling to mind the late summer days in her village on the edge of the sea.

Now, she said to herself, *I can do justice to Mr Ehret's advice.*

By the end of the following day, despite frequent interruptions from Lizzie, she had recreated her original sketch with its sinuous curved trellis of bindweed stems, but with much more detail in the botanical depictions: the veining on leaves, the shadows on a curled petal, flowers in bud, flowers in full glorious display, and flowers creased and drooping as they faded, and raindrops nestling in the apex of a stalk. Even a small black beetle which fell out of the wild flower arrangement onto her table made an appearance in the finished drawing.

Now she applied watercolour, using her old box of paints brought from Suffolk and, when this had dried, added chalk shading and retraced some of the lines with ink for added emphasis.

She propped the finished painting onto the dresser and sat back on the bed to study it from a better distance. *It is good*, she thought to herself, *much improved, the colour and shading producing greater depth and realism.* Finally satisfied with what she had produced, she rolled it into a cylinder, wrapping another sheet around it for protection, and attached a label with Henri's name and address. Now she just had to find a way of getting it delivered without prompting awkward questions.

※

The day of the Inns of Court ball was looming and Anna had begun to fret about her lack of accomplishment in dancing. In the family library she had discovered a book entitled *The Art of Dancing*, and had done her best to follow the complicated floor diagrams that demonstrated through a series of curved lines and arrows where one's feet should go. But without the music she found it impossible to gain any sense of the timing or rhythm, or, indeed, what her arms and hands should be doing. Each time she tried, the task appeared more hopeless. Although she could not bring herself to admit her failings, it seemed they had already been detected.

'We must make sure that you are fully prepared for the ball, dearest Niece,' Aunt Sarah declared at supper that evening. 'Are you familiar with the French style of dance, my dear?'

'I fear not, Aunt. I am woefully ignorant of the matter.'

'Then I shall engage a dancing master forthwith. Mrs Hinchliffe recommended an excellent fellow who taught Susannah most successfully. I shall request his services, with a harpsichord accompanist, for tomorrow and Friday morning.'

'You said *I* could take lessons also,' Lizzie whined. 'It will not be long before I am invited to a dance, and surely I too must be prepared.'

'You may watch and learn, Lizzie,' her mother said firmly. 'When the time comes we shall arrange lessons especially for you. But for now the priority is to ensure that Anna is presented at her very best, is it not, Mr Sadler?'

Uncle Joseph grunted into his glass of claret.

'Monsieur le Montagne' managed to maintain the French accent for most of the lesson, only slipping into his native cockney when Anna's ineptitude led him to extremes of frustration. He was not an attractive man, white-wigged and over-rouged – 'a proper macaroni', Lizzie observed – in an overtight silk jacket and breeches with only slightly stained white stockings. But he was perfectly polite and pleasant in demeanour, and thoroughly professional in his approach.

'In zee minuet we are making a beeootiful painting across

the floor with our feet, Miss Butterfield, like zis,' he said, demonstrating. They had pushed back the chairs and rolled up the rug in the drawing room, exposing cracked and unsecured floorboards, which made 'painting with zee feet' a tricky affair.

'We have our feet turned out slightly, like zis, which is noble. Never turned in, like zis, which is grotesque.' He frowned like a gargoyle. 'First we are on our tiptoes and then we bend, you see,' he said, dipping and rising for all the world like the drakes on the village pond at mating time, Anna thought, struggling to suppress a fit of laughter.

'We bend,' he repeated, 'and we create zee beautiful serpentine shape, like a river, with our feet, our hands and our . . . erm . . .' He ran his hands through the air as if around the curves of an imaginary woman. '*Comme ça.*'

'It is like Hogarth. He says the serpentine curve is the essence of beauty.'

M. le Montagne smiled benignly at his pupil. 'Indeed, Miss Butterfield. How clever of you. Mr Hogarth also declares zat zee minuet is zee perfection of all dancing. Now, let us try again. Remember, no hurrying, no looking at your feet. Gentle fingers, elegant arms, held in opposition to zee direction of your feet. Zat is correct. Now, one, two and three . . . sink, rise, bend.'

Over and over again she tried and failed to meet his exacting requirements but slowly, as the three hours passed, she gained confidence and made fewer mistakes. Aunt Sarah and Lizzie applauded encouragingly from the sidelines. 'You've nearly got it, Anna. By tomorrow it will be perfect,' her cousin cried.

'At least I am not important enough for anyone to take

notice of me. They will all be watching the other dancers,' Anna said, sipping from the glass of water her aunt had thoughtfully provided.

'Oh no,' M. le Montagne piped up. 'Each couple must dance separately, that is the point of the minuet.'

'You mean everyone at the ball will be watching me?' Her elation turned to terror.

'Yes, I am afraid so,' he said. 'I regret that our time is up for today but tomorrow we shall perfect your dance and I promise you will be the belle of the ball. *Au revoir, madame, mesdemoiselles,*' he said, bowing deeply to each of the ladies in turn. '*À demain.*'

Anna was exhausted from the morning's exertions, but there was to be no rest. The afternoon was fully consumed with considerations of dress and other details: which hairstyle, which shoes, which stockings, which rouge, which blacking for her eyebrows, which *parfum*, which fan – the painted silk or the lace? Letters were composed to Miss Charlotte and a visit arranged for the following morning to collect various other items that Aunt Sarah deemed vital: a silk scarf in the same yellow damask as the dress, lace lappets for her hair with yellow ribbons, and a fan to match.

Then there was a full half-hour lesson on how to use the fan.

'Refrain from placing your fingers to its tip,' Aunt Sarah said, demonstrating. 'It will be taken as an invitation that you wish to talk to the person you are looking at. And never, ever, in any circumstances, close it by drawing it through your hand like this.'

'Why is that so bad?' Lizzie asked.

'It is supposed to convey that you hate the person you are with.'

Anna laughed. 'I doubt many men trouble themselves to learn the language of the fan.'

'That's as may be,' her aunt replied, pursing her lips. 'But the other ladies will, and word will spread soon enough.'

Lizzie took up another fan and put it to her lips. 'What does this mean, Mama?'

Aunt Sarah coloured and snatched the fan away. 'Do not let me ever see you doing that again, Lizzie.'

When her aunt was not listening, Anna pressed her cousin for the meaning.

'It means "kiss me".'

'I'll avoid that one, then.'

'Do you not *want* Charlie to kiss you? If you are going to marry someone, surely that is what you most desire?'

'Hush, Lizzie,' Anna scolded. 'Let us not run ahead of ourselves.'

Later, in her room, she pondered her reaction. Why did she not thrill at the thought of Charlie kissing her? Was that not what a young woman most wanted, when romance blossomed? He was a nice enough man of good means, who talked with her most respectfully. But when she thought of him, she saw those long limbs, bony cheeks and the Adam's apple bobbing in his throat. Would she ever, even in time, find him attractive enough to want to kiss him – or take part in those other things her mother had once darkly hinted at but about which she had very little notion?

Perhaps I should be grateful that anyone is taking an interest in me, she sighed, catching a glimpse of herself in the looking glass. *Who am I to be so choosy?*

❧

By Friday lunchtime, after a further three hours of intensive tuition, she felt a good deal more confident of her dancing steps and was even beginning to look forward to the ball. But first there was the trip to Miss Charlotte to collect the finishing touches for her costume.

Aunt Sarah suggested that Betty be sent, but Anna insisted.

'It is best that I go in person, for I may need to make some choices, or perhaps wait for adjustments,' she said. 'It is only a few streets away and I can perfectly easily find my way there and back again, just as I did last time.' To her surprise, Aunt Sarah agreed.

She hoped Miss Charlotte might invite her for tea again, with perhaps the pleasant diversion of entertaining conversation. It was almost at the last moment that she realised that this visit offered the perfect opportunity: she would ask Miss Charlotte if she would be kind enough to deliver her new painting to Henri.

As she approached the shop in Draper's Lane Anna could see that Charlotte had customers. She stalled, crossing the road to the other side where she could wait less conspicuously.

Through the bow window she could see a woman

holding the hand of a small pale-faced boy wearing the beautiful plum-coloured damask coat she'd seen in the shop several weeks before. Miss Charlotte embraced the young woman briefly and then kneeled so that her face was level with the boy's, put her hands to his cheeks and kissed him on the forehead. It was a scene of charming but unexpected intimacy.

Shortly afterwards the door opened and the pair emerged. Miss Charlotte lingered on the step, waving goodbye. After ten yards or so, the boy turned his head, lifting his hand in a reciprocal gesture. Then something unexpected happened: pulling away from the woman's grip, and oblivious to her calls, he began to run at some pace back to the shop. He held out his arms and Charlotte, who had now descended the steps, crouched and opened hers so that he fell straight into her embrace.

The other woman returned to his side and tried to prise him away, but he clung to Miss Charlotte like a limpet, nuzzling his face into her neck as she appeared to whisper words of comfort. After several long moments she stood up, forcing him to release his hold, and the young woman took his hand once more. Reluctantly, he was led away and this time Miss Charlotte went immediately inside and closed the door.

It was such a touching scene that Anna lingered several minutes further before crossing the road to knock at the door of the shop. She was glad she had done so because the seamstress took some time to answer and, when she did, her eyes were reddened and her cheeks raw-looking. She recovered herself immediately: 'Oh, it's you, Anna,' she said, resuming her usual welcoming smile. 'What a lovely surprise.'

'I have come for some ribbons and lappets for the ball I am attending on Saturday.'

'Come in, come in.'

'I could not help seeing you saying goodbye to that little boy. He looked so charming in that beautiful damask coat you made for him.'

Miss Charlotte flushed. 'He is my nephew. The coat was for his seventh birthday.'

'He seems much attached to you,' Anna said.

'Indeed . . .' Her words tailed off and the smile faded. 'Now, about those lappets you wanted . . .'

When they had completed their business and were taking tea, Anna took out the parcel and explained her request.

'I am quite happy to deliver it for you,' Miss Charlotte said. 'But why do you not take it to him yourself? Unless my memory deceives me, when you were here last week Henri invited you to visit so that you might better understand how the design would work on the loom.'

'Indeed, that would be my dearest wish,' Anna said. 'But I have not told my aunt and uncle about the design and I feel sure they would consider it unseemly for me to visit the home of a French weaver.'

Miss Charlotte nodded sympathetically. 'I can certainly deliver it for you on Tuesday afternoon when it is early closing, if that is soon enough?'

'That will be perfect,' Anna said.

It was arranged that Anna would take a carriage to the Hinchliffes' after lunch on Saturday and would dress there, along with Susannah, and assisted by their maid.

In the carriage Anna was assailed by a fit of nerves, wishing herself far away and not having to face the trial of her social and dancing skills among eminent and wealthy strangers. But Mrs Hinchliffe – 'you must call me Augusta, my dear' – welcomed her like a long-lost daughter.

'We are just so delighted that you are able to join us,' she warbled. 'I am sure we are to enjoy the most delightful evening. Charles tells us that the ball attracts most interesting and distinguished guests.'

'Dearest Anna, I am almost beside myself with excitement,' Susannah whispered. 'I can barely keep still. What colour is your dress?'

'It is a pale yellow damask *robe à la française*, so the *costumière* called it. It has a sackback, which makes me feel most elegant.'

'How wonderfully *à la mode*. I cannot wait to see it,' Susannah said. 'Mine is eggshell blue, and I have the prettiest dancing shoes you can ever imagine.'

'I am sure you will be the belles of the ball,' said Mrs Hinchliffe. 'It will be our delight to escort you both.'

After tea, they both retired to Susannah's chamber, where her maid – *her own personal maid, what an indulgence*, Anna thought to herself – was deputed to help them dress. Anna hoped this might be a moment to engage Susannah in conversation; to see what they might have in common. After all, she was the only young woman of her own age to whom she had yet been introduced.

'What do you like to read, Susannah?' she asked, between

gasps as the maid tugged at her stays, trying to force her waistline into the same impossibly tiny circumference as her young mistress's.

'This and that,' Susannah replied, distracted by a lace cuff which would not sit correctly. 'These have not been starched properly, Hannah.'

'Beg pardon, miss. I will look out another pair.'

'Be quick about it, then. What were you saying, Anna?'

'I wondered if you like to read novels, you know, romances like *Pamela*, or *Clarissa*. Or what about Jonathan Swift – I love his satires.'

Susannah regarded her blankly. Anna tried again.

'Or perhaps you like poetry? Thomas Gray? I do so love his "Elegy in a Country Churchyard".'

'How does it go?' Susannah regarded herself in the mirror, turning her head this way and that.

Anna thought for a moment, then began: '*The curfew tolls the knell of parting day, the lowing herd wind slowly o'er the lea, the ploughman homeward plods his weary way and leaves the world to darkness and to me.*'

'Sounds too gloomy for me.' Susannah held out her arms so that Hannah could fit the new cuffs then stepped forward to the dresser, causing her maid to run with her, and picked up a slim volume. 'Mama gave me this,' she said.

On the front was an illustration of two beautiful young women. Each part of their anatomy, the height of their hair, the size of their eyes, the extent of their décolletages and the slimness of their waistlines seemed overly exaggerated, unlike any girl Anna had ever encountered. '*The Lady's Book of Manners*,' she said, turning to an inside page and reading out loud.

'No lady should drink wine at dinner. Even if her head is strong enough to bear it, she will find her cheeks, soon after the indulgence, flushed, hot, and uncomfortable. Alas, I surely have no manners. My uncle serves claret each evening, and I drink it!'

She read again: 'No young lady should go to a ball, without the protection of a married lady, or an elderly gentleman.'

Susannah laughed. 'Thank heavens we have Mother and Father with us tonight. She's married and he's elderly.'

For a while their conversation was lively enough but it soon dwindled, and Anna found herself struggling to find topics of mutual interest with which to fill the time. At last they were called. The carriage was waiting.

✦

Arriving at the Inns of Court, their cloaks were taken by a red- and gold-liveried footman, who ushered them into the grandest anteroom Anna had ever seen, with bright Persian carpets, deep-buttoned leather benches along both sides and, at either end, walls covered with portraits of pompous-looking men. Charles was there to greet them.

'Miss Butterfield, it is my greatest pleasure that you are able to join us.' He bowed and took her hand to his lips, whispering, 'You are looking very fine this evening.'

She blushed, in spite of herself. She had to admit he made an impressive figure, a full head taller than her and bewigged, splendidly attired in a brilliant silk brocade coat cut away in the latest fashion with white lace ruffles at neck and wrists. Perhaps it was the mirrored hall, or the light of so many candelabra, but she thought him a great deal more handsome than she remembered.

Accepting his offer of a glass of claret, she drank it down eagerly, hoping the alcohol would soothe her nerves. *To blazes with The Lady's Book of Manners*, she said to herself. They chatted for a while, although their conversation was constantly interrupted by men greeting Charles in loud, booming voices, slapping him on the back and calling him 'my boy'. He introduced her to each one, but after the initial politenesses, she was mostly ignored.

It was with some relief that she heard the orchestra tuning up, and Charles invited her to dance. The ballroom seemed to Anna at least the size of their village cricket pitch, and the ceiling the height of a church, supported by marble columns and lit by a dozen glittering chandeliers.

Before she had a moment to think, they were already taking their places and it became obvious that the very first dance was indeed a minuet. Happily, four other couples took the central floor before them, all apparently fluent in the art of the dance, allowing her time to revise the movements before it was their turn.

She remembered to keep her feet turned out, not to look down at them and, most of the time, at which moments to dance on her toes or dip her knees. When it came to the all-important diagonal pass across the centre of the floor, the climax of the dance, Charles held out his arm well in advance to indicate that this was the moment when their wrists were to touch at the turn.

As they finished, she curtseyed as elegantly as she knew how, he bowed and, as he offered his arm to lead her from the floor, the other dancers and observers clapped appreciatively. 'A triumph, Miss Butterfield,' he whispered. 'You are a most accomplished dancer.'

The rest of the evening flew by as she danced twice again with Charles, once with Mr Ehret and once with Mr Hinchliffe. Susannah waved gaily each time they passed on the floor, apparently with a new partner each time. At last, as her feet were starting to ache, she heard the announcement of the final minuet, and it was Charles who claimed her.

Before she knew it, they were all in a carriage on their way home, Susannah chattering gaily with her mother about all the marvellously handsome young men she had danced with, and Mr Hinchliffe and Charles exchanging information about the important people they had observed, or conversed with, during the evening, and the business connections they had made.

It seemed the men were far more concerned about meeting potential customers of high social standing and plentiful means than they were with enjoying themselves, and their talk left Anna feeling a little deflated. She knew that such events were, in essence, marriage markets, but she had not realised how much they could also be commercial marketplaces.

As she prepared to leave the following morning after breakfast, Charles pulled her to one side and whispered, 'I have so enjoyed your company, Anna. May I be so bold as to invite myself to Spital Square again next week?'

On Tuesday morning Anna recalled that Miss Charlotte had promised to deliver her new sketch to Henri that afternoon. She tried to imagine herself into the scene but failed: she had no idea what the interior of the house or the weaving loft would be like. *What would he think of the new painting?* she wondered. *Would he be able to incorporate her new naturalistic elements into the woven design? How would he translate her many shades of colour into silk?* She so longed to be there herself, to take part in their discussions, to observe his reactions and, she had to admit it, to hear his voice and see his smile.

As the morning drew on, she became more and more downcast. It wasn't fair that Miss Charlotte could be free to visit whom she wanted and when she wanted, while she, Anna, was unable to. *It is like being imprisoned*, she thought to herself, *within invisible walls of social propriety*.

She gazed out of her window across the rooftops, recalling the freedoms of her former life. She imagined herself running, with little Jane, across the beach and splashing in the surf at the edge of the sea, and found herself close to tears.

'I want to go home,' she said to the pigeons.

Joseph and William were missing at lunchtime, and Aunt Sarah announced that she, Anna and Lizzie had received an invitation to take tea with some friends in Hackney. 'It is a fair drive, but it will do you good to get out,' she said to Anna. 'You are looking a little peaky, my dear.'

The idea came to her then, as sudden and surprising as

a thunderclap. 'I am so sorry, dear Aunt,' she said, touching her temple. 'I do have a terrible headache. Do you mind if I do not accompany you on this occasion? I think it would be better if I rested.'

14

*When by accident or choice you venture into the insinuating
company of women, consider them all as Syrens, that have
fascination in their eyes, musick on their tongues, and mischief
in their hearts. If your inclinations render their society necessary
to your happiness, let your prudence chuse for you, not your
appetite!*

*– Advice for apprentices and journeymen
OR A sure guide to gain both esteem and an estate*

The clatter of looms in the weaving loft usually drowned
out any noise from the street, but by coincidence and good
fortune both Henri and Benjamin had stopped their shuttles at the same moment.

In that single second of silence could be heard the ringing
of the small iron bell suspended beside the front door of
the house, three storeys below. Henri put down the handle
of his harness, went to the window and peered over the
parapet. With one hand grasping the metal gantry, he eased
his shoulders further out of the window. Now he could see
the tops of the heads of two women, standing side by side
on the front step.

He called down: '*Monsieur Lavalle n'est pas à la maison cet après-midi. Puis-je vous aider, mesdames?*'

Two faces tipped upwards, pale moons in their white bonnets. In that astonished moment of recognition, Henri nearly lost hold of the gantry. '*Mam'selle Anna! Et Charlotte! Est-ce vraiment vous?*'

Miss Charlotte shouted upwards: 'Indeed, it is us. We have been ringing and knocking this past five minutes. We were about to give up.'

He leaned out even further for a better view, almost dangling from the scaffold normally used for lifting warp beams and boxes of heavy pirns.

Anna laughed. 'Take care, Henri, or you will fly down.'

In that moment he did indeed feel powerful enough to fly, his body feather-light and flooded with joy. The girl who had been invading his dreams for the past few weeks was here, on his doorstep. And she had called him Henri.

'Wait, please,' he shouted. 'I will come down.'

Only as he descended the loft ladder and the two sets of stairs did it occur to him to wonder why no one else had answered the door. M. Lavalle was out, that he knew, but where was Mariette, and Cook? It was only a fleeting thought. What did he care, when Anna was here?

As he welcomed them both into the parlour he realised the purpose of their visit. Under her arm Anna held a long cylindrical package; it must be the new sketch she had promised. After a flurry of greetings they all fell silent, listening to the ticking of M. Lavalle's grandfather clock.

'Oh, forgive me. Please take a seat,' he finally remembered to say.

The two young women sat side by side on the hard

settle. He offered them drinks, which they declined. He took M. Lavalle's chair and smiled, waiting for one of them to say something. He could not help looking into Anna's eyes, into that breathtakingly direct gaze that seemed to swallow up the rest of the world. For a few awkward moments, she seemed entirely to have forgotten the object of her mission.

'Haven't you got something to show Henri?' Charlotte prompted, nudging her.

Anna started, as if from a dream. 'Oh, yes,' she said, flustered. 'Here is my new painting. I have added water-colour and more shading. I hope you like it.'

He untied the string and outer wrapping then rolled it out onto the table by the window. They stood either side of him as Anna described how her meeting with the botanical artist Mr Ehret had opened her eyes to the need for even more careful shading to achieve the naturalism she sought. 'I realised that I must return to observing real life, so I purchased some wild flowers to copy. I also had in mind the *points rentrées* technique Charlotte showed us last week,' she said. 'I hope that you think it will be possible to weave?'

'This is truly delightful,' Miss Charlotte said. 'This shading here, for example, it works perfectly. And the colours are just right.'

Henri was spellbound. He had loved the earlier sketch, the one with which he was now so familiar, but this new coloured version was so much more vivid, so much bolder, and yet even more natural. The trellis framework of serpentine stems was still there and the rendition of the plants and flowers was so realistic that he could easily imagine

LIZ TRENOW

himself lying in the grass among them. The beetle chewing casually at a leaf appeared so lifelike that for a second he could almost see its legs moving.

'I can smell the fresh air of the countryside,' he said at last, taking in a deep breath. 'It is wonderful. Thank you.'

For what seemed like long, long minutes the three of them stood in silence, admiring the painting. They were standing so close that he could almost feel the heat of her, the flush that was flooding her neck and her cheeks. Her hand brushed his for a fraction of a second, and the hot charge of her touch burned through his hand, up his arm and into his face.

M. Lavalle had once tried to explain Gilbert's treatise on static electricity and magnetism, and Henri had thought it a strange and confusing concept: how could something unseen be so powerful? But now he understood. As Anna turned her face to his, asking him what he thought of the painting, it was as if they were magnetic poles, and it took all his reserves of self-control to resist the force. The slightest movement of his head would have brought his lips to hers.

Charlotte was the first to break the spell. 'When we met before, you spoke of showing us the weaving loft, Henri? Would that be convenient?'

'Oh yes, please,' Anna cried. 'If Monsieur Lavalle does not object.'

'He is out for the afternoon. But I am pleased to show you, if you do not mind climbing a ladder?'

Anna's face lit up with delight. 'I used to be the best tree climber in the village. A ladder will be child's play!'

In his broken English, Henri did his best to explain the

working of the two different looms – the draw loom for figured silks and the plain silk loom on which Benjamin was weaving – and both girls seemed fascinated, firing questions that forced him to think carefully about the answers. Some French terms had no English equivalent – *momme*, *drogue*, *décreusage* – but Benjamin helped with the translation.

He spoke about the subtle differences in raw silk, depending on whether it was grown in Italy, India or the Far East, and watched her eyes widen in wonder. For him the idea that silk should travel from far across the world was commonplace, but he could see that to anyone less accustomed, those countries would seem so distant, so exotic. It made him feel worldly, stronger and taller, having this knowledge.

'The silk comes in skeins, so first of all it goes to a throwster, who twists it into singles, and then into two or three threads twisted together to make tram, which is for the weft. For the warp – these threads that go along – we perhaps use organzine, which needs a higher twist to make it stronger.'

'My mother is a throwster,' he added. 'She likes the Italian silk best of all.'

'Where does your mother live? Do you live with her?'

'No, but she lives nearby. I see her every week. My master asks me to stay on when I finish my apprenticeship. He likes me to be here, I think.' He stopped short of adding that M. Lavalle was like a father to him. It sounded immodest, saying it like that.

They were so engaged in lively conversation and laughter

that when the bells of Christ Church chimed four o'clock, no one could believe that a full half hour had passed.

'Is that really the time?' Anna said. 'I must hasten home.'

Climbing down the ladder in full skirts was a more difficult proposition than the ascent. Henri went first and then guided Charlotte as she negotiated the steps backwards. Next it was Anna's turn. He took her hand to help her down the last few treads. When she safely reached the bottom, he did not let go. Charlotte was already making her way down to the ground floor.

They were alone on the landing. He looked into her eyes, lifted her fingers and kissed them.

'Anna. I . . .' His throat tightened; he couldn't find the words to say what he was burning to tell her.

'I know,' she said softly, holding his gaze. 'It is the same for me.'

His heart was thudding so hard in his chest he felt certain she must be able to hear it. 'Can we meet again?'

'I do not know,' she whispered. 'It is difficult.'

'I understand. But please let us find a way.'

She nodded. *How sweet she smells*, he thought in those few seconds; it was the *bouquet* of the countryside, of herbs and flowers and sunshine. Only by actively resisting, with both mind and muscle, did he prevent himself from pulling her into his arms and immersing himself in that heady fragrance, feeling the warmth of her body against his. He'd experienced desire for many a girl before, but this was different: he had never wanted anything so intensely.

'Charlotte . . . I must go,' she said eventually.

As they set off down the next flight of stairs, he heard

the quiet click of a latch behind him. It was the door to Mariette's room.

❧

'Why did you not come to say hello?' Henri asked her later, when he found her sitting at the kitchen table. 'It was Miss Charlotte and her friend Miss Anna. You must have heard us? They asked to see the looms.'

'So I gathered,' she muttered. 'You seemed to be having such a jolly time I did not want to interrupt you.'

He sensed her displeasure but could not imagine what might be wrong. Did she disapprove of him neglecting his work when M. Lavalle was absent? Or was it something that had happened while she was out visiting? He found it hard to care, so elated was he from the visit and his last whispered exchange with Anna. Whatever was irritating Mariette was her problem, he decided.

❧

M. Lavalle returned grim-faced from his meeting.

'The government does not seem minded to pass the bill to raise taxes on imported fabrics,' he said over supper. 'They fear other countries will follow suit and this will hit our exports. They may lower the import duty on raw silk and ban imports of silk ribbons, stockings and gloves, but I fear these measures will make little difference to most of us.'

'What can be done?' Henri asked. 'You said yourself that many will starve if this bill is not passed.'

'I'm afraid they do not care much for the plight of the weavers. It is the general prosperity of the country they are more concerned with.'

'And padding their fat arses,' Benjamin added, earning himself a fierce look. M. Lavalle did not tolerate bad language in front of Mariette.

Henri's mood was so buoyed by the events of the afternoon that he found it hard to be gloomy. 'We have the *Book of Prices*, at least. The masters will have to pay a fair wage.'

'But it is not accepted by all, and when there is only work for a few, what happens to the rest? Some masters may feel they have no choice but to pay lower rates just so they can keep their business afloat, and who can really blame them? The journeymen are threatening violence against those who will not sign, and the government is talking about settling troops in the area to protect citizens.'

Henri shivered. It sounded too much like the tales his mother told of the *dragonnades*.

Later, Henri took out Anna's painting and rolled it out flat along the table at the window to catch the dying rays of dusk. As he studied the detail, admiring once more the delicacy of the colour she had added and the remarkable naturalism of her line, he felt close to her once again, almost as though she were looking over his shoulder. He set out his paints and a tiny brush, and began translating the design into dots of colour on the squared point paper which would guide the set-up of the loom. As he worked, he found himself humming with the sheer pleasure of the task.

When the light faded he knew that his colour accuracy was being compromised and he would have to stop for the night. He rolled up the paper and held it to his cheek as if to conjure the touch of her skin against his, feeling once again the intensity of longing that he had experienced in her presence.

He lit a candle and took out a slip of paper. This time he did not care whether his spelling and grammar were correct.

Dear Anna, he wrote.

My purpos is to thank you from the bottom of my Heart for your new peinture. *It is very beautiful & natural, more even than the 1st one. This evening I start work on the design for the loom & hope to weave soon. As it is a slow time M. Lavalle allows me to set up the loom for it so God Speed I am abel to finish my Master piece by the end of next month. The Committee meet in January, that is my gaol.*

It is not easy to make the weave of all those beautiful curves but as I work I think of you, Anna. I hope we can meet again soon.

With best wishes,
Henri

At the very moment of signing his name, he regretted it. Should the letter fall into unintended hands, might it lead to difficulties with her family? *It is difficult*, she had whispered and he knew all too well why. *Such a powerful emotion surely cannot be denied*, he thought to himself, *and she feels the same. She said so. We will find a way.* But for the moment, perhaps it was best to be discreet. He rewrote the letter, signing himself simply with an H, which felt even more intimate and exciting.

***

Although it was not yet cold enough for the fire to be lit, M. Lavalle was settled, as usual of an evening, into his favourite upholstered wing chair by the empty fireplace, comfortable in his informal indoor garb: the dark green dressing gown of soft serge, his ruby velvet hat and embroidered slippers.

'Have you a few moments? I have something to show you,' Henri said. If his master approved of the new design, he needed to put forward the all-important request: the use of the draw loom and the services of the drawboy for three weeks, so that he could set up and weave the requisite five yards of his master piece.

'Later, later,' he said. 'Close the door and join me, lad. We have something to discuss.' The old man filled his clay pipe with a pinch of tobacco, and lit it. He sucked in and then breathed out a sigh of aromatic smoke.

'We have never talked of your future, have we?'

'I have been working on the design for my master piece and hope one day to become a master myself,' Henri said. 'You know that I have always had the highest regard for you, sir.'

'And I you. Very much so. In fact, I have for some time regarded you as the son we never had.'

'You have been the very best kind of father to me.'

'But the implication is complicated . . .' M. Lavalle paused, as if trying to find the right words. And then, after a few moments, they seemed to come out in a rush: 'I am getting old and tired, Henri. But I have no one to take on my business, except you.'

'Me? But sir, I could not afford to buy your business.'

'I do not mean to sell it to you, boy. I would like you to *inherit* it. As a son would.'

A pulse throbbed in Henri's temple. This was such an unexpected twist that he could barely comprehend it. He had imagined perhaps raising enough money to rent a small room and a loom, as Guy had done, in Bethnal Green where rents were cheaper, and working up slowly, maybe eventually being able to buy a house in Spitalfields with a weaving loft, and take on his own apprentices. But now he was being offered the chance to inherit an established and well-respected silk weaving business. It was beyond his wildest dreams.

'I hardly know how to respond,' he gasped.

'But, as I said, there are complications.'

'Of course. You must consider everything very carefully. The legal issues and so on.'

'You misunderstand me. Those are mere administrative details, and easy to solve. My main concern is Mariette.'

Henri frowned. How could *she* be a problem? 'You have no need to be concerned about Mariette, sir. She is very dear to me, like a sister. Of course, this would always be her home, until she marries. I would take the greatest possible care of her.'

'She is my true heir,' M. Lavalle said. 'How can I leave

the business to you whilst ensuring that she receives her rightful inheritance?'

The reality of the dilemma was beginning to dawn on Henri. Women worked as throwsters, like his mother, and he had heard of one or two who did plain weaving. But he had never heard of a woman silk master. In any case, Mariette would not expect to be a working woman; she deserved – and he knew that her father intended her to have – better things, like marriage, and a life of comfort and leisure.

'Before long she will be of an age to marry, will she not? And such a beautiful young woman will surely have her choice of suitors?'

'And now we come to the nub of it, my boy, the true nub of it.' M. Lavalle looked down at his pipe and spent some moments carefully refilling it. He seemed to be tongue-tied by this nub, whatever it was.

'Please go on, sir. I am in suspense.'

'Mariette tells me that two young women came to the house yesterday?'

This was the last thing Henri expected. What did their visit have to do with it?

'It was the costumière Miss Charlotte, who came with another young lady, the one who did the sketch that I purchased as the design for my master piece,' he said. 'She has revised and given colour to it. I have it here, sir; would you like to see? Actually, I wanted to ask you—'

'And the name of this young lady?'

'Miss Anna Butterfield.'

'Ah. I met her once, when she came to the door with a note. And from where does Miss Butterfield hail?'

There was no escape. 'She is the niece of the mercer

Sadler,' Henri admitted. 'I know what you think of the man, but this young woman is most talented and charming. There is no harm to her at all.'

'Sadler, eh?' The old man lit his pipe and puffed on it slowly. 'That thieving bastard. Well, the point is . . .' He paused again. 'Mariette seems to think there is something between you and this girl.'

Henri felt cornered. There was little point in trying to conceal the truth now. He cleared his throat. 'Well, to be perfectly honest with you, sir, I think there might be. Although heaven knows what future there would be in it, for we are of such different worlds . . .'

'It is this affection that concerns Mariette,' M. Lavalle said, puffing on his pipe.

'I am aware that she may have observed a brief encounter between myself and Miss Butterfield,' Henri admitted. 'But I can reassure you that absolutely nothing improper took place. I cannot see why Mariette should be concerned for me?'

'Are you *blind*, boy?' M. Lavalle almost shouted. 'You are so clever in all other respects and yet it seems entirely to have escaped your notice that my daughter is in love with you.'

Henri's jaw slackened with astonishment. 'But she is yet a child, sir.'

'She is fifteen, the age when many a girl is betrothed,' M. Lavalle said. 'I have sensed her growing regard for you but held my counsel, thinking that the affection might become mutual, naturally, in its own time. It was only yesterday evening that she admitted it to me.'

Henri's head was spinning. Mariette, in love with him?

'I will be completely honest with you,' M. Lavalle went on. 'I had hoped that this might, at some time in the future, be the solution to my dilemma.'

'The solution?' The realisation hit Henri like a slap in the face: M. Lavalle expected him to marry his daughter. In fact, he appeared to be suggesting that this was a condition for Henri to inherit the business. For a few brief moments Henri had imagined himself the luckiest journeyman alive, but now it had suddenly become so much more complicated.

For how could he wed Mariette, the little girl he had grown up with, had played childish games with, whom he'd long considered to be his younger sister? Once upon a time he would have been deeply flattered, and his mother would be thrilled. It would have been an excellent match for the once-penniless migrant boy.

But it did not bear thinking about. Because, now, he knew what being in love really felt like.

All that night and at his loom the following day, Henri's head was in turmoil. He seemed to have mislaid the compass that had guided him through life so far – hard work and obedience – and although he could see clearly where his duty now lay, he could not imagine how he could follow it. He needed to talk it through with the only person he could really trust. After work he travelled to Bethnal Green to see his mother, taking with him two hot meat pies, a baked potato from the stall on Brick Lane and a twist of coffee grounds from M. Lavalle's kitchen.

As usual, he found Clothilde at her throwing wheel, working by the light of a single candle. *How old and thin she looks*, he thought to himself, *withered from too much work and not enough leisure.* Orders were hard to come by, and she was often required to deliver the thrown silk within an almost impossibly short timescale. She could not afford to turn work down, and frequently stayed up all night to make sure she met the deadline. Apart from weekly attendances at church, she had little time and few opportunities for socialising.

Her pale face bloomed with pleasure at the sight of him. '*Henri, quel plaisir*,' she whispered, as they embraced. He took down two pewter plates, laying them out on the simple wooden table, and unwrapped the pies and potato from the scarf he'd tucked inside his jacket.

'Come and eat while these are still warm, Mother. Then you can get back to your throwing and we can talk further as you work. I have brought coffee, too.'

'What a treat. You spoil me.' She put down her spindle and came to the table. 'How is life with you, my boy?' she asked, tucking into the pie with her usual hunger.

'I have settled on the design for my master piece at last,' he said. 'All I need now is Monsieur Lavalle's agreement to use the loom for a few weeks.'

'And may I see it?'

'I have it here, but let us look at it when our fingers are not covered in gravy.'

They finished their meal and Henri lit a small fire sufficient to boil just two cups of water. After admiring the painting and praising the naturalness of its forms, she asked, 'And who is your designer?'

Henri began the long explanation of how he had obtained Anna's first sketch and how she had been so keen to help she had recently done a new, coloured version. He was aware of talking too much, of using her name too often, but could not stop: it gave him a frisson of joy every time. With a mother's intuition, Clothilde went straight to the point.

'This artist girl is clearly talented. But there is more, is there not, Henri?'

He nodded, lowering his face to hide the flush flooding his cheek. 'I cannot deny it. I think I am in love with her, and believe she feels the same about me.'

Clothilde smiled encouragingly, but inside her heart was sinking. How long would this latest passion last? Henri had already gained something of a reputation at church for the frequency with which he seemed to fall in love – often to the disapprobation of the girl's parents – but it never seemed to endure. She could only hope that, one day, he would come to understand that a pretty face did not necessarily make a good wife.

'When can I meet this young woman?' she said.

There was no avoiding the truth, for it would surely emerge in time. He told her about the Sadler family, and how he was afraid they would not consider him good enough for their niece, for whom they were probably seeking a good society match. He omitted to mention their bigotry about French weavers and the accusation against them of illegal imports.

As he spoke, her face clouded over. 'Beware of getting ideas above your station, son. You must give up the idea of this girl at once,' she said.

'But I *love* her, Mother. I will die if I cannot be with her.'

She laughed at his tragic expression. 'When do you *not* imagine yourself to be in love, Henri?' she asked. 'Believe me, it will only lead to heartbreak once more.'

It was like an intense weight in his chest, thickly compressing his breath: the knowledge that his mother was right and that his love for Anna was merely a fantasy, never to be realised because of the difference between their positions in society. He felt like running away, to avoid facing the truth of her words.

The pot was boiling. Henri added the twist of coffee grounds, stirred them, and poured the coffee through a scrap of muslin into two earthenware cups.

'What a luxury,' she said, lifting the cup to her nose to draw in its sweet aroma.

'There's something else,' he said, gathering himself.

'Go on.'

'Which makes this even more complicated.'

'I am all ears.'

As simply as possible, he described the conversation he'd had with M. Lavalle the previous evening.

Even before he'd finished, Clothilde was tutting with frustration. 'Just listen to yourself,' she burst out. 'I cannot believe that I have such a fool for a son. You have come from absolutely nothing, and you have been offered an extraordinary opportunity to inherit a profitable and highly respected business, a fine house *and* the chance of a beautiful young woman's hand in marriage. And you cannot decide whether to accept? You are an idiot, boy. If you were any younger, I'd put you over my knee and knock some sense into you.'

'But I do not love Mariette,' he said, his heart breaking quietly.

Her face was severe now, her voice uncompromising. 'It is time to put aside such childish notions, Henri. Few of us have the luxury of marrying for love and many would envy being the object of Mariette's affections. She is charming and pretty, and her father is one of the most well-respected silk masters in Spitalfields. What could possibly be wrong with that? You will grow to love the girl, of that I have no doubt. You cannot afford not to.'

The candle began to gutter; it was almost burned out.

'Ignore my words at your peril, *mon fils*,' she went on. 'God has handed you the blessed chance of a good life. I beg you, do not turn it down.'

As he trudged the two miles back to Wood Street in a fine drizzle, Henri could think of little else but Anna. He could not imagine never being able to see her, never again looking into her blue-green eyes or experiencing that intense shimmer of affinity and unspoken understanding.

'I *love* her!' he shouted, out loud. 'How can I give that up?'

His words echoed around the empty streets. They gave no reply, but he knew what the answer must be and where his obligations lay; his respect for M. Lavalle and all that he had done for him, the responsibility he felt for his mother and the honour due to the memory of his lost family – all this added up to a duty that he must obey.

It was a double bind: if he turned down the chance to inherit M. Lavalle's business, he would be throwing away the very opportunity which might enable him to rise in society and have even the slightest prospect of marrying a girl like Anna. And yet he could not inherit unless he denied the chance of any future with her.

'I am damned if I do, and damned if I don't,' he muttered angrily, as it began to rain more heavily.

He arrived back in Wood Street, soaked to the skin, to find a grim-faced M. Lavalle reading the newspaper. In silence, he passed it to Henri.

CUTTERS RAID
24TH NOVEMBER 1760

At Bethnal Green, on Tuesday evening, a crowd of unruly journeymen claiming to be members of the Bold Defiance broke open the house of one John Poor, weaver, threatening him and his wife with a musket and destroying many of his looms, cutting to pieces much valuable silke.

They claim that he was working for M. Chauvet and had 'broken the book', referring to the 'Book of Prices' which they are seeking to impose for their work. Ten men are being held at Newgate, pending trial.

As he read the stark words, Henri felt the blood drain from his face.

'Is this something to do with Guy?' he asked.

M. Lavalle nodded his head. 'His mother called earlier

to see me. She is in a desperate state and wanted me to help. He got in with the wrong crowd, just as I feared, and went out on the cutting raid.'

Henri had heard tell, of course, about the groups of journeymen so desperate that they had broken into the premises of silk masters who failed to pay the going rates, and slashed the silk warps on their looms. But surely Guy would not undertake anything so dangerous?

'What happened? Why on earth was Guy there?' His mouth was so dry that he could barely force the words past his lips. He began to shiver as M. Lavalle finished filling and lighting his pipe.

'It is a bad business, I'm afraid. He was with a gang going to cut the silk in the house of a weaver – this man Poor, who is working for master Chauvet. Someone threat-ened Poor's wife with a gun. Guy was caught and arrested, and he's in gaol. His mother's been told that if he is found guilty, he could be transported or even hanged.'

Henri's breath seemed to stop in his chest. Chauvet was powerful and notorious for banning his workers from joining the weavers' clubs or paying any levies. There had even been riots outside his house after which he'd employed his own guard, which is probably why they attacked one of his weavers instead. But why had Guy got involved? Surely he couldn't have been the one with a gun? He was hot-headed sometimes, but never violent. It was impossible to comprehend.

'Saleté! That's terrible news.' His own concerns seemed now so inconsequential, so frivolous.

There was no escaping the grim image of his friend, cold, frightened and hungry, shackled in a damp and dismal cell with heaven knows how many other dangerous and diseased men. He might be headstrong and a bit foolish, but he was no criminal. Like himself, Guy had worked his way up from nothing, completed his apprenticeship with scarcely a blot on his record, had managed to rent a room and a loom and gained a few good contracts as a journeyman. Of course he was young and passionate and, like Henri, fell in love with every girl in sight, but he'd often shared his dreams of owning a house and running his own business, of marrying, having a family, of living a long and prosperous life.

Now, that life could simply be snuffed out, on the decision of a judge.

'Can the church elders do anything to help?' he asked.

M. Lavalle shook his head. 'We can try to get him bailed, but I doubt that'd do any good. We shall visit him in prison and see what we can do to make his stay more comfortable. But in the end, there is nothing anyone can do to divert the course of the law.'

Just as he uttered these words, almost as if to emphasise them, there was a loud hammering at the front door.

'By Christ, who can that be at this time of night?' M. Lavalle muttered.

The answer came immediately. 'Open up, open up. It's the Guards. If you do not, we will break down the door.'

M. Lavalle opened it and without any by-your-leave five burly men in grubby uniforms and heavy boots tramped past him into the parlour. The room felt suddenly very small and cramped.

The tallest of the men, obviously their leader, fixed Henri with a fearsome stare. 'Henri Vendôme?'

'Yes, sir,' Henri said, trying to keep the quake from his voice.

'We have reason to believe that you have been consorting with a man charged with murder,' the big man said. 'Guy Lemaitre?'

'He is a fellow journeyman, a member of our church, sir. I have known him most of my life.'

'You were a signatory to this *Book of Prices*?'

'Yes, sir. I believed it might ease potential hardship and unrest.'

'Well, you were wrong, lad. Your signature is next to that of Lemaitre and others who have been involved in criminal activity. Where were you last Tuesday evening?'

'At home here, sir. My master Monsieur Lavalle can attest to that.'

M. Lavalle was hidden from Henri's view by the five huge men, but his voice was strong. 'Indeed I can, and would be prepared to swear on the Bible to that effect. I have known Henri Vendôme for more than ten years and he is a God-fearing, law-abiding young man who would not even consider becoming involved in anything illegal. Your presence in this house is unwelcome, sirs,' he went on. 'And I now beg you to leave immediately before you disturb my young daughter.'

'Very well.' The leader turned back. 'Just you make sure you stay well away from trouble, laddie.' He pushed his face so close that Henri could smell the meaty, beery breath. 'Or I swear I'll make it my personal mission to ensure that you follow your friend to the gallows.'

The other men laughed and the four pushed past M. Lavalle so roughly that he had to hold on to the door to prevent himself falling.

15

It is a good plan to have books and pictures on the centre table, and scattered about your drawing room. You must, of course, converse with each caller, but these trifles are an excellent pastime, and serve as subjects for conversation.
— *The Lady's Book of Manners*

For Anna, the days following her visit to Wood Street seemed to pass at a snail's pace.

She had read and reread Henri's letter until the paper became worn and the folds began to tear. The sweet intimacy of those last words left her breathless: *It is not easy to make the weave of all those beautiful curves but as I work I think of you, Anna. I hope we can meet again soon.*

She pressed the paper to her heart. *That moment was real*, she thought to herself. *He feels as I do.* She pictured him at his loom, working on the complex system of knots and lashes needed to create the design, smelled the sweet, musty, nutty smell of the silk and felt the rough, uneven boards of the loom loft under her feet.

But now, the prospect of seeing Henri again seemed so remote that the memories only served to make her even more miserable. That day, after bidding farewell to Miss

Charlotte, Anna had calculated that she would have plenty of time to spare. Aunt Sarah and Lizzie would be travelling all the way to Hackney for tea, so they were unlikely to return before five, she reckoned, at the very earliest.

Arriving back at half past four, she fully expected to be able to slip up to her room unnoticed and resume her 'rest' well in advance of their return. She approached Spital Square with caution to avoid being observed and entered the house as quietly as possible so as not to alert anyone in the office next door.

She thought at first that she must have imagined it. But there it was again, unmistakeably, her aunt's voice, calling from the drawing room: 'Anna, is that you?'

There was no escape. Anna paused outside the door, straightening her skirt and pinning stray curls back under her bonnet while desperately trying to formulate a plausible story.

'You are returned early, Aunt,' she said, smiling as cheerfully as possible.

'It seems they told us the wrong day,' Aunt Sarah said. 'We travelled all that way and no one was at home to receive us. It was simply too humiliating. We shall not be accepting any future invitations from that family.'

'I am so sorry. The good news is that my head feels much brighter after a short breath of fresh air.'

'That is indeed cheering news, Niece. But it does not console me. The truth is that we have been back since before three of the clock and you were already gone. You did not inform Betty that you were leaving and you have only now returned, a full hour and a half later. Please, close the door behind you and take a seat, for I am greatly disturbed and wish to hear your explanation.'

'I have been to visit Miss Charlotte, to check on some alterations she is doing. We took tea and had a delightful conversation,' Anna extemporised. 'The time flew by.'

Aunt Sarah frowned, shook her head and sighed. 'If there is one thing I dislike more than disobedience, it is duplicity.' Her voice came out in a sharp rasp. 'You are *lying* to me, young woman. I will not tolerate it.'

Anna's head began to spin. How could her aunt possibly know?

'When you did not return within the half hour, I began to worry for your welfare. Lizzie suggested that you might have gone to visit Miss Charlotte, since she believed that you may have become acquainted. We shall speak more of this later, Niece, since it is entirely inappropriate for a young woman of your standing to cultivate such a friendship with a tradesperson, pleasant though she may be. In any case, I am fully aware that Miss Charlotte's shop is never open on a Tuesday afternoon, for that is her early closing day. In the end, I sent Betty to see and of course the shop was closed. She knocked and rang, but there was no answer.'

Anna lowered her eyes to avoid her aunt's furious glare as she frantically tried to work out her next move. Should she attempt another half-lie, or was it best to come clean? Either way, she was in deep trouble.

'Have you nothing to say, girl?'

She tried to conjure her father's kindly face. His voice came into her head, quiet and clear, just as if she were listening to him reading the gospel in church: *And ye shall know the truth, and the truth shall make you free.*

'I am sorry for not letting Betty know where I had gone, to avoid your concern. But I did not *lie* to you, Aunt. I *did* visit Miss Charlotte, for I enjoy her company and I make no apology for this, for I have no other friends here in the city and find myself quite lonely at times.'

Sarah tried to interrupt, but Anna persevered.

'We *did* take tea but after that she had an errand to run, and I decided to join her. It was to deliver a design to a weaver. He invited us inside to see his looms so that we could understand better how the design would be woven. It was so fascinating that we stayed longer than we had intended.'

Sarah's jowls drooped with astonishment. She was no longer attempting to intervene.

'The thing is, Aunt, I do not feel I have anything for which to apologise. I am fully eighteen years old, I am growing used to London ways and I have the greatest regard for, and trust in, Miss Charlotte. You must not blame her for any part of this, for the decision to accompany her was entirely my own. She would not have led me into any impropriety and at no time were we ever separated. I have had a delightful and informative afternoon and cannot see the harm.'

Aunt Sarah went to the fireplace, rearranging the ornaments and cards for several long seconds before turning back to Anna, a ferocious frown distorting her normally benign features. 'You are a very wilful and headstrong young woman.' Her voice was calm and controlled but the pink spots on her cheeks belied an inner tumult. 'You should know perfectly well by now how to comport yourself in polite society. We cannot lock you in, but if you continue to act like this without regard for your reputation, I fear we may have to send you back to Suffolk. I shall have to discuss the matter with Mr Sadler, but in the meantime please go to your room and remain there until supper, or until I call you.'

Supper was conducted in virtual silence, and afterwards she was summoned to be told that her uncle would be writing to her father to review the current arrangements. In the meantime she would not be allowed to leave the house at all, except for church or another prearranged purpose.

She managed to maintain her composure until she reached her room. Once there, she threw herself onto the bed and sobbed until her head ached and her eyes were red raw.

It was another dull afternoon, with rain clattering on the windows and the drawing room cast into such gloom it seemed as though dusk was already falling, even though it was but two o'clock. She sat by the window reading as Lizzie hammered the harpsichord, making the same mistakes over and over again until she felt like a spring coiled ever tighter and tighter. *Any moment now I shall scream and throw this book at her, or worse.*

Betty knocked at the door: it was a letter from Charles, asking if he could visit that very afternoon. Her heart sank.

'Oh, my dear, this is most excellent news,' Aunt Sarah declared, beaming. 'Perhaps this will be the big moment.'

She's only thrilled because if he proposes they can be rid of me, Anna thought miserably.

Her aunt was prattling on: 'Ask Betty to bring two large jugs of warm water and my best bar of scented soap to your room, so that you will smell of a sweet summer's day. You should wear the green damask, perhaps? You need to look at your most alluring without appearing to be overdressed, and I shall lend you my best lace cuffs, my dear, and some pretty starched lappets for your hair. There's nothing like a little bit of Taunton lace to draw attention to delicate wrists and an elegant neck.'

Anna smiled politely and thanked her aunt for her kindness, but found herself strangely detached, as though all the attention was focused on another, who looked like her and spoke like her, but who was not her inside. She felt like a commodity being packaged for sale by her aunt, who was desperate to seal the deal and thus be freed of responsibility.

Alone in her room, she took several deep breaths, trying to calm her racing thoughts and think rationally. *What if he really does propose, this very afternoon? Do I have a duty to accept the first offer that comes along, because there are no other options? Would it be the end of the world, after all, being married to a well-to-do young man about town?* She would not have to concern herself about money, and such a match would surely secure a comfortable future for her father and Jane. At least she would escape the confinement of Spital Square, and could entertain herself with painting and other diversions.

Charles arrived promptly at four o'clock. Tea was ordered and the family summoned, and the dreary round of polite conversation proceeded. Strategically placed by Aunt Sarah on the chaise longue beside Anna, he perched in a dandyish pose, with chin resting on his fingertips.

'You are looking very well this afternoon, Anna.'

'Thank you,' she said, recoiling at the familiarity.

'Have you been doing much sketching lately?'

He is doing his best. I must be polite. 'No, alas. I love to draw flowers from real life but the weather has been so poor.'

'I observed you enjoying Father's garden, when you visited with Mr Ehret. Do you have much of a garden here in Spital Square?' She found herself fighting an attack of the giggles as his Adam's apple bobbed comically, like a small animal trapped in his throat. What if it turned out to be a real mouse? Perhaps it would escape, suddenly leaping out of his mouth and bouncing across the room like a crazed ball, rendering him speechless.

'No, just a small square of grass, with a tree. It does not make for much of a painting. How are your studies going?' she asked quickly. 'The law must be such a fascinating subject.'

'You would think so. But I am required to commit to memory the detail of many thousands of cases, and my poor head is struggling. It is all too easily distracted, I fear.'

The self-deprecation was endearing. *Perhaps he has a sense of humour after all*, she said to herself. 'Which cases do you find most interesting?'

'I regret to admit that it is the serious offences I find intriguing.'

'For example?'

'I have been studying cases of murder and manslaughter. What could bring a man to commit such crimes?'

'I do not think anyone in their right mind could kill another, so it follows that they must be out of their minds to do so. I cannot believe that anyone is born evil.'

'You would change your views if you met some of the villains in Newgate. Believe me, the gallows is too good for many of them.'

'Pray heaven I never have to do so.' She had read terrifying accounts of the notorious prison, and the ghoulish crowds that gathered to watch hangings. 'But is killing a man really a just punishment, if he committed the crime when not of sane mind?'

'Everyone has choices. That is what I believe. The poor can choose to better themselves by hard work, but the wicked and immoral are a curse on society, and we are better off without them.'

'Well said,' William interjected. 'And that is why you are learning to be a lawyer, is it not, Charlie, so you can teach them a lesson?' Anna could scarcely believe her ears. William, the thief, pontificating about upholding the law? She wished she could expose him then and there but had to content herself with a glare, to which he returned an insouciant smile.

After tea, Joseph and William excused themselves, citing pressures of work. Lizzie was sent to her studies and Sarah invented some urgent business with Cook. They were alone. Anna wished she could be anywhere else but here, but one of his long spindly legs was thrust out across the rug in front of her, like a barrier preventing her escape.

'Dearest Anna, I have so enjoyed our little talks,' he whispered. 'You are an intelligent and spirited young woman, and I find this most attractive.' As he took her hand and leaned towards her, she could smell his slightly rancid breath. 'My regard for you has grown and, if I am not mistaken, I believe you may feel the same?'

She looked into his face, trying to read his expression, trying to convince herself. *If he genuinely loves me then, perhaps, my love for him could grow in time?* But there was something wrong: although his lips were smiling, his eyes were cold. It was as though he were embarking upon a business transaction. In that moment, she knew that she must listen to her own heart, and what her answer must be.

What took place next was a total surprise. His hand began to shake and he seemed to falter. There was a tense silence as he looked away to the window and turned back again. He took a deep breath. 'Will you come to dine at Ludgate Hill next week?' he said.

Relief swept over her like the surf on the seashore. His last-minute nerves – or was it cowardice – had reprieved her. Or perhaps he'd realised the truth: that neither of them loved the other. Only by biting her lip until it was almost painful did she manage to stop herself from laughing out loud.

'Thank you, that would be delightful,' she replied, crossing her fingers behind her back.

'Well?' Aunt Sarah whispered, once Charles had gone.

'We had a very pleasant time,' Anna said. 'He has invited me to dinner at Ludgate Hill next week.' She watched her aunt's face deflate and then brighten once more. *How desperate she is to see me settled. She has given her word to Father and won't rest until she has done so.*

❧❧❧

Aunt Sarah was all of a flutter. Augusta Hinchliffe had sent a note to inform her that the portraitist Mr Gainsborough would be travelling to London from his home in Bath for a few days, and would be available to see prospective customers at his painting room in Pall Mall.

'Mr Sadler has agreed to the notion, and we have made an appointment for tomorrow morning,' she declared at breakfast. 'It is only sensible to be prepared for when Mr Sadler is elected Upper Bailiff, don't you think?'

Anna had heard and read so much about the man – definitely the up-and-coming artist of fashionable society. Although he made his living from portraits he was said to enjoy painting landscapes more, and certainly his trees and plants – often lightly sketched – were wonderfully lifelike. If only she too could meet Mr Gainsborough!

After breakfast, she pleaded her case to Aunt Sarah.

'Mr Gainsborough is an excellent choice. He is sure to do justice to Uncle Joseph's anticipated new status.'

'You know his work?'

'Know it? I adore it, Aunt Sarah. His landscapes and rural backgrounds are wonderful. I'd give anything to meet the man.'

Sarah smiled fondly at her niece. 'Perhaps when you and Charles are married, you could commission him yourselves?'

'What a splendid notion,' Anna said, seizing her moment.

'In that case, might this present a good opportunity to make his acquaintance in advance?'

Her aunt thought for a moment. 'I don't suppose that would do any harm. I will ask your uncle. If he agrees, you may come as my companion.'

The houses here in the West End were so much grander than any that Anna had previously entered. The carriage drew up outside an imposing red-brick mansion and she began to marvel that any artist – however famous – could earn enough to afford such a residence.

However, Mr Gainsborough's lodgings turned out to be but a small part of the building – just two rooms on the ground floor. He appeared to have no servant and opened the door himself: a tall, fine-looking man in his mid-thirties, Anna guessed, with a good head of dark hair, a long nose and full lips that seemed to give him a permanently amused expression.

They were ushered into a large room smelling strongly of oil and turpentine, almost empty save for a chaise longue, a table and a few chairs. To one side was another table covered in brushes and bladders of paint, various bottles and jars, a pestle and mortar and what Anna was pleased to recognise as a mahlstick, used to steady the painter's wrist when working in detail. Standing on the floor was a small wooden mannequin dressed as a child, and a tall easel holding a large canvas concealed with a cloth.

After the introductions they were invited to take their

seats and Mr Gainsborough disappeared into a rear room, returning with a notebook and a set of papers.

'And so, how can I help you today?'

Uncle Joseph explained the reason for the commission.

'What an honour, Mr Sadler, I am delighted,' Mr Gainsborough said. 'My family were in the same trade, in a small way. My father was a weaver of woollens.'

They chatted about the trials of the textile markets for a few moments before getting down to business. Mr Gainsborough explained the types of portrait he could offer: the most economical would be a single figure pictured from waist upwards, with plain background and no hands, ranging up to the most expensive, a full-length group or pair with landscape background, extra for animals.

He took notes and answered a few questions before handing over the set of papers. 'These contain illustrations of each type of portrait and examples of the costs. Please feel free to write to me at any time with any further queries. I should require up to six sittings, depending on the composition you choose, which can take place here or at Bath, whichever is the most convenient.'

A moment of silence fell, in which Anna desperately wished to ask him about the painting on the easel, but was afraid it might be impolite. Fortunately Uncle Joseph seemed oblivious to such sensitivities. 'May we see your latest work?' he asked.

Mr Gainsborough hesitated for a second and then went to the easel, pulling off the cloth with a flourish. 'It is unfinished, as I am sure you will appreciate,' he said.

It was an almost full-length portrait of a handsome gentleman in a pale pink silk jacket leaning proudly against a rock, with a classical landscape in the distance. The figure was striking enough, but it was the foliage in the foreground, particularly the ivy growing across the rock, that caught Anna's eye.

'It is marvellous, sir,' she said quietly. 'I have long held your portraiture in the highest regard. But I have to confess that it is your depictions of landscapes and nature that I most admire.'

Mr Gainsborough, so stiff and formal during the earlier discussion, seemed suddenly to become animated. 'I am happy to hear this, madam, for it is that which I most enjoy painting. Nature is my recreation. I find it a relaxation from the disciplined focus required for depicting the variations of the human face and form.'

'This man has a very fine face, however. May we enquire who he is?' Joseph asked.

'It is Joshua Grigby, a lawyer at Gray's Inn,' he said. 'His family is from my own beloved county of Suffolk, where I learned my love of landscape and nature.'

'You are from Suffolk!' Sarah exclaimed. 'My niece is also lately come to the city from that same place.'

'From a small village near Halesworth,' Anna added. 'I too have learned my love of painting from nature in the countryside around my home.'

'And I from Ipswich, although I was born in the south, at Sudbury. And you are an artist too? What a happy coincidence.'

'I would hardly call myself an artist, sir,' she replied, blushing deep crimson. 'Just one who loves to sketch and paint.'

'And that is what you must do, as often as you can.' His

expression became thoughtful. 'It is possible to learn techniques by watching others, but one's own eyes and hands
are the most important teachers. Nothing can replace the
exercise of observation and constant practice.'

Anna longed to continue the conversation but Aunt
Sarah was fidgeting at her side. 'This has been most
delightful but we must not keep you, Mr Gainsborough,'
she said. 'We thank you for your time.'

'It has been my pleasure,' he said, and then added to
Anna, 'They are planning a new Society of the Arts, have
you heard? It will be lodged just along the road from here.
Perhaps you will be the first lady to display your work.'

'Do not tease me, sir.' He laughed with her, but his eyes
were serious.

'I have met many fine women artists,' he said. 'There is
no reason why they should not have their work viewed in
public too.'

As they left the building, Anna felt as though she was
walking on air.

❦

That evening, still buzzing with excitement, she took up
her pen. Henri would understand her excitement.

> *Dear Henri,*
>
> *Thank you for your letter. I am thrilled to learn that
> you are nearly ready to weave my design and you know
> that I would return to see it for myself, if only that
> were possible.*
>
> *Today I met the great artist Gainsborough. Imagine!*

I admire his work tremendously. Anyway, your kind interest in my drawing has piqued my own curiosity about fabric design and I have already ordered a new, larger sketchbook to start on my next designs! But I need to learn more about weaving – perhaps you will teach me?

    Please write again soon. With my very best wishes,
    A

16

If ye should inadvertently cause offence, let your tongue be dipped in oil, never in vinegar; and rather endeavour to mollify, than irritate the wound, and avoid anger as much as possible. By mildness and good manners, the most intractable may be qualify'd, and the most exasperated appeased.

– Advice for apprentices and journeymen
OR A sure guide to gain both esteem and an estate

As they approached the prison, along Newgate Street, it soon became clear that this was no ordinary Monday morning. Church bells were tolling and a great crowd, even larger than at the demonstration a few weeks ago, had gathered outside the prison gates, making their route impassable.

It seemed to Henri that the whole of London had taken to the streets: men, women and children all primped and vested in their Sunday best as though they were off to church and then for a pleasant picnic in the park, or perhaps a trip to the pleasure gardens.

'*Grand Dieu*,' M. Lavalle said, his face grim. 'It's an execution.'

The condemned man emerged at the top of the steps,

prompting an excited roar from the crowd, part appreciation and part denunciation. Despite the chains binding him at hand and foot, the prisoner was coiffed and dressed like a dandy. He raised his arms as best he could and smiled at the assembled masses, for all the world like a king acknowledging his subjects.

Then, to a chorus of ugly jeers and crude catcalls, he was led down the steps, hauled onto a rackety old horse cart and forcibly mounted onto a long wooden box which, Henri now realised with a shudder, was the coffin in which the man's body would later be interred.

But the man seemed barely to notice, laughing and joking with the Guards and managing, most of the time, to dodge the missiles of rotting fruit and excrement. As the cart set off, surrounded by soldiers armed with pistols and swords, the crowd swarmed in its wake.

'How far is the scaffold?' Henri asked a grizzled old man beside him.

''Tis but two miles to Tyburn. But by the time they've stopped at every tavern on the route it'll take 'em three hours and they'll have bought him so many pints he'll be dead drunk when he hangs. Which is more than the bastard deserves.'

'What crime has he committed?'

'They say he murdered a woman, though he denies it. She was a tart by all accounts, but no one deserves to die like that.'

'Why do they treat such a sinner to beer?'

'It's the spectacle they come for,' the man replied. 'They want to see him piss in his breeches.'

'From fear?'

'Nah. When he's been hanging for a while, it shows he's finally dead,' was the terse reply.

Henri watched the baying crowd, feeling dizzy and bilious. No matter how evil the crime, how could humans inflict such vile punishments on their fellow men? And what if the man was innocent? He could not bear to imagine that his friend might have to suffer the same terrible journey and undignified death.

As the crowd departed with the procession, he and M. Lavalle were able to move towards the prison gates. Even before they reached the steps they could hear the angry clamour of caged souls. It seemed to Henri that they were about to enter the gates of hell – only this was on earth, but two miles from his home and only a few hundred yards from the most beautiful building he had ever seen. M. Lavalle had told him it was St Paul's Cathedral.

'We might pray there afterwards,' he'd said.

After handing over a sixpence in 'fees', they were led by a rotund and red-faced warder along several corridors towards the cells. The stench and the racket were almost overwhelming. M. Lavalle handed Henri a handkerchief. 'Hold this to your nose, lad,' he said. 'Vapours and diseases are rife in this place.'

The warder unlocked a heavy metal door and they were ushered into the cell. It was a large stone room, lit only by two small barred windows high in the walls. At first, in the gloom, they could barely make out anything, but as their eyes became accustomed they could see that the room contained thirty or more men, all of them chained to the wall and most of them naked, covered only in their own muck. All appeared to be equally starving and desperate, clanking their chains and calling out for food, water, tobacco and gin. Picking their way between them, they found Guy curled up in silent despair on the filthy floor.

Henri shook his shoulder. 'It's Monsieur Lavalle and me. We've come to help you.'

Guy turned his head, his eyes bright in the dirt of his face. 'Leave me be,' he groaned. 'There's nothing to be done.'

'We've brought you food.'

The sight of the bundle that M. Lavalle produced from inside his jacket aroused an instant reaction from the other prisoners, who strained forwards against their shackles, bellowing even more menacingly than before. Guy grabbed the parcel, tore it open and began to stuff the bread and cheese into his mouth in a ravenous frenzy. When he'd swallowed the last morsel and checked for crumbs, he grabbed the bottle of porter from Henri's hand, pulled out the cork with his teeth, and glugged it down in four long swigs, pausing only for a sharp breath between each gulp. He concluded with a raucous belch that brought cheers from his fellow inmates.

'Where are your clothes?' M. Lavalle asked.

'If you can't pay when you arrive, they take your clothes instead,' Guy said, slumping back to the ground. 'They're vultures. If you can't pay, you get nothing, no food, no drink, nothing. But who cares? I am going to die anyway, here or on the scaffold.'

'We have brought money for bail. You could be out of here tomorrow.'

Guy shook his head. 'My mother's already offered. They won't take it.'

'We shall try, at least. What are you charged with?'

'Causing affray, theft, damage to property, accomplice to murder. Every bloody sin under the sun, they've nailed it on me.'

'Is there no one among your group who would testify to your innocence?'

'It's every man for himself. Who cares about a penniless Frenchie anyway?'

Guy's face was an expression of misery so abject that it would remain seared in Henri's memory for the rest of his life.

'I thank you for your visit and the food, friends,' he said at last. 'I am sorry for the harsh words I have spoken lately. I've been a fool and deserve to die a fool's death. Look after my mother for me.'

With that, he slid to the floor and curled up once more, tucking his knees to his forehead, with an arm over his head to shut out the world. M. Lavalle began to move towards the door, but Henri found himself fixed to the spot, reluctant to leave.

'We'll get you out of here, I promise,' he whispered.

The two men silently retraced the gloomy corridors and inquired at the gates as to who they needed to see about bail. The judge, they were told, but he was not available. When they persisted, refusing to leave until they could speak to someone, they were ushered into a chaotic office piled high with papers and ledgers and told to wait.

Half an hour passed, and then another, and still no one

arrived. At last a whey-faced clerk put his head around the door and, apparently surprised to see them, asked what they were doing there, and who they were waiting for.

A further twenty minutes passed before he returned.

'There's no bail for Guy Lemaitre,' he said. 'The judge has already turned it down.'

'But can we not appeal?' M. Lavalle said.

The man held up his palms.

'Nothing I can do, guv'nor,' he said. 'That's the decision of the court.'

As they passed through the prison gates out into the blessed sweetness of fresh air, the sunshine and birdsong seemed to mock them. They retraced their steps along Newgate Street, lost in their own thoughts. By tacit understanding, they found themselves climbing the grand stone steps of the cathedral, stepping beneath the portico and entering through tall wooden doors into the hushed silence of its enormous interior.

M. Lavalle moved to the nearest pew and slipped to his knees, bending his head in prayer, but Henri remained standing, almost forgetting to breathe, as he marvelled at the majesty of the interior, the intricacy of the carving on the marble walls, and the square pillars which soared up to multiple domes brilliantly depicting biblical scenes in gold, silver and every colour in the rainbow.

The very beauty of the place brought tears to his eyes and he began to feel light-headed, as though he had entered another world. His head started to spin, and then he heard his own voice, a disembodied bellow that reverberated in the silence of the vast space: *'Pour l'amour du ciel, je vous en prie, sauvez mon ami!'*

M. Lavalle was with him now, a warm arm about his shoulders, whispering, 'Hush, hush, boy, come with me.' He found himself being led out of the building to a bench in the bright sunlight where the old man sat quietly by his side, waiting for his sobs to subside.

The visit to Newgate left Henri with a deep and persistent anger in his belly. He had long since abandoned his faith in God but now he prayed each night. Or rather, these were not so much prayers as furious railings against the injustice of the world and the cruelty of the punishment being meted out to an innocent young man. Guy's only failing was in wanting to make the world a fairer place. Perhaps he'd been hot-headed and unwise, but his motives were pure enough, so why was God treating him so shamefully?

M. Lavalle tried to reassure him that, behind the scenes, everything was being done to secure Guy's release. The French church organised a daily rota of visitors taking food and drink, and letters were written to the court tendering a considerably larger amount of bail than M. Lavalle had been able to offer.

Discreet enquiries were made among other journeymen who'd taken part in the protest that night, but no one would admit to witnessing the moment when the weaver's wife was threatened. Most of them, terrified of being in any way associated with the crime, denied being anywhere near.

Eventually an Irishman was found who claimed to be certain that Guy had not been involved, because he had seen him in The Dolphin at around the time of the raid. Everyone's hopes were lifted when the man agreed to testify in Guy's defence, but when they brought a lawyer to talk to him he had vanished, taking his wife and children with him, never to be seen again.

Weeks passed and each time Henri visited the prison Guy seemed thinner and more despairing. At last they learned that a date for the trial had been set for January.

There was nothing to do but wait.

The nights drew in, the weather became colder and occasional flurries of snow darkened the sky. Henri overheard Mariette and the cook making preparations for Christmas, discussing the cost of buying a whole goose and deciding that it was too expensive. 'Half of it's fat, anyway,' Cook grumbled. They would make do with beef. They spent the whole morning working together on a large plum cake, soused liberally with brandy so that it would last until Epiphany.

This was usually one of his favourite times of the year, when feasts were planned, friends gathered and the house was decorated with greenery collected from the woods and fields beyond Bethnal Green. It was a time when he felt that he truly belonged in this adopted land, a country in which he and his fellow Protestants had no fear of reprisals should they wish to worship freely, and in which he had his adopted family around him.

But this year Henri had little heart for such celebrations. Visions of Guy, despairing in the hell of the prison, and the sounds of the crowd baying for the murderer's blood crowded his mind each night as he waited for sleep. Even in this seemingly benign country of England, he was now so painfully aware that there were forces to be afraid of.

The only way of quelling his anxiety was through intense application to work, specifically to his master piece. Fearing the horrors of his own thoughts, he found himself toiling through the night to finalise the point-paper translation of Anna's design, and then devising the complicated organisation of the components of the loom, the range of colours needed for warp and weft, and the arrangement of lashes and simples that would bring the colours to the front of the fabric. The weave was so demanding that he made several false starts with the set-up, but finally he was able to begin weaving with reasonable confidence that the finished product would do justice to Anna's artistry.

He loved this moment, when the shuttle made its initial passes through the warp, and the first few inches of cloth with the lines of the design began gradually to emerge, weft thread by weft thread. The work was painfully slow because the design required so many changes of the treadles at his feet and of the shuttles introducing each new weft colour. The drawboy, sleepy and sluggish in the cold, made frequent mistakes, pulling the lashes in the wrong order.

It was a more complex design than Henri had ever tackled, and he found himself exhausted by the need for constant concentration to avoid making costly errors. With each inch of fabric woven the pressure for accuracy grew greater. The further into the weave, should a mistake later be discovered, the more hours of work might be lost, and precious bobbins of dyed and twisted silk yarn wasted.

As the elegant curves and images of Anna's sketch began to emerge into woven fabric, he felt her presence, as if looking over his shoulder, approving. Sometimes he found himself talking to her in his head: *Is this green right, do you think? Or should it be paler?* or *The curve is so shallow here, I cannot conceal the steps entirely. Will you forgive me?*

If he should leave the loom for a while, perhaps to take a meal, on returning his heart would leap with the thrill of seeing afresh how the design was unfolding, how the network of curled stems was taking shape, supporting those delicately furled leaves and natural-looking blooms. When, at a foot and a half in, he reached the point where the tiny beetle emerged into the weave, he found himself close to tears, his chest bursting with a tender joy.

He worked long hours each day, often perforce by candle-light at this darkest time of the year, only giving up if a warp thread broke that could not be recovered in the dim light of a candle or, more often, when the weary drawboy finally fell asleep over his lashes.

He had not replied to Anna's letter, for he had no idea what to say. Much as he yearned for her presence and longed to see her again, the tough words of his mother and the events of the past weeks had brought everything into a different perspective, harsh-lit by his friend's adversity. He had returned to the prison twice since that first visit, taking food and clothing. The church elders had offered to pay for him to have a single cell, but Guy had refused. 'How could I bear the silence of my own company,' he said, 'when all I have to contemplate is a life of misery? They are villains, this lot, but they are companions all the same.'

It could just as easily have been me in that prison, had I not the support and guidance of a good and generous master, Henri thought to himself. His own life and Guy's had been so similar, both of them having endured terrible loss and hardship before finding themselves in the world of silk by pure good fortune, and both having worked hard to come from nothing to become skilled craftspeople. How could he turn his back on the good fortune which had befallen him, by turning down his master's remarkable offer?

Nothing had been said since that first conversation. As December was usually a slow time for new commissions M. Lavalle was rarely in his office and frequently out on external duties: at the church, where they were preparing, as usual, to help the needy at Christmas, and at the Weavers' Company, where they were making ready for the intake of silk masters in the New Year. Mariette was her usual friendly self, not overly flirtatious and apparently unaware of her father's intervention.

Two weeks before Christmas, Henri completed his master piece.

'It is a triumph,' M. Lavalle said, clapping him several times on the back. 'You have fulfilled my highest expectations, lad. I cannot imagine any circumstances under which you will not be accepted by the Company in January. Welcome, Master Vendôme.'

As the old man scrutinised the weave, using his small magnifying glass, the colours and shapes glittered and glinted in the firelight, giving an appearance that the stems and flowers were actually stirring in a gentle breeze. Seeing the silk through his master's eyes for the first time, Henri realised that it was indeed beautiful, and the naturalism of the lines extraordinary.

'This is of exceptional quality, Henri,' M. Lavalle said. 'The technical complexity is utterly unlike anything I have ever seen, even from the great designer-weavers of the old days, Leman and the rest. And yet it has a wonderfully contemporary look. It'll be snapped up by fashionable ladies and become the next big thing, I'll be bound.' He laughed. 'You'll be weaving nothing but yards of this very design for the next few months. You might become sick of the sight of it, but you will certainly make a good start on your fortune.'

Henri felt the blood rushing to his cheeks. His master's praise was rarely so fulsome.

M. Lavalle put down the silk and took up his clay pipe, charged it, lit it and took a long draw. 'You have a great future ahead of you, my son, if that is what I may call you?'

He means son-in-law, Henri thought to himself. It felt comforting, as though, after all, the mantle could sit quite easily about his shoulders. 'I am proud that you should regard me as such,' he said.

'Daughter, come and see what our clever boy has produced,' M. Lavalle called. 'And bring a new bottle of port and three glasses so that we can celebrate.'

Mariette held the silk to the light. 'Oh . . . my . . .

goodness,' she whispered on an indrawn breath. '*You* wove this?'

Before he knew it she had wrapped her arms about him, in a surprisingly powerful embrace. He could feel the warmth of her body against his and her heart beating against his chest. In the joy of the moment he wondered whether he could, in fact, fall in love with the girl.

Loosening her hold at last, she turned to pick up the silk, examining the design and discovering, with a delighted laugh, the tiny beetle clinging to the curled leaf. She unfurled the length and wrapped it around her waist, like a skirt, doing a slow flirtatious twirl before the two men, wriggling her hips and fluttering her eyelashes, laughing all the while.

'I must have a dress of it, Papa. For my first ball gown.'

'We'll have to see,' he muttered.

'And you shall be my dancing partner, Henri.'

She took hold of his hand and then, humming the tune of a sprightly dance, began to skip around the room, pulling him along with her. M. Lavalle watched from his chair, beaming with approval and clapping out the rhythm as the couple made their way across the parlour and back again. Henri felt clumsy and ungainly, but was drawn along by the sheer elation of Mariette's enjoyment and his own relief at finally having completed what was surely the most important piece of work in his life.

As they danced, the fire blazing cheerfully, its light glinting off the panelling, and the heat of the port travelling through his veins, his thoughts turned to Guy. The desperate situation faced by his friend only served to emphasise his own good fortune. Fate could be so capricious, one's hold on life so fragile. But, at least for the moment, this was his: his world, his place, his people and, in time, he would wed Mariette. They loved him, he loved them. This was where he belonged.

How could he have imagined otherwise?

There was no alternative but to acknowledge the truth that had lurked in his heart like a monster: there was no future in his friendship with Anna. He'd hoped that, by ignoring it, this truth might somehow go away, but now, he knew, the issue must be settled, sooner rather than later. It was only fair to the girl, and he needed to move on, to accept the future that had been planned for him.

Later that evening he took up his quill and, with a profound sadness, began to write.

Dear Anna,

The work is nearly finished and I write to thank you again. The fabric looks well and my master is pleased. But of the matter you ask me I cannot help you more. I am sorry. You are an artist of good talent and I wish you sucess, but I know that we must not meet again.

H

17

*No lady should drink wine at dinner. Even if her head is strong
enough to bear it, she will find her cheeks, soon after the indulgence, flushed, hot, and uncomfortable; and if the room is warm,
and the dinner a long one, she will probably pay the penalty of
her folly, by having a headache all the evening.*

— The Lady's Book of Manners

The letter arrived with the rest of the family's mail, brought
by Betty to the breakfast table. As she recognised the writing
Anna felt a knot of excitement growing in her chest, almost
stopping her breath.

'Who is it from?' Aunt Sarah enquired, peering across
the table.

'A friend from home,' she lied.

'Not bad news, I hope? Here, take the letter knife.'

'Thank you, Aunt, but I will open it later. I do not wish
to disturb my delicious breakfast.'

Her appetite had vanished, and she struggled to eat the
slice of meat pie already on her plate. At last the meal was
over and she ran to her room with Lizzie hot on her heels.

'Later, Cousin,' Anna said, turning her away. 'You must
allow me my privacy.'

She tore open the letter, and at first she could not understand what it said. *We must not meet again.* As the meaning became clear, a wave of nausea coursed through her body.

'No!' she gasped, throwing her face into the bolster to muffle her sobs. *Why would he write such a thing? There must have been a terrible misunderstanding.*

After a while she sat up and read the few lines over and over again, barely able to believe what she was seeing. What could she possibly have done to deserve such a final, terrible rejection? In her mind, she interrogated every moment that she could remember of their few meetings: at the church, at Miss Charlotte's and then at Wood Street.

She recalled the moment at the bottom of the weaving loft ladder and his words: *Please let us find a way.* Surely she cannot have imagined the powerful feelings she had believed to be so utterly mutual at that moment? Her mind veered wildly, visualising possible scenarios. Had Aunt Sarah forced Charlotte into admitting who they had visited that afternoon? Had she then gone to see Henri to warn him off? No, she felt sure that Miss Charlotte would never betray her like that. And Aunt Sarah deigning to visit a French weaver at his house? Very unlikely.

She went to the window and peered down into the square, to the spot where she had encountered Henri and Guy sitting on the wall beneath the trees; where she had once seen his figure approaching the house, delivering his first letter. How long ago it seemed.

A few flakes of early snow were falling from a leaden sky and people were scurrying about their business with cloaks and shawls wrapped tightly around heads and shoulders. She turned and picked up the letter again, reading its final phrase: *I know that we must not meet again.*

'*Must* not,' she spoke out loud. Now, she understood: *It is not what he wants, nor I. He has been told, perhaps by M. Lavalle, that our friendship is unwise, or inappropriate.* Just as she knew, deep in her own heart, the social barriers were just too high to breach. *It was a stupid fantasy*, she said to herself. *And he is just being practical. Perhaps it is for the best.*

But none of this sensible reasoning could ease the desolation in her heart. Several times she heard Lizzie's feet on the stair and sent her away, claiming a headache. At lunchtime, Betty arrived with a bowl of broth and some bread, which was welcome. Worn out with weeping, Anna slept for most of the afternoon, and took supper in her room. When Betty came to take away the dishes, she brought a message from Aunt Sarah.

Dearest Niece, she wrote. *I hope you are feeling better? You will not have forgotten, I am sure, that you are bidden to Ludgate Hill tomorrow evening, for dinner?*

She *had* forgotten, and the reminder was unwelcome. Seeing Charlie again was the very last thing on earth she wanted. But she could not maintain the pretence of illness for another full day; she would have to pull herself together, paste on a smile, and face the world once more.

Halfway through dinner the following evening Anna discovered, rather to her surprise, that she was quite enjoying herself. There were others at the table – a friend of Susannah's with her parents, and another mercer and his wife. She'd accepted a glass of claret and the conversation had been lively. Charlie asked how her art was going, and she'd told him about meeting Mr Gainsborough.

'Charming fellow, isn't he?' Charlie exclaimed. 'Met him in Bath when he came to look at Pa. What a genius with faces.'

'And landscapes,' Anna added, after which they had a discussion about which was the more demanding for an artist, portraiture or nature, in which several other guests took part. It was the liveliest and most interesting social interaction she'd enjoyed so far in the city.

After dinner, the ladies withdrew and gossiped about fashion and the latest romances of their friends, which bored her into silence, but the gentlemen soon arrived and Susannah was encouraged to play the harpsichord.

'She is very talented, your sister,' she whispered to Charles, seated beside her.

'Indeed. My mother was a fine singer, I'm told, but alas this musical inheritance seems to have passed me by.'

'I am sure you have other talents,' she replied, turning back to the music. A few moments later she felt his hand touch hers, resting on the arm of the chair. His long fingers took her own, and squeezed them gently. She felt her face flushing – *perhaps The Lady's Book of Manners was correct about taking too much wine at dinner,* she thought to herself – and wondered what to do next.

Susannah stopped playing, and Charlie removed his hand to applaud. But clearly he seemed to have recovered his nerve and she feared what might follow were they to find themselves alone. But she still had no idea how to respond.

The moment arrived: the other guests went to take their

leave, and the rest of the family followed into the hallway to bid them farewell. She and Charles were left in the drawing room, standing together at the fireplace.

'Dearest Anna,' he began, taking her hand and gripping it firmly in his own rather sweaty palm. 'You probably know what my feelings are towards you?'

She nodded, her head in a spin. 'I believe I do, sir.'

'And you probably understood my intention when I came to tea at Spital Square last week? I regret that I was much daunted by the consequence of the moment, but now I am determined.' He took a deep breath and blurted, in a rush, 'Would you do me the honour of becoming my wife?'

There it was, the question she'd been dreading. If she refused him, the Hinchliffes would be insulted and her aunt and uncle infuriated. She looked up at the face that had now become so familiar. This time, his eyes were warm, lit by a fond smile, the long nose and Adam's apple far less obtrusive. The atmosphere of this room, so comfortably furnished and lit with the warm glow of firelight, was seductive. She had enjoyed his company this evening. Perhaps, given time, they could develop a comfortable friendship, even love of a kind.

She took a deep breath and began her reply, not even knowing what it would be. 'Dearest Charles,' she said. 'It is I who is honoured. But you know, do you not, that I am a penniless vicar's daughter? I could bring no wealth or property to this union.'

'I am fully apprised of your situation, but it makes no difference to my feelings for you.' He took her hand to his lips, and held it there.

'You will know, then, that my father has lately been

widowed,' she said. 'And, as he is so far away, you will have to write to him.'

'Should I not ask your uncle?'

'I think my father should be the one to agree. I am quite certain he would be most delighted to give his permission. But could you give me leave to tell him myself first? I shall be going home for Christmas. Would you mind terribly if we waited until my return before announcing the happy news?'

She found herself in his arms, his head bent so that his cheek touched hers, his breath on her neck. It was not an unpleasant feeling, comforting in a way.

'My dearest girl, you have made me the happiest man in the world,' he whispered. 'Of course we can wait for your father. Until then, it will be our little secret.'

The approaching Mercers' Company dinner brought a palpable air of tension to the Sadler household. As well as being the annual event at which the positions of high office were decided, it was also an opportunity for Company members to display their most sumptuous fabrics – in the garments worn by themselves and their wives. Sarah had commissioned a new dressmaker for her gown, but each time she returned from one of her fitting sessions she appeared more and more dissatisfied.

'Why did you not use Miss Charlotte, as usual?' Lizzie asked innocently. What she didn't know was that Anna had overheard her aunt saying that she wouldn't use her again because she was 'unreliable', and ever since had felt a bitter shame for having inadvertently caused her friend to lose a valued customer.

'I almost wish I had indeed done so, my dear,' Aunt Sarah grumbled. 'This new one doesn't seem to have the skills or the patience. I am starting to wonder whether my gown will ever be ready in time.'

At last the great day dawned, and Aunt Sarah spent most of the afternoon having her nails manicured, her high wig dressed and lavish make-up applied. At last the preparation was finished and the family gathered to admire. The new outfit – in shades of turquoise blue – was certainly eye-catching, Anna thought, if a little unsubtle. Joseph appeared in a brightly patterned brocade waistcoat and long coat in the latest style, looking tightly buttoned and uncomfortable.

'I do hope Pa gets voted in as Upper Bailiff,' William muttered, after they had departed. 'He'll be like a bear with a sore head if they choose someone else.'

Lizzie regarded him with alarm. 'It's already been agreed, hasn't it?'

'These things are never certain till they're signed and sealed,' he replied mysteriously.

Later, after Lizzie had excused herself from the table, Anna found herself alone with him. 'What did you mean about things not being certain for Uncle?' she asked.

'There is always so much jockeying for position in these organisations,' he said. 'You have to play the game, and I am not sure whether Pa has studied the rule book sufficiently.'

'Let's keep our fingers crossed then.' They had barely exchanged ten words since the night they had met in the office, but this little conversation emboldened her. 'How are things with you, William?'

'Things?' he said, pouring himself another glass of claret and offering her one. She gladly accepted.

'I mean, are you now free of those threats you spoke of? I was worried for you.'

'Thank you for your concern, Coz,' he said. 'Let me assure you that all is well.'

'Have you stopped . . . I mean, have you mended your ways? And have you paid back the money you stole from the business yet?'

'Do you take me for an idiot?' he barked, his expression sharp, defiant.

He took a large gulp from his glass and stared into it as if studying its colour before looking up and adding in a more conciliatory tone, 'I do appreciate your continued silence, of course.'

'I may call in the favour sometime.'

'A tryst with lover boy Charles, is it, that you want cover for?'

She was about to laugh but then remembered that Charles was his friend, so she smothered it.

'It'll be a good match, you know. He likes the ponies a little too much and he's had a bit of trouble with unpaid debts recently, but who am I to judge? Still, he's extremely well connected with the great and good, and I'm sure he will become very wealthy, in time. What about you?'

'Me?'

'I heard a little rumour that he's going to propose. Will you accept him?'

The directness of the question caught her off guard. 'He is certainly very charming and I thank you for your advice.'

William finished his wine, stood up and bowed. 'Always at your service, madam.'

They wished each other goodnight.

Later she woke to hear the carriage arrive, followed by doors banging and raised voices in the room below, but fell asleep again and thought nothing more of it. Her aunt and uncle were safely home, at least.

Next morning, Betty told them that Joseph and William had already taken breakfast and were now in a meeting, not to be disturbed. Aunt Sarah was still in bed, feeling poorly.

'I expect she took too much brandy,' Lizzie sniggered.

Two hours later, Anna encountered Betty preparing warmed milk and biscuits for her aunt. 'Let me take them up,' she said. 'I will try to discover what ails her.'

Her knock was met with a muffled moan and, when she entered the chamber, the shutters were still closed and the room fuggy with overnight air. In the gloom, the sight that beheld her was pitiful. Aunt Sarah's face, amid the huddle of bedclothes, was distorted with misery, her cheeks raw and her eyes reddened from weeping.

Anna put down the tray and sat beside the bed. 'Whatever has befallen you? Are you not well?'

The inquiry precipitated a fit of racking sobs. She took Sarah's hand and waited. After nursing her mother through many ailments and her final illness, she understood that simply by being there, as an undemanding presence, could provide comfort.

At last the sobs abated and Sarah fell back onto the pillow, exhausted. She accepted Anna's offer of warm milk and took a few sips.

'We are lost, my dear,' she sobbed. 'All is lost.'

'I do not understand your meaning, Aunt. Is it something that happened last evening?'

Her aunt nodded, and sobbed a little more.

'It is finished,' she said. 'Your uncle is not to be Upper Bailiff. He is utterly disgraced.'

'Disgraced? For what?' Anna's mind slipped back to the conversation about French silk. Surely it could not be that, after all these weeks?

The story emerged slowly, between Aunt Sarah's outbursts of desperate weeping and moments of allowing herself to be comforted. It seemed that on entering the Mercers' Hall Joseph had been handed a note. He put it into his pocket, unread, assuming that it was simply the confirmation that, after the dinner, he would be called to take his vows as Upper Bailiff. The dinner proceeded as expected but, when the time came, an entirely different name was called out; another rose to take the applause and receive the much-anticipated honours. All eyes were on Joseph and Sarah, of course, who were becoming more and more embarrassed and entirely unable to understand what was going on.

'I wished the floor would open up and swallow us whole,' Sarah said. 'Your poor dear uncle was so astonished and confused, he could not think what to do.'

Eventually, he stirred himself and strode out of the hall, followed by Sarah. 'Such a long, long walk, my dear, past all those sneering faces. My poor dear man died the death of a thousand insults last night. I fear for his sanity, I really do.'

'I assume that was what the note was about?'

Sarah nodded.

'What did it say?'

'It said . . .' She broke down again, unable to continue, waving a hand towards the dressing table. The sheet of notepaper – once crumpled and now smoothed out – was headed with the Mercers' Company crest and signed by the outgoing Upper Bailiff. Anna prised open the shutter so that she could read:

Dear Mr Sadler,

    In light of recently received reports that your company has once again been illegally importing French silks, presumably to evade paying the proper import tax, we regret to inform you that your bid to become Upper Bailiff is hereby revoked and, furthermore, that you will no longer be a member of the Administration Committee.

    It is also my sorry duty to inform you that the tax authorities have been alerted and will no doubt be in contact forthwith.

    If you avoid criminal charges on this matter, you may remain as a member of the Company but only on your solemn oath that you will henceforth abide strictly by the law and agree never again to bring the Company into disrepute.

The letter was shocking in its directness. If this was the payback for William's duplicity, for which her uncle had already taken the blame, why had it taken them so long to punish him? And why do it this way, humiliating him so publicly?

'Is this true?' Anna asked, feigning innocence. 'This accusation about the French silks?'

Her aunt, who was by now sitting up and nibbling on a biscuit, nodded dolefully. 'He says there was a bookkeeping error a few weeks ago, which unfortunately led to the tax remaining unaccounted for. It was a terrible shock at the time, but he went over the whole thing with the Administration Committee and they seemed to accept his apology. He cannot understand what this latest complaint is about.'

The sour smell of suspicion hung in the air. Everything was so complex, so murky. What if, despite his reassurance to her last night, William was still gambling? And what if, in his desperation, he had continued to cook the books, claiming to have paid the tax but actually creaming off the money to pay his gambling debts? If that was the case, it was little wonder that Joseph had been so utterly surprised by last night's debacle.

'What do you think will happen, Aunt?'

'Joseph and William are at this very moment trying to ascertain what could have possibly gone wrong, and after that they will have to contact the Company and the tax authorities to try to make amends.'

'What is this about criminal charges?'

'That is what terrifies me most, my dear. But Mr Sadler reassures me that if the money is paid in full, he will be able to avert such a threat.'

'Will there be much to pay?'

Sarah sighed. 'These things are not for us women to

know. Our lot is to wait and accept our fate.' She pulled her shawl more tightly around her shoulders, despite the fug in the room. 'You must leave me now, and send Betty up, so that I may ready myself to face the world. But please –' she took Anna's hand and pressed it urgently '– give me your word that you will not breathe a word of this to Lizzie. She adores her father and it would upset her so to learn that he is facing this trouble.'

Anna promised.

After the shock of his disgrace at the Mercers' dinner Joseph seemed to disappear from view, locking himself in the office to huddle over his desk both day and night, occasionally appearing in his best wig and waistcoat and bustling out, to return only late in the evening after everyone else was abed.

Sarah spent long hours in her chamber, rising pasty-faced in her nightgown for meals, and then pecking at her plate with the appetite of a sparrow. Christmas was almost upon them, but no puddings were being stirred, no goose hanging in the larder. A dark cloud had descended on the household and it seemed nothing could lift its oppressive gloom.

A few days after the debacle, a letter arrived at breakfast. Anna recognised the hand, but waited until she was alone in the dining room before opening it.

Dear Miss Butterfield, it read,
I regret to inform you that due to unforeseen circumstances it will not be possible to honour our agreement.

I would be grateful if, to avoid unnecessary embarrass-
ment, you would not make any future contact.
    With best regards,
    Charles Hinchliffe

She wanted to laugh out loud at the absurdity of it, the
language so stuffily formal. And then she became furious.
Just who did Charles Hinchliffe think he was, so high and
mighty, so viciously dismissive? He was no saint either, if
William was to be believed, with his gambling habit and
casual attitude towards his studies, both of which were no
doubt being funded by his wealthy father.

To be written off so heedlessly, not just by him but
apparently by the whole family, was not only hurtful but
depressingly reflective of the shallowness of London society,
where one is only of worth when one is useful to someone
else. The letter brought home the enormity of her uncle's
disgrace, the way it had cast a shadow over the whole family.

Her thoughts were interrupted by William, returning to
the dining room.

'Did I leave my . . . ?' he started, before noticing the
letter in her hand. 'Is it bad news?'

'It's from Charles. It seems his interest in me has suddenly
waned. I cannot imagine why,' she said with a wry smile.

'The bastard.' William sat down beside her. 'May I see?'
He took the letter and scanned it quickly. 'Christ,' he said,
thumping the table until the silverware clattered. 'I didn't
think they'd throw us off like this, so completely. They've
been friends of the family for years. And you, practically
engaged . . . how dare he impugn your honour like this?'
He put his head in his hands. 'Oh God! What have I done?'

'It's not *all* your fault, is it?' she said quietly.

'Had I owned up, we would have been paying off the customs duty week by week as Father promised the Company in the first place, and they wouldn't now be demanding such a large whack, not to mention the fine.'

'A fine, too?'

'Four hundred pounds.'

'That's an impossible sum. Wherever could you find that?'

He shook his head.

'And what happens if you can't pay it?'

'Bankruptcy, probably.'

The word felt like a slap. Anna knew what it meant, of course, but could hardly imagine it applying to Sadler & Son. 'What would happen then?'

'Unless we can pay off the debts by the start of January we'll have to sell the business.'

'And the house?'

'That, too. It's owned by the business.'

'But where would we – I mean you – live?'

He sighed. 'Where do other people live? We'd have to rent, I suppose. Get other jobs to pay for it.'

'Surely you have plenty of stock you could sell, to help pay off the debt?'

'I've tried that.'

'You tried what?'

'Selling the rest of the French silks to an out-of-town mercer. But someone recognised them and traced them back to us. It only made matters worse – more duties to pay and another fine. The only silk we have left is what we've had on the stocks for months, years even, before everyone went into mourning for the old king. No one wants it. Fashion is so bloody fickle.' He sighed again. 'It's such bad timing. Pa was about to bid for a commission to supply silk for the trousseau for the new queen.'

'There is to be a new queen? I hadn't heard.'

'No one has. It's just speculation. They won't let young George stay unmarried for long, mark my words. He has to have a male heir, remember. All the mercers in the city are poised to make their fortune when the wedding's announced.'

'Goodness. I wonder who he'll choose?'

'There's a rumour about a young German princess. But it doesn't really matter, just so long as we are ready to offer something sumptuous and gloriously fashionable. Which, of course, we won't be now.'

They fell into silence. He picked up Charles's letter and studied its few words again. 'I've made such a mess of everything. And you got caught up in it – your betrothal and everything.'

'Please do not trouble yourself about that, Cousin. I know he's your friend, but to be honest, I do not love him. And his views are so different from mine.'

'But he's such a good match. What will you do instead? Or do you have another beau in mind?'

'Please do not worry about me. I'll just go home and live a quiet life in the country.'

'Haste thee to a nunnery?'

'Not exactly.'

Having said it, she realised that her glib remark was the truth: she *was* desperate to get back to Suffolk, to see her father, and little Jane. Those familiar paths through the marshes, the sound of the sea. 'I didn't know you read Shakespeare.'

'We men have hidden depths.'

'Hidden so deep as to be invisible, much of the time.'

It was his turn to laugh. 'I'll miss your tart little comments, Coz. I've found them quite refreshing. A girl of your intelligence won't be happy in the country for long. And what about those plans to learn about silk design?'

'Oh, I dare say I will find someone to teach me,' she said, failing to convince herself. 'There's a thriving silk trade in Norwich, I'm told.'

'Come back and see us sometime, won't you?'

A girl of your intelligence won't be happy in the country for long. Anna pondered William's words with a growing sense of despondency, recalling how bored she had sometimes felt in the village, how energised by the prospect of leaving. What if he was right? And yet she had found little contentment or pleasure here in the city.

Was there *anywhere* that she would find long-term happiness?

18

*He that places his supreme delight in a tavern, and is uneasy
till he has drank away his senses, renders himself soon unfit for
everything else: frolick at night is followed with pains and
sickness in the morning, and then what was before the poison
is administered as the cure.*

*— Advice for apprentices and journeymen
OR A sure guide to gain both esteem and an estate*

Guy's trial was set for the first Monday of the New Year. It
was still bitterly cold and the snow that fell on New Year's
Day had compacted into ugly brown ice on the streets, making
it treacherous to venture outdoors. In the unheated weaving
loft, the boys' breath clouded the air and their fingers swiftly
became numbed, making it impossible to throw the shuttle
firmly, or feel for lost threads. They had to take frequent
breaks to warm themselves by the kitchen range.

On the day before the trial, Henri delivered his master
piece, carefully rolled and wrapped against the weather, to
the Weavers' Hall in Basinghall Street. An officious clerk
made him wait half an hour while producing a form on
which he was required to write his name, age and address,
and signature.

As he read the address the clerk's demeanour thawed. 'A good man, Monsieur Lavalle,' he said. 'And a fine weaver. Was he your master too?'

Henri nodded.

'We shall be most interested to see your piece,' the clerk said, smiling at last.

Henri left the building so warmed by this encouragement that he failed to notice until almost back at Wood Street that his jacket buttons were still undone and his hat and gloves still in his pocket.

M. Lavalle gave Henri time off to attend the trial. 'You may not be able to alter the course of justice but it will give the lad succour to see a friendly face. But have a care,' he added. 'You are not allowed to speak in the court, or they could arrest you for contempt.'

When he reached the courthouse there was such a crowd that Henri feared they might be waiting for another execution. On a noticeboard pinned outside, he found a list of all the trials taking place that day and, after much desperate scanning, spied what he sought: Guy's name was among a list of more than twenty, including even some women, all indicted for breaking and entering, damage to property, carrying a dangerous weapon and intent to murder at the house of a weaver named Thomas Poor. Every journeyman in the area, it seemed, had turned out to support their fellow weavers, and they were in an ugly mood.

The crush was so great it was impossible to reach the public gallery, so Henri waited in the corridor outside.

Proceedings were slow to start because every official pronouncement was met with angry jeers and chants of 'Justice for the innocent'. At last the court was silenced and, as the trial began, news passed in whispers through the crowd.

'It's John Valline that man Poor's talking about now. They called him a son of a whore, and threatened to break down the door, he says.'

'Is it Poor still talking?'

'He says they cut the cane and all the silk and the tackle, bent the reed double and twisted it like a worm.'

'He says they attacked him even though he'd paid the committee money . . .'

'Those bastards. They're saying Valline was riotous.'

John D'Oyle followed, facing the same charges. It seemed worse for him, because when Poor's wife took the witness box, she claimed that D'Oyle was among seven others who entered her bedchamber, and he threatened her with a pistol and a sword.

'A bitch of a whore, D'Oyle called her.'

'Sounds fair enough to me.'

There was a long hiatus.

'What's happening now?' Henri whispered. He could barely breathe for the anxiety, which felt as though ropes were binding his chest.

'It's Lemaitre,' the word came.

'He's my friend. Let me through,' Henri shouted, barging his way to the front of the packed public gallery. No one stopped him. At last he was able to see down onto the courtroom, and he watched in horror as Guy was manhandled into a wooden pen, called the 'dock', by two heavy-set guards at either side. Although now dressed in decent garments his friend was barely recognisable: deathly pale and thin as a skeleton.

The judge, wearing a long wig and heavy red cloak trimmed with fur, addressed Guy in a slow, sonorous tone: 'Guy Lemaitre, you are charged that on December tenth you did, with force and arms, feloniously break by force into the house of Thomas Poor, with intent to cut and destroy a certain quantity of silk on a loom, and also with intent to cut and destroy a loom, with other tackle used in the weaving trade. Furthermore that in this house you did, with others, cut and destroy a hundred yards of bombazine, the property of Thomas Horton, and were with others who threatened the life of a woman with a pistol. How do you plead?'

Guy gazed around the court with unfocused eyes. One of the guards shook his arm and the judge barked, 'Mr Lemaitre, you are required to answer the question. How do you plead?'

Guy's reply was barely audible. 'Not guilty, sir.'

The weaver Mr Poor came back into the witness box and gave his statements, much as before. Henri's heart lifted when he said, 'Apart from D'Oyle and Valline, who I knew by their voices, it was so dark that night it was impossible for me or anybody else to distinguish any man.'

'But you claim to know this man?'

'I do, sir,' Poor answered. 'I do know his face well from the committee what forced us to give money to them. The Bold Defiance, they call themselves.'

The son of Poor, a sickly-looking creature heavily marked with the pox, claimed to have seen Guy in the house that night. 'I'd know the son of a bitch anywhere,' he said. 'He'd threatened us before, with the *Book of Prices*. That if we didn't sign, it would be all the worse for us.'

The defence seemed weak, with only two people coming forward to give evidence that Guy was of good character and had never been in trouble before. *If only they had asked me*, Henri thought. *I'd have told them in more certain terms.* But then he remembered the visit of the Guards that night: he was already a marked man, and his testimony might have been considered unreliable. Although the lawyers pressed the witnesses in cross-examination, it seemed none was prepared to testify to his claim that he had not actually been in the house of the weaver that night.

Henri could not believe it was all over so quickly. As the guards turned to take Guy down, he began to panic. 'Stop,' he shouted. 'He's innocent. He was never there. Surely someone can tell this?'

The judge looked up and fixed him with a stern gaze. 'Sir,' he said. 'If you interrupt again, I shall have you arrested for disrupting the course of justice.'

Then he turned back to the courtroom, and called, 'Next.'

Henri observed the rest of the proceedings in a daze. The accused appeared either one at a time or in groups, to hear the charges and provide evidence for their innocence. It was clear the judge perceived D'Oyle and Valline to be the ringleaders, and that D'Oyle was the one carrying the gun. Guy was heavily implicated, with one or two others claiming that he had not only been there that night but had in fact been another of the ringleaders. The crowd that had been so excitable earlier now fell quiet, listening to every word spoken by the accusing, the accused and the witnesses both for and against.

Late in the afternoon the judge announced that he would be taking a short break to consider the case before sentencing. Henri stayed put, not daring to risk losing his space in the public gallery. An hour ticked slowly by on the courtroom clock and when, at last, a clerk shouted, 'All rise,' Henri found his legs so weak that he struggled to stand.

The judge entered and slowly climbed to his seat on the raised dais. He read out a list of four names and called for these prisoners to be brought up from the cells; Guy was not among them. These individuals were pronounced to be 'not guilty on all counts', and allowed to leave the court, accompanied by whoops and cheers from the crowd. Seven further prisoners were told they had been found guilty on some counts – most were sentenced to transportation.

The only prisoners who had not yet reappeared were Valline, D'Oyle and Guy. 'Those poor sods are going to cop it,' Henri's neighbour mumbled. 'Mark my words. They always leave the worst till last.' Anxiety churned in Henri's belly so violently that he feared he might be sick.

A ripple of anticipation stirred through the court as the three men emerged and took their place in the dock. Valline and D'Oyle stood strong and impassive-faced, appearing almost stoical about their fate, but Guy, pale and insubstantial as a wraith, sobbed freely and loudly. Henri felt his heart might break, seeing his friend so utterly terrified that he had lost all dignity.

The judge peered over his glasses towards the dock, cleared his throat and began to speak.

'John Valline, John D'Oyle and Guy Lemaitre,' he said in a slow, portentous voice. 'I find you guilty of all charges, including going armed with intent to murder.'

The crowd erupted, and Henri found himself on his feet, shouting along with them. Days, even weeks, of pent-up anger and frustration, and the feeling of such helplessness in the face of an implacable and retributive system, seemed to explode.

'You bastards!' he shouted. 'For shame!' When he could bear to turn his eyes back towards the dock he saw that Guy had fainted clear away, his head lolling, his limp body being held upright by the guards. One of them began to slap him in the face, attempting to return him to consciousness so that he could hear his fate.

A heavy hush fell over the room as the judge reached into his desk, pulled out a piece of black cloth and placed it on top of his wig. Henri fell to his knees with head in hands, painful sobs racking his chest. 'Please God, save him,' he whispered, over and over.

'The disruption, damage to property and threat to persons has gone on too long,' the judge was saying. 'Ordinary working men and women must be allowed to continue their trades without fear of attack and extortion by lawless men, who cloak their violence under the mantle of natural justice.

'I hereby sentence the three of you, John Valline, John D'Oyle and Guy Lemaitre, to be hanged by the neck until you are dead.' A horrified groan reverberated through the court. 'And so that it shall be a proper example to others in the vicinity who may consider it their right to resort to violence, the sentence will be executed in Bethnal Green, outside the public house which has been such a centre of foment among the lawless.'

Henri could recall little of what happened next. He was trampled to the floor as the crowd surged for the exit door of the public gallery; heard the shouts and curses of the guards as they attempted to control the crowd, and the weeping of women in the corridors as he stumbled towards the doors with the acrid taste of nausea in his mouth.

He tried to reach fresh air, but failed. There was a hand on his back, a handkerchief offered to wipe his mouth. 'Come, we will go to pray for their souls,' a kindly voice said – a voice he recognised from the French church.

'Don't waste your breath praying,' he shouted, pulling away from the comforting hand, straightening his back and glaring wildly around the hallway of the courtroom. 'How will that save his life?'

More than anything, he wanted to see his friend, to tell him that it would be all right, that he'd get the sentence overturned. He ran along the street to the prison, but the huge wooden doors were closed and hammering on them elicited no response.

'For the love of Christ, open up,' he shouted. 'Let me see him.'

At last, a small window in the door eased ajar and a voice growled through the bars, 'We're closed. I'll arrest you if you don't leave off.'

'I wish to see Guy Lemaitre.'

'Bugger off, cabbage head.'

'Let me in, I said!'

'I will, in a minute. And then you'll stay in.' The window slammed.

By now several hundred men and women had gathered outside the courtroom, shouting, 'Free The Dolphin three, free The Dolphin three.' He joined the crowd and began to chant along with them, until he and they were one, melded into a more powerful whole by the strength of so many voices shouting in a single rhythm. For a few glorious moments it gave him hope: as if, by this force alone, they could change the course of fate.

It could not last. Before long a dozen Guards appeared at the gate and fired their pistols into the air before reloading and lowering them towards the crowd. Barely knowing what he was doing, Henri moved forward, his eyes fixed on the black pinpoint hole of the nearest gun, and began to shout, 'Kill *me* then, *vas-y*. Kill *me*. I am innocent too, like my friend.'

The Guards fired again, into the crowd this time. The noise and shock was so great that Henri dropped to the ground, certain that he must have been hit. But he could feel no pain. The chanting stopped abruptly and, after a second's horrified silence, everyone around him scattered. He heard the visceral howl of someone in agony, and found himself being pulled to his feet by a group of journeymen he knew slightly, faces from The Dolphin pub, and dragged along Newgate Street, past St Paul's, along Bishopsgate towards Spitalfields. The mood of the streets was feverish, restive, with groups of angry young men brandishing torches and batons, or gathering on street corners in hastily whispered conversations.

'Do not worry,' his new companions told him. 'We're going to spring all three of them. We'll cause such a riot the Guards won't be able to hold them.'

He found himself in several different alehouses, all of them in an uproar about the sentences, and he downed every pint that was placed in front of him, desperate to blunt the vision of Guy's fearful face. There was much bragging and shouts of 'Up the Defiance', and he began slowly to understand that most of the men around him were the self-styled 'Cutters', friends of Valline and D'Oyle. A few also claimed to know Guy who, they promised, would not be allowed to die.

An uneasy voice in the back of his head told him that it was unwise to associate with these men, that he should return to M. Lavalle and tell him what was happening, but whenever he tried to leave he was pushed back into his seat and given another jug of ale. They were heading towards Bethnal Green when he began to feel light-headed and horribly unwell.

He recognised the pub sign just ahead: it was The Dolphin, where Guy had brought him to sign the petition for the *Book of Prices*. Spying an alleyway, he excused himself, saying he would join them shortly. Turning the corner, he glimpsed in the gloom a man apparently coupling with a whore. But he could not wait.

'Filthy sod,' the man said.

'*Cul pourri,*' Henri growled. '*Vas-tu la boucler?*' Shut your mouth, fat idiot.

'What's the frog bastard saying?'

The voice was somehow familiar, but Henri was too focused on his own need to concern himself further.

'You don't want to know,' the woman said, resuming her attentions on the man's lower regions. But he was not to be distracted, detaching himself and lurching drunkenly towards Henri with his manhood flapping and his fists raised.

'Stand up and fight, French worm.'

As Henri tried to stand, his stomach rebelled and he could hold it no longer. The man retreated to safety, cursing even more viciously.

Henri was straightening himself up and wiping his mouth on his shirtsleeve when they heard the unmistake-able sound of hobnailed boots ringing on the cobbles. A volley of gunshots close by left his ears ringing. He cowered to the ground with his head in his hands, uncaring of his own filth, holding his breath and praying that he was not discovered. Out of the corner of his eye, he saw the man and woman scuttling away down the alley.

From inside the pub there were desperate shouts: 'The Runners, the Runners,' followed by the heavy tramp of boots on a stairway, the violent splintering of a wooden door and more gunfire. For several minutes it seemed the Cutters were trying to fight back but they were clearly outnumbered. As suddenly as it had started, the firing stopped and the shouts evaporated like smoke.

Looking upwards, Henri could see, silhouetted against the sky, men leaping from windows across the gap between the buildings. Gathering his senses, he realised that he had just a few precious moments to escape before the Runners came out of the pub. But, as he turned, his heart tumbled into his boots. At the end of the alley, just a few yards away, was a Guard staring directly at him, pointing his pistol.

'Come out with your hands up, or I'll shoot you dead,' he said.

19

Every member of the fair sex ought to know how to sew, knit and mend, and cook, and superintend a household. In every situation of life, high or low, this sort of knowledge is of great advantage.

– The Lady's Book of Manners

As the coach rattled its way out of the city, cobbled streets gave way to the graded gravel of the highway. Now, out of the window, Anna could see woods and fields, instead of houses.

She had been in London barely six months, but it seemed as though a lifetime had passed since she had travelled this road in the opposite direction. She swallowed back the tears that threatened as she recalled her first fateful hours in the city; how she had fainted in the heat and been rescued by a stranger apparently speaking in tongues, a stranger she now knew to be Henri.

All that was over now, of course. His letter had made it perfectly clear. The pain of rejection still stabbed like a knife deep in her heart, from which she would never recover. There were times when she felt that her tears would never stop, that she would never again find happiness. She'd pored over his previous notes again and again, obsessively, until the paper had worn into fragments. His face, and most particularly his dark eyes smiling at her in that confidential way of his, appeared in dreams from which she would awake, sobbing, knowing that she would never see them again.

She could not dare to venture out into the streets for fear that she might see him, reopening the agonising wounds once more. She could not even bear to approach the show-room downstairs at Spital Square because the smell of silk reminded her so painfully of the man with whom, she now had to acknowledge, she had fallen deeply in love.

Of course, she realised how unrealistic it had been to imagine that they might ever become friends, let alone lovers. The social divides in the city were simply too rigid and clearly defined, and she was not strong enough to challenge them. The notion that she'd entertained of becoming a silk designer seemed equally distant and fanciful, the whim of a naive girl.

And how close she had come to accepting Charles, whom she did not love. She could see now that only the unexpected conjunction of circumstances – unfortunate for her uncle and aunt, but fortunate for her – had reprieved her from a life of unhappiness.

She was now desperate to leave London, to put behind her everything that reminded her of what might have been. When she'd announced that she was going home for Christmas, her aunt had appeared almost grateful. Only Lizzie showed genuine sorrow. 'Whatever shall I do without you?' she wept. 'Everyone is so gloomy all the time, except for you. My life will be a misery if you leave. Promise me you will come back in the New Year.'

She'd written to her father to say she was returning to Suffolk just for a few weeks but in her heart she knew she would stay, probably for good. She would let fortune take its course; she would probably remain unmarried, living a peaceful and impecunious life in the country. Yes, she might be bored, but surely she would find something to entertain her brain? Perhaps she could do a little tutoring, of drawing or reading, and bring in a few extra shillings to support her father and little Jane.

She gave a deep sigh and turned her eyes to the passing fields. Arriving in the city for the first time she had felt like a stranger, but it was curious how the countryside now appeared equally surprising to her eye. Of course it was in the grip of winter, the trees leafless and stark against a grey sky and rainwater lying in silver stripes along the furrows of brown fields.

The faces around her were uniformly pale and featureless, their exchanges exclusively in the English tongue. On the streets of Spitalfields she had become accustomed to hearing so many languages: most commonly English or French, naturally, but also Spanish, Gaelic, Dutch and German, and many others she could not recognise. Here, she could understand every word and the conversations were so mundane that overhearing them became irritating and wearying.

After lunch the passengers wrapped themselves up against the cold and settled into slumber for the four-hour leg to Chelmsford. Anna allowed her eyes to close. Over the past few days, events had moved so fast that she'd barely had time to take stock, to consider her own feelings.

At Chelmsford she knew just what to do, requesting a simple meal of bread, cheese and pickle to be served in her chamber, and ordering an additional candle. Somehow the lumpy bed seemed more bearable this time. *Just one more night and tomorrow I shall be resting deep in my own feather mattress at the vicarage*, she thought to herself, *with the sound of the waves in my ears.*

It was well after sundown when they reached the town square at Halesworth, but by the light of the fading sky she could see her father and sister waiting in the smithy's horse cart, bundled up against the cold, ready to transport her the final few miles to the village. Never had a sight been so welcome. Moments later, they were in each other's arms, laughing and crying in their joy with Bumbles running in circles around them, barking with excitement.

'Dearest girl, how we have missed your sunny smile. Let me look at you,' Theodore said at last. 'What a smart cloak, my dear. And that beautiful warm muff. My sister has treated you well. But your journey must have been wearying. Let us get you home at once. We have stew in the pot.'

'And it's nearly Christmas,' Jane said, holding tight to Anna's arm. 'We've got presents!'

'Remember, we must not tell until it is time to open them,' her father said, mock-sternly.

Jane snuggled up to Anna on the hard seat of the wooden cart, inside their shared blanket. The dog settled on top of their feet like a hot water bottle and Theodore squeezed in beside them. Despite a light rain wetting their faces Anna realised that, for the first time on her long journey, she actually felt warm.

This is what I've missed, she thought to herself, *the comfort of human contact.* Apart from Lizzie's occasional embraces, and the press of Miss Charlotte's professional fingers during fittings, she had barely touched another human being for the whole six months. There had been the briefest of contacts with Charlie, of course, but also – her heart lurched at the memory – the moment when Henri held her after she fainted on the street, and the time when he took her hand to help her down the ladder from the weaving loft. But no prolonged embraces, no proper, comforting cuddles. She pressed herself closer to her sister and father as the cart jolted its way along the muddy, rutted track home, and found herself grinning with happiness.

Despite her exhaustion and a bellyful of mutton stew, she did not sleep well. They had insisted she use the chamber normally reserved for visiting curates and the like: 'You are our special guest now, my dear,' her father had said. 'You must have your privacy.' She did not want to be a guest, special or otherwise. She wanted everything to be as it had always been. *But of course I cannot turn back the clock*, she thought to herself. *They have grown used to living without me, just as I have grown used to the city. With the simple passing of time everything changes, and everyone is changed.*

She tossed and turned on the soft mattress, missing the lumpy horsehair of her London garret. At some time before dawn she crept along the corridor into the room where, for nearly all of her childhood, she had shared a double bed with her sister, the feathers plumped up into a bolster between them.

As she climbed beneath the covers Jane stirred, turned over and moved across, pressing her body against Anna's, just as she had as a very small child. Then she resumed her usual snoring, as soothing and familiar as a lullaby. Anna slept, undisturbed, well into the morning.

The next couple of days were spent reacquainting herself with the village. Walking down the short main street with her sister took a full couple of hours because everyone wanted to stop and ask her about life in the city. Some of their questions were plainly absurd, such as 'Made your fortune yet?' or 'Have you met our new king?', and she deflected with a smile the thinly disguised enquiries about her romantic prospects: 'I expect you've met many fine young folk there?' She did not care if the rumours ran wild, as they always did in a village. They would soon discover that she was staying for good.

During these conversations, she noticed a new relation-ship between Jane and the other villagers. Her own absence seemed to have given her sister greater confidence to speak to almost anyone, her place more clearly defined in this secure little world. Her vocabulary was also greatly improved. For their part, people appeared to be more solicitous of Jane's welfare than before, as though they had taken on the mantle of ensuring her wellbeing and safety while her big sister was away. More than once, Anna was told, 'Jane's definitely coming out of her shell.' Sometimes they added, 'Been doing her best to look after your dear father, that she has, poor love.'

At home she learned that, in fact, although Jane had been doing the shopping, some basic cleaning and laying of fires, she had not been managing at all with the laundry and the cooking. Despite the generosity of neighbours, who often left on the doorstep home-made bread, cooked dishes and prepared vegetables, her father had been obliged to employ a cook and housemaid on weekdays. She dared not ask him where he found the money. More than likely he was just slipping further into debt in the hope – now vain, as it turned out – that his elder daughter would marry into wealth and gain the means to pay them off.

She had forgotten how chill was the wind at the coast, how the rain came at you sideways straight off the North Sea, how the mud of the paths clagged to your shoes until it was barely possible to drag them onwards. But in brighter, calmer moments, she and Jane managed some walks through the marshes and along the beach, collecting driftwood for the fires and 'hagstones' – flints with holes worn through them from centuries of abrading by the forces of the sea – to hang by the door for good luck. Her father disapproved: 'Just stupid old superstitions,' he said. So they had always compromised by hanging them at the back door so that they could not be seen from the street.

Perhaps because of her physical weaknesses Jane was often weary and it was her habit to retire early, leaving Anna and her father at liberty to talk long into the night. During one of these conversations she told him about the troubles facing the family in London, much of which had been brought about, as far as she could see, by William's gambling and theft.

'It's so cruel,' she said. 'I am sure Aunt Sarah is ignorant of the problems he has caused because Uncle Joseph has covered up for him. But perhaps this is for the best. All she really wants is for her family to be happy and for the business to prosper sufficiently so that they can move to a larger house, preferably on Ludgate Hill, and get Uncle's portrait painted by Mr Gainsborough.'

'*Gainsborough?* Goodness, they are becoming puffed up! That would cost a penny or two.'

'He's such a nice man, Pa.'

'You met Mr Gainsborough?'

'We went to his London studio and he talked about his painting and how there's going to be a new Society of the Arts, to hold exhibitions. He even suggested that women might be able to show their work.'

'Women such as my talented daughter? And why not, indeed?'

She blushed at the memory of it. 'He was just being gracious. Still, I am very unlikely to meet him again – all their plans for such things are now lost, at least until Uncle Joseph can recover his reputation. But Aunt Sarah is so very low; it's as if she has no reason for living.'

'I am sure things will turn out for the better before long. But what about William? What is he doing to make amends?'

'I think he has stopped the gambling, at least,' she answered. 'And he has been working hard to sell more of their fabric stocks, to pay off the fine. But he says much of it is out of fashion.' They sat in silence, gazing into the flames of the fire for several minutes. 'London society is beastly, you know,' she went on. 'Because of the scandal, the whole family has been ostracised.'

'And what about you?'

'What *about* me?'

He raised a quizzical eyebrow. 'You know what I am talking about. Has this horrid affair damaged your reputation, too? Is this why you were so keen to come home?'

'I wanted to be here for Christmas. I told you.'

'Of course I hoped you would come, but confess that it was a surprise. I'd have thought there would be many more exciting diversions in the city during the festive season. Young men, for example.'

'There *was* a young man, a lawyer, from another mercer's family who used to be best friends with Sarah and Joseph. I wrote to you about him, I believe? He even proposed, Pa! But he dropped me like a hot potato after the scandal emerged.'

Her father leaned across and placed his hand on hers. 'Oh, my dear, I am so sorry.'

'Please do not be concerned for me, for I am not the slightest bit sorry. He was nice enough, but I did not love him. He gambles, too, according to William. And we had nothing whatsoever in common.'

'Have you absolutely made up your mind not to return? What about this friend you wrote of, the seamstress?'

'Miss Charlotte. Yes, I shall miss her,' Anna sighed. 'She's such an inspiration. Never married, I think, or perhaps widowed; it seemed indelicate to inquire, although she has family – I met her nephew. But what I most admire is that she runs her own shop, and earns an independent living from her seamstress work. All the society ladies patronise her but at the same time she seems to have the freedom to socialise with whomever she pleases.'

'Whereas, reading between the lines of your letters, am I to understand that you did not?'

Anna nodded. 'I was not even allowed to leave the house without permission and certainly not without a chaperone. I couldn't bear it, being so constrained. It's no life for someone like me.'

Another evening, he asked, 'And what do you think now, my free-spirited daughter, should be the best kind of life for you?'

She looked up at him sharply. 'What prompted that?'

'You talking so glowingly about your friend the other night.'

'It would be wonderful to find a way of making an independent living, without having to get married for it.' As she spoke, she recalled the powerful display of affection between Charlotte and her nephew, and then remembered the sadness in Charlotte's eyes when he had gone. Being single, without children, seemed also to have its drawbacks.

'You do not wish to be married?'

'Of course I do, but to someone I love, not just because they are wealthy and speak the right . . .' She stopped herself.

'The right what?'

'The right language, I was going to say.'

His forehead furrowed. 'So who is it that speaks the *wrong* language?'

She explained how a quarter of all people in Spitalfields were French and that many were weavers, suppliers to merchants like her uncle.

'I have heard of the French Protestants who came over because of Catholic persecution. There are some in Norwich,

I believe. But you have met some of these people? How fascinating. Theirs must be a very different kind of culture from ours?'

'Not at all. They are just like us. They work and eat and sleep and go to church, and dream about their futures, just like we do. They love growing flowers and keeping song-birds, and they are the best craftspeople in London.' She found herself speaking just a little too emphatically, too fervently, and saw the understanding dawning on her father's face.

'You know some of these French, I think? In fact, I would go so far as to guess that you are rather fond of them, or is it him?' She couldn't help smiling – she had forgotten how acutely her father seemed to understand human motivation.

And so the story came out: about the market stall, and the sketch, and the French journeyman weaver who bought it as the design for his master piece, which he was currently weaving. About how Charlotte had encouraged him because she loved the design which had reminded her of Hogarth's *The Analysis of Beauty*, and believed it would go well with fashionable society ladies. And how she, Anna, had imagined that she might, one day, learn enough about weaving to become a proper silk designer, and make some kind of living, but that her visit to Henri's master's house and the weaving loft had ended in disaster.

Her father listened without speaking, as she rambled through the story. When finally she stopped, he thought for a few seconds.

'It all seems to make perfect sense to me, my darling. And furthermore –' he paused again, rubbing his temple as though considering whether it was wise to continue '– it sounds to me as though you are a little in love with this Henri? Am I right?'

Hearing her father say his name was just too much: her chin began to wobble and a tear escaped down her cheek. He gathered her into his arms.

'My dearest, I am so sorry. I did not wish to upset you. What is making you so sad? Were your affections not reciprocated?'

'I believed that they were, Pa,' she sobbed. 'At first. But it is impossible. He is a French journeyman and Aunt Sarah is trying to transform me into a society lady.'

'And if she knew you were actually in love with this lad, she'd literally explode with horror?'

The vision was so irresistible that it made Anna chuckle, even through her tears. Her father returned to his chair, and she took a few deep breaths, drying her face with his handkerchief.

'Well, do you know what?' he said at last. 'I am your father, and it is up to me to decide who is worthy of your hand, not Sarah. After Christmas, we shall go to London and make a visit to this Henri fellow and his master. How's about that?'

'It's no good, Pa. In his last note he told me that any further friendship is impossible. I just have to accept that there is no future in it.'

Christmas Eve came and went, much as always. It was a time of happiness and sorrow, the joy of traditional rituals – bringing green branches into the house, cooking and eating the goose and the pudding, the exchange of gifts followed by midnight mass and a glass of mulled beer – tinged with sadness because this was the first year her mother had not been here to share them.

The following day, as was their habit, they invited all the lonely souls of the village into the vicarage for luncheon. The wide oak dining table that usually served as a storage space for her father's books and papers was cleared and polished until it gleamed; every item of cutlery, every plate, saucer, cup and tankard in the cupboards was brought out, dusted and shaken to dislodge unwary spiders, bottles were opened, left-overs and other contributions of food unwrapped and set out upon it, every chair and stool collected from the nether regions of the house placed around it. Logs were brought in, fires were set and candles lit against the gloom of a heavy sky which threatened never to brighten.

Partway through the meal, Anna found herself with a moment free to cast her eyes around the room. The assembled company, twenty-two in all, were mostly elderly ladies in their Sunday best, white hair carefully coiffed and caps stiffly starched, and a few widowers, uncomfortable in wigs which almost certainly never left their boxes from one end of the year to the other. There was the young, sallow-faced widow failing to keep control of her four unruly children, a couple of unmarriageable bachelors and a motley assortment of other unfortunates, the blind, the deaf, and the weak of mind.

Observing the way they helped and took care of each other, she was struck by how comfortable everyone seemed, how mutually supportive, how unconcerned with difference. Of course there were the snobbish people;

people who, on this day, would be supping the wine of the De Vries family, the landowners up at the great hall. *But the rest of us just mix along, regardless of income or status*, she thought to herself. *And isn't society the better, the stronger, the healthier, for it?*

And yet, in the same moment, she found it impossible to imagine herself here in ten, twenty or fifty years' time, seeing the same group of people, doing the same things each day. Living here at the coast, in a small fishing village at the end of a single five-mile track, provided infinitely wide and varied geographical horizons but the narrowest of social prospects; no marriageable young men, little means of earning a living, few opportunities for meeting interesting people and, most crucially, nothing ever surprising or unexpected.

On the first day of January the snow began to fall and continued falling for thirty-six hours. Unless there was a sudden thaw, the village would be cut off for several days at the very least. No one was greatly concerned: this was an almost annual event, and every household stored additional supplies of food, fuel and candles against the prospect. While her father resumed his usual studies and writing, Jane and Anna spent their time sewing – many of the curtains and much of the bedlinen were in urgent need of repair – cleaning out cupboards and taking brisk, slippery walks. Jane could not read, but she enjoyed card games and draughts, which Anna usually allowed her to win.

At last, after about five days, the weather warmed and the snow turned to slush, so that now they saw an occasional cart passing down the street. Around lunchtime, the post boy arrived with mail that had accumulated in the office at Halesworth.

Anna picked up the most recent newspaper, and went to sit by the fire. As she turned the pages, a tiny headline caught her eye. The report beneath it was terse.

SPITALFIELDS JOURNEYMEN TO BE HANGED

Three French journeyman weavers were today sentenced to hang for breaking and entering, damage to property and threats to murder. All are linked to the Bold Defiance, a group turning to violent means to demand rates outlined in the so-called Book of Prices.

Just then, her father came over with a letter. 'Tucked in with my mail,' he said. 'It's for you.'

'Whoever could it be?' she said, examining the writing on the fine vellum, folded and sealed. It was a female hand, but not Lizzie's, nor her aunt's. 'I am not expecting news and I barely know anyone in London well enough to exchange letters.'

'Oh, open it, do,' Jane said. 'Stop wasting time wondering.'

7th January 1761

Dearest Anna,

Forgive me for troubling you, but I bring unhappy news. Henri is in gaol, wrongly arrested in connection with the Bold Defiance. There are fears he may face the

death penalty. M. Lavalle is desperate. I thought
perhaps you might know someone who could help? I
know you would if you could. Please come, if you can,
as soon as possible?
    Yours affectionately,
    Charlotte

Terror gripped her chest. Surely such a gentle soul would not turn to violence? And then, like an icicle piercing her heart, she recalled the placard at that rally where she'd spied his friend Guy from the carriage so long ago: *Bold Defiance: fair pay for all.* If Guy was involved with this group, might Henri might have been, too?

She checked the date of the newspaper. 10th January: three days after Miss Charlotte wrote her letter. Could Henri be one of those three, already tried, found guilty and sentenced to hang?

20

*The greatest achievement for a man, the one he must aspire to
at all times, is freedom: for an apprentice, freedom from indentures; for a journeyman, the freedom to become a Master and
employ his own men; for a Master, to achieve the ultimate, the
Freedom of the City.*

*– Advice for apprentices and journeymen
OR A sure guide to gain both esteem and an estate*

Each morning, for a split second before fully wakening,
Henri could imagine himself to be in the warm truckle bed
beside the kitchen in the basement at Wood Street.

Then he would hear the clang of a metal door, the
howling and cursing of his fellow inmates or a volley of
violent threats from a guard, and harsh reality would crowd
in. He'd become accustomed to the smells that, at first, had
made him gag, and since M. Lavalle had brought in extra
clothes and blankets, the biting cold had become almost
bearable. But the noises of the prison were the one thing
he could not grow used to.

He had been arrested by the Runners and, despite his
protestations of innocence, had been charged with damage
to property and causing affray. Now here he was in gaol,

awaiting trial. He'd been told he would likely be sentenced to transportation or even, because the authorities were so determined to crack down on the weavers' protests, the death penalty.

Not even in the most difficult times of his life, after his father and sister had drowned and his mother seemed to have lost the will to live, could Henri remember feeling such darkness in his soul. In just a few hours of drunkenness, he had let down everyone who had supported him: his mother, M. Lavalle, Mariette, Miss Charlotte – and Guy, of course.

Several times he'd tried shouting his friend's name in the chance that his cell was close enough to hear, but all he got in response was the curses of other prisoners. When he asked the guards if he could be taken to see his friend, they were without pity: 'Think you can curry favour, in your position? Get lost, French vermin.'

M. Lavalle visited and said they were trying to raise bail. But it seemed the authorities were refusing to countenance it, adamant that the prisoners should be held as an example of how all vestiges of the rebellion were being crushed. Three people had been injured that night, he learned, and sixteen arrested – some of them were in the communal cell in which he spent his first few days. The phrase 'death penalty' had been widely whispered among the group, but he tried to banish it from his mind. M. Lavalle did his best to reassure him. Henri was of good character and had an unblemished record; surely the mere keeping of company with a group of protestors was not a felonious crime?

Friends from the French church brought him food, drink and clean clothes, claiming they would soon see him released.

They even raised funds for him to have a single cell, for which he was tearfully grateful. At least he was now free of the threat of assault by other prisoners and could enjoy some privacy when visitors arrived. It also meant that he had a chance of keeping his blankets and clothes from being stolen.

A few days later a legal clerk arrived at the prison, uneasy and out of place in full wig, smart silk coat and pristine white leggings. He admitted he was not a fully-fledged lawyer and that, although he was an expert in French law, he would have to take advice on any variations there might be with the English statute. For an hour he quizzed Henri about the events of that night: who he was with, what precisely he had witnessed, what was done and said by whom, and the exact timing of when he had left the group before they went into the pub.

Henri was still so shocked at his situation that his brain had gone to pulp; he could remember barely anything. He spent the next few days trying to focus, writing down everything he could recall so that when the lawyer returned a few days later, a far more coherent picture seemed to emerge. The clerk thought that *if* they could locate the man or the whore, and *if* either agreed to testify, they could prove that he was not with the group inside The Dolphin, and there was a chance the charges might be lifted. It sounded to Henri as though his freedom, even his very life, hung upon the testimony of two strangers who were unlikely ever to be traced. The encounter left him feeling more depressed than ever.

His moods swung violently between long spells of abject misery and despair and shorter spells of cautious optimism.

He had already survived so much in his life, and his good friends would surely make certain that he did not suffer the same fate as Guy. At night, however, the doubts crept into the cell like a malign vapour, and he would find himself shaking with fear.

The visits from his mother and M. Lavalle were the hardest to cope with. The look of sorrow and disappointment in his master's face and Clothilde's expression of raw concern were almost unbearable. They tried to cheer him but his sense of shame was so great he could barely bring himself to respond, let alone be comforted. M. Lavalle said that Mariette had badgered him to allow her to come, but he'd decided it would be too upsetting for her. Instead he produced a note, which Henri opened later; he broke down into sobs as he read her words: '*N'oubliez pas que je suis toujours ton amie,*' she wrote. Never forget that I am your friend.

He was pleased to see the apprentice Benjamin, who arrived with a parcel of Cook's special meat pies and some fresh apples, two bottles of beer and a long woollen scarf that Mariette had knitted for him. After he'd sated his appetite, Henri quizzed him for news of the family, but the usually garrulous boy seemed reluctant to expand on what he already knew. 'They are well,' he said. 'We are working all hours to cover the work. The Master lends a hand when he can and even the drawboy is learning to weave. Mariette sends her love.'

'Any news of Guy Lemaitre?' Henri asked. 'Has his appeal come to court yet?'

In the gloom of the cell, he could see Benjamin's face blench. 'This is what I have come to tell you,' he said in a quiet voice. 'The Master said I must. It is bad, I am afraid. Your friend was executed early yesterday morning – hanged with the others outside The Dolphin.'

Although Henri had been half expecting this dread news, the harsh reality of it took several moments to sink in. The beer and meat pie he'd consumed with such gusto a few moments earlier seemed to curdle in his stomach. Guy, his friend, hanging on the end of a rope? The boy he had grown up with, sat with at school, played childhood pranks with, chased girls with, who in dark times had been there for Henri, and Henri for him . . . now *dead*?

'Apparently, the Bold Defiance men attacked the Guards who were building the gallows and so the authorities set the hour of the hangings to early morning, to try to avoid further violence. As soon as the news got out there was an enormous crowd assembled.'

A vision of the prisoner he'd seen on his way to Tyburn flooded Henri's mind: the man so defiant and smiling even when he was chained on the cart to his own coffin and pelted with rotten eggs and cabbages. The last time he'd seen Guy he was a pale, almost wraith-like figure who had fainted into the guard's arms in court. How must he have been on the day of his hanging? It was unimaginable.

He swallowed hard, fighting back tears. He barely dared to ask: 'Did you go?'

Benjamin nodded. 'M. Lavalle made me, because he needed to stay with Mrs Lemaitre. They had to get the doctor for her, she was that distraught. He told me I must go to pay my respects on behalf of the family.'

And now the hardest question of all: 'Was his death quick?'

'I believe so, although the crowd was so great I could barely see. The Bold Defiance planned to storm the carts before they reached the gallows, but there were so many soldiers that they couldn't get past.' He shook his head, as though scarcely able to believe what he'd witnessed.

'By the time they managed to break through and cut them down, they were already dead. They've brought Guy's body back to his mother, so at least she will be able to bury him properly.'

As Henri listened, a great chill crept through him, and he began to shiver violently. The vision was just too awful to contemplate.

'That's not all,' Benjamin said, grimly determined to complete his duty of witness. 'Then they tore down one of the gibbets and set off with it, carrying it piece by piece, chanting all the while and waving their torches, till they got to Crispin Street. They set the gibbet back together right there, outside Chauvet's house, and smashed his windows and threw their torches inside to set fire to the place. It was mayhem. Then of course the soldiers arrived and arrested dozens more. They say the prisons are over-flowing with journeymen now.'

Later, after Benjamin had left, Henri gave himself up to his misery, curling up on the floor, weeping and holding his hands over his ears, trying to block out the ghastly image of the pale, terrified figure of his friend as he went to his end. If only he'd done more to help him, to give him a little dignity and comfort in his last days. He deeply regretted failing to help him more generously, or of intervening sooner when he'd begun to tread a wayward path.

Now it was too late.

He had been in gaol nearly two weeks, had heard nothing from the legal clerk and was beginning to despair when M. Lavalle arrived with news.

'The Company Committee met last night,' he said, taking his seat on the bench beside Henri. 'To review the submitted master pieces.'

'And?'

'As you know, in the first instance, the works are presented anonymously, to prevent bias. Yours was considered to be of the highest quality, exceptional in fact, according to certain members. "Without a doubt this weaver should be admitted," they said. Congratulations, my boy.'

From the expression on his face, Henri sensed that bad news was to follow. 'What are you not telling me?'

The old man cleared his throat. 'When they came to write down the list of new Freemen, they went into a long discussion about whether they could admit someone who was currently facing criminal charges. They had to consult the statute books but, in the end, they said they would suspend admission until . . .'

'What does it matter, anyway, when my life is already lost?'

'Please do not lose heart, my boy,' M. Lavalle said. 'The legal fellow is working hard to find people to testify to your innocence and good character. We shall get you out of here soon. Imagine, you will not only be freed, but also a Freeman.'

Henri tried to smile for his master, to be glad and grateful, but somehow the idea of a double prize felt even more of a distant dream. He could not rid his mind of the conviction that his life was effectively finished.

What did my father and sisters die for? To find freedom for our family. And how do I, the last remaining child, repay them? By becoming a good-for-nothing who has thrown away every opportunity that has come to him.

In a dim memory from his childhood, he recalled one of his father's favourite sayings: *Where there's life there is hope.* But for how long would he manage to hold on to his own life, he wondered? It seemed the authorities wanted to wipe out the Bold Defiance completely. If no one came forward to prove his innocence, might he soon be following Guy to his grave?

21

There can be no doubt Providence has willed that man should be the head of the human race, even as woman is its heart; that he should be its strength, as she is its solace; that he should be its wisdom, as she is its grace; that he should be its mind, its impetus, and its courage, as she is its sentiment, its charm, and its consolation.

— The Lady's Book of Manners

Anna was all for going directly to Miss Charlotte's shop as soon as the coach set them down outside the Red Lyon.

'I will not rest easy until I know,' she chafed, but night had already fallen. The shop would be shut and Joseph and Sarah were expecting them for supper.

'We've had a long journey and we need to eat and rest, my love,' Theodore said. 'To prepare ourselves properly.'

Still tucked into her muff, where she had held it like a talisman for much of the journey, was the envelope containing Charlotte's letter and the newspaper cutting.

She could still picture the moment she'd read those words, when her world turned upside down. Henri, in gaol, possibly sentenced to death? Perhaps already hanged? How could that be possible? He seemed so dutiful, so level-headed. She had known about the journeymen's riots, of course, but could not imagine him being part of that lawless gang of thugs.

She must have uttered a small yelp, because her father had immediately come to her side. 'What is it, dearest? Bad news? You look as though you've seen a ghost.' She'd passed the note to him, wordlessly, barely able to speak for the shock of it. Then she showed him the newspaper report.

'Is the letter from your seamstress friend? The one you told me about a few days ago?'

She nodded.

'This Henri she writes of is the weaver boy? And you think that he might already have . . . ?'

She nodded again, still too numb to weep.

He put his arm around her. 'Take heart, my dearest. If he is the man you have described to me, it seems most unlikely that he would have committed any such crime. I am sure he will not be one of those mentioned in the newspaper. The law does not move that quickly. However, we must go to their aid at once.'

'Whatever can we do? We have no money to pay for his bail or buy clever lawyers.' As she said it, the idea came into her head: she *did* know a lawyer, albeit one not fully qualified.

'We could visit the young man, at the very least, to cheer his soul,' her father was saying.

She recalled the cold tone of Henri's last letter. 'I am not sure I would be welcome.'

'But can you ignore your friend's request?'

'No,' she admitted. 'I must go and do what I can, or I will never rest easy.'

'Then we shall write at once, and make preparations. I shall come with you. Let me get my Sunday duties out of the way, and we shall go on Monday.'

'What about Jane?'

'She will stay with Mrs Chapman next door, as usual.'

'I am sure we will not be welcome at Spital Square, with Joseph's troubles.'

'*Pssht.* They've still got a house, haven't they? We are family. And we won't burden them for long.'

Anna was dreading the inevitable interrogation by her aunt and uncle. Her father was adamantly opposed even to white lies, but during the journey she had managed to persuade him that revealing their true purpose would cause outrage. She could so clearly imagine her aunt spluttering, *A French weaver? In prison? Whatever business is it of yours, Theodore?*

Neither was she looking forward to returning to the sunless house in Spital Square. When she'd closed the door behind her, a few short weeks ago, she had breathed a sigh of relief, never imagining that she would return so soon. It had been a place of so much loneliness, ignominy and sadness.

As it turned out, Joseph and Sarah appeared delighted to see them and had laid on an impressive spread for supper: hot roast pheasants, cold cuts and an apple turnover for pudding. The fires were burning merrily in every room, and many candles were lit. *No sign of belts being pulled in here*, Anna thought to herself.

Lizzie flung herself upon her cousin as soon as they

entered, and had clung to her side ever since. Even William seemed in an unusually cheerful mood. After several glasses of his best claret – to celebrate the value of family, he'd declared – Joseph began to expand on his plans for turning around their business fortunes.

'Have you heard? The new king has chosen his queen. She comes to London this spring to prepare for their wedding. It's the best possible news for the silk trade, mark my words.'

'Who is she?' Anna enquired.

'A German princess,' Sarah said. 'Princess Charlotte of Mecklenburg-Strelitz. Word is she's no great beauty, so there will be all the more reason to bedeck her in the best silks. They will marry in July and the coronation is planned for a fortnight later.'

'Every mercer in the land is busy buttering up anyone who might be appointed royal costumier,' William said drily.

'But even if we don't supply her trousseau, can you imagine all the dress silks that will be required for their guests?' Joseph said. 'It is just a matter of finding the best possible designs to catch the eye of the courtiers and their ladies.' He tapped the side of his nose. 'I haven't been in the business for all these years not to know the next best thing when I see it.'

Lizzie piped up: 'And what *is* the "next best thing", Papa?'

'I don't know just yet, my dearest, but when I do I shall work day and night to make sure we get the commissions,' he said, draining his glass. 'Anyone for another?'

'Have you heard about the troubles?' William asked. 'There have been many shenanigans among the weavers since you left. Journeymen rioting and cutting, and getting themselves hanged. It's a bad business.'

'We have seen newspaper reports, but they didn't mention any names,' Anna said, struggling to keep her voice steady. William left the room and returned shortly with a crumpled newspaper.

She held it up to the candle and tried to keep her hands from trembling as she scanned the page, fearful that she might encounter Henri's name. Instead, the name which caught her eye was that of Guy Lemaitre. The report was brief and the ending brutal: *Hanged at Bethnal Green.*

She could barely breathe. If Guy had already been sentenced and hanged, might Henri be next? It was all she could do to hold her body still when what she most wanted was to scream. She took a swig of wine and then another, forcing herself to take breaths slowly, in and out, in and out.

'Load of violent villains, the lot of them,' Joseph was saying. 'They've been holding masters to ransom, forcing them to pay according to their illegal *Book of Prices.* They've got no idea of the consequences: the masters will go to the wall, and then where shall we be?'

After a sleepless night, Anna sat impatiently through breakfast listening to her father fielding the family's inquiries about their plans. He spoke in vague terms of meetings and Church business, intimating that they would not be back till late afternoon.

'My goodness,' he said, as they passed the market, swerving to avoid carts, horses, pedlars and beggars thronging the streets. 'I don't remember London being quite so chaotic before.'

'How long is it since you were here last?'

'Ah, it must be twenty or thirty years – before you were born, anyway.'

'They say this part of the city has doubled in size just in the past few decades,' she said. 'Everyone wants to come here for the work.'

'From all over the world, my ears tell me,' he said. 'Doesn't anyone speak English around here?'

※❀※

Miss Charlotte welcomed Anna with a delighted embrace.

'Charlotte, tell me at once, I must know,' Anna cried. 'I have read dreadful news of Henri's friend Guy. But is Henri well?'

'Indeed it is terrible news of Guy. But take heart, Anna. Although Henri is still in gaol, he is not yet come to trial and by all accounts is well.'

'Thank heavens.' She clasped the door jamb, giddy with relief, only then sensing her father behind her, still waiting on the step. 'Oh, do forgive my rudeness. Miss Charlotte, please meet my father, Theodore Butterfield.'

Miss Charlotte dipped her knee. 'Sir, it is a pleasure. Anna never told me that you were a man of the cloth,' she said. 'How should I address you?'

'Theo,' he said. 'That's what everyone else calls me.'

'Will you take tea?' Charlotte said. 'And I can relate to you all that has happened.'

As they were ushered into the rear parlour, Anna recalled

that happy afternoon of conversation about William Hogarth and his views on beauty. How long ago that seemed. When they were seated, Charlotte began, 'It was Mariette, Monsieur Lavalle's daughter, who first brought me the news. She was so upset, poor little thing. He was arrested the day his friend Guy Lemaitre went to trial – had you met?'

'Briefly, just once, with Henri,' Anna said. 'I cannot believe he has been hanged.'

'It was a shock for us all.' Charlotte looked down at her hands. 'Especially Henri. He went to the trial but after they were sentenced he went crazy and ended up drinking with a group of those Bold Defiance men. He says he was drunk and didn't know who they were. He'd already left the group by the time the Runners arrived, but they found him nearby and arrested him anyway.'

As the story unfolded Anna could hardly believe what Charlotte was telling her. The devastation of hearing Guy's sentence must have caused Henri to lose his senses.

'Mariette said the people at the French church are doing all they can to get him released,' Charlotte went on. 'I really have no idea what to do for the best. Which is why I got in touch with you. In case you might know someone . . .' She tailed off.

Theodore's face darkened. 'This is why we have hastened here, dear Miss Charlotte,' he said. 'I suppose Henri has already been asked whether he knows of anyone who might testify to his innocence?'

She nodded. 'I believe Monsieur Lavalle has pressed him on this point, but he says he was so befuddled by the ale that his memory is poor.'

'Is it possible to visit him?' Anna asked.

'I am told that Newgate is a terrible place – a very hell on earth, someone described it. Monsieur Lavalle would not allow Mariette to go because it would be too upsetting. If you decide to visit, you will have to be strong.'

'I can be as strong as an ox, with my father by my side,' Anna said.

'I know how much you mean to Henri,' Charlotte said, a wan smile warming her cheek. 'He will be very happy to see you. Promise you will return to let me know how he is?'

Anna's strength seemed to evaporate as they entered the prison.

The gatekeeper, an overweight, unshaven man with grease stains down his jerkin, grabbed her father's proffered sixpence with a burly hand and then, painfully slowly, scanned a long, well-thumbed list.

'Condemned cells,' he grunted. 'That way.'

'That can't be right,' Anna cried. 'He is not yet come to trial.'

'What it says here, miss,' was the curt reply.

Panic filled her heart and she clung to her father's hand as they walked the dank, gloomy passageways. *It truly is a very hell on earth*, she thought to herself. The howls and curses, the clanging of doors, the foul stench and the surly, aggressive guards made her wonder how anyone could survive the place.

It reminded her of the time when, as a small child, she

had been locked into a pigsty by some older boys. The terror of being unable to escape the foetid gloom, the air so vile that you could barely breathe, and the ear-splitting squealing of the terrified pigs had caused her nightmares for weeks afterwards.

She almost wept with relief when the gaoler at the condemned cells claimed no knowledge of a M. Vendôme, and redirected them back to the main block.

When they eventually found the right cell, and persuaded another gaoler – with more pennies – to unlock the door, she could barely believe that the pathetic human form gazing vacantly at them without recognition, his clothes filthy, his skin scabbed and cheeks hollow, was Henri. Under the layer of grime his face was deathly pale.

'It's me, Anna,' she said tentatively, holding out the small parcel of bread and cheese they had brought at Charlotte's suggestion. As she took a step towards him he cowered as if fearing a blow and then, to her horror, fell to his knees and buried his head in his hands. '*Non, non, non,*' he said, through muffled sobs. '*Je ne supporte pas que vous me voyiez dans cet état.*' I cannot bear for you to see me like this.

She put a hand on his shoulder. 'Miss Charlotte wrote to me. I had to come.'

Slowly, he turned his face and pulled himself to his feet, stiff as an old man, shaking his head. '*Je ne crois pas.* I have dreamed of you so much. And now you are here,' he whispered.

'This is my father, Theodore Butterfield,' she said.

Henri gathered himself, and made a small bow. 'Reverend, sir, I thank you. I do not deserve this kindness.'

'It appears, from what we have heard, that you do not

deserve to be here at all. My daughter holds you in high regard and we have come to ask if there is anything we can do to ease your situation or to get you released.'

Theodore's little speech seemed to strike Henri dumb. He stared at him, mouth agape, for several seconds, until Anna said, 'Henri, what is it? He's my father. He will not hurt you.'

Henri sat down heavily on the bench, shaking his head and rubbing his ears with his hands. 'Forgive me, sir. Your voice . . . I recognise it. Have we met?'

'I do not believe so,' Theodore said.

'The man . . . that night. With the . . .'

'The night you were arrested?' Anna prompted.

'No, it is impossible,' Henri said, shaking his head again, as if to clear the confusion. 'That man was younger.'

'You recognised my voice?' Theodore pressed.

'Please excuse me, sir, it is the way you say some words.' Henri seemed to mutter to himself, and she could hear that he was repeating 'deserve' and 'released', imitating her father's slight fudging of the sibilant consonants.

'Who *was* this man?'

'He was with me when the Runners arrived,' Henri said. 'But he disappeared and I do not know who he is.'

'And why do you need to find him?'

'Because he could tell them I was not with the Bold Defiance men.'

As he spoke, Anna had a flash of intuition. The slight lisp ran in their family. Being more like her mother, she had not inherited it. But Theodore's sister Aunt Sarah had it, and Lizzie and William also spoke that way. Surely it could not have been *him*, in the street that night?

'Can you remember what the man was doing?'

Beneath the filth, Henri's face seemed to colour. '*C'est embarrassant.*'

'Was he with a woman?' Theo asked.

'*Précisément.* How you say, a working woman?'

With a prostitute? Little about William would surprise her any more. Her mind raced as she realised that, much as she would dearly wish to offer Henri some crumb of hope in this desperate situation, for the moment she must keep her suspicion to herself. If she was to have any chance of eliciting the truth from William, she would have to do it discreetly.

They stayed a few moments more, talking about M. Lavalle's efforts to get the charges lifted. 'Do you have a lawyer?' Theodore asked.

'A legal clerk from the French church,' Henri said. 'But he does not succeed yet.' He smiled ruefully. 'I am still here.'

It was the smile that brought Anna to the brink of tears. In it she saw something of the real Henri, the one with whom she had fallen in love. Watching him converse with her father, man to man, she realised that although complete strangers from utterly different worlds, the two were really quite alike: the modest demeanour, the self-deprecating humour, the sharpness of mind concealed within a thoughtful manner, the economical mode of expression in which a few words could convey layers of meaning. And how, when talking with you, their eyes would meet yours, clear and uncomplicated, without demur. Nothing was hidden. You could trust them entirely.

As they took their leave, Theodore asked whether Henri would mind if he blessed him.

'*Je serais honoré,*' he said.

Her father placed his hands gently on Henri's bowed head, whispering a short prayer, and Anna found herself sending up her own, heartfelt plea: *I don't care if he is never mine but please, God, release him to live his life to the full. He is too good to die in this terrible place.*

Theodore led her in the direction of St Paul's Cathedral. 'Come, my darling, we need some peace. We shall pray for him.'

Anna was too overawed by the splendour of the interior to pray with any devotion, but the stillness was comforting. After a few minutes, her father rose from his knees and they sat in silence for a while.

'You are right. He is a good man, Anna,' he said, taking her hand. 'We must do our best for him. I'd like to meet this legal fellow, to see what he has managed to discover, if anything.'

'Henri's master, Monsieur Lavalle, would surely introduce us.'

'Do you know where he lives?'

They knocked at the door of 37 Wood Street for as long as they could without seeming impolite but, despite the clack and thud of looms working overhead, no one answered. Anna was reminded of the time she and Miss Charlotte saw Henri clinging to the gantry, nearly falling from the loft window. But today, as a bitter cold wind funnelled showers of sleety rain between the tall buildings, the windows remained firmly closed.

They returned briefly to Miss Charlotte's shop, where they offered her reassurance as to Henri's wellbeing, and then made their way home to Spital Square, exhausted.

That evening, after supper, Anna managed to corner William. 'I must speak to you privately,' she whispered. 'Later tonight. It is urgent.'

He took a step towards the door. 'I am going out,' he said.

'Remember our pact?' she said, placing a firm hand on his arm. 'It still holds, William.'

He scowled. 'Very well. I will return by half past ten o'clock. Shall we meet in the office? We are less likely to be disturbed there.'

'That is less than two hours,' she said, glancing at the clock on the mantel. 'Mind you are back in time, William.'

He was late, of course, and she waited with increasing impatience as the candle burned lower and lower. She lit another and took out some of the pattern books to pass the time, turning the pages in a desultory fashion, but found it impossible to concentrate. So much rested on this meeting.

Finally the handle turned and he entered, breathless and dishevelled.

'So what's all this secrecy about, then?' It was clear he'd been drinking but this might even work to her advantage.

'Take a seat and listen carefully.'

'Yes, ma'am,' he said, tugging at an imaginary forelock.

As she explained her suspicion that he had been in the

area of The Dolphin the night of Guy's trial, he began to shake his head.

'Bethnal Green? Never go there,' he said. 'Not a place for a man of my standing.'

'You see, someone I know saw you there. In an alley close to the pub.'

He shook his head more violently this time.

'You were with a woman, William. Don't deny it, or I might find myself having to tell someone that you consort with whores.'

The smug grin fell from his face. 'So?' he snapped. 'Every man does it, Anna, you poor little innocent. And anyway, you'll never prove it.'

'As I said, someone recognised you. They know your voice, and your face, too.'

'And this someone is?'

'A silk weaver who was wrongly arrested that night, and who desperately needs your testimony to prove his innocence.'

'A frog, I'll warrant. Send the lot of them home, I say. We'd be better off without them.'

Anna rose from the chair and began to pace, trying to control her fury. 'Yes, a Frenchman. A man who I know to be honest and respectable. A man who does not dissemble, or cheat, or lie. He is a dear friend, and that is the reason Father and I have returned to the city. A terrible miscarriage of justice has occurred and his friends have asked for our help.' She stopped and glared at him. 'If you do not admit to this, I will tell Uncle Joseph about the cash you stole.'

Now William stood too, bearing over her just as he'd done in this very room all those months ago. This time she was not afraid. 'You little . . .' he hissed. 'You expect me to help that filthy cur in the alley who puked all over my boots? I can't believe it.'

He's admitted it, she thought to herself, silently enjoying a sweet moment of triumph. *There is no way back for him now.* 'I do, William,' she said calmly. 'If you testify that you saw him in the alleyway that night when the Guards arrived, there will be no mention of the whore, nor of the stolen cash. You may not even have to appear at the trial.'

'I will do nothing, you understand, *nothing*, if there is *any* chance my name will be splattered all over the newspapers. I will only talk if we can do this discreetly.'

'If we move quickly, we may be able to get the charges lifted altogether. But at present he only has the support of a legal clerk. We need a proper lawyer, with contacts at the Inns of Court and at the prison.' She paused for a second, allowing him time to catch up with her thoughts. 'I think you know who I have in mind.'

He looked blank for a moment and then his eyes widened with incredulity. 'Charles? *Phuh!* He threw you over, didn't he? And he hasn't spoken to me since Pa's disgrace.'

'But you know about his gambling debts, don't you?'

After a second of confusion, William burst out laughing. 'God's teeth, Anna, you are a little minx. First you blackmail me, then you ask me to blackmail my friend.' She maintained her severe expression, and his laughter stopped as suddenly as it had started. 'You're not serious?'

'I have never been more serious in my life.'

He sighed, shaking his head in disbelief. 'Very well. I will visit him. But only if you come too.'

She let out a slow breath and the tightness in her neck and back began to ease. *We're nearly there*, she thought.

William sat down again. 'So let me get this right. You've returned to London to get this cabbage head out of gaol? Just why is he so important to you, Cousin Anna?'

She refused to be drawn. 'A mutual friend wrote to me, asking for our help.'

'I did not know you were friendly with frogs.'

'You have no cause to be rude about the French. They weave fine silk, do they not, and you have made a fair penny from their labours?' Anna relit her candle from the nearly exhausted stub on the table, ready to take her leave. It was cold in the room, and she was weary from the day's emotions. 'Besides which, the mutual friend is Miss Charlotte. She is not French.'

'Miss Charlotte?' He paused, his mind seeming to wander elsewhere. 'Now there's a thought.'

'What kind of thought, William? It is late and I wish to retire.'

'You heard Pa at suppertime last evening, blathering on about how well he knows the market and how only he knows how to find silks that will steal the new queen's heart?'

She waited.

'The truth is he doesn't have a clue. He's out of date and all his contacts are too old. They dressed the last queen, decades ago, for heaven's sake! This one is only eighteen and will want the very latest fashions – or at least that's what her costumiers will be advising her to want – as will the courtiers and other guests. We need advice from someone who really knows.'

It was Anna's turn to be incredulous. 'You want me to ask Miss Charlotte if she will advise you? Have you forgotten how poorly she was treated by your mother and her cronies? They deserted her and took their business elsewhere, if you remember.'

'Look,' he said, rising to his feet and lighting his own candle. 'You have asked me for a favour – *two* favours. The least you can do in return is ask her for me. We desperately need a couple of good commissions to get us out of debt, Anna. The fine has been deferred for two months but if we don't pay it we'll be in the Marshalsea before you can say Mecklenburg-Strelitz.'

The response was cool, but at least he agreed to meet them.
Come to my chambers 12 noon tomorrow. Charles.

She was dreading it: begging a favour from the man who had spurned her, having to endure his pitying looks and patronising tone. But if it achieved a reprieve for Henri, then anything was worthwhile.

It was a crisp sunny day as she and William walked to Gray's Inn. She had only been here in the dark before – for the ball – and was surprised by the spacious beauty of the place. The chambers buildings, clustered around peaceful courtyards and cloistered walkways, reminded her of the cathedral close at Norwich she had once visited with her father. An air of privilege and learning suffused the green spaces and ancient buildings. It was a far cry from the chaotic, noisy streets of East London just a few miles away.

Charles's rooms were less impressive: on the third floor,

chilly, cramped and sparsely furnished, and clearly shared with several others. Fortunately, they found him alone.

'Miss Butterfield, William, welcome to my humble lodgings,' he said, pulling up two rackety chairs. 'To what do I owe this unexpected pleasure?'

William looked at Anna. 'You start.'

She explained the bare bones of the story: that she had a friend who had been wrongly arrested and needed the help of a lawyer to get him out of prison. 'We have found a witness to attest to his innocence, but the witness cannot risk appearing in public should the case go to court. So we must get the charges dropped, before that eventuality,' she explained.

Her little speech elicited a surprising response. Instead of the surly reluctance she'd expected, Charles leaned forward and listened attentively. When she finished, he leaned back in his chair and smiled genially.

'It sounds just up my street, this little case. I'm flattered that you have come to consult me,' he said. 'I have been looking forward to my first real commission – so far all I've had is the dross the others don't want to deal with. The experience will be very helpful when I come to apply for acceptance at the bar.'

Anna steeled herself. 'There is just one small matter, Charles. You know our situation only too well. Neither we nor the defendant have any money to pay you. We are asking you to do this *pro bono*, that's the legal phrase, isn't it?' Her father had used the words the previous evening, when she'd told him of her plan.

The smile fell instantly from Charles's face. 'And you have the nerve—'

William interrupted. 'You and I have been good friends, have we not, for many years? And in that time we have both had our ups and downs?' Charles narrowed his eyes as William went on. 'It was last year, wasn't it, that you fell on hard times yourself, my friend? When you were in it up to your neck and you came to me desperate to borrow money? I didn't have any, of course, but I knew someone who could help you make the debts go away. Or has that slipped your memory?'

Charles began to pace the small area in front of the fireplace.

'In my situation, as a pupil,' he gestured around the scruffy little room, 'I have to be totally above board, in everything I do. I cannot take on *pro bono* cases at will, without the say-so of my masters. And they are unlikely to agree, because I have to prove I can earn money for the chambers. Surely you understand my difficulty here?'

'We understand it only too well,' William said. 'And it certainly wouldn't do for word to get out that you resorted to threatening someone's life to relieve you of your debt, would it?'

Anna's mouth almost fell open – Charles threatened to kill someone?

'It wasn't *me* who did the threatening.'

'But it was *you* who paid the man who did the threatening,' William said. 'And that man will sing, if I ask him.'

Charles stopped pacing, ripped off his wig and threw it across the room. He rubbed his head and sighed loudly.

'Bloody hell, William. You leave me with little choice. But I will remember this, mark my words.'

'Just do the business and we'll be square,' William said

calmly. 'Now, Anna, would you like to brief our learned friend?'

On the way back from the Inns, William suggested they call in at a coffee house. Anna had never set foot inside one before, and was curious. The place was very warm, with a huge cauldron hung over a roaring fire, and rough wooden benches around tables crowded with groups of men reading newspapers or engaged in intense and sometimes heated discussions.

Their entrance attracted a fair number of stares: the only other woman was behind the serving hatch. 'I suppose it's not done for women to frequent these places?' she said, as they searched for an empty table.

'Men come here to conduct business mainly. Mother would have a fit if she knew I'd brought you here,' he said with a grin. 'But who cares? I thought you might enjoy seeing another side of city life.'

'I want to keep company with people because I like them, not for how far they can pull me up the social ladder.' It felt good, admitting this to William. Despite his insufferable prejudices and insalubrious habits, they had one thing in common. He, too, was a bit of a rebel.

The coffee arrived and she took a sip of the dark, bitter liquid, stronger than any she'd ever tasted before. 'You kept that quiet: Charles threatening someone to get out of paying his debts.'

'I like to keep my powder dry,' William said with a smirk. 'It was satisfying to see the creep squirm.'

'Will he keep his side of the bargain, do you think?'

'I'm certain of it. The alternative would be unthinkable, in his position. You've had me over a barrel with this business, Anna, but in a strange kind of way I'm enjoying it. Of course I consort with prostitutes, what man doesn't? I'm no saint. I drink a pint or two, and sometimes associate with some pretty unsavoury characters. But if I can get an innocent man freed without having my name all over the newspapers, it will be worth it.'

'Even a Frenchman?'

'We hate the French because we've been at war with them for years, and because there are just too many flooding into our city and taking our jobs. But I've nothing against individuals; I have to admit they are bloody good weavers and designers. And talking of designers, it's time for you to deliver your part of the bargain. Drink up. We're going to call in on Miss Charlotte on our way home.'

The seamstress was busy with a customer, so they were offered seats in the back room and waited quietly, listening through the open door as Miss Charlotte pulled out bolts of fabric for the lady to consider.

'It's called the new naturalism,' they heard her explain. 'Delicate colours, fine design and, above all, natural forms. Nothing too large or overly obvious, of course. And see the curved lines, just like in nature. Straight lines and geometric designs are too severe for a beautiful young woman like you.'

'It's all so charming, I cannot choose,' the customer sighed.

'Of course you could always consider calico,' Miss Charlotte said. 'On cotton, the designs can be printed. It's very *à la mode*.'

'Oh no, it has to be silk. Mama would not have me seen in cotton, not for formal, anyway.'

William whispered, 'It's the perfect lesson.'

'But will you-know-who and her friends want to have just what everyone else wants?' Anna whispered back. 'Or will they be after something different, to be distinctive?'

'How can anyone know what that difference needs to be?'

'That's the thing about fashion,' Anna said. 'Everyone has to guess what the next big thing is likely to be, before it has arrived.'

When the young lady left, Miss Charlotte joined them.

'What news of Henri?'

'Nothing, as yet,' Anna said. 'But things are looking hopeful. Charlotte, meet my cousin William, silk mercer, of Sadler and Son.' He bowed, she curtseyed. 'We have been to see a friend of William's who is a lawyer at the Inns. And we believe we have found a witness who will testify that although Henri was in the area of The Dolphin, he was not with the Bold Defiance men.'

'A witness! Oh, I can hardly believe it.' Charlotte flushed with pleasure, fanning her face with her hand. 'How wonderful. You must tell me as soon as you have news.'

'I promise,' Anna said. 'But I have brought William here on another matter.'

'Of course. Please, come and sit down.'

As William explained about the search for the perfect samples of fabric to tempt a princess, the smile on Miss Charlotte's face grew wider.

'Every mercer in the land is on the same quest,' she said. 'But you are the first to consult me. I am most flattered, sir.'

'What would be your advice, please?'

'I can tell you what the ladies like to wear today and could have a stab at predicting what they will want to wear tomorrow. But the princess is German and will have her own ideas; who knows what she may fancy? Fashion is always a gamble and you need a little touch of magic to stay ahead. But one thing is certain: whatever she chooses will instantly become the very latest thing among society ladies. Everyone will seek to copy, but whoever gets it right in the first place will make their fortune while the others are trying to catch up.'

'We'll just take a little bag of that magic dust, please,' he said. 'I am sure you have some tucked away in your storeroom, do you not?'

Charlotte grinned. 'Indeed, I wish I had. But what I do have is up here.' She tapped her forehead. 'Give me some time to think on it.'

As they rose to leave, her eyes suddenly widened. She clasped Anna's arm. 'I've had an idea: did Henri finish weaving your design, do you know?'

'He wrote that he was starting, but . . .' Anna shook her head. 'Surely, you are not thinking . . . ?'

'It's perfect. Modern, very naturalistic and a little quirky. The line of beauty, remember? Those subtle *points rentrées*? It just might catch the eye, among all those other submissions.'

'What the devil is all this about?' William muttered.

Anna ignored him, too astonished to explain. 'Charlotte, are you seriously suggesting that my design might be suitable to be considered for the royal trousseau?'

Charlotte nodded. 'If he has woven it well, and since it was for his master piece I feel sure that he will have done, what is there to lose?'

22

Above all things learn to put a due value on time, and husband every moment, as if it were to be your last. In time is comprehended all we possess, enjoy, or wish for; and in losing that, we lose them all.

> – Advice for apprentices and journeymen
> OR A sure guide to gain both esteem and an estate

The visit from Anna and her father had, briefly, given Henri heart.

If I ever get out of here, I will do everything to regain her friendship, he promised himself. But this flicker of hope was followed by an even deeper despair when an official arrived to tell him that his trial had been set for the following week. The prospect of release seemed more distant than ever, and he had almost lost hope of ever getting out of prison alive, save for the journey to the gibbet.

So when a tall, gaunt-looking fellow in a newly powdered wig and perfectly white hose stepped into his cell and introduced himself as Charles Hinchliffe, lawyer, he could hardly believe what he was seeing. Accompanying him was another man, smaller and altogether less impressive, whose face seemed familiar.

'Henri Vendôme? I have come to get you out of here,' the lawyer said, without preamble. 'We believe that this man here, William Sadler, may have been a witness to your innocence.' Now the mystery was solved Henri became even more confused. Surely this was Anna's cousin, the brute who had punched him in the street outside the Red Lyon that day? How could *he* possibly be a witness?

The answer came as soon as Sadler opened his mouth. Henri now knew, with a powerful certainty, that he was indeed the man who had cursed him in the alleyway next to The Dolphin that terrible night. A genuine witness, at last, after all these weeks of waiting! Could this be truly happening, or was it a dream? But how had they come to be here? What had made William come forward? Who was paying for this smart society lawyer? Nothing was explained, and he was too astonished to ask.

Mr Hinchliffe asked Henri to recount the story of that night, telling nothing but the whole truth. Henri, his head reeling, did his best. Then he enquired as to whether Henri recognised William as the man he had encountered that night, outside The Dolphin pub, and he agreed that he did. Though it had been dark, the voice was unmistakeable, he said.

The lawyer then turned to William and asked whether he recognised Henri as the man who had been in the alleyway that night, and he acknowledged that he did. There was no mention of the other circumstances, or the whore. Would the two of them be prepared to swear to it under oath, on the Bible, in front of a judge? They both agreed.

Charles went on to explain that after making their statements they must both agree never to speak of this discussion, or reveal each other's identity in this matter to any other party in the future. This was to be an entirely clandestine arrangement. They concurred and shook hands. Shortly afterwards, Charles and William departed.

That afternoon, the guard brought Henri some clean clothes and a bowl of water with some soap and a cloth to wash his face. 'Make yourself respectable, quick sharp, laddie,' he said brusquely. 'Can't have you appearing before his honour looking like something dragged in from the gutter, can we?'

To catcalls and curses from the other inmates, he was led along many corridors and through several doors to a small room in which sat a large, florid-faced man in a shoulder-length wig, who was introduced as the judge. Also in the room were William Sadler, Charles Hinchliffe and a clerk who scribbled down every word spoken.

He was required to place his hand on a Bible and swear that he would tell the whole truth and nothing but the truth, and then asked to repeat his story. The judge asked a couple of questions: how could he know it was William Sadler, given it was so dark? And could he swear that he had not at any time that evening entered The Dolphin? He answered both as well as he could.

When the judge was satisfied, the clerk pushed forward a piece of paper which he was told to read and sign. William Sadler then had to repeat the process, swearing to tell the truth, recounting his side of the story, answering a few questions, then signing his statement. Without further explanation, Henri was dismissed and returned to his cell, scarcely daring to imagine what, if anything, might happen next.

Then, this morning, he'd woken to the sound of his cell door opening and the guard saying, 'Wakey, wakey. You're free to go.'

Surely he was dreaming? 'What, now? This very minute?' he heard his voice saying.

'Right now. Come on. Scram, before they change their minds.'

After three weeks in the gloom of the prison, the sunlight was blinding.

As he stumbled down the steps onto the street, familiar faces and voices emerged out of the glare. His mother, Clothilde, was wrapping a sweet-smelling woollen blanket around his shoulders and enfolding him into her arms, the warm, firm hold that had comforted him since birth. '*Mon trésor, mon petit garçon*,' she whispered, over and over again. 'Thank the Lord. You are back with us at last.'

Mariette was by his side, kissing his cheek and taking his hand, her high-pitched voice squeaking words he found unintelligible. M. Lavalle stood to the front of him, placing a hand on each of his cheeks and, in an unexpectedly intimate gesture, leaning forward to kiss his forehead. '*Mon fils*,' he said. 'My son, my son.' Beyond him, in a row, were Benjamin, the cook and the drawboy – the entire household – all of them grinning from ear to ear.

Henri could hardly take it in. Much as he had longed for it, he now found himself recoiling from human contact, consumed by the awareness of how filthy and stinking he must be, of how he must go home to change from these sordid rags, to shave and scrub away the grime of the prison, the smells of human excrement and fear.

In a daze, he allowed himself to be dragged along, as his eyes slowly adjusted to the sunlight. And then he saw her, running at full tilt towards them, skirt hitched and showing her boots, her bonnet loosening and flying back from her head.

As she approached, the image seemed to take on a magical quality, a brilliance and intensity, as if she were some kind of ephemeral being. The world appeared to slow down, the voices distanced as though he were inside a glass bowl. *Am I imagining this?* he asked himself. *Is it a mirage?*

But no, it was real. She stopped, a few yards away, and he stopped, and the whole entourage stopped.

'Henri,' she whispered, her cheeks glowing pinkly. 'I am so sorry to intrude, but I just had to see you.'

He forgot how dirty and smelly he was, forgot his mother, his master and Mariette, and stepped forward, taking her out-held hands.

'Anna,' he said. 'Is it you?' His eyes were drawn into that deep blue-green gaze, until he sensed a movement behind her and looked up to the tall, stooped figure with a clerical collar arriving at her side.

M. Lavalle's voice boomed in his ear. 'Henri, may we be introduced?'

'Allow me,' Theodore said. 'Anna is a friend to Henri and I am her father, Theodore Butterfield, pleased to meet you.'

Henri gathered his wits. 'Anna, Reverend Butterfield, please meet my mother, Clothilde, my master Monsieur Lavalle and his daughter Mariette.' He turned to M. Lavalle.

'I suspect it may be Anna and her father that I have to thank for my release.' As he looked back into Anna's face she gave the hint of a nod.

'Then we owe you the greatest honour in the world, my friends,' M. Lavalle said, doffing his cap. 'May we invite you to visit us once Henri has had time to recover from this ordeal?'

'And take a bath,' Henri said, once more aware of his filthy state. Everyone laughed.

'*Très bonne idée*, you smell terrible,' his mother said. 'But what do we care? You are back with us, that is all that matters.'

Theodore put his hand on Anna's shoulder. 'It would be our greatest pleasure to visit you. But for now, we must leave you in peace. Come, Anna.'

It was only when she turned to leave that Henri realised, throughout all of this conversation, they had not loosed their hands. Letting go felt like a small bereavement.

Everything had happened so fast, he mused to himself as he lay back in the tin bathtub of steaming water in front of a roaring fire. Everyone else was banished upstairs. Only Cook, who had bathed him since he was a raw ten-year-old apprentice, was allowed to stay, replenishing the hot water from a kettle steaming on the range.

Also on the range was bubbling a stew of mutton and dumplings, and in the fire below were potatoes baking in their skins. Even though he'd already eaten a small snack of bread and cheese and taken half a pint of porter that had made his head swim, the delicious smells were causing his stomach to rumble all over again. But the luxury of soaking in this warm, sweet-smelling bath was too glorious to hurry.

As they sat down to luncheon, Henri recounted what he could of the events of the past few days. When they asked who the elusive witness was he said, truthfully, that he had sworn on the Bible to preserve the man's anonymity. And where did this grand lawyer come from, they asked? Who was paying his fee? Again, he could not answer.

He wanted to know how M. Lavalle and his mother had known to come to the prison at the precise moment of his release. His master explained that an anonymous note had been thrust under the front door late last night. All it said was: *Henri to be freed 8 a.m.* It was all very mystifying but, given the happy outcome, everyone around the table agreed it was hardly important any more.

He felt an overwhelming gratitude towards Anna and her father, certain that they must have engineered his release. Had she somehow divined from their conversation in the prison that her cousin William was the witness, the man with the lisp? Had she persuaded him to come forward in his defence? But who had paid for the lawyer? He doubted that a vicar would have that kind of money, and surely it could not have been the miserly uncle, Joseph Sadler?

Much later, after all the stew had been eaten, several jugs of porter had been drunk, much news had been shared and many embraces and kisses exchanged, Henri excused himself and retired to his room. But, weary as he was, he found himself afraid to sleep, for fear of waking to discover that it had all been a dream.

Listening to the sounds of the household around and above him, the clatter of Cook in the kitchen, the familiar squeaks of the floorboards, the murmur of voices and the smell of M. Lavalle's pipe tobacco, he found himself smiling in the darkness at this unexpected, extraordinary turn in his fortunes.

The tuneless tinkle of the harpsichord started up – Mariette practising for the visitors. 'Oh, Mariette,' he sighed. She had greeted him like an overexcited puppy, barely able to stop herself from touching his sleeve, holding his hand, pasting chaste kisses onto his cheek. He was pleased to see her too, of course, but just as a brother would on being reunited with his sister. Never in a hundred years could he imagine her as his bride.

Prison had changed him, cleared his mind. In the bleakest moments, he'd promised himself that if he ever managed to gain his freedom, he would live to the full whatever future was granted to him. He would stop being so concerned about what others thought and allow his own conscience to lead him, rather than always doing what others expected. Above all, he would lead a quiet life, a domestic life, he hoped, well away from politics and protest.

Despite M. Lavalle's assurances he felt it unlikely that he would receive his mastership, given his reckless behaviour and prison record. The suggestion of inheritance would, he was sure, receive no further mention: for how could his master entrust his precious business to such an irresponsible fool? But he was certain, still, that silk weaving was in his blood. He would apply himself to his craft and set up his own business as best he could, and work hard to recover the respect of those he loved: his mother, M. Lavalle and the family and . . . Anna.

Even the thought of her brought butterflies to his stomach. M. Lavalle had already sent an invitation to Spital Square, for tea the following afternoon. His mother and Miss Charlotte were coming too.

He visualised Anna on the step with her father, welcoming her in, taking her cloak and smelling on it her sweet, wild-flower fragrance, sitting close to her and talking openly, without having to whisper in that clandestine way when they had met before. Then, after tea, he would show her his master piece, the realisation of her very own design, and watch the look of wonder and joy creep over her face.

Henri woke with a start, not knowing how long he had slept. No slivers of light pierced through the wainscot and the house was silent. He peered through the door into the kitchen. The fire was out, the bird asleep in its covered cage. It must be the dead of night.

Lighting a candle, he pulled on his breeches and slippers and wrapped a blanket around his shoulders. He'd been dreaming about weaving – it was nearly a month since he'd held a shuttle in his hand and yesterday he had been so busy eating and talking that he had not even found a moment to visit the weaving loft. Avoiding the creaky treads, he made his way up two flights of stairs and then climbed the ladder to the loft. He pushed up the hatch, climbed through and then, carefully feeding the knotted rope through his hands, hinged it gently to the floor with only the slightest clunk.

The dry, nutty smell of the silk was so familiar, so comforting, it felt like being welcomed into the arms of a lover. Holding his candle high, he scrutinised the work on the three looms. Benjamin was weaving a dusty pink damask, he could see, and the small plain loom was, as usual, being used for narrow-width black satin facings. And then he saw to his astonishment that on his own loom was the brocade that he had been weaving to Anna's design. He shook his head, bewildered. Surely he remembered taking the piece off the loom? He had delivered it to the Weavers' Hall with his own hands.

Peering at the take-up beam, he guessed the roll held around six yards. He had never woven this much; he'd only had time for a single repeat of the figure, as required for the Company. He was still puzzling over this when he heard the creak of the ladder, and turned to see M. Lavalle's night cap appearing through the hatch.

'I thought it must be you,' the old man said, blinking sleepily.

'Pardon me if I disturbed you, sir. I am just reacquainting myself with the looms.'

M. Lavalle climbed the remaining treads and stepped to Henri's side.

'I hope you don't mind. I asked Benjamin to continue weaving your brocade. He's done a good job of it, don't you think?'

'It is just as I would have woven it,' Henri admitted uneasily. 'But may I ask, sir . . .' The question stalled in his throat. What if the answer was negative? He tried again: 'I have failed you, master. If you were to send me away, I would understand.'

'Failed me? Send you away? Don't be ridiculous!' M. Lavalle's laugh filled the room. 'Come. Take a seat.' He lowered himself stiffly to the loom bench, patting the board beside him. 'You acted foolishly, that I grant, and you have paid dearly for it. But let that be the end of the matter. Surely you can see how pleased we all are to have you back with us? You are like a son to me, and will be always welcome in my house and my employ. What you decide to do when you achieve your mastership is, of course, your decision.'

'How can I thank you enough?' Henri said. 'I cannot imagine any life but the one I have enjoyed here for the past years. Except . . .' Again he stalled. How could he tell this kind, generous man, upon whom he looked as a father, that he could not accept his generous offer of inheritance? That, in effect, he did not want to be his son?

M. Lavalle leaned across, taking Henri's hand in his. 'This is about Mariette, is it not?'

Henri nodded. Words failed him.

'There was a time I imagined that you two might marry,' M. Lavalle said quietly. 'But I have changed my mind. In fact, I would not consent to it, even if you asked me. It would result in a life of unhappiness for both of you.'

Henri turned to him, confused. 'But why . . . ?'

'It was quite obvious to me, to your mother, indeed to anyone watching you in the street yesterday, that your affections lie elsewhere.'

'My mother?'

'It was she who made it clear to me. "We are going to have to let him follow his heart, Jean." Those were her words, and straight away I knew she was right. I believe that Mariette understood it, too, for she said she had never before seen such a look on your face.'

Henri sighed, a long exhalation that seemed to draw all of the tension and fear from his body. 'It is true,' he admitted, almost under his breath. 'I am sorry to disappoint Mariette's feelings for me, if she had any.'

'She is young yet, and there are plenty of handsome young men to catch her eye. But is your regard for Miss Butterfield reciprocated, do you believe?'

'I believe that Anna feels the same for me. But whether her family will allow her to marry a lowly French journeyman, that I cannot tell.'

'It will depend on her father, of course, but from the little I saw yesterday he seems an open-minded sort. Besides, you will soon become a master weaver with your own profitable business – surely a good catch for any young woman?'

'My own business? But I thought . . . ?'

'My offer stands, even if you are not to be my son-in-law. I cannot think of anyone else to whom I would want to entrust the business,' M. Lavalle said.

Henri felt his eyes fill with tears. How could so much happiness be handed to him, in such a short space of time, when less than twenty-four hours before he was mouldering in prison, expecting transportation, or even death, to be his fate? He wiped his face with his sleeve and turned to face his master.

'How can I ever—' He had no time to finish because he found himself in a powerful, warm embrace.

'No words are needed, my son,' M. Lavalle whispered into his ear.

It was not only the lack of sleep which left Henri feeling as though he were in some kind of dream.

Observing his mother being charmed by Anna's passionate talk of art and nature, listening with one ear to M. Lavalle and the reverend animatedly discussing whether politics and morality could ever be bedfellows, and watching Mariette and Charlotte excitedly poring over copies of *The Guide to Modern Fashion*, a sort of ecstasy seemed to flow through him, thrilling and comforting at the same time. Everything that he could possibly desire, his friends, his family and those whom he loved, as well as the silk and his weaving, were right here in this house.

Every chair in the house had been brought to the parlour, where a blazing fire glinted cheerfully off the dark-wood panelling. Cook served tea in the best porcelain, along with some delicate *langues de chat* biscuits, a speciality to impress the English guests.

From time to time, he and Anna would exchange discreet glances and the smallest of smiles which made his heart seem momentarily to stop beating. He could see, without a doubt, that she felt happy here with him and in the company of his household.

Once tea was over, M. Lavalle took out the package containing the yards of Henri's master piece fabric that had been returned from the Weavers' Company. He was nervous now, wondering what Anna would make of his interpretation. The piece was held up and passed around the room, everyone severally exclaiming over it, complimenting Henri on the delicacy and intricacy of the weaving, and Anna on the elegance of the design, the trellis pattern of columbine, the bold-faced daisies and nodding bluebell heads, the curled petals of the dog rose.

He could see, all over again, how the silk threads shimmered and glinted in the firelight, giving the appearance that the stems and flowers were actually stirring in a gentle breeze. The intensity of the colours seemed even more brilliant than he had remembered: the deepest pink stripes in each columbine petal, the bold yellow-gold at the centre of the daisy, the deep purple of the bluebells, the leaves of each plant each in a different shade of green.

When it reached Anna she glanced at him with a shy smile and, without a word, took the silk over to the window. All eyes were upon her as she held it close to her face, examining it section by section. Henri was transfixed: a beam of late afternoon sunshine reflected from a window on the house opposite and fell directly onto her, lighting up the blue of her dress and the halo of curls loosened from her bonnet.

He could bear the suspense no longer. 'Do you like it, do you approve my work?'

The look on her face as she turned was something he would remember for years to come. She seemed, literally, to be illuminated, her eyes wide in wonder and wet with tears, her smile broader than he had ever seen it.

'It is wonderful,' she said simply. 'I would never have

believed that all those details could be translated into the weave of a fabric. You have perfectly reproduced my very rough painting and turned it into a true work of art. Look, even my little beetle is here.' A single tear escaped down her cheek, and she wiped it away with the back of her hand.

Everyone laughed, and Henri felt that he might burst with pride. For a second, he was transported back to the market, hanging over the rails of the gallery overlooking the flower stalls, his heart beating wildly as he watched the shapes coming to life at the point of Anna's graphite. From the moment he'd first held it in his hands the design had almost taken over his world: working out how he could make the loom weave it with the most faithful similitude, the meticulous scrutiny needed to translate it onto squared paper, the painstaking choice of yarn colours, the careful weaving and the satisfaction of watching the finished cloth emerging, inch by slow inch, rolling onto the take-up beam.

All the time, as he'd worked, Anna's presence had been close, in his mind. And now she was here, in his house, with his family, holding his fabric, the fabric they had created together, the fabric that bore all his love for her. He could not imagine any place, or any company, in which he might find greater happiness. He looked up and realised that everyone was waiting for him to say something, but he found himself overwhelmed, unable to speak for the tears choking his throat.

Charlotte broke the silence. 'Anna, were you going to ask about the silk for you-know-who?'

'Yes, of course,' Anna said, seeming to gather herself as

if from a trance. 'I almost forgot.' She returned to her chair and handed the silk back to M. Lavalle. 'You see, my uncle Joseph Sadler and my cousin William have a proposition to make.'

She glanced at Charlotte, who nodded encouragement. 'They have an appointment with the royal costumiers who are preparing for the wedding of the king and queen,' she went on. 'And they wondered whether you would agree to them submitting this fabric for consideration.'

'*Mon Dieu*,' M. Lavalle exclaimed. 'This is, how you say, a bolt from the blue. But they have not yet seen it for themselves.'

'They have received a commendation from Miss Charlotte,' Anna replied.

'I am astonished – and delighted, of course. Henri, would you allow them to consider your work?'

Henri's head was spinning. These Sadlers were full of surprises. First William gets him out of gaol, now he wants his silk to clothe a queen.

'How can we refuse such an honour?' he managed to stutter.

'Please convey our thanks. We are much flattered,' M. Lavalle said. 'Henri will bring the piece to them in the morning and if they are still interested, then we will meet to discuss terms.'

'It is a remarkable piece of work, Henri. I cannot imagine how you could weave such a complex thing,' Anna's father said.

'Would you like to see the loom for yourself?'

There was barely room to move once M. Lavalle and Mariette, Henri and his mother, Anna and her father as well as Miss Charlotte had all safely climbed the ladder and negotiated the hatchway into the cool air of the weaving loft. Henri had never seen the attic room so crowded. Benjamin took his bench and began to demonstrate the weaving with the drawboy at his place by the side of the loom, and everyone watched with rapt attention as the pattern emerged with each pass of the shuttle.

Henri glanced anxiously at Anna, standing next to him. Her cheeks were flushed and her eyes glittering, as if on the brink of tears again. 'Are you unwell?' he whispered.

'I am better than I can ever remember,' she whispered back. 'It's simply that . . . seeing my design come to life . . . it is just so exciting. I'm so happy that I could cry.'

'In my humble view, this is the very finest level of crafts-manship,' M. Lavalle was explaining to Theodore. 'And when the Company grants Henri his Freedom he will be able to employ others on his own account. He will run the business for me, and I can spend the rest of my days at leisure. That is my plan.'

Clothilde laughed. 'You will never let go that easily, Jean.'

'I must say that it sounds like an attractive prospect,' Theodore said. 'Regrettably, vicars are not allowed to retire, they must minister to their flock until their very last days or be thrown onto the street.'

'Then you must depend on your daughter to earn a fortune from her designs,' M. Lavalle said. 'Anyone can see she has a talent for it.'

Henri took care to ensure that he and Anna were the last to take their turn down the ladder. As she went to prepare for the descent, he took her hand, holding her back.

'I want . . . I cannot thank you enough for all you do for me.'

'You don't mind, do you?' she said. 'About offering the silk to my uncle? It was Charlotte's suggestion.'

'Don't mind? I am most . . .' He struggled for the right word. 'Delighted. Very much flattered.'

'I am glad.' Her smile seemed to him the most beautiful sight in the world.

'But more than that, I want to ask . . .' He faltered. 'I think you know . . . ?'

She nodded, turning her face to his so that he found himself lost in her gaze all over again.

'Would you . . . ?' He could hear his own heart beating in his chest.

And then, so quietly that he could barely hear it, she whispered, 'Yes, Henri. I would.'

He lifted her chin and their lips met, so quickly and chastely that afterwards, as he tried to reimagine the moment, he found himself wondering whether it had actually happened.

'Are you coming, Anna?' he heard her father call from the floor below.

'Do you think he will consent . . . ?' he whispered. His lips, indeed his whole body, seemed alight with desire.

'You will have to ask him,' she smiled back, gathering her skirts for the descent.

EPILOGUE

Those moments, and those of the days that immediately followed, are etched as clearly in Anna's mind as though they were yesterday. *Can it possibly be forty years ago?* she wonders.

She looks up from her tapestry to where, on the opposite side of the hearth, Henri is dozing in his favourite chair – once the favourite of the late Jean Lavalle. The way her husband's head has fallen sideways, the eyes closed and jaw slackened, the hands slumped in his lap and yet still keeping a grasp on the newspaper, brings a fond smile to her face. He is an old man now, his face lined and his beard grizzled; that once luxuriant dark hair is greyed and thinning beneath his favourite velvet cap.

We are both growing old, she thinks, scowling at her wrinkled fingers, the roughened skin of her arms, the liver spots on the backs of her hands. She cannot remember how long it is since she troubled to take more than a passing glance at her reflection in the glass, preferring to deceive herself with the memory of how she once was.

The house feels little changed by the passage of time and the many events it has witnessed. Firelight glints off the wooden panelling in just the same way as it did that day, forty years ago; the clock ticks in the corner, the shutters rattle when the wind is in the east and looms thud and clatter in the loft. The sweet, nutty smell of raw silk still pervades the air.

The ground floor remains dedicated to the business – the showroom in the front and their shared office and studio at the back – although their eldest son, Jean, has recently persuaded his father to support the rental of a new 'manufactory': three large warehouse rooms on the other side of Brick Lane where the silk is stored, throwsters throw and warps are wound. There is less 'leakage' that way, he says.

He is talking about setting up his own looms in the manufactory, too, so that they can meet the requirements of new laws setting weavers' pay. That way, he says, they will not have to support the costs of weavers working at home, as they will weave at his looms and he can pay them by the piece. 'It's so much more efficient, Papa,' he says. 'And we can keep a closer eye on quality.'

The business has survived turbulent times. In the face of new import freedoms many, even some of the most successful, foundered, thousands of weavers were put out of work and their families starved. Other companies moved out of London altogether, to avoid paying the rates demanded by the new acts. Henri always claimed that the survival of Lavalle, Vendôme & Sons was entirely due to the extraordinary achievements of their in-house designer.

The princess was not clothed in Henri's silk for her nuptial celebrations, but it was chosen by one of her ladies-in-waiting, which was enough to catch the eye of the new queen. Herself an amateur botanist, she took the new naturalism to heart and promulgated it widely amongst her acolytes. Straight lines and geometrical patterns were sent into the wilderness as the artist Hogarth's *The Analysis of Beauty* became the benchmark for artistic endeavour. The serpentine curve became *de rigeur* in fashion, furnishings, furniture and all other decorative arts.

Her paintings have never been hung on walls, as Mr Gainsborough suggested, but for nearly four decades Anna Vendôme's designs have been worn and highly sought after by society ladies. As the orders flooded in, Henri was compelled to employ more than a hundred weavers to keep up with demand. Their silks were even exported across the Atlantic, to be worn by the wealthy aristocrats of the newly independent United States of America.

The mercers Sadler & Son profited too, becoming one of Henri's major customers, although they saw little of the family in society. Aunt Sarah finally achieved her lifetime ambition of moving to Ludgate Hill, just along from the Hinchliffes. She is now a grandmother several times over with Lizzie well married into a wealthy family, and William's two sons following him into the business.

How did I manage to do it all, Anna wonders, *while giving birth to seven children, burying four of them and raising the remaining three into adulthood?* Mariette fell in love with and married the son of a silversmith whom she met at the French church – they live just a few streets away. She and Anna are like sisters, and supported each other in caring for M. Lavalle and Clothilde – who was eventually persuaded to move into the house when she became too frail to work – as they neared the end of their lives.

Then, just as things were becoming easier, Theodore died suddenly while delivering a sermon in his dear old village church. Just as he would have had it, people said at the funeral, but it was no solace for Anna, who has missed him dearly every day since. Jane came to live with them, and remains with them still, which is great consolation, for she is a dear thing, uncomplicated and undemanding, and has been a wonderful helpmeet with the children.

Throughout all of this sorrow and the heavy demands of domestic life, Anna has always managed to steal a few hours for her painting and designing. She loves to work in the office alongside Henri and their two sons, observing the coming and going of traders and weavers, enjoying and sometimes joining their conversations about trade, money and politics.

Occasionally she will persuade her husband, or one of her children, to accompany her to the new Royal Academy of Arts exhibitions to see Mr Gainsborough's work, or to the British Museum where she can study and sketch the natural curiosities collected by Sir Hans Sloane. Before he died, Mr Ehret introduced her to the books of botanical studies held in the library there, which have become a constant inspiration for her work. Dear Mr Ehret. In his will he left Anna two of his prints, which hang on the walls of the salon with pride. Whenever she looks at them, she recalls how he taught her to observe line, shading and colour, right down to the tiniest detail. *What a great debt I owe the man*, she thinks to herself.

She remembers her own vague, unfocused longing on arriving in London, how the appreciation of the fascinating and surprising world all around her only led to greater frustration because, as her aunt would have it, a young lady entering polite society could not be allowed to have an occupation outside the home. She would never have been able to endure spending the rest of her life as an ornament for a conventional husband, but at the time could see no way of avoiding that path.

Despite the unpromising start, she has enjoyed the most wonderful life in this city, she thinks to herself, a life full of family love, and of artistic and intellectual interest. She could not have asked for more.

And it is all on account of one man, the one now sleeping peacefully in his chair on the other side of the hearth. He snores lightly, shifts in his chair and opens his eyes briefly, smiles at her and then falls asleep again. Even after all this time his smile can still ambush her heart, causing it a momentary pause, a contraction of love.

She had known, of course, from the very moment that he rescued her on the street, and he claims that was the moment he knew, too. But she feels sure that, were it not for his moment of drunken foolishness, followed by his arrest and imprisonment, they would now be unhappily married to others. Both acknowledge that Charlotte was the agent of their good fortune, and frequently tease her about it.

As their friendship deepened, and the trust between them became stronger, Anna felt able gently to probe the seamstress about her personal life: how she managed to remain single and run her own independent business. At first she was reticent, but one day, when they had taken a good meal and a few glasses of claret together, Charlotte confided her greatest, most intimate secret.

She was the fourth daughter of a respectable family that had fallen on hard times when their father died prematurely,

she said, and had been forced to find herself a job as seamstress to the household of a noble family. Unfortunately the
duke had a roving eye, which soon enough settled on the
seventeen-year-old Charlotte, and he pressed his attentions
upon her so forcibly that she had submitted for fear of
losing her job.

A few months later, finding the situation insufferable,
she began to resist him, with the inevitable consequence
that she was told to leave. Her oldest sister, now married
to a country vicar, took her in but, within a few short weeks,
it became clear that the duke's attentions had left an
unwanted legacy.

The vicar feared that the scandal could lose him his living,
but his wife, who for six years had failed to bear him a child,
persuaded him that they could adopt the baby, pretending
that it was theirs. Charlotte was sent away for her confinement
while her sister wore cushions of ever-increasing size beneath
her dresses. Thus it was that Peter – for that was his name
– became Charlotte's 'nephew'.

'He has a better life than I could ever have provided,
and I see him every month. Although,' she added wistfully,
'I feel our parting each time like the cut of a knife.'

'Did you never want to marry, so that you could take
him back?'

Charlotte paused and poured herself another glass of
wine. 'No, I am happy as I am. I have worked hard to set
up my business and if I married, I might have to give
it up. Besides, how can I ever trust any man again?' she
said. 'And how could I take my son away from my sister,
when they have loved him as their own for so many years?'

Peter was now grown into a handsome young man with

children of his own who frequently visited their 'great aunt'. Anna, invited to meet them one day, could plainly see the likeness of her friend reflected in their faces, and Charlotte's pride and happiness in their company was a joy to behold.

To everyone in the family but her father, theirs had seemed such an unlikely match. Anna can still recall the look of utter horror on Aunt Sarah's face when Henri turned up at Spital Square that morning.

'Mr Henri Vendôme, madam,' Betty announced.

'Tell him he has come to the wrong address. The business entrance is next door,' her aunt said firmly.

'No, Aunt, he has come to see Father,' Anna cried, dropping the book with which she had been trying unsuccessfully to occupy herself for the past half hour. She flew down the stairs to where Henri was waiting on the doorstep, nervously shifting from foot to foot, smart but uncomfortable in his best blue serge, his hair neatly tied back beneath what looked like a new cap. Under his arm was a brown paper parcel containing the silk brocade.

'Come in, come up,' she said, beckoning him with a conspiratorial wink. 'Father knows.' When they reached the top of the stairs, Theodore was already on the landing. Anna pushed Henri forward and the two men shook hands.

In an unsteady voice, Henri began, 'Sir, I have come to ask—'

'Don't stand on ceremony, boy,' Theodore said, clapping him on the shoulder. 'Anna has already told me the reason for your visit. Of course you have my consent. Knowing how she feels about you, I could not be more delighted.'

At that point, Sarah emerged from the salon door with Lizzie behind her. 'Whatever is going on out here?' she snapped.

'Sister dear, meet my future son-in-law, Henri,' Theodore announced. 'Henri, this is my sister Mrs Sarah Sadler and my niece, Elizabeth.' Henri offered his hand, but it was ignored. Aunt Sarah's mouth gaped, her jowls flapping loosely, as though she had seen an apparition.

Lizzie had a fit of the giggles, and was burbling congratulations when her mother seemed to gather her senses. 'Have you lost your mind, Theodore?' she gasped, before turning to Anna. 'Have I not warned you about the unsuitability of this sort of friendship?'

Anna stood firm, holding tightly on to Henri's hand in case he felt minded to bolt. 'Come into the drawing room,' she said, pulling him past Sarah and Lizzie through the doorway.

'Sir, I must ask you to leave while we discuss the matter,' Sarah said. Anna could hear her uncle's footsteps coming up the stairs.

'Hello, hello. Do we have company?' he bellowed. At the sight of Henri, he stopped in his tracks. 'And who is this, may I be so bold?'

'My fiancé, Uncle,' Anna said. 'Please let me introduce you to Monsieur Henri Vendôme.'

Henri held out the parcel that he'd tucked under his arm. 'I am pleased to meet you, sir. I have brought the silk as discussed, for consideration for the royal wedding.'

'Then why did you not call at the tradesmen's entrance, boy?'

'He is my *fiancé*, Uncle, as I said. He has gained permission from Father for my hand. Isn't it wonderful? And he has kindly brought the fabric he has woven from my design that William told you about at breakfast, remember?' Anna took the parcel from Henri and ran to the window, ripping open the string and paper, and allowed the silk to unfold, glittering and gleaming in the light just as it had done at Wood Street the previous day.

'Good God,' Joseph said, coming to the window to see for himself. 'That is a very fine piece of silk, young man, and a most striking design.'

He pulled his magnifying glass from his waistcoat pocket and lifted the fabric close to his face.

'Did you weave this yourself?'

'I did, sir. It is my master piece.'

Joseph put his eye to the glass once more. 'Excellent work. I very much admire your use of *points rentrées*; seems to have gone out of fashion of late, but this makes for very fine definition of your curves. Tricky stuff. Remind me again, who is your designer?'

'For goodness sake, Uncle,' Anna burst out. 'Were you not listening when I told you at breakfast? It is *my* design.'

He frowned at her. 'But how . . . ?'

'I will explain later, but for now, will you all please welcome into your house Henri Vendôme, the young man I intend to marry?'

The old grandfather clock strikes ten o'clock, interrupting her reverie. The fire has burned low, and she considers putting on another log. But tomorrow will be another full day, and they both need their rest, now that they are old.

She puts down her tapestry and steps over to the sleeping man, gently takes the newspaper from his hands and kisses him on the forehead.

'Come, husband,' she whispers. 'It's time for bed.'

A note on the history that inspired *The Silk Weaver*

When I was researching the history of my family's silk business, which started in Spitalfields, East London, in the early 1700s (and is still weaving today in Sudbury, Suffolk), the first recorded address that I could discover was in Wilkes Street, then called Wood Street. Wonderfully, the house is still there.

Just a few yards away, on the corner of Wilkes Street and Princelet Street, then Princes Street, is the house where the eminent silk designer, Anna Maria Garthwaite, lived from 1728 until her death in 1763. It was here, at the very heart of the silk industry, that she produced over a thousand patterns for damasks and brocades, many of which are today in the Victoria and Albert Museum. I was thrilled to realise that my ancestors would have known, and possibly worked with, the most celebrated textile designer of the eighteenth century, whose silks were sought after by the nobility in Britain and America.

She was noted for her naturalistic, botanically accurate designs and credited in the *Universal Dictionary of Trade and Commerce* of 1751 as one who 'introduced the Principles of Painting into the loom'. She lived in the Age of Enlightenment, when scientists and artists were obsessed with exploring and recording the natural world, and when botanical illustrators such as Georg Ehret became minor celebrities.

In an unpublished manuscript in the National Art Library, unfinished at her death, the late Natalie Rothstein, formerly curator of textiles at the V&A, hints at a tantalising connection between the artist William Hogarth and the weavers of Spitalfields: his famous series of prints, *Industry and Idleness*, published in 1747, shows weavers at their looms. Six years later he published *An Analysis of Beauty*, in which he proposed that the serpentine curve – as seen in nature and the human form – was the essence of visual perfection. It is quite possible, Rothstein suggests, that he had been inspired by Anna Maria's designs.

Yet no one, not even Natalie Rothstein, has been able conclusively to discover how Anna Maria, who showed a youthful artistic talent, learned the highly technical and complex skills of designing for silk. Or how a single woman by then in her middle years managed to develop and conduct such a successful business on her own account in what was a largely male-dominated industry. It is this mystery that sparked the idea for the novel.

It is said that at that time, a quarter of all those living in Spitalfields and Bethnal Green spoke only French – they had their own institutions, including a French church, which has since been a synagogue and is now a mosque. Although, as Protestants, the Huguenots were officially welcomed in England, there is much evidence that these refugees were subject to racism and mistrust, much as refugees fleeing persecution in their own lands are today.

But now, a word of warning: although inspired by real-life events and people, this novel is pure fiction and I have taken enormous liberties with history, in particular the timing of events. Anna Maria hailed from Leicestershire, not Suffolk, and did not come to London until she was forty. Her fame was at its height in the 1730s and 40s and she died in 1763 at the good old age of seventy-five.

Although there were always rumblings of discontent among weavers, the 'cutters riots', and most notably the trial and hanging of D'Oyle and Valline, did not take place until the 1760s, around the time of Anna Maria's death. It is in this period of extreme industrial unrest that I have chosen to set the novel, even though Anna Maria probably witnessed little of it.

So if you are an expert in the history of that time, or the life of Anna Maria, I beg your forgiveness. Novelists do not write history, but merely take inspiration from its characters and events. But for the curious, and just to prove that I *do* know the difference between fact and fiction, here is a timeline of the events that inspired me, and some of the books and websites that have helped me build a picture of life in Spitalfields at that time:

1681   First major wave of Huguenot persecution in France, when 'Dragonnades' were first used – and consequent migration.

1680s   French church *L'Eglise de l'Hôpital* first established in Spitalfields. It was rebuilt in 1742 and since then has been a synagogue and a mosque.

1685   Revocation of *Edict of Nantes* by Louis XIV, which meant that Protestant worship was no longer tolerated in France. By 1690 more than 200,000 Huguenots had emigrated.

1688	Anna Maria Garthwaite born at Harston, near Grantham in Leicestershire, on 14 March.
1712	Huguenots admitted to Weavers' Company as 'foreign' masters.
1719	Riots in Spitalfields, Colchester and Norwich over imports of calico.
1722	First Walters silk weavers, Benjamin and Thomas, recorded as working and living in Spitalfields.
1726	Anna Maria left Grantham to live in York with her twice-widowed sister Mary.
1728	Anna Maria and Mary moved to Princes Street, Spitalfields, in London.
1737	German botanist and botanical artist Georg Ehret settled in London.
1746	Joseph Walters, silk weaver, married at Christ Church.
1755	*An Easy Introduction to Dancing* published.
1759	Thomas Gainsborough and his family moved from Suffolk to Bath.
1760	King George II died on 25th October, succeeded by his grandson George III aged 22.
1761	On 8 September George III married Princess Charlotte of Mecklenburg-Strelitz, whom he met on their wedding day. The coronation followed a fortnight later.
1762	In May, 8,000 weavers paraded to St James Palace. Next day 50,000 weavers assembled and marched to Westminster. In August, journeymen weavers organised the *Book of Prices*.
1763	Anna Maria Garthwaite died in Spitalfields.
1763	Thousands of weavers took part in wage riots, breaking into the house of a notorious master, destroying his

looms and cutting his silk, and later staging a hanging of his effigy. Soldiers were sent to occupy parts of Spitalfields.

1764   Huguenots led campaign against the import of French silks.

1765   Siege of Bedford House: weavers marched with black flags in protest at the Duke of Bedford's opposition of a bill that would have prohibited the import of French silks. A new act was passed making it a crime punishable by death (a felony) to break into any house or shop with the intent to maliciously damage silk.

1768   The Royal Academy founded – and accepted women artists. Thomas Gainsborough was a founding member.

1769   A group of journeymen formed the Bold Defiance, which met at The Dolphin Tavern in Cock Lane (modern Boundary Street, in Bethnal Green), to protest against masters who ignored the *Book of Prices*. In September, Bow Street Runners and troops raided The Dolphin and made four arrests.

1769   In December, John D'Oyle and John Valline found guilty of attacking the looms of Thomas Poor, a weaver working for the notorious master Chauvet. They were hanged at Bethnal Green. Rioters tore down the gallows and rebuilt them in front of Chauvet's house, smashed his windows and burned his furniture. Two weeks later more alleged 'cutters' were hanged.

1771   Further silk weavers' riots in Spitalfields.

1772   First recorded address of Walters silk business (Joseph I and his son Joseph II) in Wilkes Street, Spitalfields.

1773   First of three Spitalfields Acts passed, regulating weavers' wages.

1774   Thomas Gainsborough and his family moved to London.

Here are just some of the books, exhibitions, libraries and websites that helped my research:

Robin D. Gwynn, *The Huguenots of London* (Alpha Press, 1998)

Douglas Hay and Nicholas Rogers, *Eighteenth-Century English Society* (OUP, 1997)

Alfred Plummer, *The London Weavers' Company 1600–1970* (Routledge & Kegan Paul, 1972)

Roy Porter, *English Society in the Eighteenth Century* (Penguin, 1991)

Natalie Rothstein, *Silk Designs of the Eighteenth Century* (Bullfinch Press, Little Brown, 1990).

Natalie Rothstein, *The English Silk Industry 1700–1825*, unpublished mss in The National Art Library at the Victoria & Albert Museum

Amanda Vickery, *Behind Closed Doors: At Home in Georgian England* (Yale University Press, 2009)

Amanda Vickery, *The Gentleman's Daughter: Women's Lives in Georgian England* (Yale University Press, 2003)

Sir Frank Warner, *The Silk Industry of the United Kingdom* (Drane's, 1921)

Cecil Willett Cunnington, *Handbook of English Costume in the Eighteenth Century* (Faber, 1964)

The National Art Library at the Victoria & Albert Museum, London

Denis Severs' House at 18 Folgate Street, Spitalfields
www.dennissevershouse.co.uk

Georgians Revealed exhibition at the British Library (London, 2013) and the accompanying book of the same name

John Roque's Map of London, 1746 **www.locatinglondon.org**

The Proceedings of the Old Bailey, 1674–1913 **www.oldbaileyonline.org**

Spitalfields Life daily blogs by 'The Gentle Author'
   www.spitalfieldslife.com

The Fashion Museum, Bath **www.fashionmuseum.co.uk**

The Georgians exhibitions at Kensington Palace and Buckingham
   Palace gallery

The Huguenot Society and Library at Gower Street
   www.huguenotsociety.org.uk

The Worshipful Company of Weavers **www.weavers.org.uk**

extracts reading groups
competitions books new
discounts extracts
competitions extracts
books new discounts
new extracts
events books reading groups
extracts new events
new titles reading groups
interviews
events extracts extracts
discounts events books
new books events interviews new books extracts
events new
discounts extracts discounts
www.panmacmillan.com books
extracts events reading groups
competitions books extracts new